Wanton's Web

Alex Matthews

INTRIGUE
PRESS

For information, please contact Intrigue Press, P.O. Box 456, Angel
Fire, NM 87710, 505-377-3474.

ISBN 1-890768-12-X

First Printing 1999

Grateful acknowledgment is made for permission to reprint a line of
dialog from a Mixed Media comic strip. ©Tribune Media Services. All Rights
Reserved. Reprinted with Permission.
Grateful acknowledgment is made for permission to reprint a line of
lyrics from the song Me And Bobby McGee
Words and Music by Kris Kristofferson and Fred Foster
©1969 (Renewed 1997) TEMI COMBINE INC.
All Rights Controlled by COMBINE MUSIC CORP. and Administered
by EMI BLACKWOOD MUSIC INC. All Rights Reserved. International
Copyright Secured. Used by Permission.

This book is a work of fiction. Although Cassidy McCabe and the author
have many circumstances in common, none of the actions or events is based
on real events in the author's life. Names, characters, places and incidents
either are the product of the author's imagination or are used fictitiously.
Any resemblance to actual events or persons living or dead is entirely
coincidental. Although the author and publisher have made every effort to
ensure the accuracy and completeness of information contained in this
book, we assume no responsibility for errors, inaccuracies, omissions, or any
inconsistency herein. Any slights of people, places or organizations are
unintentional.

Library of Congress Cataloging-in-Publication Data
Matthews, Alex.
    Wanton's Web / Alex Matthews.
        p.   cm. -- (The fourth Cassidy McCabe mystery])
    ISBN 1-890768-12-X (hardcover)
    I. Title. II. Series: Matthews, Alex. Cassidy McCabe mystery:
4th.
PS3563.A83958W36   1999
813'.54--dc21   98-51072 CIP

For my husband Allen, who makes all things possible.

Many thanks to all the people who helped in the birthing of this book: my husband, Allen Matthews, whose fourth career has become book promotion; my elder son, Ross Brown, who took time from his busy career to copyedit the galleys; my younger son, Robin Brown, who provided consultation on the viewpoint of young males; my lifelong friend Susan Sullivan, who turned her artist's eye to the design of book jackets; my editor, Chris Roerden, who would not accept less than my best; my fellow critique group members, Nancy Carleton, Jan Fellers, Carol Hauswald, and Denise Stybr, who faithfully refused to let me get away with anything; my publicist, Barbara Young, who applied her vast energy and enthusiasm to book publicity; my fellow DL member, who gave me exactly the right words for the title; Chicago Police Detective Anne Chambers and Oak Park Police commander Robert Scianna, who tried to set me straight about police procedure. Everyone gave freely of their time and expertise. Where errors exist, they are mine.

Also by Alex Matthews:

Secret's Shadow
Satan's Silence
Vendetta's Victim

1. Spiderwoman

A blurry twilight was softening the concrete angles along Lake Street as Cassidy McCabe and her friend Maggie Benton stepped outside the air-conditioned movie theater into a breezy July night.

You're in such a spin about what you and Zach are up to—could've been watching Godzilla Meets the Three Stooges for all you know.

Pausing on the sidewalk, Maggie cocked her head. "I assume, of course, we're going to eat ourselves into oblivion with double dip cones at Edie's."

Cassidy nodded and the two women started strolling toward the ice cream shop a block east of the Lake Theater in the heart of demalled downtown Oak Park.

Maggie wants ice cream. I want my guardian angel to come sit on my shoulder and promise I'm not about to make another hideous mistake.

"They've got too many flavors," Maggie complained in the husky voice Cassidy envied. "I wouldn't want just chocolate, strawberry, and vanilla, you understand. But ten'd be nice. I could cope with ten. When I look at all those choices, I get immobilized. I just stand and stare at the lucious array in front of me and then I go into overload."

About the same height as Cassidy's five-two, Maggie had a delicate face surrounded by soft, curly hair and an air of contentment that flowed from her like a magnetic field.

They passed a Starbucks, tables on the sidewalk, a half-dozen coffee drinkers lounging in the balmy air. A caffeine junkie herself, Cassidy felt tugged at by the rich aroma. The night swirled with soft lights, clumps of straggling pedestrians, sounds of clogged traffic creeping along Lake Street.

Do it now. Otherwise you'll act like a tongue-tied idiot tonight, then have to make up some stupid excuse to get together next week. So just say it. Get the old voice box in gear and start pumping out words.

Cassidy ran the tip of her tongue across her upper lip. "Zach and I are planning to get married."

"What?" Maggie stopped short and grabbed Cassidy's arm. Her clear gray eyes stared in surprise. "Well, what do you know!"

Cassidy swallowed and said in a small voice, "Does that mean you think it's a bad idea?"

Maggie threw her arms around Cassidy in a quick hug. "Don't even try to fish for reassurance," she said, resuming her ice-cream bound journey. "You're not getting one word out of me—either pro or con— about what I think you should do. Just give me all the juicy details right now."

"We're thinking of early September." Her mouth went dry. *Never imagined I'd get so nervous just talking about it.* "We're going to keep it tiny, but I would like you to stand up with me." Holding onto her short magenta dress to keep the skirt from blowing, she added, "You're the first person I've told."

"Me, a bridesmaid. I never expected to get so traditional. But you're my closest straight friend, so for you I'll do it."

A rusted-out Ford prowled past, the radio amping out rap, a young black driver in dreadlocks jumping to the beat. When their ears had recovered, Maggie asked, "So, how sure are you?"

"Umm." Cassidy pressed her palm to her cheek. "Eighty percent?"

"What's that uncertain twenty?"

"Oh, my history of getting left. Zach's history of leaving. You know that can't be just coincidence." She paused. "Plus the fact that the first husband I picked turned out to be such a jerk."

Maggie let out a light, puffy laugh. "Can't you for once stop acting like a therapist and just enjoy being in love and planning a wedding?"

"The other thing is, my life's been going too well. It makes me nervous. I keep waiting for the other shoe to drop."

"Well, of course it will sometime. But why not enjoy the good stuff till it does?"

Same thing you always tell clients.

Yeah, but letting your guard down is too much like tempting the fates.

Cassidy breathed in air smelling of trees, car exhaust, and a hint of pizza from the shop across the street. Letting her worries go in a long sigh, she felt the tension in her neck and shoulders drain away. "You know, I've always wondered why people who are living together and getting along fine want to up and spoil it by getting married. And here I am, doing it myself."

They stopped for the light at Lake and Forest. "The perversity of human nature, my girl. People can't stand for their lives to stay in balance. They get bored and have to stir something up."

"Well, and it's a damned good thing they do, or we therapists'd be out of business."

❦ ❦ ❦

Cassidy dropped her friend off at the small brick house Maggie shared with her partner, Susie, then drove north on Ridgeland, east on Briar to her corner two-story. *If it seems too good to be true, it probably is.* She and Zach had been living together nine months, and their life had fallen into an easy rhythm that allowed her to pull in her claws, sleep more soundly at night, and sing along with Bette Midler and Bob Seger on the radio.

Even the climate reflected her current state of contentment, providing day after day of bright, mild air without the usual stickiness that in previous summers had made her feel like soggy Kleenex. *The weather gods in my corner? Not hardly. More likely compensating for that killer heat wave a few years back that racked up so many bodies Chicago ran out of places to put 'em.*

She parked her Toyota in the garage and started the ten-yard trek along Briar toward her back gate, and past that, her tall, box-shaped house, a yellow glow radiating from every first floor window. Among the many things Zach's mother had failed to teach him was the economy of turning off switches. Although night had officially fallen, the village's white street lights and the city's rosy aura kept darkness at bay. Cassidy watched a flock of grade school kids Rollerblading in the street, said hi to a couple of neatly dressed teens moseying in the direction of Austin Boulevard, the border between her integrated suburb and an all-black section of Chicago.

The too-good-to-be-true part was the change in Zach. She'd initially pegged him as a man to be stayed away from, the kind of irresponsible, noncommittal jerk that had always been her downfall. *Even told you flat out on the first date, intentions were strictly dishonorable. A short fling, then bye-babe, been-nice-to-know-you.* That had been his modus operandi for nearly twenty years, but somehow, this time out, he'd gotten sidetracked and moved in with her. *Once he got his waterbed installed in your house, turned out to be the kind of guy who brings coffee in the morning, talks out problems, and now, the most amazing thing, actually eager to put a ring on your finger.*

Overall, most of the rough edges had smoothed out. She'd finally paid off the debt bequeathed to her by her ex, Kevin, her client load was increasing, and Zach was mowing the grass before it achieved ankle length, as she'd let it do in previous summers. At thirty-eight, Cassidy had navigated some pretty unpleasant shoals. *Kevin's bimbo-fever yanking you into a divorce, a bread-and-water stint in graduate school, a two-client private practice start-up. And then, against all better judgment, getting involved with Zach. At the beginning, seemed you had to be either crazy or masochistic to have anything to do with him.*

She opened the back door into her client waiting room, a space partitioned off from her large kitchen by a free-standing oak closet. She'd done her best to make the room inviting, with mauve wicker chairs, airy wallpaper, a filmy raspberry-sherbet fabric draped around the window. Despite worn linoleum that curled at the seams and a kitchen twenty years overdue for remodeling, she had managed by dint of much elbow grease and little money to overcome the sense of slumminess her old house was always in danger of slipping into.

Before starting toward the stairs in front, she made a quick stop in the half-bath off the waiting room. Checking the mirror, she pushed wayward auburn curls back from her face. The reflection she'd been seeing for several months now was softer and more relaxed than in the past. During the difficult years, her narrow face had always appeared bony and drawn. Tonight the image was rounder and fuller, the deep-set hazel eyes, high cheekbones, and pointed chin actually striking her as attractive. *First time ever thought I was pretty. Not sure if the difference is how I look or how I see myself. Must be the steady diet of love and sex.*

Coming around the oak room divider, she noticed a nearly empty bottle of Jack Daniels on the kitchen counter next to the sink. Above it the cabinet door hung open. *Nothing unusual. Zach always has a drink or two in the evening. 'Cept he usually manages to close the cabinet behind him.*

On her way through the track-lighted living room, she glanced out the wide front window. The back of Zach's head was visible above the wicker couch on the dark, enclosed porch, their favorite place for summertime sitting.

As she opened the oak door, the smell of bourbon hit her full force. *Don't like this.* Zach looked up. Starshine, sitting erect in the casement window next to the screen door, jumped down, extended her front legs in a long stretch, and greeted her with a Mwat.

He was fine when I left.

He's not fine now. When she'd kissed him good-bye at four, he'd glanced up from his computer screen, given her his usual lazy smile, and returned to whatever he was doing. She'd gone off to visit her mother, then to meet Maggie for dinner and a movie, with no sense of anything amiss.

She sat beside Zach, her back teeth clamped in anger at the alcohol fumes rolling off him. "Well," she said, keeping her voice even, "what's up?"

The midsummer night was soft and buttery, the air perfumed with flowers and freshly cut grass. A light breeze jangled the wind chimes and rustled the trees lining both sides of Hazel.

"There's something I have to tell you." He spoke slowly. The words were not exactly slurred but she could tell he was a little drunk. *If it seems too good to be true ….*

"You want to talk." *Changed his mind. Decided to nix the marriage plans. Damn him—should have told me before I said anything to Maggie.*

"Need to fix another drink before I get started." Starshine sprang onto his lap but he pushed her away. It was the first time Cassidy had ever seen Zach, devoted as he was to the cat, treat her so indifferently. Starshine stepped daintily onto the picnic bench that served as a makeshift table and shook her paw to register annoyance.

"Another? How many have you had already?" She hadn't intended to ask but the words bypassed her brain and jumped out of her mouth.

" 'Bout half a bottle."

Amazing he's even conscious. High tolerance. Too high.

He rose and started heavily toward the kitchen, Cassidy and Starshine trailing behind. "I know, you don't like it and you're probably right. This is probably not a good time to get wasted. But I'm gonna need one more to get through this."

Through what? He doesn't want to get married? He's moving out? What?

Starshine yammered for food and Cassidy spooned some smelly stuff into the cat bowl on the green linoleum counter as Zach mixed two strong drinks. Leaning carefully against the cartoon-covered refrigerator, she studied him for clues. Bronze-skinned, wide through the shoulders and chest, he wore jeans and a threadbare black tee-shirt, a Sam Adams bottle depicted on the front. *If it seems too good to be true ....* The clock above the sink registered nearly ten.

He held out a dark amber tumbler.

Don't take it. How can you yell at him for drinking if you drink along with him?

She reached for the glass.

They returned to the wicker couch, Cassidy jamming her rear into the far corner, drawing her legs up tight so no part of her body touched Zach. She took a long swallow. Starshine sat erect on the bench, withholding attention to show that Zach was as yet unforgiven.

He slumped forward, his right hand balancing the drink on his knee, his left rubbing the back of his neck. "A kid showed up at the door 'bout half an hour after you left. Had this flashy yellow Miata parked in front of the house. Asked if I was Zach Moran, then stood and stared at me."

"He stared at you." Cassidy said it automatically, using his own words the way she did with clients to make sure she didn't lead them.

Leaning back, he dropped his burly arm onto the wooden armrest and raised his glass. "I asked what he wanted and he told me he didn't want anything, didn't want to have anything to do with me. But his mother said he had to come. Then he handed me a letter."

Tiny needles prickled in her chest. *Oh no, oh no, oh no.*

"He came inside and we sat down and had a beer." His words halted, stalling like a car.

Don't tell me. I don't want to hear this. Taking shallow breaths, Cassidy sat absolutely still, a frozen animal with danger zooming toward her like headlights.

Zach's voice picked up again. "His name's Bryce Palomar. He's seventeen." He shook his head. "God, he seemed young. He was trying to pull off this tough guy act but he's just a scared kid." He leaned forward, ran a hand over his face. "I was twenty-three, Xandra twenty-five. I never knew, never even suspected."

"Xandra?"

"His mother."

Cassidy's feelings disconnected the way they did when clients told horror stories, giving her time to take it in. "So this kid who arrived at the door is a son you didn't know existed? That is, if the mother's telling the truth."

Starshine sat up tall, her ears pricked, and said Mwat, a bid for attention. When they didn't respond, the calico bounced to the floor, leapt and twisted her body, performing contortions in an effort to capture her tail.

"According to the letter, Xandra thinks she's in some kind of danger. She wanted Bryce in a safe place so she forced a promise out of him to stay with me a few days. He's pretty pissed, but she got him to agree. She didn't tell him about this unspecified risk factor, just that she needed him gone for a while, he has to stay here, she'll explain later. All this in a sealed letter, which I presume he didn't read."

Zach sat straighter, slugged down a portion of his drink, rattled the ice, and thumped the glass down on the armrest. "It's amazing to me she could even get a seventeen-year-old to do what she wanted. Although from the way he talks, I get the impression he's pretty fond of her. Which is bizarre in itself, considering how teenagers usually feel about their mothers."

"You don't know he really is your son."

"Wait till you see him."

"He looks like you?"

"He's got the same dark skin. Xandra was fair, as I recall."

What does this mean? Sliding out from the corner, she stretched her leg sideways, rubbing her ankle against Zach's. "Where is he now?"

"He went off on his own. Hates the idea of staying here but says if his mother really wants him to, he will. What *we* want doesn't enter into it." He stared off into space. Following his gaze, Cassidy looked absently at the row of stately houses on the opposite side of Hazel, a couple walking a lab.

"Kid's got a real chip on his shoulder." He shook his head. "Years ago, Xandra told him the Moran byline at the *Post* belonged to his father. He seems to think I walked out on her when she was pregnant. I told him I didn't know about the pregnancy, but he wasn't interested in hearing anything I had to say. Anyway, for as long as he can remember she's been telling him I was a real sonovabitch, she didn't want him going anywhere near me. Only now she's changed her mind."

Maybe he was a sonovabitch with Xandra. That was years ago. Now he cuddles with you at night, remembers your birthday. Even willing to spend time with your mother, which definitely qualifies as above and beyond. "Any idea where he might've gone?"

"I tried to get him to talk but his mother'd told him to keep his mouth shut and he wouldn't give up anything. So I instructed him to empty out his pockets on the table, and after considerable bullying, he finally did. I was able to get the address off his driver's license, but the phone's unlisted. He had a fat roll of cash and a handful of credit cards, so Xandra must be doing okay in her line of work, which doesn't surprise me. Anyway, he was really pissed by then, so he announced he was leaving the house but he'd be back later."

Her eyes narrowed. There was something in his tone of voice. "What is her line of work exactly?"

He gave her a long look. "She was employed by an escort service when I knew her. She'd be too old for that now but she's probably in some related field."

Cassidy caught her bottom lip sharply between her teeth. "So, were you a . . . client? Customer? What is the proper term?"

"Are you kidding? Xandra was high-end merchandise. I couldn't afford her then, probably couldn't now."

Her spine stiffened. *Maybe you're being too understanding again. Maybe he still is a sonovabitch.* Gritting her teeth, she forced herself not to speak, not to do anything that would make it easier for him.

Starshine sprang to the rim of the couch. Feeling catly fangs nipping at her ear, Cassidy swatted her away.

Zach picked up his glass, realized it was empty, set it down. "This is not something I ever wanted to tell you." Leaning forward, he dropped his head, rubbed the back of his neck. "When I was in college, I used to get high on a regular basis, and by the time I graduated, I was pretty messed up. It was mostly pot, but I was using enough of it that I wasn't functioning very well. I got a job at a suburban paper, very small time, and just drifted along." Pulling himself up straight, he rubbed his forehead.

Must be totally thrown by all this. He always acts so in command— easy to forget he's not made of steel.

"A friend took me to a party at a Gold Coast highrise and I met Xandra. She said she was a model, we did a couple lines of very good coke, and she took me home. The whole deal was way over my head. Xandra had a powerful kind of seductiveness different from anything I've ever encountered before or after. I couldn't get enough of her. Or the drugs that came with her."

Cassidy's lips clenched in a tight line.

He dropped a hand on her knee. "Don't take this the wrong way. I'm happy with you. You're good for me, and Xandra was like a dose of exotic poison. Getting involved with her was the beginning of a fast downhill slide. But she was some kind of sexual spiderwoman, and she knew how to get what she wanted."

Cassidy shivered slightly. "She wanted you?"

"Briefly."

"Why? If you couldn't pay her price, I mean."

He leaned back and grinned, for a moment looking halfway like his normal self. "At the time, I assumed it was my irresistible studliness. I was a tad cocky back then."

A cat scream came from the feral colony across the side street, the sound so piercing it raised goosebumps on her arms. Starshine, her tail puffed, leapt onto her window ledge, paused, then disappeared outside.

"What do you think now? Why'd she pick you?"

"You're not doing my ego any good." He rubbed the back of his neck. "All I know is, we had a hot month or so—three months, I guess it was. I was crazy about her, I thought she was crazy about me. One day we were doing it five times a night, the next day she said—'it's over, get out of my life.' "

He's never done it five times in one night with you. "What about now?" Her voice sounded small and insecure, a side of herself she hated.

"If you saw her again, would that testosterone craziness kick back in? Is she so hot you couldn't stay away from her?"

He took her hand from her lap and squeezed it. "I am going to see her. I'm going down tonight. The only reason I waited is, I didn't think it was fair to go off without telling you."

She made herself take three long, slow breaths. "This is not a good idea."

"I can't let Bryce just hang out at our house without knowing what's going on."

"This is crazy. She might not be home. Might not let you in. Maybe she dumped the kid here the way mothers leave children in bus depots, now she's taken off for parts unknown."

"Maybe. But I have to go see what I can find out."

"Then I'll have to drive."

"Shit, I was afraid of something like this. You're gonna make me sorry I told you."

"I won't let you drive with all that alcohol in your system."

He sighed heavily. "All right, but only if you promise to stay in the car."

She didn't want to stay in the car. She wanted to see what this woman looked like and how Zach acted around her.

He said, speaking slowly and distinctly, "Do I have your word you'll stay in the car?"

He could've just gone but he didn't—he waited to tell you. "Okay, I'll keep my butt planted."

She scrutinized his face in the murky light filtering through the picture window behind them. Smooth dark hair, high forehead, large hawkish nose, long diagonal scar across his left cheek. His expression, typically calm and observant, revealed extreme tension, lines cutting so deeply he looked years older, fifty instead of his real-time forty.

She pressed her middle finger and thumb against her forehead. "There's something you're not telling me, isn't there?"

"Not tonight. I can't tonight."

2. Champagne Bottle and Hostility

She backed the Toyota onto Briar and headed for the Eisenhower Expressway, which took them east into Chicago. *Feels strange, you behind the wheel, Zach sitting there not talking. He's usually so male about driving.* When they reached the downtown area, he told her to turn right on State Street, then parceled out directions until they arrived at a townhouse in Dearborn Park. The block was parked solid so she drew up in front of a fireplug about fifteen yards from Xandra's gate.

"Wait," she said, as Zach turned toward the door. "You didn't answer my question. Is seeing her now going to stir up all those lusty old feelings from the past? You didn't let me drive just to make sure you don't end up back in the sack with her again, did you?"

His wide mouth pulled down at one corner. "That's one thing you absolutely don't need to worry about."

❦ ❦ ❦

She looked at her watch. Eleven-forty. Thirty-two minutes since he'd turned in at the townhouse gate. *Stop checking the time.* She stared fixedly at the wrought-iron fence. Moments later the gate swung outward and Zach came through it.

Opening the Toyota door, he slid into the passenger seat, a look of intense concentration on his face. He said, his voice rough with emotion, "Get this car moving. We've gotta get out of here."

Putting her hand on the key, she stared at him in surprise. "What happened?"

"If you don't get going *now,* I'm taking the wheel."

As she pulled away from the curb, the sound of a siren emerged from the distance. "Why the big rush? You get in a fight or something?

She call the cops on you?"

He covered his face briefly with one hand. "The situation in there . . . I don't know what to say . . . I'm gonna tell you everything, but you've gotta give me some time." She saw a shudder run through his body. "When we get to Oak Park, pull off on a side street and I'll explain. Bryce might be at the house and I want this over with before we get there." He looked at her directly. "Just don't try to drag it out of me now."

She'd never seen him so shaken. A rush of anxiety sluiced through her. *Why not just spit it out? What's he doing—trying to decide how to doctor his story? Only two things I can think of he wouldn't want to tell me. If he made a pass at her—or if she called the cops 'cause he wouldn't leave.*

Stopping at a light, she peered at him closely. His skin had gone gray; his face sagged. *He does need some time. You can't hammer on him now. You're just gonna have to muzzle your mouth and wait.*

The ten miles of expressway between Dearborn Park and the village had never seemed so long. Finally reaching Austin Boulevard, the border between Oak Park and the city, she cut left on Harrison and parked beside an Amoco station, then turned toward him.

Making a visible effort, he straightened his shoulders, glanced at her face, then looked away. "Nobody answered when I rang, but the door was unlocked so I went on in. She was . . . her body was sprawled on the living room floor. There was blood everywhere." He covered his eyes briefly, as if trying to shut out the mental picture.

"Her body? Are you saying she's dead?"

"She'd been bludgeoned. She was half on her side, the back of her head all caved in." He took a deep breath. "Somebody'd clubbed her. Her head was just this big, bloody hole. A champagne bottle with hair and blood on it was lying next to the body, a couple of glasses on the coffeetable. Looked like a romantic evening gone wrong."

"You just left her there? You didn't call an ambulance?"

"What good would it do? She was already dead."

"How can you be sure? What if she was in a coma or something?"

"Jesus, you think I don't know when somebody's dead? Her eyes were fixed. The skin temperature hadn't fallen much but it'd been at least an hour 'cause some of the splatters were starting to dry."

Cassidy stared at him, the enormity of what he'd done gradually dawning on her. "You left the scene? You didn't phone it in?"

"I called anonymously just before I left. Tomorrow morning I'll contact Area Four and explain why I didn't hang around."

"Why don't you begin by explaining to me." She spoke through clenched teeth, furious that he'd walked away from a murder scene and equally furious that he'd manipulated her into going along with it.

He shifted to face forward, his back slumping against the seat. "God, I hate it when you back me into corners and make me say things." He shook his head as if to clear it. "The truth? I'm too fucked to talk to cops tonight. A fact I never like admitting to anybody. I want to believe I can handle anything, anytime." He paused. "But tonight, I can't. First it was having that kid arrive and announce that I'm his father and he hates me. Then it was getting stupid and drinking too much—my brain's still half scrambled from all the booze. And then," he rubbed a hand over his face, "finding her. It's too much at once. It's got me reeling."

"Okay, I can understand you're not able to be on top of things the way you like." *Vulnerable—that's what he's feeling. But you better not say it out loud.* "Nobody'd expect a precise account, all neatly packaged as if you were writing a story. But even if you are fuzzy-headed and incoherent, it'd still be better to go back and talk to the police now instead of waiting till tomorrow and really pissing them off. The first few hours are critical. They need to have all the facts."

He glared. "Don't talk to me as if I were one of your clients." Looking away, he continued, "The problem is, there are some facts here you still don't know about. The rest of it. The part I was planning to tell you later."

The rest? Oh God, what else? She said in a low voice, "Does this other part implicate you?"

He shook his head. "I don't know. Probably not." He turned to look at her. "When I said I was too fucked to talk to the cops, what I meant was, I need some time to figure out exactly what I'm gonna say. There are some things here that could make me look bad, and I'm just too messed up to sort it out right now."

Her hand went to the base of her throat. "I was assuming you hadn't seen Xandra since she kicked you out. Was I wrong?"

"The last time I saw her she was pregnant with Bryce, only I didn't know it."

"Then how could you be implicated?"

"I'll tell you in the morning. I'll tell the cops in the morning. Just let me off for tonight."

Closing her eyes, she took several deep breaths, trying to get her own thoughts straight. Something niggled at her. "That half-hour. You were in there a full half-hour."

"Christ, I hate having to be accountable all the time."

Anger flared in her chest. "You want to move out?"

"I'm just all shot up with adrenaline is all." He shook his head. "Another reason to stay away from cops. I don't want to move out, but given the way things are going, it might be better for you if I did."

"Stop trying to distract me. What about that half-hour?"

"The first few minutes I just stood there staring at her body, not quite believing it was real. After that I wasted some more time trying to figure whether to call it in or not. Then I decided to take a quick look around, see if I could get a lead on how she knew she was in danger."

"Zach, your prints'll be all over!"

"I used a handkerchief. The only prints'll be consistent with my having walked in and found her."

Here he is, middle of a crisis, the old investigative reporter kicks in.

The same as you start acting like a therapist when everything goes up for grabs around you.

"See anything?"

"It was what I didn't see that was interesting. Everybody keeps an address book or Rolodex close to their phone, but I couldn't find anything with names and numbers on it." He muttered, "I need names."

"You're planning to investigate."

"I haven't gotten as far as a plan. It was more like an automatic response. Once I came out of my stupor, it occurred to me that I don't know a thing about her life. Bryce won't talk to me. If I did decide to dig around a little, I'd need contacts."

"Bryce." She let out a deep sigh. "God, it's gonna be hard telling him." Pressing her knuckles into her cheek, she said, "That poor kid. First his mother sends him off to his sonovabitch father, then his father has to deliver the news that his mother's dead."

Zach said, his voice low and resolute, "We're not gonna tell him tonight."

"Oh no you don't. You already tricked me into leaving the scene. You're not gonna talk me into putting Bryce off too." *He setting it up so he can weasel out of contacting the police altogether?*

"If I tell Bryce tonight, he'll go tearing off to the townhouse, then the police'll descend on me. It'll look like I was covering up the fact that I fled the scene. But if I call the cops in the morning, then tell Bryce, at least I'll get credit for turning myself in."

"You can't just withhold his mother's death. Bryce has the right to know. Besides, how'll you ever get him to trust you if you don't tell him now?"

"At the moment, Bryce's trust is not a high priority." He rubbed his face again, then took her hand. "Cass, I need some time."

Need—not a word I hear from him very often.

"Six hours, that's all. By tomorrow morning I'll have it all straight in my head and then I'll tell everybody everything. But you try forcing me tonight, I'd probably end up in some bar killing off another bottle. I know that'd be a real dumb-shit thing to do, but that's how out of control I feel."

Swallowing back the sudden thickness in her throat, she gazed into his bleary eyes. "So you're saying you've hit the wall. I seem to be a little slow on the uptake here." She smiled a wobbly little smile. "I guess I don't do any better at remembering you're not Superman than you do." Looking out the windshield at a brick apartment building, she said. "Okay, we'll do it your way."

❦ ❦ ❦

Nearing the corner where her house stood, Cassidy noted an unoccupied yellow Miata parked in front and a red convertible with a teenage boy and girl in it by the back gate. As they passed the convertible on their way to the garage at the far end of the lot, Zach said, "Well, he's here. And he brought company."

Walking from the garage toward the convertible, Cassidy scrutinized the car's youthful occupants, clearly visible under the streetlight A light-skinned black girl with short curls, beautifully molded face, and long slender neck lounged behind the wheel. A lean boy with dark crewcut and angular face sat erect in the passenger seat. From the stiff way he held his body Cassidy got an instant impression of hostility. *God, I don't envy Zach. An angry kid he never heard of, suddenly he's the only parent.*

She squeezed his hand, then raised her eyes to his face. He looked exhausted but otherwise okay. She had no doubt he'd been telling the truth about feeling out of control—Zach would never admit to such a thing unless he had to—but she wouldn't have known if he hadn't told her. A master at concealment, he only rarely allowed anyone to see below the surface. *First time I've ever known him to be so raw. Now he's got this pissed off kid in his face. Sure to make him feel like he's gotta be at his most unflappable best.*

Starshine zoomed toward them, rolling on the sidewalk and awaiting her usual greeting. When Cassidy failed to show proper respect by hunkering down and lavishing compliments, the cat sprang to her feet, flicked her tail, and stalked toward the door.

Zach approached the convertible's passenger side. "I see you made it back."

Bryce said in a defiant voice, "I told you I'd spend the night."

"You sure you don't wanna come home with me?" Giggling, the girl looped her arm through the boy's. "I'm all done working for tonight."

Bryce turned to face his companion. "I promised Xandra I'd stay with the asshole."

Zach hooked his thumbs into his jeans' waistband. "Who's your friend?"

"I said I'd sleep here. That doesn't mean I have to explain anything."

Twisting around to reach behind Bryce's back, the girl extended her hand, her nipples distinctly outlined by the red fabric clinging to her body like Saran wrap. "It's Tiffany. And I'm sorry Brycie's being so rude."

Zach took her hand. "I'm sorry he is too."

She settled back into her seat, nuzzled up close to Bryce, and stage-whispered into his ear. "He's kinda cute, especially with that scar. You should be nice to him."

"Shut up," he said affectionately. Wrapping an arm around her neck, he gave her a quick kiss. "I gotta go."

He grabbed a duffel bag and hopped out of the car. The girl pulled a U-turn, throwing a quick wave over her shoulder as she sped away. With Bryce on his feet, Cassidy could see that his lanky frame sported a fresh knit shirt, khaki pants, and clean Reeboks. A well-tended kid, the kind who usually had a parent breathing down his neck to make sure his clothes were pressed and his manners scrubbed. When he tossed a look in her direction, she introduced herself but got no response. *Well, this is gonna be fun.*

Starshine sat on the stoop waiting for the door to open, then raced inside ahead of the others. The humans paraded after her, Zach first, Bryce second, Cassidy bringing up the rear. Starshine jumped onto the counter to check her bowl. Cassidy saw the boy glance at the Jack Daniels bottle, which the cat was sniffing. *Trying to get a fix on his father. Should've put the bottle away. Don't want him getting the wrong idea. Or the right one either.*

Switching on the lights in the living room, Zach pulled a key out of his pocket and handed it to Bryce. "You'll need this." He nodded toward the blue paisley sofa beneath the front window. "Why don't you sit for a minute?"

The teenager shot a scowl at Zach, glanced over his shoulder as if thinking of leaving, then perched on the cushion. Cassidy and Zach sat in the side-by-side armchairs opposite the entryway and staircase.

"I laid out a sleeping bag and air mattress in the extra bedroom so you're set for tonight."

Sleeping bag? Air mattress? Must've pulled 'em out of those boxes he brought over from his condo. Like a Noah's ark of inanimate objects—a pair of everything that exists packed away in that mess in the basement.

"Okay." Bryce dispensed words grudgingly, giving Zach as little as possible.

Leaning back, Zach pressed his fingertips together on his chest. He watched the boy in silence. *Zach can withhold with the best of them. These two'll be stalemated indefinitely.*

Cassidy ventured, "I guess you're really pissed about having to stay here."

Bryce glanced her way. "She should've let me go by my friend's." His eyes were brown and surly, nothing like the steady, blue-gray ones she looked into so often. He was a couple of inches taller than Zach, who stood a hair under six feet. The boy's frame was lighter, his face more rugged. The only similarity was the color of their skin, deep bronze on both faces. *Zach has to be the father. That unusual skin tone—couldn't be a coincidence.*

Cassidy said, "I'm curious why she insisted you come here. Don't you have any other family you could go to?" *Somebody else that could take him?*

Bryce glanced at her briefly, then looked away. "Nah, I'm all she's got."

Nobody. Oh Lord. Cassidy felt the sadness in her throat again. *He's stuck with us, we're stuck with him.*

Folding an arm beneath her breasts, she grasped the other elbow. "I know you're really angry at your father, but what about me? You mad at me too?"

He shrugged. Starshine sidled around the edge of the room, disappeared behind the sofa, then peeked out from its far end.

"So if I'm not the one you're mad at, could you maybe talk to me?"

Bryce glared over their heads toward the dining room. "I just wanna do my time and go home."

A picture popped into her mind of an exotic, chalky-skinned mannequin lying on a blood-soaked carpet, its eyes blank. She turned away to hide the sudden rush of sympathy. "You worried you might get stuck here longer than you expected? That your mother might not be able to let you come home right away?"

For one instant she glimpsed the anxiety in his eyes, then the shuttered expression returned. "Nah, she said it'd just be a couple of days. Besides, I'm only gonna sleep here."

Zach gave her a sharp look, the visual equivalent of kicking her under the table. She read his thought: Stop playing therapist.

"I can see why you'd be pissed at Zach. Here he disappeared on your mother when she was pregnant. He didn't know about it, of course, but that doesn't make it any easier for you. And he's never been any part of your life at all."

Bryce blinked, surprised at what she was saying.

"You're probably right. He probably was a real jerk back when he got your mother pregnant. But it's possible he might've learned a thing or two in all this time." She flicked a glance at Zach, who had his detached expression firmly in place. "I understand you hate having to sleep here. But as long as you have to put up with us for a few days, I wish that both of you," she shot a look at Zach, then Bryce, "would consider the possibility of getting to know each other a little."

Zach cleared his throat. "Did I mention she's a shrink?" His eyes met Bryce's. "She has trouble turning it off." He let out a long breath. "It's late. Let's go upstairs."

🍎 🍎 🍎

She crawled into bed next to Zach, who was usually half asleep by the time she finished her nightly washup. His arms went around her, pulling her backside up close. She snuggled in deeper. "I feel so sorry for him."

"I'm not looking forward to tomorrow either."

Monday morning. Maybe we could just skip it. Take one of those amnesia drugs and zone out till next week.

Normally they cuddled a minute, then each rolled over to their own side of the waterbed. Tonight, his grip didn't loosen even when she heard his breathing deepen into sleep.

🍎 🍎 🍎

Cassidy opened her eyes and looked at the clock on the bureau. *Six? I never see that number in the morning. What am I doing awake at this hour?* Then she remembered. Since Zach's side of the bed was empty, she got up, started to pull a tee-shirt over her naked body, thought of Bryce, and dressed instead, absently picking a lavender shirt and grape-colored shorts. On her way out of the bedroom, she glanced at the two doors across the short hall. The door to the left, Bryce's room, was closed. The one to the right, Zach's office, was open.

She found Zach downstairs in the dining room, elbows propped on the teak table, a nearly empty mug in front of him. She padded into the kitchen, poured the remains of the pot into her purple cat mug, added large quantities of cream and sugar, then sat kitty-corner from him. The coffee tasted stale. "How long've you been up?"

"Hour or so."

"Working yourself up to telling everybody everything?"

He folded his arms on the table. "Digging up other people's secrets is part of my job, and I've been known to say that anytime anybody has something to hide, it's sure to come back to haunt them. Now it's *my* old garbage getting resurrected, and it's like my own words circling around to bite me in the ass."

Tell him you don't want his smelly old garbage. Let's pretend it never happened, wait till the police notify Bryce. Zach and I can act surprised.

"We both deal in other people's secrets. I'm a good listener, remember?"

As she reached for her mug, he folded his hand around her wrist, his way of saying "thank you." She caught a look of embarrassment, maybe even guilt, in his smoky eyes. *This is gonna be bad. We have to find some way to get through it.*

"Okay, here goes." Zach gulped the last of his coffee. "I already told you how Xandra dumped me all those years ago. Well, when it happened, I didn't believe her. I was strung out on coke, convinced she was the love of my life, certain I'd be able to change her mind if I could just get her to listen. Trouble was, she hung up every time I called, so I started following her around. I really believed it was all some kind of misunderstanding." He stared straight ahead, gave his head a shake, looked down at his mug. "People didn't talk about stalking so much back then."

Cassidy swallowed, trying to get the lump out of her throat.

"That went on a couple of weeks, maybe longer." He ran a hand over his face. "It's hard to remember. I never let myself think about it before this. Anyway, one day I was standing there ringing the bell, and she up and opens the door, invites me in just like nothing'd happened. I figured she'd been pissed, now it was over. She seemed glad to see me, we did some coke and fell into bed. Afterward, she lit a cigarette, looked me in the face, and told me to get out. Said if I ever bothered her again, she'd call the cops on me."

He gazed through the dining room window. The light outside was pale and crystalline, completely at odds with Cassidy's mood.

"Tell me."

"I got a little rough. Shoved her around. Maybe I slapped her, I don't know." He rubbed a hand over the back of his head, dropped it on the table, looked out the window again.

Cassidy's stomach churned. *He's not that kind. Yes he is, he just told you. Her fault. No, you don't. Don't you ever even think things like that.* "Zach . . ." She couldn't find any words.

"What I did, it wasn't that much. I'm not trying to let myself off. I know I was a complete shit. But I also know I didn't do what she said."

3. Insect Under A Microscope

Her hands shaky, Cassidy wrapped both of them around her mug to raise it. "What did she say?"

Zach sighed. "Later that day she turned up at a hospital with a broken arm and her face smashed in. She said I did it and the police came and got me. My family, very grudgingly, came to the rescue. They paid for a hot-shot attorney who pled it down to a misdemeanor. I never saw her again but they showed me the hospital pictures and I know somebody else got to her after I left."

Taking a swallow, she realized the coffee was a mistake the instant it hit her stomach. She set the mug carefully on the table. A woman wearing headphones jogged down the middle of Briar. *Sure he believes that's all he did. Not sure I believe it. Everybody minimizes. I minimize how much chocolate I eat.* Her words slow and neutral, she said, "When people do things they regret, sometimes they change the memory so it's easier to handle."

His eyes narrowed. "Don't pull that shrink stuff on me."

He needs to know how you feel.

Don't know what to say. Can't say it's all right. Can't hide behind the this-must-be-hard shit. Can't yell at him.

"I'm pretty horrified."

"Yeah, I thought you'd be." He looked away.

"Guess I'm going to need some time to get used to the idea." She laid her hand on his forearm. "This what you couldn't sort out last night?"

"I couldn't focus enough to make a decision. The first story you give the police is extremely important. If it's inconsistent, if you leave out parts and it doesn't make sense, they come after you like gangbusters."

"So we have to have everything down pat before we talk to them."

"Now, as you can imagine, this is a story I'd go to great lengths to avoid having to tell. Last night I almost had myself convinced that it's all ancient history, they can't use it in court, I'm not under any obligation to tell you or anybody else."

"But you changed your mind."

"Yeah, what I was thinking last night was a crock. Just trying to find a way out of it. The police have a sheet on me from the arrest, and even though Xandra's name isn't on it, some old geezer is bound to remember who the victim was. Then they'd know I was hiding something and that'd make 'em wonder what else I was hiding. If something's gonna come out anyway, it's always better to do it yourself."

"So you're telling the cops everything."

He nodded.

"I'm gonna make more coffee." She set the dial on the grinder, poured water, wiped up spills. Starshine rubbed against her ankles, then sprang onto the counter. As Cassidy scratched the cat's cheek, her green eyes squinted and an adoring purr vibrated from her body. *She doesn't care what any of us did nearly eighteen years ago. Long as we feed her today, she pours out love. Or something.*

Cassidy's kitchen window had a view of the Stein house and yard next door, including a direct line of sight into her neighbor's kitchen, where two brown-skinned teens were arm wrestling over their cereal bowls. Dorothy Stein, the rosy-skinned adoptive mother, threw her a quick wave.

Oh God, why can't I have a normal life? A mob of off-the-wall kids instead of a boyfriend with old garbage oozing to the surface like an oil spill.

Something felt unfinished. She poured fresh coffee and sat at the table again. "What about that half-hour when you were in her place? What do I tell the cops?"

"They'll question us separately and we both tell it straight. The drinking, the half hour, everything. That way there won't be any inconsistencies, any little holes."

"It's going to look bad."

"Yeah, but there isn't any evidence so they won't be able to do anything."

Not an arrest. Just stories in the newspaper. Problems for Zach at the Post. *Clients looking at you like you must be crazy.* Just yesterday she'd asked Maggie if marrying him was a bad idea.

He put in a call to the police, then went to wake Bryce. The teenager sat at one end of the table, Zach at the other, Cassidy in between.

Zach gazed steadily at Bryce. "I have something to tell you that's gonna be very hard for you to hear." Pausing, he glanced at Cassidy.

Oh shit. "You want me to—"

"No, I'll do it." He took a long breath. "Last night we drove down to your place because I wanted to talk to your mother."

Bryce jerked to his feet, skittering the chair backward on the hardwood floor. "I'm not discussing her with you. I'm getting out of here."

"Take it easy." Zach folded his arms on the table. "Now sit. There's something I have to tell you."

The boy hesitated for several beats, then lowered himself into the chair, his body rigid.

"When I got down there, your mother was lying on the floor. Somebody'd come in after you left and bludgeoned her. By the time I found her, it was too late."

"What do you mean, too late? You fucker, what'd you do to her?" He jumped up and started toward the front door. "I've gotta get down there."

Zach said, his voice level, "The police'll be here any minute. If you leave, they'll pick you up and haul you into the station."

Pivoting, Bryce thundered back toward them, pressed his palms flat on the table, and thrust his face toward his father. "Goddamn you, what'd you do to her?"

"I'm not the one who hurt her."

The boy collapsed into his chair, thumped his elbows down, and buried his face. A garbled moan came from behind his hands.

Cassidy slid her arm uncertainly across the table, wanting to touch him, not sure that she should.

Zach rose and gripped her shoulder. "Let's go wait on the porch, give him some time to himself."

She hesitated, then followed him out.

On the porch she felt the air beginning to swell with humidity like a body bloating up. *Reverting. Everything's reverting to its normal state. The weather reverting to its usual oppressiveness. My life reverting to chaos and crisis.*

❦ ❦ ❦

A Ford sedan stopped in front of the house and a man and woman approached the porch. The woman, walking in front, was fortyish, with a thin, fine-lined face and straight blond hair chopped at jaw-length. She wore a sleekly styled jacket and mid-thigh skirt.

The man, in his thirties, was short and slight, his wiry frame thrusting forward in a straight-ahead stride that said DON'T GET IN MY WAY. His suit coat was overdue for the cleaners and his pants bore only a ghostly reminder of a crease.

Zach and Cassidy rose from the wicker couch. Opening the screen door, Zach introduced himself.

The woman came onto the porch, followed by her partner. "I'm Detective Hathaway and this is Detective Torres."

Stepping backward to position himself in front of the door to the house, Zach said, "You know about Bryce?"

Hathaway nodded, her face impassive.

Torres moved closer to Zach. Curly brown hair sprouted above a wide forehead, thick nose, and square chin. He looked like great sports bar material, but the sharpness in his alert blue eyes reminded Cassidy that sports bar enthusiasts were not necessarily dumb. "Bryce." His voice snide. "That would be the deceased woman's son." His voice came out a couple of decibels higher than necessary. He took another half-step forward. "You found the body last night, called it in anonymously, then had second thoughts, is that it?"

Pissed off 'cause Zach left the scene. I knew there'd be trouble over it.

The senior detective cut a look at her partner and he pulled back somewhat.

Zach said, "Bryce just heard about his mother. So if you could talk to Cass and me first, that'd give him some time to pull it together."

Hathaway, in her precise voice, addressed Cassidy, "And you are?"

"Cassidy McCabe. We live together." She started to say "We're planning to be married," then thought better of it.

Hathaway said, "Let's go inside."

They're not gonna give him an inch.

They stood in the living room, Bryce emerging from the dining room to lean against the archway. Zach handed Xandra's letter to Hathaway. After discussing the available space, she took him into the therapy office, Torres sat down in the living room with Bryce, and Cassidy was sent to wait on the porch.

Starshine settled on her lap, gazed up, and purred rapturously. *She actually providing comfort just when I need it the most? Could it be all that stuff about catly intuition isn't entirely bogus after all?*

Half an hour later Hathaway came out to sit on a molded plastic chair across from Cassidy, pad in hand. "Okay, let's hear your version."

She recounted the events, then asked, "What will happen to Bryce?"

"We'll call DCFS and they'll find some place for him to go."

"Zach's his father."

"So the letter says."

"Couldn't he stay with us?" *You really want a hostile kid in and out of the house?* "Temporarily, I mean."

Hathaway brushed at the sleeve of her impeccable gray jacket. "I get the impression he doesn't have any great desire to be here. Given his age, if he were to decide he wanted to stay, DCFS would probably go along. Unless, of course, we arrest Moran." She leveled her eyes at Cassidy, her neck perfectly aligned with her spine, not the least sympathetic tilt to her head. "Now, back to the matter at hand. How long have you two been living together?"

Cassidy lifted her chin, mirroring the other woman's body language. "Since November."

Hathaway's gaze met Cassidy's, her gray eyes as unresponsive as Starshine's when the cat didn't choose to acknowledge her human's existence. "What do you know about Moran's history?"

Quite a bit, considering my dead client Ryan was Zach's brother and he used to bitch about Zach's screw-ups fairly often. "He's got twelve years in at the *Post*, and he's been pretty noncommittal with women until now."

The corners of the detective's mouth tipped slightly. "But this time it's different."

Thankful for her training in therapist neutrality, Cassidy kept her face blank.

"Have you ever seen his temper come out?"

"We've been living together nine months. Of course I have. The worst he ever got was when I did something really stupid and he walked out of a bar and waited for me in the car." She wanted to get on a soapbox about his outstanding ability to manage anger and superb impulse control but stopped herself from saying more.

"What about his drinking?"

As she opened her mouth to speak, Cassidy realized she'd paused an instant too long. "What exactly is the question?"

She saw a faint glimmer of distaste in Hathaway's cool gray eyes.

Thinks I'm one of those women so gaga over her man I can't see that he's slime. God, I hope she's not right.

🍎 🍎 🍎

By ten-thirty the detectives were gone, Zach was at the *Post*, and Bryce had slipped off somewhere when she wasn't looking. Starshine, who sat on the dresser demanding attention, was pleased at the departures. She liked having clients in and out. They opened doors and fussed over her. All other territorial intrusions were unwelcome.

As Cassidy pulled on a plum skirt in preparation for seeing clients, Starshine struck at the moving fabric.

Stepping out of range, Cassidy spoke to the calico, who watched with big green eyes and appeared to listen. "Talking to that detective made me feel like I'd committed some grievous sin but was too ignorant to know what it was. Even though I think I've managed to get through twenty-four of the worst hours of my life without doing anything egregiously stupid."

As Cassidy moved back to the dresser for earrings, Starshine bumped her head against her human's side, a request for petting. Cassidy stopped buttoning her top and provided the sought-after chin scratch.

"I distinctly dislike being put in a one-down position, a pretty unavoidable event when you're on the answering end of somebody else's interrogation."

Starshine patted her arm, indicating she wanted to be picked up.

Cassidy hoisted the calico onto her shoulder. "Being a detective is sort of like sitting in the therapist's chair, except the cop never has to be empathic. God, I hope my questions never make any client feel like an insect under a microscope, the way Hathaway's did me."

❦   ❦   ❦

Cassidy sat in her director's chair across from her client, Judy, who had taken a place on the new sectional that curved around the two windowed walls of the office. The sleek contemporary furniture was a gift from Zach, who'd insisted on replacing the ratty old vinyl sofas for her birthday.

Judy said, "I know this divorce is for the best. Not just for me but for Bob as well. I mean, what kind of life would it be for him if I stayed out of pity?"

The client was a forty-two-year-old bank executive with short, black hair, darkly lashed blue eyes, a soft mouth and strong chin. Cassidy thought of her as a rosebud corsage, feminine but with hidden thorns. Judy fixed gleaming, hyacinth eyes on Cassidy and said, "Unfortunately, other people don't understand."

"Which other people?"

"My mother, for one. She's always preaching this unconditional love schtick. She's real old-school, a confirmed believer in sticking together through thick and thin, which is what she did."

Unconditional love. Such a wonderful ring to those words. But just beneath their sugar-coated surface, a license to abuse. "You-gotta-love-me-no-matter-what" translates to, "I-can-do-anything-I-want-and-you-can't-leave."

Cassidy asked, "What do *you* think about unconditional love?"

She sighed. "It feels like slavery. If I thought I had to love Bob even though he can't hold a job, even though I've lost all respect for him—well, I couldn't, that's all. I don't see how you can make yourself love someone who constantly lets you down."

The east window above the client's head let in a diffuse, late afternoon light. "Feelings just are," Cassidy said. "They occur spontaneously. It's not a good idea to try to make yourself feel anything."

"I used to think I was free of the traditional stereotypes. Thought I wanted a sensitive guy, that it was good for men to cry."

Most of us today think we want that. Do we?

Crossing one knee over the other, Judy smoothed her short, red skirt. "But the way Bob's been acting about this divorce, it really gets to me. When his voice sounds depressed or he has tears in his eyes, I get this terrible sense of disgust. I just can't get past seeing him as weak. I should be able to accept that it's okay for him to have his feelings, but I can't."

Cassidy nodded.

Judy said, her voice low, "I keep having this awful sneaky suspicion that when I decided to marry him, I was just settling. I was getting older. There weren't a lot of opportunities. I'm afraid I talked myself into it. That I never really loved him."

"What would be so bad about not having loved him?"

Judy stared out the window on the wall to her right. Cassidy's waiting room radio, the white noise she used to muffle voices, played softly: "Walkin' through Memphis ...." She heard the back door open, then close. The clock on the windowsill behind Judy's head said five forty-five. *Zach home early? Bryce sliding into the house?* The muscles in her neck tightened as thoughts of the murder, which she'd pushed aside while doing therapy, rushed back in.

After showing her client out, Cassidy paused by the door, some of the questions raised by the session echoing in her mind. *How would you handle it if Zach got all weepy on you?* She tried to picture it but couldn't. The odds of Mike Tyson becoming a feminist were higher.

A little voice she did not want to acknowledge whispered in the back of her mind, *You wouldn't like it. He'd seem pathetic.*

We all want to be so PC and perfect, but deep down inside the bad old attitudes linger on.

She headed across the kitchen and into the dining room. A pizza box and a bag of peanut butter cups sat on the table. *So the door-opener was Zach. And he brought Reese's.* He knew that during times of stress, she reverted to her childhood habit of scarfing peanut butter and chocolate.

The phone rang. Retracing her steps, she lifted the receiver off the kitchen wall and heard a familiar "Hello." Helen's voice was laden with the same heaviness it had carried for the past several months.

"Hi Mom. How you doing?" *Damn, why'd I pick up? I sure don't need her problems on top of my own.* The first floor, which had no air conditioning except in her office, was clogged with heat.

"Well, dear, I was feeling kind of blue. I know you usually have clients at night but I thought I'd take a chance and see if you and Zach might want to go out for a bite to eat."

Her mother had launched an anti-Zach campaign shortly after they'd started dating, her animosity stemming from her insecurity over his wealthy, privileged background and from his apparent disinterest in meeting Cassidy's family. Helen operated under the assumption that anyone who'd grown up in a North Oak Park mansion was bound to be a snob. Then, five months ago, Zach was instrumental in stopping a vicious psychopath. Afterward Helen decided that having a thoroughly competent male join the three generations of McCabe women—Cassidy, her mother, and grandmother—was not all bad.

She finds out about the dead spiderwoman and the surprise kid, she'll flip back to her original out-with-him, the-sooner-the-better stance. Cassidy stared through her window into the Stein's kitchen, where a couple of kids appeared to be cooking. "I'm sorry you're having a bad day, Mom. And I wish I could spend some time with you .... " *You don't have clients tonight. You could see her.* She felt a familiar pang. "But I've already got plans."

"I understand." Helen sighed. "I know you have your own life and I don't mean to drag you down. As soon as I pull out of this awful funk, I'll get started volunteering at the housing center again."

Some months back, Helen had been exposed to HIV. Although the tests had come up negative, the experience had undermined her. And to make matters worse, her then-fiancé had blamed her for the exposure and broken off their engagement. Cassidy was of the opinion that Helen had every right to be depressed, although having her mother as an unofficial client wasn't easy.

Glancing at the clock above the window, she shifted from one foot to the other, impatient to go upstairs and talk to Zach. *Can't you give her five minutes?*

"So, what have you been feeling down about?"

"Oh, I just keep thinking about Roland. You said he wasn't good for me and I know you're right, but just for that little while my life was so exciting."

If only she'd try medication. Or get an official therapist, who'd certainly have more influence than you do. Unfortunately, she'd rather wallow.

After the phone call, Cassidy ripped open the Reese's bag and bit into a peanut butter cup, chewing slowly to stop herself from gobbling half the contents. A moment ago she'd been dying to get upstairs, but now she felt a sense of dread at being drawn back into Zach's old garbage, his history of cocaine abuse, obsession and violence having stirred up some small part of her that was truly pissed at him.

Thank God, I didn't say a word to Mom about the wedding. Whatever might be going on with Cassidy, her mother was generally the last to know. Before telling Helen anything, Cassidy had to work herself up to facing her mother's displeasure, and nothing was higher on Helen's current disapproval scale than men and marriage. Even though Zach was presently in favor, Cassidy suspected Helen would have a hard time with her daughter's getting married when her own wedding plans had failed.

Gazing through the window at her neighbor's tidy vegetable garden, Cassidy recalled the night three weeks earlier when Zach had asked her to marry him, a warm memory to tamp down her anger.

It had been a clear, mild night. Having finished early, she'd planted herself at her desk with the intent of filling out the managed care forms she'd been avoiding. Zach appeared in the doorway to inform her that he'd put an iced bottle of champagne on the porch and would like her to join him. Happy to be rescued from the forms and curious about the champagne, she trotted down behind him.

When the glasses were filled, he clinked his against hers and said, "Here's to us." Starshine jumped down from the open window and settled on Cassidy's chest. A warm breeze lapped at her skin.

Zach gave her a long look, then said, "I know this is gonna come as a shock, but I've been thinking it might be a good idea for us to get married."

She stared in surprise, anxiety twitches starting in her stomach.

Appearing a little self-conscious, he went on, "As long as we're planning to stay together, it just seems like it'd be better to make it legal. There're a lot of advantages. You know, things like health insurance—" His voice trailed off.

"Health insurance?"

"Yeah, I realize that's not very romantic, but I don't know how to say these things."

"You could practice. It'd be good for you." *Good for both of us. You don't do much better at romantic than he does.*

"Having decided a long time ago that I wasn't the marrying kind, I trained myself never to say anything that might imply otherwise. I've been trying to talk about feelings more but it doesn't come easy."

And the reason I don't say how I feel is that Kevin and I used to babble love words all the time and it didn't mean anything, so I swore off them for the rest of my life.

Zach pulled her closer. "I like how we are together. I like the things our bodies do in bed. I want this to be permanent."

"Well, me too. But why marriage?"

"It's not nice to ask *why* when you've just been proposed to."

She made a face. "You sound like my mother. So, why marriage?"

"I can't explain. It's just a feeling. Just this sense of wanting to nail down what we've got. Which doesn't make sense, I know, considering we'd be changing the status quo, maybe even making it worse. I know all that, but I still want to marry you." He placed his hands along the sides of her head, snarling his fingers in her hair, and lifted her face for a kiss. "So, what do you think? You wanna do it?"

She felt a brief surge of panic. Pulling back, she gazed shakily into his calm blue eyes. *Don't take chances. Too risky. Couldn't stand to see this fall apart.*

But there were no guarantees, neither in getting married nor in not getting married. *Only thing you can count on is change. So, since there's always gonna be risk, the single relevant question is: which would you rather be—a girlfriend or wife?*

A wife, no question. Girlfriend has such a teenybopper ring to it.

She'd tried to focus on the fact that Zach, a self-proclaimed bachelor, actually wanted to marry her. That alone ought to give her a terrific boost. *So why am I not out there dancing in the street?* She'd felt an odd little shiver. *If it seems too good to be true . . ..*

Shaking her head, she pulled herself back to the present. She imagined saying to her mother, "We're planning to get married as soon as Zach's out of jail and Bryce's off to college." Picturing Helen's horrified face, she tossed the candy wrappers and went upstairs.

4. Beer Cans and Doorbells

Zach and Bryce were together in her bedroom, hardly surprising since the only television in the house resided there. Zach lounged on the left side of the waterbed, his legs pointing toward the opposite corner, in sole command of the remote. Bryce slouched in Cassidy's chair in the middle of the room, his legs propped on the end of the bed. Behind him stood two executive desks, Cassidy's and the one Zach had moved over from his Marina City condo. A television anchor was interviewing some expert on the topic of kids shooting their classmates.

Leaning against the doorjamb, she waited for the two males in her bedroom to break out of their trance.

Can't imagine why Zach wants to cover news all day, then come home and watch it on TV. Her mouth pursed in distaste. *Less I know about the ravages around me, the better.*

Zach glanced up, his face distracted. "I bought a pizza."

She didn't respond.

A minute passed. "Oh yeah, you don't like to talk with the television on." He cut the power.

Bryce kept his eyes on the blank screen, not looking at either of them.

Male bonding. "You guys ready to eat?"

They paraded downstairs. Bryce took a chair at the opposite end of the table from Zach's. Cassidy arranged dishes and napkins. Zach got out three beers.

Zach finished his first slice and said, "After dinner I thought maybe we could pick up a few things to make that other bedroom more comfortable. Another television, a mattress, maybe even a bed."

Cassidy stared at him in surprise. His full attention appeared to be on the chunk of pizza in his hand. *He tiptoeing around the question of whether Bryce is gonna stay with us? Not like him to come at things sideways. Could it be he actually cares how Bryce feels about him?* She shook her head. Nobody's opinion ever seemed to matter much to Zach.

She glanced at Bryce, who sat, head lowered, devouring pizza. He hadn't said a word since she first came upstairs. *I do believe Zach's met his match at remoteness.*

Cassidy wiped her greasy hands on a napkin. "Bryce . . ."

Several beats later he raised his head.

"We need to know whether or not you want to stay with us. From what Zach just said, I get the impression he'd like to have you spend some time here."

A reaction she couldn't identify flickered in his dark, sulky eyes, then they closed off from her. "I dunno."

Several more beats passed.

You should get out of the middle, let them work it out on their own.

Work it out? They'll never get as far as a conversation.

Zach went into the kitchen to get another beer.

"Bryce, you have to tell us what you're going to do. You can't just slip in and out like some kind of ghost. You have to officially decide where you'll be staying for the next couple of weeks. If you don't, I'll call my friend who's a high mucky-muck at DCFS and they will come and get you." *Lies are beginning to come way too easily.* She raised her glass, filled her mouth with beer, swallowed slowly. "My preference would be to have you stay."

That true? You really want a punk kid around?

Bryce went into the kitchen for a second beer.

Zach shouldn't be feeding him beers. He's only seventeen.

Probably been drinking since he was seven.

Dropping into his chair, Bryce said, "Okay, I'll sleep here for a while."

She would like to have demanded that he appear on a daily basis for dinner, but since neither she nor Zach ate regular meals, that would be unrealistic. "Shall we start with a commitment for the next two weeks?"

"I guess."

After dinner Bryce got a third beer, then leaned against the wall to watch the other two clean up. Zach was clearing the table and Cassidy was rinsing out Coors cans for the recyclable tub when the front doorbell rang.

The can she was holding clattered into the sink. *God, I'm edgy. Seven o'clock. Probably some guy raising funds to fight Com Ed.*

Zach headed for the door, Cassidy and Bryce at his heels. Detectives Hathaway and Torres were waiting on the porch. They advanced into the living room uninvited.

Hathaway looked directly at Zach. "I want you over at Area Four for a lineup."

Oh shit, oh shit, they've got something.

Zach stood in front of Hathaway, hands on hips, feet planted widely. Cassidy moved up next to him. Bryce remained somewhere in the background. After a long pause, Zach said, his voice tight with anger. "What's going on?"

Jaw set, shoulders squared, Torres edged in closer. "All those police stories you write, you need us to spell it out?"

A glance passed between the two detectives that Cassidy thought surprisingly intimate, but it happened so fast she couldn't be sure. Hathaway moved slightly and Torres pulled back.

"I told you," she said with exaggerated precision, "I'm taking you in for a lineup."

"What does this mean?" Cassidy asked, her gaze bouncing between Zach and the detective.

Leveling his eyes at Hathaway, Zach said, "I presume you have a witness."

She just looked at him.

Zach said in an even tone, "I explained already. I went into the townhouse around eleven."

Torres shifted his weight impatiently. "Yeah, yeah, yeah. Now let's get going."

"You know," Zach said, "I'd really hate to have to get an attorney. If you force me to call my guy down to the station, it's just gonna slow things down for all of us. He'd insist on my not answering questions, and that'd keep you from getting what you need and me from convincing you I didn't do it." He paused. "Now, if you were to tell me the when and the where on this witness of yours, I probably wouldn't feel the need to bring my guy in."

Hathaway raised her chin slightly, looked out the window, then back at Zach. "Some guy matching your description was seen entering the premises at half-past six."

When did you get home from the movie? After nine-thirty. You don't know for sure he wasn't at the townhouse earlier. She glanced back at Bryce, hoping he'd say he'd been with Zach at the time. But the boy lounged against the archway, his face blank, his stance making it clear he considered himself strictly a bystander. She put her hand on Zach's forearm. "Maybe you *should* get that lawyer." *You—not we? You on your way out too?*

"After I just made a deal with these two?" He shook his head. "Wouldn't be fair." He moved one foot forward, letting his body go looser. "Besides, I've already told the cops everything I know, so there's not much a lawyer can do for me at this point."

Torres snorted. "Oh, I'll bet there's a thing or two you haven't gotten around to mentioning yet."

Cassidy said, "Let me come with you."

He shook his head. "These two want me all to themselves."

A slight smile played at the corners of Hathaway's thin mouth. "You do know the drill, I'll give you that." Her sardonic eyes caught Cassidy's as she turned toward the door.

She's got it all scripted out. I'm the stupid, stand-by-your-man ninny. Zach's the slick creepo who bashed his old girlfriend, then got his new girlfriend to alibi him. And she's the enlightened feminist who'd never be any man's fool.

When the front door closed, she turned to Bryce. "What time did you leave here?"

" 'Round five-thirty. He could've been at the townhouse by six-thirty easy." Bryce's arrogant tone grated on her nerves. Heading for the kitchen, he opened the refrigerator, extracted another beer, and started toward the stairs.

"Sit down at that table right now."

He gave her a long, defiant stare.

"Sit."

Can't you cut him slack? His mother just died.

I'm too pissed.

He slowly folded his lean body into the chair.

She stood over him. "Give me that can. You've had enough."

"*He* drinks."

"You're seventeen. Hand it over."

He waited thirty seconds, then yielded. "You done now?" He started to get up.

She pushed him back down. "No, as a matter of fact, I'm not. I've got a little something to say about this attitude of yours, which I'm getting pretty sick of. Here Zach was, minding his own business, didn't even know you existed. Then Xandra suddenly decides you have to go stay with your father. She plunks you into the middle of our lives, proceeds to get herself killed, and now they've hauled Zach down to the police station. He doesn't deserve any of this. He especially doesn't deserve to have you acting like he's pond scum, because that's not what you really think, anyway."

"That *is* what I think." He stood. "You don't know anything about him. You just wanna believe he's this great guy 'cause you looove him." He made the word sound ridiculous, a malady only simpletons would fall prey to. "I saw how that detective looked at him. She thinks he went down and whacked Xandra after I took off, then got you to drive him over later so he could explain the prints and everything. That's what she thinks." He pulled himself up tall, towering over her by at least a foot. "And you can't come up with a single reason to say it's not true." He pivoted and headed for the stairs.

"Where're you going?"

"To watch television."

Not leaving? He's hooked into this too, as desperate as you are to find out what happens at the lineup. But maybe looking for a different outcome. Hoping his father killed his mother? Shit—what a miserable place to be.

"Wait," she called after him. "Take the TV and the swivel chair into your room." *Your room? It isn't his room. He doesn't belong here. I wish he'd just disappear and I'd never have to see him again.*

She poured herself a glass of Carlo Rossi, then went to sit on the front porch. But as soon as she was settled, the memory of what she'd heard the night before began replaying in her head. The air was hot and sticky, the humidity she'd noticed that morning having run right up to the top of the scale. Drumming one fist on the wooden armrest, she tried to shut off the sound of Zach's voice telling her about his sexual spiderwoman. The tape was restarting for the tenth time when she got up and headed for her bedroom.

The door to Bryce's room was open, the sound of high-volume car chases pouring out of it. From the hall she could see the teenager in her swivel chair, his feet on Zach's chair, a beer in his hand.

Do I have to take it away from him just to prove a point?

Shit, I'm not his mother. Why should I care if he gets wasted?

She went into her bedroom and closed the door. Sitting on the bed, she pulled her knees up tight, wrapped her arms around them, and squeezed her eyes shut. *Wish I had somebody to talk to.* Her grandmother was a real trooper, someone she could always count on, but Cassidy hadn't confided in Gran since she was six years old. She and her mother were getting along better than they used to, but not so well that she wanted Helen to know about Zach appearing in a lineup. Even with Maggie it would be too hard to say, too hard to admit that her life was unraveling again, just when she seemed finally to have gotten it together. She'd always kept her problems to herself, not letting anybody know when she was in trouble. Now the pressure of holding it all in was so intense she felt she might burst.

She took a large swallow of wine. It was only in the past few months that she'd allowed herself to open up totally to Zach. Zach was the one she wanted to talk to. *This is why you should never start needing anybody. As soon as you need them, they're not there.*

Finishing her wine, she wandered downstairs in search of Starshine, who also was not there.

🐛   🐛   🐛

Cassidy stood on her stoop and scanned her well-lit yard for the small calico. For the three years she'd lived in the house alone—and before that, for the eight years she'd lived in it with her ex-husband— her yard had been the battleground for a losing war with overgrown grass and weeds. When Zach, a thoroughly urban male, left his city condo to move in with her, she had never expected yardwork to be one of the perks. But he amazed her by taking on the challenge of dandelions in May and fast-growing grass in June, and now, for the first time in her tenancy, her yard looked almost as good as her neighbor's.

No sign of Starshine. She called "Kitty, kitty" with some degree of hope. The cat had, on occasion, been known to come when beckoned by the sing-song incantation that humans considered the magic words for luring felines. *Maybe she's visiting her friends.* After producing a litter around the time Zach moved in, Starshine had been neutered. Since then she'd resumed her old habit of yowling at the door until Cassidy gave in and opened it. With motherhood behind her, the calico was free to develop a social life of her own, which meant hanging out with the colony of feral cats that clustered around the bungalow across Briar where a neighborhood cat lady fed strays.

Cassidy went to the sidewalk and stared across Briar, the street running alongside her west-facing house. On the opposite side, two large orange cats hunkered in the yard belonging to the feeder of strays, a bevy of kittens played in the woman's driveway, and an additional three cats were visible on the lawn of the corner house.

Starshine sat erect on the ledge beneath the cat lady's front window, her take-charge demeanor reminding Cassidy of the night more than a year before when she'd come home to find the stray calico in possession of her stoop. Starshine had been a diminutive, half-grown cat at the time, and even now she remained so petite she seemed like a teenager next to the hulkish ferals. Discovering her tiny Starshine on the neighbor's window ledge made Cassidy nervous. She disapproved of the calico's new-found urge to socialize, fearing that the thuggish street cats would pick on her dainty pet or give her fleas, as had happened when Starshine consorted with them before.

Cassidy said sharply, "You come home right now."

The cat surprised her by bouncing off the ledge and strolling across the street to roll on the sidewalk in front of her.

Sitting on her heels to scratch the snowy chin, Cassidy said, "I should set limits with you. Make you stay in the house. Everybody says it's dangerous to let cats go outside."

The calico nipped her hand.

Cassidy went back inside her chain link fence to sit on the stoop and watch Starshine perform her bug-jumping dance, the cat making slow, exquisite leaps as she pounced on invisible insects.

❦ ❦ ❦

At ten-thirty Cassidy and Starshine were on the waterbed, Cassidy stewing about Zach, the calico placidly grooming herself, when the front doorbell rang for the second time that night. Her shoulders jerked; her nerves snapped tight.

On her way out of the bedroom, she noticed that Bryce's door was closed, although the sound of the TV indicated he was probably still inside. She dashed downstairs and flipped on the porch light. Detective Torres' face peered at her through the small window in the oak door.

Torres came inside with two uniforms behind him and handed her an envelope. "Search warrant."

Panic stabbed her chest. Inhaling through clenched teeth, she pulled herself up tall. "What are you looking for?"

"It's all there." He jerked his chin toward the envelope. Planting his hands on his hips, he stood with legs apart, jacket open, gun showing. His probing blue eyes were beginning to look tired; a dark stubble had appeared on his cheeks. "Now if you don't mind, I'd like to get to it. This place is so big, we're gonna be stuck here half the night."

Make him tell you about Zach. "Wait a minute. I haven't read it yet." She pretended to study the document. "Before you go tearing through my house, at least tell me what happened at the station."

"The witness ID'd your boyfriend." A note of satisfaction in his booming voice.

She felt the blood drain from her face. "That can't be true. He wasn't there."

"Yeah?" His mouth widened in a cynical smile. "You ready to get on the stand and testify to that?"

"Is Zach under arrest?"

"Not yet. Hathaway's got him in the box. He'll be tied up awhile, but then you won't be getting to bed too early yourself." Beckoning to the two uniforms, he walked them through the first floor and basement, directing one to start on the lower level, the other in Cassidy's office.

She crossed her arms and stood in front of the door. "You can't open my client files."

He moved about an inch too close, just inside her personal space. There was something in the jut of his chin and the square of his shoulders that suggested a runty kid who'd made it his life's work to whip all the guys who were bigger than he was.

She stood unmoving until he finally shrugged and said, "Okay, leave the files. I'll be upstairs."

The kid's upstairs. "I need to tell Bryce what's going on."

"I'll have to go with you."

Knocking on Bryce's door, she heard a loud "Yeah" above the sound of the television. She went inside. Torres watched from the hall. The boy was sitting where she'd seen him before, remote in hand, crushed beer can on the floor. His gaze remained fixed on the screen.

"The police are here with a search warrant. At some point they'll need to go through your room."

His eyes slid up to hers. Although glazed from too many beers, she saw something in them that hinted at worry.

Chest tightening, she added, "The witness picked him up out of a lineup."

Bryce's gaze went back to the television. "Yeah, I thought they would."

"Why? Why are you so dead set on believing he did it?"

"The guy's a jerk. Xandra told me all about him."

"That was nearly eighteen years ago."

"People don't change."

If he's right, I'm wasting a hell of a lot of my time and the clients' money. Gritting her teeth, she returned to the hall.

Torres nodded in the direction of her bedroom. "I'll start here."

She shifted from one foot to the other, debating where she needed to be. *More important to watch Torres poke through my panties or make sure that cop downstairs doesn't get into my files? The files, definitely.* She hurried back to her office.

Five minutes later Torres appeared in her office doorway. "Got something here I need to talk to you about."

5. A Big Red Book

Her eyes zoomed in on the plastic bag in his latex-gloved hand. In it was a red leather book about the size of a small telephone directory. Her stomach churned. *How could he have found that thing—whatever it is—when I've never seen it before?*

A young cop who'd just finished checking behind the pictures on her wall looked over his shoulder at Torres. "Find something?"

"Yeah." He gave Cassidy an appraising look. *Wondering if I'm really surprised to see it.*

"Well, Ms. McCabe, let's go sit in the living room."

Cassidy lowered herself onto the edge of the paisley sofa.

"So, about this book here .... " Torres, sitting in one of the small armchairs, moved his eyes to the staircase where Starshine's triangular face could be seen peeking around the corner. "You got a cat." He tapped his fingers on the floor and softened his voice. "Here, kitty, kitty." Starshine took a half step out from behind the wall.

She's an alien in disguise and if you don't put that book back and forget you ever saw it, she will turn you into a horned toad. Which would be a distinct improvement.

Starshine surprised her by slipping around the edge of the room and coming up to stand a few inches in front of the cop's scuffed shoes. He held his hand motionless as she sniffed his fingers.

Cassidy glared. *What's this? You switching sides to go with the winner?* Feeling a sense of dread, she firmly reminded herself that she did not believe in the prescience of cats. *Just don't forget who operates the can opener around here.*

Starshine rubbed his legs, then disappeared behind the sofa.

Torres leaned back, one hand on the chair's armrest, the other holding the bag in his lap. "I'm a sucker for cats myself." Warmth flickered in his eyes. "Got five of 'em crowded into a small apartment. I know it's too many, but you find these starving strays in the alley, what're you gonna do?"

"*Practice some restraint?*" *Restraint, as in not being totally hooked on a guy who just might possibly be a batterer/murderer?*

Torres removed the red book from its bag. "This here's a combination daily planner-address book and it's got the Palomar woman's name in it. You ever see it before?"

Her heart thudding, she shook her head. "Where'd you find it?"

"Under the waterbed mattress. For all his fancy job, I gotta say that boyfriend of yours is not real bright."

Fancy job? That why he's got it in for Zach? Sees him as one of the big kids he's gotta whip?

The detective took out his pad. "You stated Moran exited the townhouse at eleven-forty and got back in the car. He have the planner with him then?"

She pictured Zach walking toward the Toyota. *He didn't have it. What does that mean? Oh shit—I don't like this.* She started to clutch her arms beneath her breasts, realized her body language was all wrong, and stopped herself. Straightening her back, she rested her hands loosely in her lap. "I don't know."

"Yeah?" Torres cocked his head in an exaggerated show of curiosity. "What was he wearing?"

"Tee-shirt and jeans."

"You telling me he wasn't wearing a jacket, he had no way of concealing this big book on his person, but you don't know whether he had it or not?"

Making a great effort, she got her therapist part in control, looked him in the eye, and waited.

Torres scratched the back of his head, his fingers digging into thick, unruly curls. "So, if he didn't have it with him when he came out of her place at eleven-forty, how do you suppose it got under the mattress?"

"Someone else brought it into the house?" Keeping her gaze on his face, she searched for the slightest indication that she might have hit a nerve, but all she saw was amusement.

His latex-gloved hands started flipping through the planner. Cassidy clenched her teeth and sat motionless. *Why's he handling it?*

Wouldn't he need to get it dusted for prints first?

Oh, I get it. Wants to catch me off guard, convince me Zach's guilty, break me down, get me to tell all.

Torres looked up. "Now here's something interesting. Got a note here on January twenty-seventh. 'Talked to Z.M. Said he couldn't make it tonight, maybe some other time.' Z.M. Not real common, wouldn't you say? So, what do you think happened on January twenty-seven?"

He talked to her? And didn't tell you? You should get him for that. Tell the cop he was washing the blood off when you walked in the door.

Willing her hands not to move, she whispered, "I don't know."

"Here's a bunch of pages tore out. Evidently the original version had something in it Moran didn't want anybody to see. What do you think?" His coarse-featured face broke into an unpleasant grin. "Here's another note. 'Called Z.M. He's playing it cagey.' Now what do you suppose that one's about?"

She didn't answer.

He leveled his tired blue eyes at her. "He tell you he talked to her on January twenty-seventh and March fifteenth?" A long pause. "Sure sounds to me like your boyfriend and this babe had something going on the side."

She shook her head. *Talked to her. All Zach did was talk. This jerk's trying to rattle me. Can't let him see that it's working.*

"So, you're gonna stonewall, is that it? Might as well get back to work and see what else I can dig up." He went upstairs.

Why would they talk? Is it possible he was *playing around? Maybe Hathaway's right. Maybe you are so stupid-in-love you can't see he's slime. It wouldn't be the first time.*

Stop that! her therapist voice commanded. *There's no point going nutso now when you can make him tell you later.*

🍎 🍎 🍎

When the police finally left at three-thirty in the morning, Cassidy went to sit on the porch, which had cooled considerably. This time the tape of Zach's voice did not play in her head. It had been crowded out by the events of the past few hours. Starshine jumped onto her window ledge perch from the steps outside. The wind chimes jangled lightly and sirens screamed from Austin Boulevard. Bryce had left his car in front of the house, apparently indifferent to the village practice of ticketing overnight parkers.

Should've called the police and gotten a parking dispensation.

Given what's happening in the rest of our lives, who cares?

"Come sit with me," she coaxed Starshine, who looked out at the street, ignoring her. "C'mon, make me believe cats really do intuit when their beloved humans need an extra dose of TLC."

Relenting, Starshine leapt delicately over to the picnic bench, twisting her head to lick her shoulder.

Crossing her legs, Cassidy jiggled one foot. "Zach and I've been in some sticky situations before. But in the past the bad guy always was an outsider. Now there's some possibility that the bad guy is the man who shares my bed. And I'm far too close to see it clearly, because, as Bryce so aptly put it, I 'loove' him."

Nobody's ever totally objective. Emotions always get in the way.

Yeah, but you have to try.

Starshine sat up straight and said Mwat.

"I'm glad you're in the mood for conversation. I really need somebody to talk to and you're my favorite confidante 'cause I can always take your response to mean anything I want."

Maintaining her Egyptian princess pose, Starshine elegantly licked a paw.

"Okay, the question is, what were Zach and Xandra up to? No, wait, I'm not gonna think about that. The real question is, how did the planner get into the house? Zach could've driven to Xandra's before I got home, killed her, and taken it. Or Torres or Bryce or some other unknown party could've brought it in. Zach had no reason to bash her, so the latter is more likely."

No reason you know of.

A sharp wind riffled across her skin; she rubbed her arms against the chill. "Okay, he might have some motive I'm not aware of. So the next question is, could Torres be right about Xandra and Zach?"

Twisting her ears, Starshine stared at her with wild black eyes, looking as if she were angry that Cassidy would even consider the possibility of Zach cheating on them.

Zach wouldn't have an affair. He wanted to sleep with somebody else, he'd just leave. He certainly wouldn't be planning to get married.

Xandra was available only now and then. Lotsa men want a wife at home, sensational sex somewhere else.

She shook her head. *Not Zach. That's not his style.*

"All right, assuming he could withstand the temptation to do it one more time with his sexual spiderwoman, that leaves yet another question. Do I think Zach could've killed his former lover and be lying about it?"

Learning to trust him had not been easy. For the first six months of the relationship, she'd constantly had her guard up, always alert for the first sign he was lying and cheating the way her ex used to. That hadn't happened. He'd withheld information plenty of times but never told a straight up lie.

That you know of. Besides, he's never had this kind of reason before.

Starshine hopped up to the rim of the couch and began yanking Cassidy's hair.

"I guess you don't like the direction this is going. I guess you figure, as long as he brings home cat food and tells you you're beautiful, we shouldn't care what else he does."

Plopping into her lap, the cat made her chin available for scratching.

"All right, the data's insufficient for a definitive conclusion here, so once again we have to rely on intuition." She tried to visualize an enraged Zach swinging a champagne bottle at the white-faced mannequin she had previously pictured as the dead spiderwoman, but the image wouldn't gel. What came to mind instead was the memory of Zach, as angry as she'd ever seen him, standing abruptly and walking out of a bar.

A small voice whispered, *Is that really your intuition? Or just what you want to believe?*

She tried again to consider the possibility of his having clubbed Xandra, but there was no part of her that could accept the idea.

"Okay, the decision's made, then. Keeping in mind that I could be wrong, I'm going to believe what he tells me unless I see clear-cut evidence to the contrary."

❦ ❦ ❦

Fifteen minutes later Zach, who'd entered from the rear of the house, came out on the porch. Adrenaline surged as she jumped to her feet, dislodging Starshine, who fled out the open window. "Torres found Xandra's planner under the mattress."

"Tell me about it. When Hathaway got the call, she went straight for the jugular."

"The witness, the planner. This is looking worse and worse."

He asked, his voice slightly hoarse, "Do you think I went down there earlier and killed her?"

She shook her head.

Pulling her into his arms, he nestled his cheek against her hair. "I ever tell you how much I love you?"

No, you jerk—at least, not nearly often enough. Stepping back, she gazed into his exhausted face. "You look beat. I'm dying to talk, but I guess I could hold off till you've had some sleep."

"No, let's get it over with. After six hours with Hathaway, what's one more with you?" They settled in their usual places on the couch. Zach hunched forward, dropped his head, and ran a hand over the back of it. "Somebody's setting me up and doing a damn good job of it. This is fucking deja vu."

She rubbed the tense muscles at the back of his neck. "You talked to Xandra several times, didn't you?"

"Three. She called three times."

"Why didn't you tell me?"

"Remember Emily?"

"Emily's the cop you were involved with before you met me."

Leaning back, Zach put his hand on her knee. "You gave me the third degree when you found out Emily'd called to see if I was interested in getting back together. Well, the last thing I wanted was to have you grilling me about my history with Xandra. Intellectually, I can agree that it's not okay to keep secrets. But I grew up never letting anybody know anything, and it's a hard habit to break."

His telling the story in bits and pieces was familiar to her, since clients often relayed embarrassing information on the installment plan. But she was not quite ready to let him off. "Okay, I can see why you didn't say anything at the time. But yesterday morning you told me what seemed like the worst of it. Why didn't the phone calls come out then?"

"Because it was easier to talk about something that happened nearly eighteen years ago. Because I stupidly thought you wouldn't find out. Because I was afraid you might get jealous and pissy and I need you on my side right now."

"That's not fair. If I could handle all that really offensive stuff about stalking and pushing her around, why would three phone calls send me over the edge? Or did you do more than talk?"

"That's all. Xandra surprised the hell out of me by calling at work last January. First I'd heard from her in all these years. She acted like nothing had happened, like we were simply old buddies who'd lost touch. Then, in a very sexy voice, she suggested that I might want to stop over some time."

Cassidy's jaw tightened. "And you didn't tell her to get lost? Or that you were madly in love with somebody else?"

"I figured she was up to something and I was hoping to find out what it was. I never saw her, but I didn't slam the door shut either."

She peered above the overgrown bushes in front of the porch at an unfamiliar cat sauntering toward her yard from the other side of Hazel. The darkness seemed to have lifted slightly, but since the house faced west they would not be seeing any sunrises. "You must've been curious. Wondered what she'd look like after all these years. Probably felt some urge to take her up on her offer."

"Well, sure." He looked away. "I had a thirty-second fantasy that we could go back to the way it was at the beginning. Then reality set in and I remembered that getting anywhere near Xandra'd be about as safe as sightseeing in Chernobyl."

He's living with me and he had a fantasy about her?

Yeah, but he didn't go. Remember all the times Kevin popped up with surprise invitations and you actually went?

Cassidy sighed. "Well, I don't like it but at least you told me the truth. Although I have to say, I'm up to my limit with these bombs you keep dropping. What else are you hoping you won't have to tell me?"

He shook his head. "That's all."

"Xandra had you arrested for beating her up, then brainwashed your kid into thinking you're slime. And now, all these years later, she tries to entice you back into the sack." Cassidy stroked her chin. "Maybe she started thinking she might need a safe house for Bryce as early as January. Maybe it was a test, and by not jumping into bed you convinced her you're someone she could entrust her son to."

He shrugged.

Piercing cat shrieks, nearly identical to a baby's high-pitched scream, came from Briar. Cassidy stood abruptly. "Where's Starshine?" A moment later the calico, tail puffed, jumped up to sit in her window.

Dropping back onto the couch, Cassidy said, "Torres assumes you were seeing her on the side."

"I figured they'd pull her phone records so I told Hathaway about the calls yesterday morning. I know it's lame saying it now, but I *was* planning to tell you."

Compressing her lips, she exhaled noisily, then decided to let it go. She made an effort to get her bleary mind to focus. "If somebody's going all out to bust you, we definitely need a lawyer." *You did better this time, kiddo. Said we.*

"Not yet."

"Hey, I'm supposed to be the idiot who throws herself headlong into danger. It's your job to be the sensible one. Why wouldn't you want a lawyer?"

"Two reasons. First, criminal attorneys cost a ton of money, and in case you haven't noticed, I'm not famous for banking my salary."

Probably hasn't even finished paying back the money he borrowed to buy off that guy who wanted to break my kneecaps.

"Second, the police don't have enough to charge me."

"What about the witness? Doesn't that position you in the right place at the right time?"

"Most witnesses don't hold up too well against a good defense attorney. And as to the time . . ." He tilted his head slightly. "The witness puts me entering her townhouse at six-thirty, and I had to be out of there by nine in order to be sloshing down bourbon on the front porch when you got home. If the time of death falls outside that window, I'm off the hook. But it probably won't 'cause the guy who's setting me up knows when she died and wouldn't want to fabricate my arrival more than an hour or two before the murder. He couldn't've known whether or not I'd have an alibi, but unfortunately he got lucky on that score."

"Bryce knew you were alone at five-thirty when he left here. And he's also a prime candidate for bringing the planner into the house."

"Bryce. God knows, there are kids who kill parents. But the way he talked about her . . . It's hard to reconcile that sense of affection in his voice with the thought of his bludgeoning her a couple of hours later."

"It may not've been Bryce. I'm sure there are plenty of other possibilities." She gazed at the rippling movement of the elms lining the street.

"You know," she went on, "it makes me very nervous to see you getting complacent about this. The parallels between that past arrest and this current situation are uncanny. The police're gonna think you and Xandra were sleeping together. Then she sends Bryce to your house out of the blue, and you're pissed she didn't tell you earlier. You have a few drinks, then drive to her place to find out what's going on. She invites you in, you share a bottle of champagne, then she pulls the same stunt all over again—tells you to get lost. You're drunk, you lose control and club her. Almost the exact scenario as before."

"What're the odds of the same person orchestrating that first frame, then coming up with an almost identical replay nearly eighteen years later?"

"Wait a minute. I'm not done yet. Anyway, she keeps a journal or something in the planner, so you grab it, bring it home, tear out the incriminating pages, and stash it under the mattress. But you're too blitzed at the time of the murder to think about the prints, so later on, after you sober up, you realize you have to go back and wipe everything off. Maybe when I come home you act drunker than you are because you know I'll insist on driving, and that way I can substantiate the when and the why. Maybe you didn't stay at the scene because your blood-alcohol level wouldn't't've been consistent with the too-drunk-to-drive story. And in addition, they've got the prior charge to prove that this is an obvious case of history repeating itself."

He lowered his chin, his eyes nailing her. "What're you doing? Talking yourself into believing that's what happened?"

"Not for a minute." She wrapped her hand around his. "I'm just looking at the situation from a prosecutor's point of view."

"Yeah, but they can't bring that prior into court. And don't forget the letter. Xandra knew she was in danger. And whoever she felt threatened by, it was somebody other than me since I'm the one she sent Bryce to."

"Oh, that's right." Shaking her head, she tried to get it all straight. "What about the champagne bottle? If this really was a crime of passion, maybe the killer forgot to clean it off."

"Considering he didn't forget to plant evidence or pay somebody to pick me out of a lineup, it's hard to believe he'd forget the prints."

"I suppose Hathaway's not telling you anything about the witness?"

"I was lucky to get as much as I did. Cops generally won't talk to suspects at all." He stared into the distance. "However, I think it's safe to assume the witness was hired by the killer. It's even possible he is the killer, although our frame artist probably wouldn't want to call attention to himself by stepping forward like that."

A woman walked two small dogs on the other side of Hazel. *That has to be an android. No real humans get up at this hour.* The adrenaline had drained away and she was beginning to feel as tired as Zach looked. She leaned against his arm. "We've gotta get some sleep. But before I can get my mind to turn off, I need to know what plans you've cooked up for running your own investigation."

"Two possibilities. First thing tomorrow I'm gonna talk to this P.I. in Uptown who was a member of Chicago's finest till he turned up too many drug test positives. He worked vice a lotta years and he knows the roll call. The other thing is, I've gotta find some way to make Bryce open up to me."

🕷 🕷 🕷

The sultry white mannequin lay in the center of a round pool filled with bubbling red liquid, Cassidy and Zach sitting on the short marble wall that encircled it. A champagne bottle and two glasses stood between them. Zach filled the glasses and raised his, but before he could complete the toast, the sparkling liquid in the champagne flutes turned red. Overcome with disgust, she flung hers into the pool. Zach smiled, drained his, and tossed the empty glass in also. A glittery, iridescent spider crept along the side of the wall toward him.

The alarm shrilled. Cassidy jumped up to turn it off. Zach, who did not have Tuesday morning clients to see, opened his eyes briefly, then went back to sleep. She gulped coffee and hit the shower. Even with adrenaline pumping, the lack of sleep made her feel as if she was a thin, brittle shell on the outside, all hollow within. Just before her client arrived, she scribbled a note to Zach: "I'll be done at noon. I have something I need to talk to you about so don't leave."

She finished her two sessions, then returned to her director's chair to consider the battle she was about to have with Zach. *He's gonna hate it. It'll take all your persuasive powers, plus some verbal arm wrestling, to get him to agree.*

You can do it. Zach tries to control everything, but when it's really important, when you know you're right, you've always been able to make him do what you want.

Yeah, but there's a price to pay. First we have to fight, then he's pissed afterward. And this is a time we absolutely need to pull together.

However, this one's essential. You have to make him do it.

Stepping into sauna-like heat on the other side of her office door, she went to look for Zach, who sat at the dining room table, a mug of coffee and a folded newspaper in front of him. The fact that the paper was folded, that he was not reading it, made her stomach jittery. She filled her purple cat mug and sat beside him.

Zach drummed his fingers on the paper. "Looks like we've both got something on our minds." He glanced at her, then away. The twitchiness in her stomach got worse. He said, his voice tight, "You go first."

"What is it? A story in the paper?"

"It'll wait. Your item's at the top of the agenda."

6. Everybody Knows

"Okay, here goes." Inhaling deeply, Cassidy moistened her upper lip. "I know there's no way I can talk you out of investigating Xandra's murder—even though the cops are gonna get more pissed than they are already when you start interfering in their case."

He gave a who-cares? shrug.

"But it's really important that you not go off on your own and leave me out of it. You told me yourself that you've gotten in trouble in the past when the line between your professional and personal life starts to blur." *As if you don't sometimes dive head first into the muddy waters of your clients' turbulent lives.* "And in this instance, you're way too involved to trust your own judgment without having someone to bounce things off of."

Running a hand over his face, he said, "Just when I was thinking maybe I oughtta move out."

She felt a sudden throb in the back of her head. "What?"

"The newspaper story. The situation's getting very messy."

"How bad is it?" *Oh shit. Clients, family, friends—everybody's gonna know.*

"That was *my* agenda item—to tell you about the story. The only thing they withheld is your name. They had to do it. If the *Post* left anything out and it showed up in the other paper, it'd look like they were covering for me.

Besides, it's better to have the whole thing come out all at once. If the story showed up in dribs and drabs, it'd seem like I was withholding information." His mouth pulled down at one corner. "You know, like I do with you."

She reached for the paper.

He held onto it. "Since you make it a practice not to read newspapers, it actually occurred to me that maybe you didn't need to know. Then I remembered what happened the last time I neglected to tell you about a story, and I decided that was one mistake I didn't care to repeat. However, now that I've explained what's in it, maybe you oughtta just maintain your habit of never opening a paper."

Do I have to see this thing in print? Is wallowing in humiliation really required?

There's no way out. You've gotta know what other people are reading.

She pulled it away from him. Biting hard on the inner lining of her lip, she skimmed, then reread the most damaging parts.

Sources close to the investigation say that Moran admits to becoming intoxicated and that, when his girlfriend returned to their shared residence, she refused to let him drive. Moran says his girlfriend drove him to Palomar's residence, then waited in the car while he went inside. He found the body, then spent half an hour searching her house. Before leaving, he placed an anonymous call to the police.

Another section farther down was even worse.

Moran says that the last time he saw Palomar alive was nearly eighteen years ago. On that same day she was beaten severely and hospitalized. Palomar accused Moran of having committed the battery, but the charges were pleaded down to a misdemeanor.

I hate sex-and-violence trash, no matter who it's about. Hate it a lot more when it's about us.

"What possible justification could there be for printing something like this? There's no reason anybody needs to know this kind of sleaze."

"I'm a reporter. The public's entitled to read about anything that'd reflect on my ability to represent situations accurately."

"Yeah, but this doesn't represent our situation accurately. It makes you look guilty when you're not."

He gave her a grim smile. "I'm the only one who can be entirely sure of that. Since you know me pretty well, you're willing to believe what I tell you, but you can't expect the public to simply take my word for it. The good citizens have a right to read the story for themselves and make up their own minds. You can't ask papers to only print news about the guilty. This story casts me in a questionable light, but when the cops arrest somebody else it'll all go away."

This is the story everyone'll read and remember.

Leave it alone. You don't need to attack his profession on top of everything else.

She huffed mildly and said, "So how's the paper gonna handle the fact that you're a suspect?"

"My editor wants me to lie low for a while. I can take off as much time as I want for my own investigation or I can hang around the office and do rewrites, but he doesn't want me working my regular beat till this is cleared up. At this point my byline would not be an asset to the paper, and my presence in this house isn't doing you any good either."

Laying her hand on his arm, she said, "You're not going to leave. We're going to get through this together. But you have to promise to let me know what you're up to."

He removed her hand. "I refuse to drag you into it." An edge came into his voice. "Besides, I don't want you getting in my way. I intend to follow every possible lead and I don't need you telling me what I can and can't do."

She unclenched her back teeth. "Isn't it a little late to decide you don't want me dragged into it?" *Guilt—the only leverage I've got.* "At least half my clients have chatted with you out in the yard. That means my family and friends, plus a lot of the people who hand me checks, will know what's going on. Everyone'll assume that once again I've been stupid enough to pick an extreme loser. And it'll get a whole lot worse if you're arrested. Whether you live here or not, every action you take will have repercussions for me, so I think that gives me the right to know exactly what you're gonna do before you do it. You are simply too close to this case to see things clearly."

"Shit!" He got to his feet. "The one thing I won't put up with is somebody telling me what to do." He slugged down the rest of his coffee. "This is why you get left, you know that?"

She felt as if she'd been punched in the stomach. "Yeah," she said bleakly, "I do."

❧　❧　❧

An hour later Cassidy sat in the swivel chair she'd taken back from Bryce's room, her heels propped on the radiator, a dull ache in her chest and Starshine on her lap. She gazed out her west window at three children playing in the yard across the street. Behind her was a north window, and between the two windows her massive corner desk. Atop the desk were piles of paper, a phone, and an answering machine. The desk Zach had brought over from his condo stood against the west wall three feet from hers, its chair still in Bryce's room.

Starshine jumped to the windowsill to gaze after a robin that had flown past the glass. "At least you can't get in the car and drive away. The worst you do is go across the street and visit the neighbors."

The phone rang but she ignored it, letting the machine silently record the message as she'd done with the preceding three calls. She'd turned the volume down because she didn't want to hear the sympathy and curiosity she knew many of the voices would convey.

Could be a client. You've gotta play the messages.

Even therapists are entitled to an occasional breakdown.

Starshine turned her head abruptly to point her ears and nose toward the doorway. A moment later Zach stood in front of her, a scowl on his face. "Okay, you win. I'll keep you apprised for the time being, but this agreement is *not* written in stone."

"You mean, you're not going to pack your suitcase and go home to mother?"

"I thought about it—the suitcase part, not the mother. I gotta tell you, I was fucking tempted."

She gritted her teeth. "Well, that's what you do, isn't it? When things get tough, you walk."

"I haven't done it with you. You've given me more grief than just about anybody, and sometimes I need to get the hell out and cool down. But I always come back."

"Someday you won't. You've walked away from everybody else, including your own family. Someday I'll do something to push you over the line and you'll be gone."

"Are you saying it's better to stay and suffer the way you did with Kevin than break it off when it isn't working?"

She briefly compressed her lips, then said, "Sometimes it's better to leave. Obviously. But we have opposite problems. I stay too long, you leave too fast."

"Here's the real bonus to having a shrink for a girlfriend." He sat on the edge of the bed. "You get lectured at all the time. You hear about everything you're doing wrong and how you need to change."

Craning her neck to gaze at the ceiling, she pushed down her rising anger. "All I'm saying is, if you've got a basically good relationship it's worth a little effort before you throw in the towel."

"Isn't that what I've been doing?"

He's right. You're not giving him credit.

A growly edge came into his voice. "What do I have to do, spend the rest of my life proving I'm not Kevin?"

Shaking her head, she sighed. "I'm sorry I had to get so pushy. I only did it because—"

"Because you know I've taken undue risks in the past and with everything that's going on, I might not be as cautious as you think I need to be." He stood. "Point taken. Now I've got work to do."

"Does that mean I get to come with you?"

"That's why I came back. I'm headed out right now to meet with that P.I. I told you about, and I'm here to give you the option of riding along."

Session in two hours. She grabbed her calendar and picked up the phone.

After rescheduling, Cassidy changed into her best black jeans, faded but no holes, and a silk garnet blouse. Zach upgraded to his professional image, a black tee with no beer inscriptions and a well-worn jacket. On special occasions he might don a button-down shirt but he did not own a suit or tie.

🐛 🐛 🐛

The Nissan pulled up to the curb on an Uptown street lined with Vietnamese restaurants, Mexican groceries, and at least two unsavory-appearing taverns per block. Cassidy saw a scruffy person pushing a shopping cart filled with plastic bags. As she stepped out of the car, he scooped up a can and tossed it into one of the bags.

Zach steered her toward a grimy plate glass window inscribed: "PETE IZLOTTO, PRIVATE INVESTIGATOR."

Inside, a fiftyish man sat in an ancient swivel chair in front of a scarred oak desk, a phone clamped to his ear. The chair was tilted as far back as it would go. His face pointed toward the ceiling. His no-socks feet in loafers were splayed out on the desktop. Izlotto's gravelly voice lobbed brief questions into the receiver. In front of the desk stood two wooden armrest chairs, and behind the chairs an old bakery case displayed a grow light and a row of small, velvety plants. Symphonic music played in the background.

Clasping her upper arm, Zach nodded toward the case. "African violets. The only thing I've ever seen Izzie wax enthusiastic about. And the music?" He listened a moment. "Vivaldi, I'd guess. He read in some arcane book that violets do better in an environment enriched with classical music. He thinks if he pampers the little darlings enough, they'll bring him more blue ribbons in plant shows."

Cassidy, who didn't know Vivaldi from elevator music, could not have named that tune for the life of her. But Zach, as much as he cultivated the role of seedy reporter, had grown up in a family reeking with culture and class and for all she knew had been toilet trained to the strains of Beethoven piped into the bathroom.

"Hey, Zach," the gravelly voice said in a welcoming tone.

Cassidy turned to watch Izzie lumber toward them. Short and stocky, with a large head, short neck, and massive shoulders, he reminded her of either a musclebound wrestler or a grizzly on its hind legs, she couldn't decide which.

"So . . ." The P.I. shook Zach's hand. "Did you do her?"

Zach laughed. "Nobody's ever accused you of being indirect, have they, Izzie?" He shoved his hands into his jacket pockets. "Those violets winning you any prizes lately?"

Looking straight at Zach, Izzie paused before replying, a style of speech Cassidy regarded as ponderous. *Has to have full audience attention before any utterances leave his lips.* She took note of his thick black hair, tinted glasses, rugged features, and strong chin. *Hides his eyes behind dark glass. This is a guy who'd never go into therapy.*

Izzie said, "I stopped showing them. Hauling 'em around the country was bad for their health." He turned his gaze on Cassidy. "You going to introduce me to your girlfriend?"

"Hadn't planned on it."

"Cassidy McCabe." She stuck out her hand and he enveloped it in his large paw, giving it one decisive pump.

"Zach here will not be pleased that you told me. He's of the opinion that since he has to buy information from me, he loses points if he gives anything away."

Zach added, "I'm also of the opinion that anything I say can and will become a commodity on the open market."

Izzie took off his glasses, thrust his large head toward Cassidy, and pinned her with an intense squint. "Do you think he did her?"

Staring at me like there must be something he can pry out of my head. What he'd really like to do is suck the data directly from my brain cells into his computer. If the technology existed, he'd have it.

She said, "I believe I've been put on notice I'm not supposed to tell you anything."

"Okay." Replacing his glasses, he folded his arms across his barrel chest. "I guess therapists are as good as anybody at keeping their mouths shut."

Therapists? How much does he know?

Izzie gestured toward the chairs in front of the desk. "Sit and we can do a deal."

As they settled onto the hard wooden seats, the P.I. returned to his own chair, once again pushing it backward to maximum tilt. From where she sat, Cassidy had a clear view of his cheap plastic soles, almost no view of his face.

Izzie said, "I suppose you want everything I've got on Xandra and company."

"How much?"

"Five bills."

"Am I mistaken," Zach drawled, "or did your rates just double?"

"Am I mistaken," Izzie reprised, "or did your need to know just quadruple?"

"You gonna take advantage of my situation here, Izzie?" Propping his elbows on the armrests, Zach pressed his fingertips together.

"Just doing business. Besides, you can afford it."

"I haven't got my inheritance yet."

Izzie raised his head from the backrest to meet Zach's eyes. "No, but you've been drawing down a regular salary for years, you're living in your girlfriend's house, you have the condo rented out, and you've managed not to fuck up too bad with designer drugs, gambling, or other expensive vices. So I'd have to say you're not hurting."

"You just dropped all that on us to remind me that you've got good sources and to whet my appetite about Xandra. I'd guess you picked up everything with one call to the *Post*. Whitmore, maybe. He wouldn't mind seeing me take a fall."

Cassidy glanced from one self-possessed male face to the other. *It's all a game. Posturing for position. Izzie shows off how much he knows, then Zach one-ups him by knowing how he got it. That's why Zach's such a news junkie—so he can beat out other males in the information game.*

"We're both in the same business, you know. Gathering data and selling it." Sitting erect, Izzie removed his glasses and fixed Zach with his intense stare. "So, we got a deal?"

Zach handed over five hundred-dollar bills, then pulled a spiral pad and pen out of his jacket pocket.

"Xandra was running about a dozen girls. She's had her own business over ten years now. She kept herself very private, very clean. Her only known vice is that she always liked to keep some boy on the side. Nobody even knew the paternity of the kid till you got your name inside a news story instead of on the byline. Now here's something you may be able to use. It happened twice she got herself beat up good enough to land in the hospital. The first was that time she nailed you for it. The second was just this past January."

January? That's when she started calling Zach.

"That second time it happened she didn't give anybody up. She pulled the old falling-down-the-stairs routine, but it was common knowledge somebody'd busted her up real good. The person you want to talk to about that is Adonis Domingo. They've had an on-again, off-again arrangement for at least three years, which is longer than most of her guys lasted."

"He the one who beat her up?"

"I doubt it. Last I heard they were still going strong, and I don't think she'd have kept him around if he got physical. She never let anybody get the upper hand."

"How do I find this Adonis?"

"He's a musician. Plays at Bluestown, tends to hang out there a lot. He also tends to run off at the mouth, which made him Xandra's biggest security risk. Especially when he got to drinking. He may be worth the five hundred alone."

Zach tapped his pen against the pad. "Was Xandra strictly independent? Or did she have a backer or some kind of protection?"

"Independent, as far as anybody knows. But like I said, she was an expert at keeping things zipped up, except for the occasional leak on her boyfriend's part. However, the fact that neither she nor any of her girls ever spent a night in the slam makes me suspect there might be somebody with connections lurking in the background."

Cassidy frowned. "Are you saying the police knew Xandra was a madam but somebody applied pressure to keep them from arresting her?"

Turning to face her, Zach said, "It could be somebody used clout to fend off the law." He shrugged. "But you gotta remember, the cops—who certainly knew about her operation—had no reason to bust her unless she screwed up. If they'd arrested her for pandering, her big bucks attorney would've had her back in her townhouse in hours. Prosecution would've run up a big bill for the taxpayers and all they'd've gotten in the long run is a fine. There's no point hauling in offenders like Xandra unless the police can use 'em to get at some bigger fish, and apparently she kept her operation clean enough to avoid such secondary problems."

I seem to be up for simpleton of the year award.

Zach leaned back, laid his arms on the chair's armrests, and narrowed his eyes at Izzie. "What else?"

"That's all. I told you, she ran a tight ship. But Adonis should be able to help you along."

"What about her girls? I need names and numbers."

"No can do."

"You telling me the renowned Pete Izlotto isn't able to dig up a list of working girls? You know all about who I'm living with but you can't give me the names of Xandra's hookers?"

"The story only came out this morning. I know my job but I've gotta have some lead time." He dropped his feet to the floor and sat erect, indicating he had run through his stock of merchandise.

"How 'bout throwing in a call to that blues club to see if our guy's there now."

"Sure." Izzie made the call and confirmed that he was. Ambling around the desk to give Cassidy's hand a parting shake, he thrust his large head forward and said, "And would I be correct in assuming that the reason you're tagging along with Zach here is, you're not sure whether he did her or not and you want to hear what everybody has to say about it?"

In the Nissan Zach let out a dry chuckle. "For once Izzie guessed wrong. The reason you're glued to my side is, you wanna keep me in line. And maybe you're also hoping to break the case before I do. Sometimes I think investigations get your competitive juices going, make you determined to bust the bad guy first."

❧ ❧ ❧

Bluestown, on Clark Street half a mile north of Fullerton, was surrounded by a United Nations mix of restaurants—Middle Eastern, Japanese, Ethiopian—a feminist book store, a vintage clothing shop, and a Starbucks. Several pedestrians were out, some thoroughly professional, others beyond the dress-code pale. This area, one of the trendiest in the city, was parked solid at night but easy pickings in the middle of the day. After five minutes' circling, Zach stashed the car a mere three blocks from the club.

As they hiked toward their destination, Cassidy was relieved to find that the temperature, as the radio always said, was cooler by the lake. By the time they arrived, she could feel a trickle of moisture between her breasts, but at least here on the north side a breeze from the lake provided some natural air conditioning.

A tinted window scattered with unlighted beer signs fronted the Bluestown building. Although a hand-lettered sign proclaimed the club closed, Cassidy could see a chunky man standing behind the bar and a thin, slouchy man leaning over it, a guitar case propped next to him. Zach rapped on the door and the bartender, paunch hanging over his belt, opened it.

"You the guy Izzie sent?"

Zach indicated that he was, and they wended their way through a maze of chair-stacked tables to join the musician. Grayish light filtered through the window. Her stomach winced at the smoke and stale beer smells that clogged the air.

Leaning sideways against the bar, Zach said to the man with the guitar, "Adonis Domingo?"

The musician, evidently not on his first drink of the day, made an

BUSINESS REPLY MAIL

FIRST-CLASS MAIL PERMIT NO. 3415 OAK PARK IL

POSTAGE WILL BE PAID BY THE ADDRESSEE

ALEX MATTHEWS & ASSOC
P O BOX 4021
OAK PARK IL 60303-9903

Dear Reader,

I would like some feedback about Wanton's Web. If you answer the following questions and return this card, I'll enter your name in a drawing for a free pre-publication copy of my next book.

Alex

1. What I liked best about the book was _____

_____

_____

_____

2. What I liked least about the book was _____

_____

_____

_____

Your Name: _____ Phone: _____

Address: _____ City, State, Zip: _____

effort to pull himself up straight. He looked to be in his early thirties, perhaps ten years younger than Xandra, and just missed being hand-some. Wiry black hair framed a mocha face with woeful brown eyes, a broad nose, and a day's growth of stubble. "You must be the guy they wrote about in the paper." He was clearly trying to assume an alpha-male demeanor, but the soft voice lacked muscle and he couldn't pull it off. "Only reason I agreed to meet with you is, I wanted to see what kind of dude busts up his woman when she's pregnant, then walks out on his kid."

7. Code of the West

Cassidy positioned herself beside Zach. *Why try to act the tough guy when it so obviously doesn't suit? Code of the West? If Zach killed his girl, he's got to play gunslinger whether he likes it or not?*

Laying his left arm on the bar, Zach hooked his right thumb into his jeans pocket, his stance nonchallenging. "Can't believe everything you read in the paper."

"You're a reporter yourself, aren't you?"

"Guilty as charged."

The bartender wiped his rag in front of Domingo. "You gonna talk to this guy or not?" He gazed at Zach. "Personally, I hope he decides to bend your ear for a while, 'cause mine's all wore out."

Zach pulled out his wallet. "Before you go, why don't you get another drink for Adonis here, then mix up two Jack Daniels and sodas."

Cassidy said, "Make mine plain coke." *Only three-thirty. Too early for Zach to start his daily drinking.*

The bartender peered at Domingo. "You sure you want this dude feeding you drinks while he grills you on your love life?"

Domingo grinned like a kid caught with his hand in the cookie jar. *He wants to tell us. Dying to.*

"Let's sit." Zach took the chairs off a table in the middle of the room.

The bartender delivered drinks, then disappeared into a back room.

Cassidy rested her bare arm on the red formica table, discovered it was sticky, and rubbed at the beery-smelling residue with her napkin.

Zach looked at Domingo. "Xandra sent me a letter saying she was in danger. Who might've wanted to harm her?"

"Hey, dude, before I answer any of your questions, you gotta 'splain some things to me." He tried again to square his shoulders and stiffen his back, but he couldn't sustain it. He was naturally loose-jointed and floppy, a man with just enough starch in his spine to hold himself upright.

"What do you want to know?"

"What I don't understand is how you could run out on your kid like that. I been with Xandra over three years, and I watched that boy. He was desperate for a father. When I'd be over there, he'd always be hanging on me, looking for attention. I did what I could, but then she'd throw my ass out and it'd be months before I'd even see him again."

"She tell you I abandoned him?"

"It was all there in the paper."

"I didn't know he existed till Sunday night." Zach took a swallow of his drink.

"Oh." Domingo gazed down at his glass for several seconds. "Yeah, that sounds like Xandra, all right." His shoulders slumped, his puffy eyes welled.

This guy does not look good.

How could he? He just lost his woman—best lay in Chicago, according to Zach.

"Yeah, but you did bust her up." Domingo looked squarely at Zach, his face showing a touch of admiration. "Punched her out when she was pregnant. I can understand how you'd get pissed, man. I mean, the way she'd all of a sudden dump me, then a coupla months later just wag her little finger, and there I'd be, back in her lap."

Domingo shook his head sadly. "There were times I'd get so mad I couldn't see straight. We'd yell and scream, but man, I never touched her 'cause I knew if I did there'd be no going back. But you—you didn't care, you just busted her up." Again, the admiring glance.

Zach said, "You probably won't believe this, but it wasn't me who did all that damage to her when she was pregnant."

Domino continued as if he hadn't spoken, "I don't know how many times I swore I was finished, but every time she'd coax me in that sexy voice of hers, off I'd go again." His eyes filled. Pulling out a well-used handkerchief, he blew his nose.

Cassidy leaned forward. "What kept you coming back?" *What's the secret formula? If I could bottle it, I'd make my fortune.*

Domingo gazed at Zach. "You know, don't you."

"It was like an addiction."

The musician glanced sheepishly at Cassidy, clearly afraid that Zach's admission had hurt her feelings.

She laid her hand on Zach's arm. "That's all right. It happened a long time ago." *Actually, I'm dying to figure out what she had the rest of us don't.*

The bartender started toward them. "You want anything else?"

"Sure," Zach said. "Bring us another round." He tossed down the rest of his drink. "So, what can you tell me about this danger Xandra was in?"

"She didn't talk to me 'bout nothin'." The sheepish grin reappeared. "Always said I couldn't keep my mouth shut." He stared at his glass, his hand moving it in a slow circle on the table. "She did seem jittery that last week. Every time I called she was too busy to talk, but I just figured she'd picked up somebody new, she was getting ready to dump me again. But she wasn't mean like usual, so maybe it was something else."

The bartender set down fresh drinks. When he left, Zach said, "I hear somebody put her in the hospital last January."

Adonis hunched his shoulders over the table. "It happened one of those times after she threw me out. I felt real bad about it." His mouth trembled. "I mean, here we been together all this time, I couldn't even keep some jagoff from busting her up. But what was I gonna do? I been outta the picture a coupla months when it happened. Then she lands in the hospital, and what does she want? Wants me to come sit by her bedside, that's what."

Zach folded his arms on the table. "So who put her there?"

"One of her johns from the old days. When she started her own business, she stopped seeing guys personally, but I guess this john'd just moved back to town. He insisted Xandra had to do him but she wouldn't give him the time of day." He wagged his head. "I can see how it could happen, man. She had this way of making you feel so small."

This guy's more conflicted than the Israelis. Half of him wants to play gunslinger and protect his woman. The other half wants to applaud whoever beat her up.

"What's his name?"

Domingo shrugged.

Zach leaned in toward the musician. "Did he keep after her? Was she afraid of him?"

"She seemed kinda scared in the hospital, but once she was back on her feet, she went out and hired herself a bodyguard. This guy, he didn't follow her around or nothin', but a lotta times he'd come over late in the evening or he'd go with her if there was a situation that made her nervous. She told me, if that john ever tried anything again, she'd put out a contract. She wasn't afraid of nobody, man."

"What was the bodyguard's name?"

Domingo shrugged again. "All I ever heard was Rudy. Mostly he just sat in the kitchen, drank coffee, and read newspapers."

"Who else had it in for her?"

"She pissed off a lotta people." Domingo's head swayed back and forth. "But I guess Luther Corbin'd have to be at the top of the list."

Zach straightened abruptly, his face registering surprise. "*The* Luther Corbin?"

Cassidy asked, "Who is he?"

Zach shot her a look of irritation.

He's getting downright peeved over my refusal to do current events homework.

Eyeing the musician, he said, "Corbin one of her johns?"

"No way, man." Domingo smiled slyly and waited a beat, creating a buildup for his punch line. "But his youngest kid, she was working for Xandra."

Whistling under his breath, Zach said, "I'll bet Corbin was pissed. So, what'd he do about it?"

"Threatened her. First he said he'd get her ass thrown in the joint. When that didn't work, he swore he'd kill her. Xandra just laughed it off."

Cassidy observed Domingo closely, trying to assess how much of what he said was reliable, how much was just his wanting to play the expert. She scanned his slumped shoulders, watery eyes, tremulous mouth. *He's probably got her figured out just about right. After all, he spent years studying her every move.*

Picking up his glass, Zach rattled the ice cubes. "Who else had a grudge against her?"

"There was Nikki." Domingo cocked his head thoughtfully. "Nah, that was the other way around. Mostly it was Xandra that was pissed."

"What about?"

"And she shoulda been pissed, too." Domingo straightened his back in indignation. "Here Xandra gave Nikki her start. Taught her how to walk and talk, all the tricks of the trade. Then Nikki, she just takes off with half her customers."

Sounds like the beauty salon business. Or psychotherapy group practices.

"So what'd Xandra do about it?"

Domingo shrugged. "She was pissed. That's all there was to it."

Eyes narrowing, Zach went into an alert mode that meant something had snagged his attention. "If Xandra was pissed and didn't do anything, she'd mellowed a lot from when I knew her." He pulled out a pad. "What's Nikki's number?"

"Uh-uh. I'm not giving you anything like that. I don't mind swapping stories, but I ain't giving out names and numbers."

Zach laid a fifty on the table.

Domingo stared wistfully at the bill. His right hand sank to the table, his fingers edging jerkily toward the money. He shook himself, wrapped his hand around his glass and took a long swallow. "Can't do it, man." The sheepish grin. "I swear, she'd come back to haunt me."

"You sure she's not haunting you already?" Zach's voice went soft and deep, the way Cassidy talked to clients who were in pain. "She keeping you awake at night because of what you did?" He leaned in closer. "If you did it, man, I don't see how anybody could blame you. After what she put me through, I'd sure understand. Here she's been jerking you around for years, throwing you out, reeling you back in, and all you wanted was to break loose from that spell she had over you."

A sheen of sweat came over Domingo's face. He gulped at his drink.

Zach's low voice continued. "Maybe you shared a bottle of champagne, had a good time in bed, then all of a sudden she says 'Get outta my face.' And you're over the limit, man, you can't take it anymore. So you pick up the bottle and you bash her. You don't even mean to do it. It could happen to anybody. Anybody can get pushed to the point they do something they never thought they'd do."

Domingo hunched over the table, his head shaking in a slow,

repetitive motion.

Cassidy stared at Zach. *That true? Is clubbing someone to death within the realm of possibility for everybody?* She examined herself and rejected the idea. She wasn't violent enough. But what about Zach—especially with all that alcohol in him? Was he capable of it?

You never know what somebody else might be capable of.

Maybe he could've done it, she told herself firmly. *But he didn't.*

The musician finally met Zach's gaze. "I didn't do it, man. Maybe I thought about it, maybe I even wanted to, but it wasn't me." His forlorn brown eyes filled. "I loved her too much."

🍎 🍎 🍎

Zach held the passenger door open for her but she stood on the sidewalk, arms crossed, legs apart, making no move to get in. "You sure you should be driving?"

"What?"

"You just gulped two bourbons in the space of forty-five minutes." *And who knows what watering holes we may be headed for next?*

His jaw clenched, he said, "Get in."

As she slid into the passenger seat, she was aware of her unconscious tugging at her, trying to get her attention. Something about the interview with Domingo. But as soon as she tried to focus on it, it slipped away. The pent-up heat inside the closed car made it difficult to breathe, much less think.

Zach started the engine and pointed the car south, then fixed her with an angry look. "I let you drive to Xandra's 'cause I knew you were right, but I'm not handing over my keys every time I have a drink. I know we're both edgy but I've had about all I can stand of you ordering me around. In fact, this relationship might hold up better if we stayed the hell apart for a while."

Pain flashed through her, followed instantly by anger.

He's gonna keep acting like a shit, let him leave.

Two hours ago you made him give you interference-rights in his investigation—something he hates. Now you expect sweetness and light?

She turned her head away from him to stare out the side window at the Century Mall, a spectacular old movie theater converted into shops. The ornate terra cotta facade was adorned with carved columns that rose four stories into the air.

Facing forward again, she said, "I wish you'd drop this staying-apart crap. I don't think you want that any more than I do."

He drove in silence for a couple of blocks. Finally he looked over at her and said, "You're right, I don't want us to be apart. I also don't want you scrutinizing my behavior or telling me what I can and can't do." He paused. "Whenever I get pissed, my first impulse is to walk away." He put his hand on her knee. "But I don't intend to act on it and I'll try not to say it anymore."

She laid her hand on his. "Maybe I overreacted about the bourbon. It just seems like your drinking's increased lately and it bothers me."

"You think Domingo would've talked to me if I'd sat there with a coke in my hand? When I'm interviewing suspects in bars, I need to drink along with 'em, but this isn't gonna become a way of life."

"So, what's next?"

He pulled out his cell phone. "An appointment with Luther Corbin." Getting the number from directory assistance, he made the call. "His secretary slipped us in for eleven tomorrow morning."

"The Luther Corbin you sneered at me for asking about?"

He glanced at her, his face amused. "Your refusal to read newspapers borders on reverse snobbery, you know."

"But it allows you to put on your mantle of superiority and fill me in." *Why would anybody want to spend half their life following every little detail the way Zach does?*

"Corbin's a prominent black minister who heads an African Methodist Episcopal church in Pill Hill. He's very influential in the black community, a spokesman for liberals of all stripes. He also wields a lot of clout with politicos."

"His daughter's one of Xandra's hookers? That must be quite an embarrassment." She pictured the slinkily dressed teenager in the red convertible. "That girl Bryce was with. Could she be the one?"

Zach shrugged.

"Doesn't seem like Corbin'd be eager to discuss the fact that his daughter's a call girl." She lifted her heavy, cinnamon hair up off her neck to cool herself.

"I've always treated him well enough in the paper, and we have a relationship of sorts. Here's hoping that'll be enough to get him to talk."

He glanced at her quickly, then away. "There's one other thing. I wrote an obit for Xandra that'll be coming out tomorrow. This isn't standard procedure, but I added a line saying that anyone who wants to send flowers can contact Bryce at our address."

She shook her head. *Using Bryce to get something. He should leave the kid out of it.*

You don't stop causing trouble, you'll get yourself thrown off the case.

Making an effort to keep her voice mild, she said, "The fact that Xandra sent Bryce to you—a person no one would ever connect him with—seems to imply that the kid's in danger too. Isn't it a little risky, making his location so public?"

"The news story didn't specifically state that Bryce is with us, but if anybody's looking for him, he'd have to be a moron not to figure it out from what was in the article." He looked straight ahead, avoiding her eyes. "The reason I did it is to see who sends condolences. If anything comes to Bryce in the mail, I wanna confiscate it."

She compressed her lips, resolutely keeping her mouth shut.

He glanced at her again. "You don't like it."

"Doesn't sound to me like the best way to win his trust."

"You are constitutionally unfit to be an investigator." He chuckled. "Way overburdened with scruples."

Too many scruples for Zach, not enough for the ethics committee. A month earlier she'd had to face a social work hearing occasioned by a grievance filed against her for violating client confidentiality.

His beeper went off and he read the number. "Shit. Area Three."

"Hathaway?" Her chest tightened.

"I won't know unless I return the call, which I'm not inclined to do. They want to rake me over any more coals, they'll have to run me down to do it."

"How'd she get your beeper number?"

"I gave it to one of the other dicks over at Area Four. A guy leaking info on a murder investigation."

❦ ❦ ❦

Starshine met them at the stoop and raced through the house, her furry little bottom bouncing up the stairs one step ahead of them. Inside the bedroom, the air felt like warm soup. Zach punched on the window air conditioner, then retrieved his desk chair from Bryce's empty room. Starshine curled up on the waterbed and went to sleep. Cassidy sat and stared at the relentlessly blinking light on her answering machine.

Zach stood beside her. "Looks like you've stacked up a few messages."

Pulling a legal pad out from one of the piles on her desk, she drew a gloomy cartoon face at the top.

"I take it you're not looking forward to hearing them." Dropping into his chair, he swiveled to face her.

Heaviness settling in her stomach, Cassidy pushed PLAY. The first two were from her seven and eight o'clock clients canceling their sessions for that evening. Neither mentioned rescheduling.

The third was from Maggie. "I understand how you disappear into your cave when lightening strikes, so if you don't want to talk, that's okay. You must be feeling sick about that story in the paper, but don't blow it out of proportion. Everybody in Oak Park does *not* know about the two of you, and rumors are *not* running rampant all over the village. So keep your chin up, kiddo, and give me a call when you're ready."

The fourth was a social worker from DCFS. She identified herself as Sara Perkins and asked to see them at their earliest possible convenience regarding placement for Bryce.

The fifth was from her client Judy. "I feel really strange bringing this up, but I saw the article about Zach Moran and that murdered woman and . . . Well, I met him once coming in. And after reading all those things in the *Post* . . . Well, it's bothering me a lot and I need to talk about it."

"Oh shit."

The sixth was from Gran. "Your mother and I are real worried about that newspaper story. So anyway, we thought we'd drop over around five to see how you're doing and then maybe we could all go out to dinner. We'll ring the front doorbell, and if you're seeing clients we'll just quietly slip away. I'm not sure bringing your mother's such a great idea but I couldn't fend her off."

The seventh was from Hathaway asking Zach to return her call. The machine beeped and finally came to a halt.

He said, "Forget Hathaway. Whatever it is she wants, I'm not making it any easier than necessary."

"Oh shit," Cassidy repeated, plunking her elbows on the desk and covering her face with her hands. "Dealing with clients is gonna be tough."

"What're you gonna say to that woman who wants to talk about it?"

8. Want Him Here

"This is tricky." Cassidy chewed on her bottom lip. "I can't go into any kind of detail about my love life, but I also don't wanna simply refuse to discuss it. The fact that she knows I'm involved in a murder is certainly disruptive to the therapy."

"Didn't you say you aren't one of those blank-screen therapists who never discloses anything personal? I thought you do sometimes talk about yourself." Zach's smoky eyes showed concern.

"If a client's beating up on herself for being disorganized, I might say I'm disorganized too, just to normalize it. But I always have to maintain a clear boundary."

"Boundary. One of those fuzzy shrink words that nobody quite understands."

"In this instance, it means I can't talk about you, our relationship, or the case." Cassidy hunched over her desk and drew a box around Judy's name, retracing the line several times to make it heavy and dark. "Telling clients *anything* about us is getting way too personal. Plus it makes me look like an idiot, which won't exactly boost their confidence in my therapeutic skills."

His shaggy brows pulled together. "So what're you gonna do?"

"I'll have to think about it." She shook her head. "At least with Judy I have a starting point. Those two other clients that canceled—I don't even know what their story is. It could be just coincidence. Or it could be they know about us, and they've decided that a therapist who gets into this kind of trouble is not the best source of wise counsel."

"And knowing you, you're probably not gonna blow it off and say 'who cares?' the way I would."

"Well, of course I don't like losing the income." She glanced over at him. With his chair swiveled in her direction they were only about a yard apart.

He frowned. Money was a sore point between them. He thought they should throw everything into the same pot and not worry about it; she thought she should pay her own way.

"But it's not just the money." She sighed. "I hate it that people will be gossiping about us. And I also don't like it that clients may quit before they're ready, which isn't in their best interest." She drummed her pen on the legal pad.

"And here I was hoping to keep you out of it." He shook his head. "Not one of my more rational moments."

At least he never says "It could be worse" or "Don't worry about it."

"I don't know how you stand being a therapist. I hate ambiguity. Give me something clear cut any day." Reaching for the phone and list of messages, he moved them to his desk. "Like this DCFS person. That's something we can take care of right now." He called and arranged for Sara Perkins to come by the house at eight-thirty that evening.

"Clear cut?" Cassidy cocked her head skeptically. "Bryce's placement is one of the most complicated issues of all. Should he stay with us? Would he be better off elsewhere? Do we even want him? He's not exactly a joy to be around. Is he safe here? Can we take care of him adequately, considering the way he just disappears on us?"

Zach looked her straight in the eye. "I want him here. He's got more information about Xandra than anybody else and I have to find some way to make him talk."

"He's just been through one of the worst traumas a kid can experience." She pressed her knuckles into her cheek. "And he's not letting either of us get close enough to help him with it. He really might need to be someplace else."

The lines running from the base of Zach's nose to his jaw deepened. "Right now, all I can think about is clearing this case, and that means keeping Bryce where we can get to him."

She studied his face. *That all of it? Or is there some part of him that wants to get to know his son?*

You keep worrying about Bryce's needs, Zach's needs. What about you?

What I need is to get this messed-up kid out of my house. She pictured a ten-foot-tall social worker stuffing Bryce into her car and driving away. It surprised her to discover that this image did not make her altogether happy.

❦ ❦ ❦

At five o'clock the front doorbell rang and the two other McCabe women—Helen and Gran—settled into the living room armchairs, Cassidy and Zach on the sofa. The air was thick and humid, making her armpits sticky, her silk blouse cling to her back. Noting the grim expression on her mother's face, she concluded that it was the combined effect of unbreathable air and maternal displeasure that was sending her irritability into the danger zone.

Gran, her small face framed by a blond Doris Day wig, was tiny and wizened but full of vitality. Gazing at Zach, she said, "Here I was, reading this story in your very own newspaper, and I saw the name 'Zachary Moran.' Then it hit me—that's our Zach they're talking about." She cocked her golden head and asked, "Is it true? What the article said? Just imagine—a real madam, like that Heidi person out in Hollywood, only not so rich and famous."

"Yep, it's all true."

"But you didn't do it, did you?" She shook her head vigorously, knocking her wig slightly askew. "No, of course not. I shouldn't even have asked." Her eyes, peering out between folds of wrinkles, were bright with curiosity; her voice brimmed with exuberance. "And it also said you have a son who simply landed on your doorstep," she snapped her fingers, "just like that."

"Mother," Helen interjected, her voice laden with disapproval, "how can you talk about that horrid story as if it were something to get excited about? This could ruin Cassidy's career, destroy her reputation. And it makes all of us look like a bunch of silly women who've been taken in by some dreadful con man."

"Now Helen," Zach drawled, "I've been accused of plenty of things, but conning women's not one of 'em. That's Cassidy's ex you're thinking of."

Can see why Mom'd take this so hard. First her fiance turns out to be an abusive creep, then Zach's made to sound like a similar type. All that anger toward Roland—bound to get transferred to Zach.

Can understand it, but that doesn't make it any easier listening to the dreck coming out of her mouth.

Helen, a plump woman in her sixties, had avoided men from the time her husband abandoned the family thirty-three years ago until the previous fall, when a sudden fling at dating had led to her disastrous engagement. At that point she'd updated her image, transforming herself into a chic senior. But now that her wedding was off, she'd reverted to her former style of dressing: beige pant suits, gray perms, and sturdy shoes.

"So," Gran leaned forward, "you gonna let me meet this unexpected son of yours?"

"If I can catch him." Zach shrugged. "We never know when he's gonna turn up."

"What about the police?" Gran asked. "They don't really think you killed that madam, do they?"

"I don't know what they think, but I do know they don't have enough evidence to book me."

"That doesn't mean he didn't do it," Helen muttered.

" 'Course, not getting arrested's not good enough," Gran continued. "We've gotta prove you innocent. Now I know you two've run your own investigations before and I'll bet you're already in the thick of things. I just hope you can find some way to put me to work, like last time. I'm pretty good at manning the phones, you know."

Helen frowned at Gran. "I don't see how you can even think of such a thing." She turned her scowl on Zach. "Every time you drag Cass into one of these horrid situations of yours, something terrible happens. You brought this on yourself by getting involved with that disgusting girl in the first place. Isn't it bad enough that you've disgraced Cass in front of her friends? You should just take yourself back to that Chicago condo of yours and leave her out of it."

Cassidy gave her mother a fierce look. "You better stop right now, Mom, 'cause I'm not putting up with this. One more word and I'll have to ask you to leave."

Zach leaned back, laid his arm along the rim of the sofa, and said to Helen, "Have you ever been able to keep Cass out of anything she wants to get herself into?"

Helen withdrew deeper into her chair.

"What I think we oughtta do is just the opposite. This family's gotta stick together." Gran's tiny fist pounded the armrest. "We need to hold our heads high and let the world see we got nothing to be ashamed of. And I say we start tonight by going out to dinner at Philander's where all the upper crust folk like your family eat." She gave a nod to Zach.

Cassidy felt warmed clear through by Gran's words.

Zach said in his laconic tone, "I normally avoid places where I might run into my family, but I guess I could make an exception."

"I'm not sure I want to be seen . . ." Helen started.

The other three stared at her for a good thirty seconds.

She sighed heavily. "All right, I'll go."

Cassidy wanted to tackle the unpleasant task of returning client calls before dinner, so they agreed to meet later at the restaurant.

🍎 🍎 🍎

Sitting at her desk, she phoned the two clients who had canceled. The first rescheduled; the second said he wanted to take a break from therapy. She had just finished setting an appointment with Judy when she heard the front door close. *Well, the kid's back. If we can just hang onto him, maybe Gran'll get to meet him after all.*

Cassidy started downstairs with Zach coming out of his office to follow her. Finding Bryce in the living room, he told the teenager they needed to talk. Cassidy noticed that the boy's appearance was either deteriorating or normalizing, she wasn't sure which. He'd arrived looking preppy and was now sliding into grunge.

"We're having dinner with Cass' mother and grandmother," Zach said from the sofa. "We'd like you to come along."

Bryce, in one of the armchairs, gazed out the window. "Count me out."

Hearing the flatness in his speech, Cassidy took a closer look. His eyes were bloodshot and his face was slack, the expression for once neither sulky nor defiant.

"Well, well." Zach rested his outspread hands on his thighs. "This a daily habit or you just taking the edge off?"

"None of your business." The same slow monotone.

Zach asked, his tone conversational, "Are you trying to get me to throw you out? 'Cause I will if you don't follow house rules. And I'm telling you, you're not using *anything* while you stay here. In fact, now that I think about it, it was a mistake handing you those beers. In the future I don't want you even drinking unless Cass or I say you can."

"It's only pot."

"Yeah, I know. I know a lot about pot, and having used my share of it, I'm in no position to preach to anybody else. But this is Cass' house and she doesn't like it, and I'm at a point in my life where I don't favor it much myself. So no drugs for the duration or you're outta here."

Cassidy looked at Zach in surprise. *First he says he wants the kid here no matter what. Now he gives him an ultimatum. Don't understand but I'm glad he did.*

"And as far as tonight goes," Zach added, leaning slightly forward, "I want you with us. Now go change into something decent, and when Cass' mother makes snide remarks, just keep your mouth shut and let us handle it." He stood. "I believe I'll even put on a clean shirt and jacket myself."

❦ ❦ ❦

In the car on the way to Philander's Cassidy said, "We better skip the wine tonight since we've got a DCFS worker after dinner."

"DCFS—shit!" A low grumble, Bryce talking to himself. Then he piped up in a louder voice clearly intended for Zach, "How come you drink all the time but I can't take a few tokes? Everybody knows alcohol is worse than pot."

Keeping his eyes straight ahead, Zach said, "The matter is not open for discussion."

Zach's drinking—not open for discussion? The kid's only been here a couple of days, he's already picked up on it.

Suddenly the question she had refused to face squarely since their first meeting over a jug of Carlo Rossi forced itself into her consciousness. *Is he alcoholic?* Chest tightening, she huddled in on herself, gazed blindly out the window, tried to think about something else.

Drinks daily but it's never out of control. Matter of fact, you usually have a nightcap with him.

A memory drifted into her mind of a client whose husband had kept his drinking in check till he lost his job, and then he'd slipped rapidly into unmitigated drunkenness. The trouble with being a therapist was she heard too many stories, knew too much about the bad things that could happen.

Zach abused drugs till Xandra got him arrested, then decided to quit and just did it. Same way he quit cigarettes. He can take care of himself.

Or—another way to look at it—he has an addictive personality. Didn't so much quit drugs as switch to alcohol. Always uses something. And the higher the stress, the more he's gonna use.

Zach's been through extreme duress more than once in his life, never self-destructed. Now leave it alone and let him handle it, 'cause if you start checking the bottle in the cabinet, you are in big trouble yourself.

Turning south on Oak Park Avenue, they passed a freshly painted Victorian, the gingerbread highlighted in burgundy and dusty rose. Cassidy stared at it absently.

"Something I wanted to ask you, Bryce," Zach said. "Cass and I visited Adonis Domingo today and I'd like your read on him."

Her unconscious tweaked her, the same feeling she'd had right after the interview. *Missed something.* She tried to dig it out but it was gone.

"What're you talking to him for?" the boy asked in the same listless tone.

Cassidy twisted around to answer. "We need to find out who killed your mother."

"You don't have very far to look."

"So, what do you think of your mother's boyfriend?" Zach persisted.

"That jerk? What a loser. I mean, he can play the guitar all right, but the rest of the time, forget it. I kept telling her to dump him."

Cassidy's brow creased. "Why do you suppose she'd hang around with somebody like that?"

"She always had to have her little plaything." Even with his emotions flattened by pot, Cassidy could hear the note of bitterness. *What's this? A crack in his mother's veneer of perfection?*

Zach glanced over his shoulder. "Domingo seemed to think the two of you were buddies."

"He doesn't know anything. I had to be civil 'cause Xandra'd've killed me if I wasn't, but I couldn't stand the jagoff. He kept panting after her like this lost little puppy and he was always begging her for money. I hated it that he took money from her."

"You think he might've whacked her?"

"Nah, he's too much of a pussy. You're more the type to knock somebody around."

"That a compliment?" Zach laughed. "What about the bodyguard, Rudy? You know his last name or where we could get hold of him?"

"All I ever heard was 'Rudy.' He sorta stayed out of sight, never said much. He did make me think about getting into bodybuilding, though."

"Why do you suppose Rudy wasn't there the night she was killed?"

"Who knows? Lots of times when she wanted to be alone, she'd tell him to get lost. And if Lenny was around, she wouldn't need him."

"Lenny?" Cassidy asked.

"Her driver. He was sort of a bodyguard too, even though he was kinda old."

Cocking his head, Zach said, "I forgot about the driver. I wonder if this is the same one she had back when I knew her. How long has this Lenny been with her?"

"How would I know?"

Could the driver've beaten her up nearly eighteen years ago? Not a recommended strategy for long-term employment.

Zach asked, "What'd be the best way to track this Lenny person down?"

"Beats me."

The kid's brain was so smoked he lost his concentration and actually answered a few questions. Now it's come back to him that he's not speaking to us.

Zach tried another tack. "So who do you think might've done it?"

"You know what I think."

❦   ❦   ❦

Cassidy, her stomach twitchy over the impending DCFS decision, invited Sara Perkins into the living room. She was in her fifties, an angular woman with iron-gray hair pinned up in back, stray tendrils falling loosely around her strong-boned face.

Zach rose to greet her. Bryce remained hunched in his chair, the sulky look back on his face now that the pot had worn off.

"It's good of you to see me on such short notice." She shook hands all around.

Cassidy sensed confidence and amiability. *Seems like somebody who'll listen to all sides, not just run to the rule book, go rigid on us, and proclaim: Can't let a kid stay with a parent who might've committed a crime.*

They sat together in the living room while Sara Perkins explained that Bryce, as a minor whose mother had been killed, was now under the guardianship of the state, and that she, as his caseworker, was responsible for determining his placement. These were procedures Cassidy had learned in graduate school, but having worked solely in private practice, the details were fuzzy in her mind.

Perkins set herself up in Cassidy's office to interview each of them in turn. Following the interviews, she brought them together to discuss her recommendation. Since Perkins had commandeered the director's chair, Cassidy had to join the other two on the sectional curving around the two outside walls. *Feels odd, sitting in the client's seat, someone else in my place.* The spiffy new furniture Zach had bullied her into accepting made her unwashed canvas chair, her frequently-spilled-upon wicker table, and her straggly, unpruned coleus look even shabbier by comparison.

She wondered what Perkins must think of her, a social worker living with a man who'd once been arrested for battery and now was under suspicion of murder. *Appears nonjudgmental, but every one of us is trained to give off that impression, and half the time it's bullshit. Social workers are exemplary at nodding and smiling on the outside, feeling totally disgusted on the inside.*

"Well . . . Perkins fastened her warm gaze on Bryce. "I understand you're very angry at your father and you don't like having to stay here."

"I hate him," the teenager mumbled. Scrunched into the small space between the wicker table and the sectional, he sat with head lowered, hands hanging between his legs, widespread knees high in the air.

Perkins checked Zach's face, which had taken on its detached look.

Does Bryce's attitude matter to him at all? Cassidy knew Zach's feelings for her and Starshine ran deep, but she also knew he could disconnect from people without a qualm. *Really wish I could sit him in the client's chair and dig out everything going on inside of him about his kid.* The chances of Zach's tolerating her playing therapist were about as great as Limbaugh's starting a Hillary fan club.

Perkins turned her attention to Bryce. "Considering how strongly you feel, it would probably be better to move you into another home."

9. DNA

The teenager instantly straightened, his eyes darting to Perkins' face. "What're you talking about? Just go live in somebody else's house? Somebody I don't even know?"

"Well," the DCFS worker said evenly, "what other option would you suggest?"

Eyes dropping to the floor, he waited a beat, then mumbled, "Guess I'll stay here."

Cassidy gave him a sharp look. *Lesser of the evils? Curiosity about his father?*

Perkins rested one elbow in the other hand. "You told me you think Zach killed your mother. If you really believe that, why would you want to live with him?"

Bryce shrugged. There was a long silence.

"I think," Perkins said slowly, "it would be best if you went someplace else."

Zach shifted on the flat-cushioned seat. "You know, I am his father. I can understand your reluctance to take any risks, considering I'm still under investigation. But I haven't been charged with anything yet, and from where I'm sitting I'd say the odds are pretty high I won't be."

"Innocent until proven guilty, of course." Perkins nodded. "Actually, the main reason I'm recommending Bryce's removal is his high degree of animosity toward you. He doesn't seem to be doing any active grieving and I'm concerned that his anger may be blocking it."

A cacophony of cat shrieks erupted from outside. Cassidy's shoulders jumped. Zach excused himself and went to the back door to call Starshine. Returning to his seat, he said, "She came streaking into the house so I guess she's okay."

Exhaling noisily, Cassidy took a deep breath and said to Perkins,

"I've been worrying about Bryce's anger myself." Glancing at the boy, she saw resentment etched deeply in his face. *Hates that we're talking about him.* "The problem is, if he leaves now, these two," she gestured toward Zach and Bryce, "will cut each other off and the chances are, Bryce'll never work through all the hostility he has toward his only remaining parent. He has a number of conflicting needs, but I think the most important one is to get to know his father and develop some kind of relationship. If he stays here, he may come to see that his mother's version of Zach isn't the whole story."

As Perkins gazed into space, taking some time to think it through, Cassidy glanced from father to son. Zach's face was round and smooth, Bryce's narrow and craggy, but both had the same bronze skin and walled-off expression. *If these two are ever going to get together, it'll be my job to make it happen. What have I gotten myself into?*

Finally Perkins looked directly at Bryce. "When you said you wanted to stay, is it that you *don't* want to go someplace else or that you *do* want to be here?"

Bryce responded, his voice so low they could barely hear him, "I wanna be here."

This isn't forever, is it? This may be what's best for Bryce, but it sure as hell isn't what's best for me.

When Perkins left, Zach turned to face the teenager. "Okay, I'm officially in charge now, and I've got a couple more rules to add to the no-drugs deal."

Bryce scowled. "I don't have to do what you say. You may have gotten Xandra pregnant, but that doesn't make you any kind of real father."

"I know you think you're old enough to do whatever you want. I felt the same when I was your age. But I have to make sure you're safe, and I can't do that unless I can keep track of you. That means you have to learn to live with a curfew. I want you in by midnight unless you call ahead and get an official dispensation from Cass or me." He pulled a card out of his wallet and jotted something on it. "Here are my pager and cell phone numbers. I want the same from you." Handing the card to Bryce, he took out his spiral pad.

"All I have is a cell phone." Bryce stared at the floor, shifted his weight, then recited a number.

Zach stuffed the pad into his jacket pocket. "The other thing is, there's a space behind the house where you can park at night so you don't collect any more tickets."

"You don't have to worry." Bryce stiffened his shoulders. "I got plenty of money. I can pay my own tickets."

"Fine. You pay the ones you already tossed in the trash, but from now on, you park in that slot so you don't pick up any new ones."

🍎 🍎 🍎

Upstairs Cassidy pulled a long plum tee over her head, then sat in bed to wait for Zach, who was downstairs making sure Bryce moved his car. She was determined to stay awake long enough to clear up a puzzling little inconsistency.

After he settled in beside her, she said, "I was amazed to hear you lay down the law with Bryce. First you say you want him here at all costs, then you threaten to throw him out if he doesn't follow the rules."

Zach drew her under his arm. "I get the impression Xandra kept him on a tight rein, so I figured I had to take a stand on the drugs or he'd never see me as any kind of parent figure. The only way I'll ever get him to talk is if I can engender a little respect."

She ran her hand down his arm. "I halfway expected him to get back in his car and drive away." *Halfway hoped, don't you mean?*

Zach shrugged. "I need him here but not enough to let him trash our lives. After that debacle when Xandra had me arrested, I swore I'd never want *anybody* at all costs again."

She knew Zach was right. She'd advocated a similar stance to clients. She just had never quite been able to incorporate that mind-set for herself.

"I'm exhausted." She slid out from under his arm to lay her head on the pillow, then realized something was not right. Opening her eyes, she looked at Zach. "Where's Starshine?" The calico typically was ensconced at their feet by this time of night.

"In the house somewhere, but I haven't seen her since she came tearing in from that cat fight. Probably still in shock from the ruckus outside."

🍎 🍎 🍎

Wednesday morning the front doorbell bonged, dragging Cassidy out of a deep sleep. Struggling to open her eyes, she groggily took in two things: the clock on the bureau said 7:30 and Zach's side of the bed was empty. *He can take care of it.*

She was sliding down toward an unfinished dream when she heard Zach's voice say gently, "You have to get up. Hathaway's paying me back for ignoring her page by requesting your presence in the living room."

"You deal with her." Cassidy kept her eyes closed.

"She wants to talk to both of us and she's not likely to leave till she does."

Anger knotted in her stomach. "Shit." She stood and glared at Zach. "You should've returned the damn call." *Last thing I want before coffee is to see that woman's condescending face.*

Raking fingers through her thick mane, Cassidy pictured the sleekly groomed detective as she stared despairingly into her closet. In front of her hung a rack of clothing that had not been organized in years: items wrinkled from having been scrunched together, everything covered with cat hair, nothing washed or ironed.

*Was that you being judgmental about the condition of Torres' attire? Next to the straight-out-of-*Vogue *senior detective, you look like a refugee from Les Miserables.*

Don't be ridiculous, her therapist voiced chided. *People like Hathaway always turn out to be self-critical and obsessive. Even their friends can't stand 'em. No matter how put together they look, they're too driven to enjoy it.*

Yeah, but with sex goddess Xandra on one side and bandbox perfect Hathaway on the other, that insight fails to comfort.

Gritting her teeth, she grabbed a violet shirt that was only slightly stained, pulled on dirty jeans, and went downstairs. Hathaway, her back straight, her gleaming leather pumps aligned neatly on the floor, was seated in an armchair.

Feeling fuzzy-headed from sleep, Cassidy sat next to Zach on the sofa.

Hathaway fixed her cool gray eyes on Zach. "We need a sample of your DNA."

Cassidy's shoulders tensed. *There's more. Oh God, it just keeps getting worse.*

Zach pressed his fingertips together on his chest. "Autopsy results?"

"Semen in the vaginal canal." Hathaway's gaze moved to Cassidy's face. Her thin mouth curved into a small smile.

"So," Zach said, "if my DNA isn't a match, you cross me off the list?"

A way out. Zach didn't screw her so he's not the one.

Hathaway didn't answer.

"No, of course not. You could always say I showed up after the other guy left."

"Obviously you know what the results will be." Hathaway crossed one leg over the other and smoothed her short linen skirt. "So if the test is certain to come up negative, it's clearly in your best interest to give us a sample."

"I don't think so."

What's that mean? That he did sleep with her?

Zach scratched his jaw. "If the lab work's straight up, I'd be off the hook in terms of having fucked her. But with a witness saying he saw me when I wasn't there and evidence planted in my house, my trust in the department is running a little thin."

"Isn't it a bit flimsy to say the lab might falsify results?"

"Maybe, but I'm tired of being cooperative."

"C'mon Zach." Hathaway tilted her head and coaxed slyly. "You can prove you didn't have sex with her." She looked pointedly at Cassidy. "All you have to do is give us a sample."

"I don't have to prove anything. That's your job."

Hathaway's voice turned cool. "You know I can get a court order."

Zach shrugged.

"Wouldn't it be easier to come now than have me pick you up at the *Post*?"

"If you're gonna play games with us at seven-thirty in the morning, I'm inclined to make you talk to a judge." Zach draped his arm along the top of the sofa. "Time of death?"

The detective's gaze snicked to Cassidy again, then went to the window, her interest in the conversation apparently waning.

Doesn't matter if Hathaway won't talk. It had to be during the time Zach was alone or she wouldn't be here.

"No comment? How 'bout prints then? You obviously didn't get any off the bottle, 'cause if you did you'd be sitting in somebody else's living room right now. Was it smudged or wiped clean?"

She smiled her supercilious smile. "You know I'm not going to tell you anything."

Cassidy's teeth ached from being clenched so long. Watching Hathaway sit so precisely in the chair, she felt a deep sense of loathing. "Why insist that I come down?"

The detective lifted one shoulder in a slight shrug.

Cassidy held her head a notch higher. "You wanted me to hear that Xandra had sex before she was killed because you thought I might get jealous and give up evidence against Zach. Not a bad strategy, except I don't have a single piece of information that'd help you build your case."

"So, I understand Bryce is still with you." Hathaway stood.

"Right."

They rose also as Hathaway started toward the door.

"He needs to make arrangements for the body. We'd like it picked up as soon as possible." She glanced over her shoulder at Zach. "But then, you know all about police procedure, don't you?" Stepping out onto the porch, she added, "We've unsealed the house so the boy can get his things."

After the door closed, Zach faced Cassidy squarely. "You wanna ask?"

"Did you?"

"Never saw her alive. And if I had, I wouldn't have wanted to." He grinned. "Well, I might've wanted to but I wouldn't have done it."

She made a face. "First I have to put up with Hathaway, then you."

Resting his hands on his hips, he looked at the floor, then out the window. "Hathaway's campaign getting to you?"

She folded her arms across her chest. "I'm absolutely sick of having police walk in as if they owned the place. But as for believing you, I made a decision I'd accept whatever you tell me unless I see proof positive to the contrary. So, even though your refusal about the DNA test nearly gave me a heart attack, I'm gonna take your word for it."

He pulled her into his arms for a quick hug.

"You really think they'd falsify lab results?"

"It's not likely but also not impossible." He placed his hand on her back, steering her toward the kitchen. "I only did it to give Hathaway a hard time. I knew she'd go for a court order. She'll be hunting me down again before the day is out. But it'll take six weeks to get the results, and I expect to have the real guy nailed long before then."

In the kitchen they poured the coffee Zach had started before Hathaway arrived. As Cassidy's brain cells came online, she noticed the absence of catly demands, remembered the calico's defection from their bed the evening before. Alarm tugged at her. "Have you seen Starshine since she came running in from that cat fight last night?"

"I was just headed toward the basement to look for her when I got interrupted."

Basement's the worst possible place to try to find anything. Undoubtedly why she heads down there whenever she wants to hide out.

But she never hides out during breakfast.

They descended cracked cement steps into a dimly lit space crowded with tools, furniture, and ancient artifacts, all the debris that makes its way into the basements of people with streaks of pack rat. One entire corner was stacked with boxes Zach had hauled over from his Chicago condo. This mysterious heap was like a magician's magic hat, a treasure trove from which he seemed able to extract absolutely anything, including the sleeping bag and air mattress for Bryce.

They spent considerable time peering into odd crannies before she spied a small box lying on its side atop a picnic table, a furry rump poking out the open end.

Apprehension tingled in Cassidy's chest as she called out softly, "Starshine?"

Coming to stand beside her, Zach rested his hand on her shoulder. "She must've been hurt in that fight."

Cassidy tilted the box gently, sliding the cat out onto the table. Starshine moved as little as possible, her head facing away from them, tail and legs tucked in. The only acknowledgment she gave was a twist of the ears and a low growl.

Scrutinizing the cat's body, Cassidy found no mark of any kind. She ran her fingers along the furry spine, eliciting a deeper growl. "Guess she's telling us to leave her alone." *Oh shit, hope it's not internal bleeding.*

"I'll check the yellow pages for the closest animal ER."

❦ ❦ ❦

In the vet's office, Cassidy placed Starshine on the examination table. The cat looked at her with huge, betrayal-filled eyes that seemed to say, "How could you do this to me?"

The vet, a young woman in a white smock, took the calico's temperature and probed her body. "Some other cat nailed her. You can just barely see these marks here." The woman extended Starshine's leg to its full length, pointing to two tiny punctures above the knee. Enormous black pupils turning venomous, the cat struggled to bite the vet's hand.

She were big enough, she'd snap all three of our necks in a minute. Cassidy pictured a tiger-sized Starshine sitting among their mangled bodies, a self satisfied smirk on her face. *Why do we get so attached to these predatory creatures who'd have us for lunch if they could?*

"She's going to need antibiotics for a full week." Leaving the room, the vet reappeared with a bottle of pills. "I'll give her the first one, then you make sure she gets them morning and evening for the next seven days. No quitting just because she perks up. She'll probably seem back to normal in a day or two, but if she doesn't take all the pills, the infection's likely to return."

Cassidy watched closely as the vet pried Starshine's mouth open, placed a pill at the base of her tongue, then held her jaws closed for about thirty seconds.

Gripping a squirmy Starshine, Cassidy stopped at the front counter on their way out. "Let me get this." She fumbled to open her handbag.

Irritation crossed Zach's face as he pulled out his wallet and laid down a charge card.

In the car Starshine sat on Cassidy's lap, ears flattened, whiskers retracted, her face turned steadfastly away from both of them. "Wonder how long she's going to punish us for abusing her like this?" Cassidy experienced a faint echo of the guilt she used to feel when her mother sulked.

Zach put his hand on her knee. "She never holds a grudge past mealtime, just like I never do past sex."

Yeah, but we haven't had any since I made him promise not to go off on his own. That mean he's still pissed?

Don't be ridiculous. You're both too exhausted to even think about sex.

❦ ❦ ❦

After depositing a subdued Starshine on the waterbed, they changed clothes: a burgundy dress scattered with cat hair for Cassidy, a collarless jacket for Zach. As they left for their appointment with the minister, Cassidy pictured Izzie whipping off his glasses and probing her brain cells with his intrusive stare. *Wonder what he'd give to learn the distinguished Luther Corbin has a call-girl daughter.*

The church was located in Pill Hill, a wealthy, mansion-studded black neighborhood on the south side. Zach parked behind a tall building, its intricate, airy spires soaring into the dazzling sunlight overhead. Inside, a secretary ushered them into the minister's plush and polished office. Opposite the door stood a desk the size of a city block, a fawn-colored leather couch facing it, a floor-to-ceiling bookshelf to their left, a wall with a wide window to their right. Cassidy noticed a number of gold-framed family photos standing amid the books. Scanning the pictures, she couldn't tell whether any of the prim, girlish faces resembled the slinky red convertible creature or not.

"Zach, good to see you." The man who rose from behind his desk reminded her of a small mountain. He was well over six feet, with a large, balding head, prominent features, thick shoulders and chest. The self-assurance in his voice, the directness of his gaze, everything about him conveyed power. Benevolent power perhaps, but power nonetheless. This was not a man who would take defeat lightly.

Especially not from a white madam who was thumbing her nose at his religion and defiling his little girl.

Shaking Zach's hand, Corbin asked, "And your companion here?"

She looked curiously at Zach to see if he was going to play the not-introducing game, but he responded promptly. "Cassidy McCabe. We've partnered up on a couple of investigations."

"Glad to meet you." Corbin extended his large hand, gestured to the sofa in front of his carved mahogany desk, then eased back into his swivel chair. Behind the minister's gray-wreathed head, a rosy stained glass window glowed with midmorning light. "Should I ask how things are going or skip over your personal problems and move directly to whatever brought you here?" Although his deep voice resonated with congeniality, Cassidy sensed an underlying uneasiness.

Leaning back, Zach let his hands rest loosely on his thighs. "I think you know why we're here."

"You'll have to spell it out."

Noticing a minuscule tightening of the craggy face, Cassidy tried to imagine how humiliating it must be for Corbin to hear what Zach was about to say. *When you read that news story, you wanted to disconnect the phone and go into hiding for six months. Think how much worse it's gotta be for this big-shot minister. Guy already knows his daughter's a hooker. Now he's gotta hear that other people know it too.* Picturing the girl in the red convertible, Cassidy felt distinctly sorry for Luther Corbin.

Zach spelled it out.

The minister sat, fingers tented beneath his chin, moving not a muscle. Three beats passed, then he squared his shoulders and said, "I'll deny it, of course."

"I'm not interested in writing you up or embarrassing you. All I care about is finding the guy who did it so I can get the cops off my back. The sooner this case is nailed shut, the better for both of us." Zach leaned slightly forward. "The police talk to you yet?"

Corbin nodded.

"Well, you're lucky one of my fellow media scavengers hasn't picked up on it already. Soon as some cop leaks the word to a reporter about your daughter and the threats to Xandra, it'll be all over the ten o'clock news. But if I can lock this case up fast enough, the news-hounds'll go sniffing somewhere else."

Corbin hunched forward and said, a knifelike edge to his voice, "This a threat, Zach?"

10. Retaliation

Pulling himself up straight, Zach said, "That's not how I operate."

Cassidy regarded him with a warm, interior smile. *Use threats if he had to, but only as a last resort. Not out for power over people—least, not over people other than me. Now Corbin—I bet he wouldn't cavil at an occasional threat.*

Zach went on to say, "I'm asking for your cooperation. I want everything you know about Xandra, including how to reach your daughter, all on deep background."

Deep background. Journalist version of confidentiality. I tend to forget—reporters do have some ethics after all.

"And the reason you're gonna tell me is, you've got as much at stake in getting this case closed quickly as I do."

"Why shouldn't I assume the police'll get it closed quickly by arresting your ass?"

"Because I didn't do it. The police are wasting a lot of manhours looking for evidence that doesn't exist."

"I don't know." The minister tilted his large head from side to side. "If the man who killed that bitch madam was standing in front of me today, I'd probably offer to shake his hand." His fingers drummed a staccato beat on the neatly stacked desk. He wore a wide gold wedding band on his left hand, two sizable rings on his right, one apparently a school ring, the other a great knobby protrusion of diamonds and rubies. "Okay. On the somewhat preposterous theory that you'll be able to wrap this case up faster than the police, I'll talk to you."

Zach took out his pad. "How'd your daughter come to be working for Xandra?"

Corbin turned his head to look out the window to their right, then dropped his eyes to the desk where both hands were twisting a large gold pen. "It was Gordon Wiess getting revenge." He closed his eyes briefly. "That's the hardest part to swallow. That my beautiful eight-een-year-old is . . . doing what she's doing because I whupped Wiess' sorry ass in a construction dispute."

Zach scribbled a note, his face taking on its alert-reporter look. "That battle over the Westin Memorial Library?" He gazed into space. "Almost two years ago, wasn't it? Wiess called in a bunch of favors to get that new library built in his northside ward, then you launched your southside campaign for increased minority hiring. You pinned him to the mat with strikes and protests, and in the end he had to bring in black subcontractors. Isn't that about how it went down?"

"We shook hands and played kissy face in front of the cameras, but Wiess is not a man who takes kindly to being beaten on his own turf. I'm not surprised he came after me," he paused, cleared his throat, "but I never imagined he'd do it the way he did." Corbin lowered his gaze, then looked up again. "His plan for retaliation started at the new library's opening gala. Wiess hosted the event, of course, since the entire project was a tribute to his power in the council. He had to invite me to prove he was a good loser, and I had to attend to prove the fences were mended."

Where do alpha males learn the rules? Is it written in some book women aren't allowed to read?

No, wait—women do it too. Everyone who wants to be a player simply mimics the next echelon up. Thank God Zach only enters small-scale information contests. Other than that, he'd rather write about games than play them.

Corbin smoothed a hand over his crown. "So there I was, sipping champagne and schmoozing my opponents when I noticed Wiess standing in a huddle on the other side of the room with a good-looking redhead and that police lieutenant . . ." He paused, forehead furrowed as he searched for the name. "Uh . . . Steve Frasier, that's who it was. I wouldn't have paid any attention except at one point they all looked over and stared at me."

Zach tapped his pen against the pad. "You didn't know who Xandra was at the time?"

"Our paths had crossed at a few black-tie charity events, but I didn't know her name, certainly didn't know how she came into possession of the generous sums she donated."

"So what happened next?"

"Xandra came over a few minutes later, announced she was a friend of the alderman's, then proceeded to hit on me. And I didn't have to use guesswork to know what she was suggesting, either. It crossed my mind to wonder if Wiess was trying to get blackmail pictures or something, but if that were the case she'd never have made a point of telling me they were buddies." Corbin placed a hand on his balding head. "It was only later I deciphered the message Wiess was sending that night." He gazed out the window, lips clamped, jaw tight with anger.

Shifting in her chair, Cassidy asked, "So you think Wiess used Xandra to get back at you? And the reason Xandra made a play for you at the opening was so you'd know that recruiting your daughter was a deliberate act of revenge?"

Corbin glanced in her direction, a frown furrowing his brow. *Guess you're not supposed to speak until spoken to.*

"Well, now, that does seem to be the obvious interpretation, doesn't it?"

She added, "And I suppose it gives him leverage for the future. If you ever get in his way again, he can threaten to leak the story about the prominent minister's call girl connection."

He nodded, his expression changing subtly, as if she'd demonstrated sufficient intelligence that he might consider taking her seriously.

If Wiess was behind the daughter's recruitment, the fact that Corbin started a political battle was what triggered the revenge. "So . . ." she eased in slowly, "does all this make you feel responsible for what happened to your daughter?"

Zach looked at her in surprise. The minister sat very erect. "Are you implying this was my fault?" He scowled down at her from what seemed a great height. "How can you even suggest such a thing. It was clearly Xandra's doing. Weiss and Xandra. That godless whore! She seduced my little girl, offered her money and worldly pleasures to turn the temple of her body over to the corruption of men."

"So you don't feel responsible?"

The bluster draining out of him, he hunched forward. "Not completely." He was silent several moments, then raised his head and gazed at her directly for the first time, a haunted look coming into his dark eyes. "I suppose there's some part of it I might feel responsible for."

Seems to me those big shoulders of his are carrying around a ton of guilt. More to it than he made a bad mistake by getting on Wiess' shitlist? She asked in a low voice, "Which part?"

Corbin turned toward the window again, his face knotted in concentration. She could see the wheels turning as he decided whether or not to continue. Finally he spoke, his face still averted, as if he were talking to God instead of her. "I've taken a very strong stand in favor of African-American men staying with their families. I've preached over and over that the key to raising healthy kids is father-involvement, and I've tried to be the kind of family man myself who'd stand as a model for what it means to be a good dad. With the first three, I demanded excellence, set tight limits, and it all worked. But with Tiffany, everything backfired." He picked up the gold pen, dropped it on his desk.

Tiffany? That's what Bryce called his girlfriend. So Corbin's daughter is the girl in the red convertible. "What made it different with her?"

"When she was small, I simply doted on her. She was so bright and pretty and high spirited. Then she got to be a teenager and it was like she'd turned into a devil-child. I did everything I could, but nothing worked."

"So part of it was Tiffany's getting wild. What else was it?"

He rubbed his face with both hands, then said, his voice barely audible, "My wife says it was me. That it's my fault it happened."

"Do you think it's your fault?"

He swiveled back toward Cassidy, despair crossing his face. "I think Xandra's attempts would've failed if I hadn't already gotten into a war with her."

He was silent for several moments. Cassidy thought she'd pushed as far as she could go, that he wouldn't say any more.

He cleared his throat and continued, "About the time she hit puberty, I got involved in community organizing and wasn't home much. That's when it began. She started running with a bad crowd and I reacted by getting tough with her. She'd break curfew, I'd ground her for a month, she'd sneak out the back door." He picked up the pen again, jiggled it between his fingers.

"It all fell to pieces. Xandra couldn't have gotten near her if Tiffany hadn't already started using drugs and sleeping around." He wiped his palm over his forehead and crown. "My wife thinks that first I got too busy, then I got too strict. Maybe if I hadn't tried to jerk the reins in so tight, if I'd given her a little room . . ." He pressed his fingers to his forehead.

"So you're blaming yourself as well as Xandra and Wiess." Cassidy shook her head. "What an awful burden."

A moment passed, then Zach said, "When did it start?"

"It's been about eighteen months since Tiffany first ran away. She was only sixteen. God, can you imagine? A sixteen-year-old. Anyway, I hired a private investigator to find her, and he gave us the news. She'd moved in with another of Xandra's hookers, a woman in her twenties named Nikki Stiletto. I went storming over to Nikki's condo and was surprised to find that this other woman, even though she's a hooker herself, was fairly sympathetic. She said she didn't think a girl Tiffany's age should be in the business and actually told her to go home."

Bet Xandra foisted Tiffany on Nikki, Nikki was sick of having this other girl's cosmetics all over her bathroom.

Corbin shook his head. "We dragged her back to our house, but then a month later she showed up high again. I got into a big fight with her and off she went, running back to Xandra. This same scenario occurred a few more times, and then finally my wife and I were forced to admit that there was no way we could make her stop hooking, especially with the drug problem she had. Anyway, Tiffany moved out of the other girl's place and is living on her own now."

Zach said, "We need to talk to her."

Corbin directed his gaze at Cassidy. "You'll tell her that we love her? That we still want her back?"

"I'll do what I can." *Which is probably nothing. I know it. He knows it.* "People usually don't get clean until their life is so bad they can't stand it anymore."

"Tiffany won't speak to me, but my wife calls her from time to time." Corbin gave them the girl's phone number and address, then flipped to a card in his Rolodex. "Nikki'd be a good person to talk to. She seemed more sensible than I would've expected."

Zach looked up from his notes. "Xandra's boyfriend told us you'd threatened her."

"Damn straight. I told her I was gonna make her die by inches. Make her wish she'd never laid eyes on my little girl." Cassidy could see the rise of color beneath the dark skin. *Anger to block out guilt.*

"There were times I stood outside Xandra's townhouse and fantasized about getting my hands around her pretty, white throat. But I've been a follower of Martin Luther King my whole life." He shrugged his massive shoulders. "I couldn't do it."

Zach nodded. "How much did you tell the cops?"

"I said the boyfriend was full of shit."

❧   ❧   ❧

In the car Zach glanced at her. "I'm always amazed at the things you get people to say."

Feeling smug, she asked, "So you didn't mind me inflicting my presence on your interview?"

"You could say that."

"So now maybe you won't argue when I ask you to let me have a copy of those phone numbers and addresses?"

His shoulders stiffening, Zach stared straight ahead for a couple of beats. "That mean I'm not allowed to go off on my own but you are?"

She sighed, trying to identify exactly why she felt such a strong urge to have them. "I feel like a tag-along. If you control the information, you control the case. Maybe I'll have a sudden stroke of brilliance and want to call one of them. I'd just like the same access to information you have."

"You've got every bit as much of a problem with getting impulsive and taking risks as I do." He turned onto the Eisenhower Expressway. At midday, when traffic was light, they could shoot straight west from the Loop to Oak Park in under fifteen minutes.

Okay, so I got myself involved with some Satanists and a psychopath. At least I never got arrested.

"We both need to get better at thinking things through. I'm not planning to do anything reckless. I may not even use the numbers. I just want to have them."

He handed over his pad. Copying the information, she asked, "You know anything about that police lieutenant Corbin mentioned?"

"Steve Frasier? Yeah, he's detective commander of violent crimes over at Area Three. I've used him as a source plenty of times."

"Any chance he might've set it up for our own personal detectives—the Hathaway-Torres team—to go after you?"

"Not likely. He works out of a different area and they don't overlap much. Besides, unless we assume Torres brought the planner into the house, our detective duo isn't really doing any kind of extreme persecution here. Much as I want to feel put upon, they're simply acting like competent detectives. They're making a basic error in chasing the wrong guy, but they're just following the evidence."

She glanced absently at the fortress-like abandoned post office that spanned the expressway. "So, who we gonna tackle next?"

"The guy least likely to want to see us on his doorstep is Wiess, but since he's an alderman, he probably won't tell us to fuck off outright. Fortunately, politicians have to talk nice to reporters. Anyway, I'm inclined to take him on, but I want to check the newspaper files first, see what I can pick up in terms of background. I'll drop you off, then head on down to the office."

"If Bryce turns up, is there any reason not to discuss funeral arrangements? Do a little something to appease Hathaway?"

"Go ahead. You'll deal with him better than I would anyway."

She gazed at a battered blue convertible in front of them, the seats crammed with dreadlocked teenagers, the exhaust pipe spewing black clouds. "You think Corbin might've done it?"

"He certainly had motive. Given the right opportunity, what do you think?"

Earlier she'd questioned Zach's assertion that anybody, if pushed far enough, would be capable of killing. She'd even glibly dismissed the idea that she herself could club someone to death. *Unadulterated denial. Conveniently forgot I already killed two people.* She remembered the haunted look in Corbin's eyes, the guilt her sensors had picked up on. *He feeling remorse for something worse than overstrict parenting?*

❧ ❧ ❧

Parking in front of the house, Zach said he would go in with her to check messages before heading out for the *Post.* He opened the screen door and stepped onto the porch with Cassidy behind him.

Watching as he scooped up the mail, she suddenly remembered that Zach was not the only one with a threat hanging over his head. Her threat was not so grave as a murder arrest, but it was the result of a crime of sorts, an ethics violation that had landed her in a hearing conducted by her professional organization, the National Association of Social Workers. After pleading guilty to breaching a client's confidentiality, she'd been told that the committee would send out a report in thirty days informing her of the action she would have to take to avoid sanctions.

Report's due any day. You went into the confessional of the social work grievance committee and now they're gonna mete out your penance, same as a priest handing down thirty Hail Marys.

The committee's just doing its job—like Hathaway and Torres. You've got nobody to blame but yourself.

"The report there?"

Zach looked blank for a moment, then his face clouded. "Not yet."

She knew that the memory of the grievance filed against her for violating confidentiality was almost as painful for Zach as it was for her, because it was his news story that had caused it. The story included privileged information he had originally received from her, although he'd intended to protect her by getting a police source to provide the same facts. His maneuver had failed and a grievance was lodged against her, resulting in the hearing she'd attended a month earlier. The night before the hearing, they'd sat on the porch and discussed how she would handle it.

❦   ❦   ❦

Zach put his hand on her knee and said, "Look, there's no reason for you to have this on your record. I can go with you and testify that the information in the story all came from a cop, which is a true statement."

"Yes, but it's also true that I gave up confidential information. The first time because I wasn't watching my mouth, the second because I decided we couldn't just ignore a Satanic murder."

He ran a hand over his face. "Yeah, but I talked you into it. I hate to see you take the fall because I wasn't careful enough with my story."

"I'm not willing to lie about it. These are my ethics and I breached them and I need to be responsible enough to take my licks."

The hearing had not been easy. Although she still believed the situation merited her action, standing in front of her fellow social workers and admitting that she'd made an unethical choice was deeply humbling.

Every day now she approached the mail with a sense of dread.

❦ ❦ ❦

Upstairs, the blinking light indicated that one message had been recorded. "This is Jenny, remember me? Well, you'll be happy to know I've decided to see a doctor for the HIV after all, and the reason I did was Hobbes. Give me a call and I'll explain."

Zach kissed her good-bye and left for the *Post*.

Cassidy moved her Rolodex to the front of the desk, less cluttered now that Zach had taken on the role of mail-opener, and found Jenny's number. Hand on the phone, she mentally reviewed Jenny's case. *Spent three months in therapy last winter. Knew she was infected but refused to see a doc. Not much desire to live. Adopted Hobbes, one of Starshine's terror squad kittens.*

Cassidy's mouth curved in a fond smile as memories of the kittens crowded into her mind. *Hobbes got her to change her mind about a doctor? That's a story I wanna hear.*

When Jenny answered, Cassidy swiveled toward the window and propped her feet on the radiator. "It's really good to hear from you—especially the news that you're planning to see a doctor."

"It was pretty scary to make the appointment. Even worse than the first time I called you." She let out a raspy laugh. "But I finally got up my nerve."

Cassidy pictured the large woman with her plain, square face, unadorned except for her brightly speckled glass frames. "And it was Hobbes that got you to do it?"

11. Sugar-Frosted Flakes

"I know that sounds strange but the fact is, he did. Ever since I got the little rascal, I've had something to come home to. First time in my life I ever felt that way."

Something to come home to? Shredded sofa, knocked-over knick-knacks, pillaged plants. Cassidy envisioned the overgrown kittens who had nursed Starshine to within an inch of starvation and left a trail of wreckage in their wake.

"I hope you mean that having Hobbes is a change for the better."

"Oh my, yes. Every night he greets me at the door. He's just so excited to see me—rubs against my legs and purrs his head off. I have to let him climb in my lap and put his face right up into mine before I can even take my shoes off. And it isn't just food he wants either." Her voice radiated pride. "It's love first, food second for Hobbes."

Cats make the perfect sociopaths. Cunning and manipulative as they come. "Then he's being a good kitty? Not destroying your house?"

"Oh, well, who cares if the furniture has a few scratches? Nobody sees it except him and me anyhow."

Cassidy grinned, her chest swelling with warmth. *Feels good to make a difference. Even if it was the kitten, not the therapy.*

Jenny's voice went on. "So the two of us spend every evening together, and when I go to bed, he snuggles right up next to me. He used to insist on sleeping on my face but I finally broke him of that."

"So how did he get you to make a doctor's appointment?"

"When I first came to see you, I didn't much care if I lived or died. There just wasn't anywhere I could get any happiness. But now, every single day I look forward to coming home to Hobbes. He gives me this big bright spot I never had before. And—what's even more important—I have to take care of him. I started thinking how bad it would be for him if I got sick and had to give him away. If somebody did that to me, I'd feel like they didn't love me at all. So I finally decided that even though I'll probably die of embarrassment telling the doctor about the HIV, I just have to do it. I have to stay healthy as long as possible for Hobbes."

"Jenny, you just gave me a great big bright spot yourself." *Have to send her a copy of WHY CATS ARE BETTER THAN MEN.*

🐱 🐱 🐱

A few minutes later Judy arrived for the special session she'd requested to discuss her reaction to the story in the *Post*. They settled in their usual places, Cassidy in her director's chair, Judy on the sectional, the wicker table that stood between them sporting a forgotten, limp-leafed coleus.

Propping the toe of her burgundy pump on the table's edge, Cassidy said, "This isn't going to be easy for either one of us. I want to do what I can to help you resolve your feelings, but my personal life has to stay off limits. There's only one thing I can say, and that is, I don't believe Zach did anything wrong." *At least not lately.*

Judy ran her fingers through her short, black hair, Cassidy taking note of the angry spark in her client's deep blue eyes. *She's this upset, it's not just about me. Something in my situation reminds her of herself. Some part of her she's really pissed at.*

Judy argued, "You don't think he did anything wrong? But the article said he was arrested for battery when that madam was pregnant with their child."

Making herself breathe deeply, Cassidy paused before responding. *Can't get into it about Zach, no matter what she says.* "I'm sorry, I can't discuss any of the details. Now what is it about the situation that triggers feelings for you?"

Her client's mouth compressed in a tight line. "It seems like this Moran person did a number of questionable things. He was involved with a hooker, she accused him of beating her up, she had his baby but he never took any responsibility, and now he's implicated in her murder."

Ouch! Sounds even worse when you stack it up like that.

Judy leveled her eyes at Cassidy. "Given all that, it's hard to believe he could be so innocent. And if he isn't, why would want to you stay with him?"

Gotta stop feeling defensive and keep the focus on her. "What about my staying upsets you?"

Clasping her hands in her lap, Judy said, "Well, I can't understand it. I mean, the only reason I can come up with is—you don't think it'd be right to make him leave when he's in so much trouble."

Completely ignored my saying I don't think he did anything wrong. She's desperate to get out, can't imagine my wanting to stay in. "What is it about my not thinking it's right to make him leave that upsets you?"

"Well, it just seems . . . " She caught herself and seemed to reword her comment. "I mean, I guess it makes me question your judgment."

"What else about it is a problem?"

"If you're only staying out of guilt or obligation . . . " A strange look came over her face.

Cassidy tilted her head. "What happened just then?"

"I suddenly realized—those are the only reasons I'd stay in my marriage. Guilt and obligation. The only two things that'd keep me from leaving."

"And what about my doing that would be a problem for you?"

Judy said in a low voice. "Because if you're staying out of obligation, maybe that's what I should be doing. If you can tough it out, why can't I? Maybe you're the better person, and my decision to leave means I'm basically self-centered." Her darkly lashed eyes moved to the window. "That's why I'm so angry and keep thinking of reasons to blame you. Thinking that you're stupid, using poor judgment, that sort of thing."

Cassidy leaned forward. "So there's a guilty part of you that says it's wrong to walk out on your husband when he's having a hard time. And another part that wants to leave and hates feeling guilty. By not forcing Zach to leave, I've come to represent that guilty part inside of you."

"I guess that's right." She paused, looking inward. "But I'm still angry. I'm still having thoughts like—how could she get involved with such a jerk in the first place."

On the outside, Cassidy kept her face neutral. On the inside, she winced. "When have you had that thought before?"

Creasing her brow, her client focused intently. "Omigod. That's exactly what I kept asking myself when I first started wanting out. How could *I* have gotten involved with a jerk like Bob."

"Okay, now we know where these feelings are coming from. Next you have to answer the question—what would be best for you in the long run? To continue with me or find another therapist?"

A long silence. "The problem is, I'm still angry. If I can't stop feeling this way, I won't want to be here." She moved her head from side to side. "Can I take some time to think about it?"

After Judy left, Cassidy watered her coleus, then stood at the sink to watch four teenagers, each with a different shade of skin, clip, mow, and trim the yard next to hers. Her neighbors' children had originally hailed from all over the world.

The feelings she'd held at bay during the session washed over her. *Nobody could read that article and not assume Zach's guilty of something. Well, he was, a long time ago. Guilty of abusing drugs, obsessing over Xandra, stalking and pushing her around. Paper makes it sound worse. How many of the people I know think I'm nuts? Only the ones who can read.*

God, I hate being judged. I wanted to defend myself, argue with her, insist I'm right. She rubbed her temples. *Sometimes this job is not a walk in the park.*

Letting her voices run amok was not helping, she realized, so she pulled herself up straight and marched toward the stairs.

On her way through the living room, she glanced out the window and saw a familiar red Chevy head south on Hazel. The car circled the cul-de-sac at the end of the block, returned, and stopped in front of her house. Gran hopped out, reaching into the back for two handfuls of plastic grocery bags. Her grandmother, a wiry five-footer, struggled to carry her load toward the porch.

Cassidy dashed out and removed the bags from her hands. Gazing in amazement at the tiny acorn face, for once framed by her own sparse hair instead of a wig, Cassidy said, "Whatever are you up to?" She took the bags into the living room, Gran trotting at her heels.

"Uh oh, I'm busted," Gran said cheerfully. "I was gonna leave these on the porch and sneak away, but you caught me red-handed."

Poking inside the bags, Cassidy said in disbelief, "Kraft macaroni and cheese? Peanut butter and jelly? Three big boxes of sugar-frosted cereal?" She stared wide-eyed. "You don't think we're going hungry, do you?"

"Well, no, not exactly." Gran, whom Cassidy had never seen show the least sign of embarrassment, seemed almost flustered. "I, um, I just figured you had a lot on your mind and maybe didn't have time to shop."

Cassidy grinned. "You thought my usual diet of salad on the run might not be the best way to Bryce's heart. Well, I have to admit, the kid's stomach hasn't been getting the attention it deserves."

"Since you always were such a dainty eater yourself, I wasn't sure if you realized that teenaged boys are mostly eating machines." Gran's lips flattened in a self-deprecating grimace. "Sorry 'bout that sugar frosted crap. I sure do know it's not nutritionally correct and it'd be okay with me if you wanted to toss all three boxes. I just lost my head is all."

"Well, you're right. I don't know a thing about teenagers." *Don't think I ever was one.* "Less than nothing. We're talking minus numbers here. And if you think sugar-frosted is the way to go, I'll give it a try. A Reese's binger like me can't throw rock candy at anybody else's junk food preferences." Sitting on her heels, she pulled out more items. "Pistachios and beer for Zach. Peanut butter cups and cheese for me. Pounce for Starshine. Oh, and you even put in an envelope of cartoons for my refrigerator. Gran, you're such a peach."

"Well, and so are you." Gran picked up half the bags and started toward the kitchen, Cassidy following with the rest. "Now catch me up on what's happening. I'm dying to hear about the case."

Cassidy dumped her load on the counter, then turned toward her grandmother. *Gee, what fun. I get to treat her to a dissertation on court orders, DNA, and the fact that the cops think Zach slept with his spiderwoman before she died.* Her smile turned instantly from genuine to plastic, which, she realized, would not be lost on Gran.

Just as evasive words were forming in Cassidy's brain, Gran waved a dismissive hand. "Never you mind. I'm just poking my nose in where it doesn't belong. Anytime I get to prying, you just feel free to yell 'MYOB' like Ann Landers always says."

Cassidy leaned back against the sink. "I promise I'll tell you later. It's just hard to talk about right now."

"Don't you ever tell me anything you don't want to. I know

perfectly well that you and Zach'll do what's best, and it'll all come out right in the end." She patted Cassidy's arm. "Well, I gotta be off to my swimnastic class at Ridgeland."

"That's what I should be doing. Exercising and staying out of trouble."

"No you shouldn't." A twinkle came into Gran's faded eyes. "Getting into trouble's half the fun. I was hoping to meet some sexy guy with a cute rear end but no luck—they're all women. I even tried on one of those thong bikini things in case some hunk caught my eye, but I didn't buy it."

"Why not? I'll bet you looked great in it."

Gran cackled loudly. "What I looked is ridiculous. Like a scrawny old plucked chicken with a couple of red rubber bands stretched around it."

After Gran left, Cassidy put away the groceries, then taped the new cartoons on the fridge among her *Sylvia* collection. Her favorite was a Mixed Media strip listing THE FIVE WORST JOBS FOR CATS. In the first frame, the bubble above the cat psychiatrist said, AS IF I CARED ABOUT YOUR STUPID PROBLEMS.

❦ ❦ ❦

Heading upstairs, she discovered Bryce's door open, the television on, the boy lounging in the two chairs he'd once again taken out of her bedroom. She studied his face to see if it bore the slack-muscled stamp of pot smoking. Since he appeared as sullen as ever, she decided he probably wasn't high.

"The police've released your mother's body."

"So?" He flipped the remote into the air and caught it.

Turning off the TV, she said, "Let's go sit on the porch and talk."

The early afternoon sun had transformed the enclosed porch into an oven. Sinking onto the wicker couch, Cassidy considered other options. *Bedroom's currently lacking chairs. Living room's stale and stuffy. My office'd make it seem like I was doing therapy on him.* Although the insides of her knees were already growing damp, she decided she could stand the broiler effect for a short duration.

Bryce took the plastic chair opposite the couch, turned it sideways so that his profile was facing her, and stretched his long legs out in front of him.

"Just tell 'em to cremate her."

"How about a memorial service?"

"No service." He slanted his face toward the street.

Thank God he's not a client. I'd be lucky to pry out ten words in an hour. "The service is important. It gives people a chance to say good-bye."

He turned to meet her eyes. "I said—no service."

Helplessness washed over her. *Whatever made me imagine I wanted children?* "I think you're just avoiding the finality of her death. You don't want a funeral because that'd make it seem real."

"I know it's real." His voice went husky. "Seeing her blood all over the living room made it fucking real, all right."

"You've been inside the townhouse?" *Of course he has. You think police tape'd keep out a teenager?*

"You done now?" He started to get up.

"Bryce . . ." She paused, trying to get the words right. "I'd like to see your house. Would you take me there?"

He gave her a leering grin. "You wanna see the blood too?"

"I want . . ." *Why do you want to go?* "I'd like to get a fix on your mother."

"You wanna find out how she wrapped your lover man, plus every other male in the universe, around her little finger?"

"Something like that." She tilted her head slightly. "Will you take me?"

He gazed out the window for several beats. "Sure, why not?"

"Just let me change first." Upstairs she dug her black jeans out of the laundry basket and topped them with a purple shirt.

❦ ❦ ❦

Cassidy clung to the Miata's armrest as Bryce sped east on the Eisenhower. The radio was blaring the same kind of assaultive sound waves Zach used to impose on her before she'd trained him to keep it off when she was in the car. *Musical taste hereditary? Nah, Zach's predilection for rock is just a holdover from his delinquent youth.* She snapped off the deafening noise that had put her into a near shell-shocked state.

Bryce glared. "What'd you do that for?"

"You know, all you've ever heard is your mother's side. Why not at least give Zach a chance to tell his version?"

He stared out the windshield.

Cassidy gritted her teeth. "So what exactly did Xandra say about him, anyway?"

"I don't wanna get into it but I'll bet he didn't tell you everything."

"What do you think he didn't tell me?"

"It's ancient history." He shrugged. "I don't care about it anyway."

Here I am, using all my clinical skills. Every social-worker trick in the book—pacing, joining, mirroring—and he still won't open up. How the hell does he manage to evade all my therapeutic wiles? "Okay, I give. Let's try something else." She nibbled her lower lip. "Did you get to know any of Xandra's girls?"

He surprised her by responding in a conversational tone. "Only Nikki and Tiff. Nikki lives just three blocks away and she used to hang out at our place all the time. She worked for Xandra for years—right up till last fall when she took off with half the johns. I hated how she dicked Mom over. But before that, I always liked her. She was kind of like a big sister."

"You miss Nikki?"

He turned a disdainful look on her.

Empathy is not working with this kid. "I heard somebody put your mother in the hospital last January. You around when it happened?"

"I was supposed to be at that shithole boarding school but when Xandra tried to ship me off, I told her flat out I wouldn't go. So yeah—I was at home."

"Who beat her up?"

Gazing straight ahead, Bryce tightened his hands on the wheel and shrugged.

"You know, don't you?"

12. Blood and Perfume

Bryce snapped the radio back on. "I know what she said, but I don't see any reason to go blabbing stuff Xandra wanted kept to herself."

Cassidy turned the music off. "Did she tell you she started calling Zach shortly after that beating? I think she realized in January that the guy who beat her up might kill her and she wanted to reconnect with your father so she'd have some place to send you." She tucked a loose strand of auburn hair behind her ear. "It doesn't make sense that she'd have you stay with Zach if he was the person she felt threatened by. This guy who put her in the hospital—he's obviously the likeliest suspect. So the reason to identify him is to help nail the creep who splashed her blood all over the living room."

"Nah, you're just desperate to let the asshole off the hook. Same as Adonis was desperate. People who are desperate'll believe anything."

Kid's not as dumb as his mono-speak might lead you to believe. Plus, he's got a point. Just 'cause you're on Zach's team, don't start wearing blinders. Given how wrong you were about Kevin, it's always possible you could be equally wrong about Zach.

Cassidy cocked her head quizzically. "But if she really thought Zach was an asshole, why call him?"

"She does that kind of thing all the time. One minute she's claiming Adonis is the worst lowlife on the planet, the next minute they're all over each other in the living room." He paused. "Just 'cause Xandra can't stay away from assholes doesn't mean I have to like 'em."

He says seeing the blood made it real, but still talks about her in the present tense. "Hey Bryce," she said in a humorous tone, "do me a favor and stop poking holes in my favorite theories."

🍎 🍎 🍎

When they opened the townhouse door, Cassidy smelled a strange mixture of blood and perfume. The blood she was prepared for; the perfume she wasn't. The heavy floral scent brought up images of women who knew things she didn't, women who were lush and voluptuous and could get whatever they wanted from men.

As she followed Bryce inside, the sight of dark stains on the white carpeting and furniture stopped her in the doorway and sent shivers down her spine. The perfume made it worse, made Xandra seem like a real person whose essence still floated in the room but whose tangible self had been reduced to bloodstains on the floor.

She glanced at the teenager, whose body had stiffened as they stepped inside, noticing that he kept his head turned away from the area of greatest concentration, a spot near the round glass coffeetable. There was more blood than she would've thought, splatters extending halfway across the room. But except for the blood, everything was in order, and she wondered if Bryce had straightened up.

Walking along the perimeter, he led her around an L into a room containing a giant-screen TV, which was the center of a unit filled with objects she took to be the kind of electronic toys rich people plied their teenagers with.

As he turned to face her, she observed that his usual hostility had shifted into something approaching pleasantness. *Drop him into his own environment, he reverts to his natural state of being.*

"I'm gonna watch TV. You can poke around all you want." He picked up a remote and slumped onto a billowy couch.

Xandra's house reminded her of a castle in the clouds, all fluffy and white with pink and blue accents and an incredible feeling of plushness. The carpet was thick, the walls upholstered in damask linen, nothing stark and no sharp edges. *Little oasis of Magic Kingdom smack in the middle of the big, bad city.* Moving into Xandra's peaches and cream bedroom, she wondered what it meant. *Pretense of innocence? Adolescent princess fantasy? Denial of sordid realities?*

In the bedroom the perfume was stronger, the sweet scent of old roses. On the wall across from the gauzily canopied bed hung a photo montage of Xandra and Bryce, starting with the young mother and her baby and proceeding to a recent picture of mother and son dancing. Peering closely at the shot of them dancing, she noted that Bryce wore a painfully earnest expression, while Xandra appeared coy and girlish.

Everyone says she was so strong. That's what she showed the outside world. But I'll bet when she and Bryce were alone, she let herself be weak, leaned on him, made him be the caretaker.

Cassidy was pleased to discover that Zach's spiderwoman was not as supermodel beautiful as she'd expected. Her face was a little too round, her eyes too small, and in the latter photos, she appeared almost chunky. Cassidy restrained an urge to take one of the plumper pictures home to Zach.

She went through a doorway into a small room that was clearly the dressing area, with hanging clothes lining two walls, a rack of shoes beneath them, built-in drawers on the third, a full-length mirror on the fourth. She picked up one gold-strapped sandal with a stiletto heel so high Cassidy would have fallen on her face if she'd tried to wear it. Dozens of glamorous outfits hung neatly, looking as if they'd just come from the cleaners. Standing in front of a mirror, she held a black lycra gown with peek-a-boo cutouts up against her body. *You look like Little Miss Muffet impersonating a Cosmo girl.*

She turned to the drawers, pulling each one out and surveying its silky, designer-label contents. At the bottom she came across the Victoria's Secret drawer. She held up a red satin bra with size C cups, a hole for each nipple, an edging of lace around the holes. *Is this how she got men wrapped? Is Zach bored with our bedroom gymnastics, yearning for a little spice?* She envisioned herself in red bikini panties and a bra with holes. Then she tried to put Zach in the picture, but whenever she moved him into the frame he broke out laughing.

The sound of an unfamiliar male voice coming from the other side of the apartment caught her by surprise. Feeling her cheeks grow hot, she returned the bra to its drawer and headed back to the TV room. A man, fiftyish, gray crew cut and muscular build, sat beside Bryce on the sofa. As she came into the room, the two males rose.

"This is Lenny," the teenager said, a brightness in his voice she hadn't heard before. "He's worked for Xandra forever. Even got a room in back where he crashes sometimes. He taught me softball when I was a kid." Turning to the older man, he added, "This is Cass. I already explained about her."

She tried not to speculate on what Bryce might've said.

Lenny nodded. "I was basically her driver, but I pretty much did whatever she wanted."

Cassidy hooked her thumbs into her jeans' waistband. "The police tell you the place was unsealed?"

"They called yesterday, so I came in and picked up. I got a cleaning service ordered for tomorrow." He glanced at Bryce. "So, how you doin', kid?"

"It's really boring in Oak Park." He shifted his weight. "Sorry, Cass, I didn't mean . . . They just don't have anything to do out there." He gazed at Lenny. "Hey, man, maybe I could come down here and live with you."

The kid's DCFS worker would love that. What she'd really like is if Bryce started running Xandra's girls. Then he'd have gainful employment as well as a driver.

Shoving his hands in his pockets, Lenny stared at the floor. "Nah, that wouldn't work. I can't stay here all the time. I got my own apartment, remember? Plus I got my kid brother bunking with me."

"Oh, well, it's okay," Bryce said. "I only sleep there anyway."

"Look, you can call me anytime." Lenny clapped a hand on the boy's shoulder. "Hey, I gotta couple hours to kill. How 'bout you and me have a go at that new Doom game?"

Bryce started rummaging in a cabinet, then turned to Cassidy. "If you're in a hurry, I could call a cab."

Me in a hurry? I never have anything better to do than watch males shoot at cartoon figures and contemplate my sexual inadequacies as compared to Zach's spiderwoman.

She started to tell him she'd take the cab, then something clicked in her head. "Did you say Nikki's only three blocks away?"

🦋 🦋 🦋

A willowy woman with creamy skin and gleaming raven hair opened the door.

"Are you Nikki?"

She nodded. Her hair was pinned up in back, one stray piece laying along her right cheek. Her face, without benefit of makeup, was exquisite. Her intelligent, dark eyes gazed curiously at her visitor.

"I'm Cassidy McCabe and I just became an overnight surrogate mom for Bryce."

"He's with you?" She opened the door a little wider. "I've been wondering what happened to him. Is he okay?"

Cassidy gave a half shrug. "Not really. Murder makes everything not okay."

Nikki's arched brows pulled together. "How come he's at your place? Are you his father's girlfriend—the one they mentioned in the article?"

Cassidy nodded. "Xandra sent him to stay with Zach just before she was killed."

"The way he used to talk about his father, I never thought Bryce'd want anything to do with him."

"He doesn't." Cassidy smiled wryly. "At least that's what he says. But he's decided to stick it out with us awhile longer." She shifted her weight. "Anyway, the police are looking at Zach as their prime suspect, but I'm convinced he didn't do it. What we need is a strong alternative theory, and the first step is finding out everything we can about Xandra. So, would you be willing to talk to me?"

"You want me to tell you all that same stuff I told the cops?" She frowned slightly, looking as if she hadn't quite made up her mind whether to believe Cassidy or not.

Cassidy tilted her head to one side. "Would you?"

Nikki hesitated, then opened the door wide. "Personally, I don't care whether they pin it on your boyfriend or not. But it wouldn't be cool for Bryce to end up with no parents."

They sat across from one another in a living room that was Spartan in comparison to Xandra's, minimally furnished with a flat-cushioned sofa and chairs, glass and wood tables, earth tones and clean, bare surfaces. Nikki, in shorts and a crop top, a dozen silver bracelets on her left arm, settled back on the sofa and crossed her sleek legs at the ankles. A diffuse light filtered in from the picture window behind her.

"You know why else I'm going to talk to you? Because I think the kid got a raw deal. My parents died when I was ten and I spent eight years in foster homes. That's not the same as no father, but it makes me understand what it was like for Bryce. I heard what Xandra used to tell him, and I always wondered why she wanted the kid to hate his dad so much."

Eyes narrowing, Cassidy said, "So she could keep him all to herself? To gain total control?"

Nikki smiled. "So how do you know all this stuff? Were you a fly on the wall or what?"

"Xandra's forced herself into my consciousness of late." The living room walls were a light, stippled amber, the carpet a matching color in a darker shade.

"It'd be cool if Bryce's father turned out not to be the scumbag Xandra said he was." Her lively eyes crinkled. "And it's also cool that she's the one who brought them together."

Cassidy rested her forearms on the rounded arms of the low-slung chair. She noticed a light, clean-smelling fragrance in the air. "This sounds like a cliché, but on cop shows the first question they always ask is, did she have any enemies?"

"Did she have anybody who wasn't?" Laughing, Nikki raised her hand to poke at her pinned-up hair, setting off a jangle of silver bracelets. "Just like that old movie, *Murder on the Orient Express.* Everybody had a motive."

"Including Bryce?" *Could that be why he's so gung-ho to see Zach arrested? So the police won't start checking him out?*

Nikki sobered. "He adored her. We all loved her almost as much as we hated her." She cocked her head. "Would the kid hurt his mother?" She paused. "I don't know. She sure had him jumping through hoops."

"What'd she do?" Cassidy gazed through the window behind Nikki's head at a tall, yellow brick townhouse with a tiny, third-story balcony overflowing with yellow, pink, and crimson flowers.

"Turned her attention on and off like a flashing red light. When she focused the spotlight on you, it was dazzling. She could make you feel like the most fascinating creature alive. But it never lasted. Someone new would come along and off she'd go. She just bounced from person to person making sure she had everybody on her leash. She'd throw you a few crumbs, then turn her attention elsewhere, and there you'd be, always left begging for more."

Never give anybody as much as they want. The perfect formula for creating love slaves. Which is fine, unless you want a reciprocal arrangement—he loves you, you get to love him back.

"So Bryce adored her because she was always just out of reach." *That's how it goes. The neglected, deprived kids hang on tighter than the ones who get lots of love and attention.*

"Yeah, and at the same time he hated that she pushed him away by making him go to boarding school. When he was home over the summer, he used to grumble about it a lot." She shook her head, the loose piece of hair falling into her eyes. Jerking her chin upward, she tossed it back into place. "Up until he was eight, he had this live-in nanny who was always there for him and this dazzling mother who flitted in and out of his life. Then, over the summer, she informs him that come September he has to go live in this boarding school in Connecticut. A few weeks later she plunks him down in a totally strange place and won't even let him come home on weekends. Least when my parents died, they didn't do it on purpose."

"Did he say he was pissed at Xandra for sending him away?"

"Never said a word against his mother, just that he hated the school. He made out that she was only doing it to protect him from her lowlife associates. People like me." She laughed. "That part's true. Xandra always tried to keep him separate. She wanted to put him in a glass bubble but she couldn't do it."

Cassidy glanced at an arrangement of bright yellow sunflowers in a glass vase sitting on a niche in the wall. "Are there any other girls I should talk to?"

"Tiffany Corbin. The rest sort of floated in and out and didn't really know anything." She rattled her bracelets again. "There were two things Xandra worried about. One was Bryce's getting into drugs, the other, his getting into the girls' pants. Well, guess what? Her precious little baby is no longer a virgin. Tiff gave him his initiation last fall."

No surprise there. She asked, "Tiffany told you?"

Nikki nodded. "She was the reason he wouldn't go back to school last January. First time he ever stood up to his mother. But he sure wasn't about to tell her why and she never found out."

"What makes you so sure?"

Nikki broke into an impish grin. "Because Tiff is still among the living."

Their eyes meeting, Cassidy grinned back. Despite the lifestyle gulf between them, she found herself liking this beautiful young woman whose calling was procurement, a very different sort of therapy from her own. She had a same-wavelength feeling about Nikki and sensed that Nikki was having a similar response to her.

Frowning slightly, Nikki added, "That girl's got a serious coke habit, and I think Xandra was right in trying to keep the kid away from hookers. Everybody except me, of course." She sat forward, her voice turning serious. "I'm afraid he may start using. This whole little world I live in stays high all the time. Only reason I didn't get into it myself is, I was in college and had courses to pass."

"Did that include Xandra?"

Nikki shook her head. "She was death on drugs. Xandra and I are the only two people I know who aren't—weren't—into coke. Most of the girls are totally trashed by the time they're twenty."

Cassidy cocked her head curiously. "I can't help but wonder how you got into this business."

"I was waiting tables, working my way through college, and some girls I knew told me I could make more money on my back than my feet. This call-girl, clubby culture runs on money, power and looks. Only difference between me and the others is my money goes into an investment portfolio instead of coke and Fratelli shoes. I'm like Scarlett O'Hara—I never want to be poor again. Anyway, these girls introduced me to Xandra, and here I am."

Here's a woman who knows how to make the most of her assets. She'll accumulate money like the cat lady draws strays.

"Did you adore her like everybody else?"

"I was her pet for a while. She fussed over me, gave me a whole new look, taught me everything she knew, and it was obvious she loved doing it. As for me, she was the mother I didn't have. Then some new girl came along and I got dropped off her radar screen."

"That why you broke off from her?"

Leaning back, Nikki propped her left elbow on the sofa's armrest, rattling her bracelets again. "Not right away. I was still too hooked into her, still hoping to get my mommy back. I finished college, saved some money, and fantasized about going off on my own, but she still had her hold on me. What finally pushed me into leaving was seeing what she did to Tiffany. Here that girl had a family who loved her, she could've had a life, and Xandra deliberately set out to destroy her. Anyway, I walked out ten months ago and I'm mostly doing okay."

"Did you cut off all contact?"

"That's the odd thing. She never talked about my taking off with half her johns, but I knew she would've cheerfully killed me, and I also knew she was doing her damndest to fuck me over. But I couldn't stay completely away. Every so often I'd get this urge to see how they were doing." She paused, then said in a wistful voice, "After she was murdered, I cried all day."

Cassidy nibbled her lower lip. *What else?* "You know about the beating in January?"

"Heard about it."

"Any idea who might've done it?"

Delicate lines traced themselves in Nikki's forehead. "She said it was a john, but since she never wanted anybody to know anything, I thought she might've made that up."

"So who could it've been?"

Nikki gazed into space, her almond eyes narrowing. "If it was anybody she saw on a regular basis—like her musician boyfriend—he would've been instantly gone. So I'd have to guess it was somebody outside her usual circle. Maybe it was a john after all." She shook her head. "All I can say is, whoever it was would've really needed to watch his back afterward."

"So she was big on retribution. What about you? How come you're still among the living?"

Nikki laughed. "I watched my back a lot."

❦   ❦   ❦

The townhouse door was unlocked so Cassidy let herself in. Bryce, alone in the television room, was clicking the remote to make the animated hero shoot bad guys.

If only life were so simple. If only the bad guys wore black hats and we never had to wonder if we'd met the enemy, as Pogo so aptly put it, and he was us.

Cassidy sank into the enveloping plushness of the sofa end opposite Bryce's. *Confront now or later? Do it here, where he's programmed to be polite.*

"Bryce?"

"Yeah?" His eyes never wavered from the screen.

"Nikki told me about you and Tiffany."

"So?" He still didn't look at her.

"Are you using coke with her?"

"You're a therapist. Can't you tell?"

"I don't do substance abuse."

"That why you don't care if Zach drinks all the time?"

He sure learned how to push my buttons fast enough. She got her therapist part firmly in control and asked, "Does it bother you that he drinks?"

He continued clicking for several moments. "So, you wouldn't be able to help somebody with a drug problem."

"Tiffany?"

He took so long to answer she thought the conversation was over. Then he finally muttered, "I'm worried is all."

"About the coke?"

He turned and looked squarely at Cassidy, a glimmer of fear in his eyes. "She's in trouble."

"How can you tell?"

"After Xandra got whacked, Tiff started really bingeing on a lot of different drugs. Before that, I'd been trying to get her to quit, and she said she was ready to do it. Now I can't talk to her at all." He glanced at the floor, then turned his face away.

Hiding something. "What else?"

"Promise not to tell the asshole?"

"I won't keep secrets from Zach. But if Tiffany's at risk, you ought to tell somebody about the rest of it."

He let out a sigh, his face suddenly looking much younger. "She was really high yesterday. I was scared she might . . . you know."

"O.D."

"And she was saying some pretty weird stuff." He paused. "She kept asking me about this key. Somebody told her she had to get me to explain where it was. But I don't know about any key." He shook his head. "This somebody, whoever it was, insisted I could get the key for her. It seemed like this guy might've threatened her, but when I tried to get her to say who it was, she got all upset and begged me to leave it alone."

Cassidy leaned forward. "Why don't you take me to her place and both of us together can ask her about it."

A desolate look came over his face. "What good'd that do? I'm the only person in the whole world she cares about and I can't get anywhere with her."

"I don't think there's anything more painful than watching someone you love self-destruct."

His eyes starting to glisten, he turned quickly away.

"Let's go talk to her. It can't hurt to have two people telling her the same thing, and it might be easier for you if you're not the only one who knows what's going on."

He stood and took out his keys.

13. Morning After

They drove to a lakeshore highrise, a tall, narrow building girded with balconies. Insouciantly parking in a tow-zone, Bryce took her to the fortieth floor and opened the door with his key. In the living room, closed miniblinds dampened the light. As Cassidy surveyed the discarded gowns strewn across furniture and the empty vodka bottle on the floor, she picked up a faint odor of vomit intermingled with the stronger smells of smoke and sex.

The morning after—except it's late afternoon. I've had a few booze-type mornings after, but don't have a clue what a cocaine morning after'd be like.

"Wait here." Bryce disappeared into a hallway at the rear of the living room.

Cassidy pushed aside a sequined dress and sat on the blue velvet sofa. Several minutes later Bryce returned, his arm around the waist of a girl who faintly resembled the beautiful teenager in the red convertible. She held a cigarette in one shaky, crimson-taloned hand, raised it to her mouth, then blew out twin streams of smoke.

A line from an old Kristofferson song ran through Cassidy's head: ". . . wonderin' if the goin' up is worth the comin' down."

"This is Cassidy," Bryce said as he maneuvered Tiffany onto a loveseat and sat beside her. Her only article of clothing was a huge, ragged tee-shirt proclaiming BLACK IS BEAUTIFUL, a shirt her father might have worn to protests in the sixties.

Shoving Bryce away, Tiffany stubbed out the cigarette in an ashtray on the end table, rubbed her fingers across her mouth, and said in a shrill tone, "What'd you bring her here for?"

The boy moved to the opposite end of the loveseat. He said, his voice abrupt and angry, "Cass wants to talk to you."

She gave a little sniff, a logos coke addicts display the way Izod shirts sport alligators. "You're that fucking social worker who's trying to get everybody to like each other."

Boy, have you got a lotta credibility here.

Tiffany said, "You trying to save my soul, Brycie? Living with the asshole giving you religion?"

Usually don't like going one-up, but this girl's bringing it out in me. Besides, what else is there? Taking a superior tone she never used with clients, Cassidy said, "Why do you care if I'm here? You afraid of what I might say?"

"You think you're better than me, don't you, white girl?" Tiffany's face twisted in anger. "You think screwing an asshole reporter and taking money to listen to people whine makes you better than girls who fuck for a living." She combed her fingers through her short, curly hair.

"Yeah," Cassidy said. "As a matter of fact, I do."

"Just look at you in your Salvation Army clothes and old-lady tennis shoes. I bet you never had any millionaires panting to get at *your* body. And when did any guy ever blow five bills taking *you* to Le Français? Or hand over a couple of grand to spend the night? Who're *you* to look down on me?"

Lot easier not to get defensive now that she looks as if she's been sleeping under a rock. Remembering what Nikki had said about girls being trashed by the time they were twenty, Cassidy stood and opened the blinds, letting in a stream of light. "Bryce, go find a hand mirror." Arms crossed, she leaned against the wall next to the window. *That's good. Always helps to act like you know what you're doing. Especially when you don't.*

Standing, Bryce glanced darkly from Cassidy to the girl on the loveseat. "This is useless. Why don't we just leave?"

Catching his eye, Cassidy said in a low voice, "Just work with me on this."

He hesitated, shrugged, then started toward the hall.

Tiffany screamed after him, "You get outta my house and take this bitch with you!" When he didn't respond, she turned her body so that it angled away from Cassidy, twitched her foot, and rubbed her mouth.

Bryce returned with a gold-framed mirror.

"Hold it in front of her face."

"Aw shit," he muttered, his tone more defeated than angry.

"C'mon, Bryce. Let her get a good look."

Tiffany clawed at him with her long crimson nails but he secured her wrists with one hand and positioned the mirror with the other.

Detaching herself from all sympathy, Cassidy said in a steely voice, "How long you think you're gonna have what it takes to get five-hundred-dollar dates? I'd say you're not looking so hot right now. Imagine what the mirror'll be showing a couple of years from now."

"Stop," she shrieked. "I don't have to listen."

"So don't listen. I'll talk to Bryce. Take a good look at your girlfriend. Notice the yellowish cast to her eyes? I'll bet she isn't eating right or taking care of her skin or teeth or hair."

"Don't do this to her," Bryce whispered.

"I'm talking to you." She nodded at the boy. "I want you to look into the future and get an image of what this girl is gonna be like a couple of years from now. She'll be too sick to keep herself up, so she won't be bringing in much money, and what she does get will go for crack. She certainly won't be able to afford the good stuff by then. She'll need to work all night just to feed her habit. She won't be shopping at Nordstrom any more, so maybe she'll be decked out in some Frederick's of Hollywood trash. Just picture her in some cheap spandex miniskirt, desperate to get enough money for the next hit. By then she'll have been beaten up a few times, so she may have a broken nose or missing teeth. Her shoulders are slumped, her hair's unwashed. Some fat guy takes her into an alley and does her behind a dumpster."

Cassidy paused. Bryce had gone pale beneath the bronze skin, and Tiffany was breathing rapidly through her mouth.

Lowering her voice, Cassidy continued. "Okay, Tiff, you've got the picture. Now step into the skin of that future you. Feel the constant craving gnawing at your insides. Smell the fat man's filthy body, the reek of the dumpster. Imagine the rough concrete beneath your back, feel the weight of the man crawling on top of you, hear his grunts as he pushes inside you."

"Stop," Tiffany whimpered, pulling at her nose.

"You know it's going to happen."

"Just leave me alone. I don't wanna think about it."

Cassidy sat down on the sofa opposite the teenagers. "Not thinking about it will kill you."

"She's right." Bryce put his arm around Tiffany's shoulders. "If you don't stop, that's where you'll end up and I can't do anything to change it."

"I don't want it to be like that." She let out a sob. "But I can't quit. I tried. It's just too hard."

"Maybe Cass can help."

A shudder ran through Tiffany's body, then she pulled away from Bryce and turned an insolent look on Cassidy. "You gonna play social worker and say I can just go into treatment and everything'll be fine?"

"Everything won't be fine, but your chances would improve if you'd accept help from the people who love you."

"Yeah, right. You'll call my dad, he'll come get me, all my troubles'll be over."

"He could take you to a doctor who'd bring you off gradually. It wouldn't be easy but it's probably the only way."

Her voice went sarcastic. "Put me in the hospital, you mean."

Cassidy regarded her steadily. "Your choice. The hospital now or the street later." *And no hope at all unless you really work at it.*

The girl's large brown eyes filled and ran over. She rubbed at her face, sniffled, and said, "You really think I could do it?"

"Your choice."

Tiffany turned to Bryce. "Will you stay with me? Come to the hospital and hold my hand?"

"What do you think?"

"Okay." She sniffed, twitched her shoulders, then looked at Cassidy. "You can call him."

Cassidy took a deep breath. *You tough enough to do the next part?* Leaning back, she crossed her legs. "I'll make the call if you tell me who wants the key." *This is ridiculous. She'll just call him herself.*

"Fuck it," Bryce said. "Make the damn call."

Tiffany's knee started a jittery little dance. Her eyes flitted to the door. "Can't talk about it."

"Tell me who wants the key."

"Fuck you." Tiffany walked her fingers along the boy's arm. "You call him, Brycie."

Cassidy waited. Looking away, Tiffany combed her fingers through her hair. Bryce reached for the phone on the end table, then turned back toward the girl. "I don't know," he muttered. "Maybe you should tell her about the key."

"No, you're wrong," Tiffany said, shaking her head. "They'll hurt me if I say anything. And I don't know who it was anyway."

Picking up the receiver, Bryce handed it to Tiffany. "You call your dad. He won't give you a hard time or anything."

Tiffany whispered, "You don't know him." Glancing at Cassidy, she tugged her shirt farther down over her thighs. "If I'm gonna go in the hospital, I suppose it doesn't matter anyway." She paused, her eyes darting around the room.

Taking a deep breath, the girl said, "It was one of her johns. I never saw him. He just called me on the phone," she waved her hand vaguely, "a day or two ago. Xandra was blackmailing him and he needed some key to get whatever it was she had on him. But I don't know who the guy was or what kind of key he was looking for. Just that he thought Bryce knew where it was. He was gonna give me two thousand dollars if I could find out for him." Her knee started to dance again. "But he said something bad'd happen if I told. He called that one time and said he'd get back to me. And I better have the key for him when he did."

"Thanks." Cassidy asked for the minister's number, dialed, and miraculously got through to Luther Corbin, who said he'd be right over.

They sat for five minutes, Tiffany talking sporadically about the money she earned and the men who sought her favors. She drifted into silence, raking her hair and tugging at her shirt, then suddenly said, "I hate hospitals. Can't stand being locked up. Hate how the docs poke and pry at you." She stood abruptly. "I gotta pee."

Cassidy glanced at Bryce. "Maybe you better go with her."

"No, I'm all right." She gave him a sweet smile. "You gotta trust me, Brycie."

Don't let her leave.

She doesn't want to quit, forcing her into the hospital will just be a huge waste for everyone. Besides, where can she go? High-rises have only one door and no fire escapes.

Tiffany walked through the doorway and disappeared from sight. A long time passed, then Bryce went after her.

"Shit!" His voice came from the far end of the apartment. A sick feeling settled in Cassidy's stomach.

He reappeared, eyes flat, mouth angry. "She told me that one time when her dad came to get her, she went out on her bedroom balcony and climbed over to the balcony next door. I knew she had a way out. Why didn't I stop her?"

🍎 🍎 🍎

Corbin stepped through the front door, his eyes scanning the room.

"I'm sorry," Cassidy said. "It's my fault. I knew I shouldn't have let her go to the bathroom alone."

"Damn!" Corbin's face hardened. "So why the fuck did you?"

Heaviness settling over her, she wrapped her arms beneath her breasts. "I just ... I figured, if she really wanted to run, barring the door wouldn't do any good."

"Damn!" Squeezing his eyes shut, he rubbed his face with both hands. He took a long, shuddering breath, sighed, and said, "You're probably right. It's probably better not to drag her off to the hospital unless she's willing to go." He paused. "My wife and I don't need any more disappointments." Lowering his large head, he swallowed, then pulled himself up straight and cleared his face of emotion. "At least you tried."

🍎 🍎 🍎

After Corbin left, Bryce turned away from Cassidy and muttered, "You said I should go with her and I didn't. Why didn't I just go with her?"

She sighed. "Let's have a fight over who deserves the most guilt."

He snuck a quick look at Cassidy, then turned away again. "What's gonna happen to her?"

"If she's lucky, her life will get so miserable she'll finally be forced to quit." She paused. *Tell him the truth. The truth is always better.* "Otherwise, she'll die or end up on the streets."

He blurted angrily, "Tell me something I don't know." He paced back and forth a couple of minutes, then stopped and said more calmly, "Thanks for what you did. I just gotta make myself stop thinking about it."

🍎 🍎 🍎

Having hit rush hour, they didn't arrive at the house until after six. In the kitchen Bryce asked, "What's for dinner?"

The good news is he wants to eat with us. The bad news is there is no dinner around here.

Cassidy dug her wallet out of her handbag. "What would you like to pick up?"

"McDonald's?"

"Forget that I asked and go get three low-fat subs."

She handed him money and he left. Her seven o'clock client would be arriving soon and she needed to check on Starshine and confer with Zach, whose Nissan was parked in front. Upstairs, Zach sat in front of his monitor in the room next to Bryce's. He'd laid out his computer and printer on top of a fifties-style dinette table.

Looking up, he said, "Hathaway's hot on my trail. She started beeping around three. She's probably already tried to catch me at the *Post* and the house, but so far I've managed to stay one step ahead of her."

The more he pisses her off, the nastier she's gonna get. Cassidy said through clenched teeth, "If you go quietly, maybe she'll stop making surprise visits at odd hours."

The creases between the base of his nose and his jaw deepened, an expression she knew well. It meant he was not going to let anything deter him from the course he was on. Since Cassidy often got that way herself, she could understand.

"I'm gonna make her work for it."

"Next time she shows up, tell her I'm on vacation in Bermuda." Cassidy squeezed his shoulder. "How's Starshine?"

"She's still on the waterbed." They went into the bedroom. Raising her head, Starshine greeted them with a friendly Mwat.

Zach stood behind Cassidy. "She's definitely more responsive than this morning."

Kneeling beside the bed, Cassidy scratched the cat's cheek and was rewarded with a heartfelt purr. "She loves us now, but once we start pushing pills at her we'll be on her hit list again."

"You want me to be the bad guy?"

Picturing Zach in a black cowboy hat, she smiled up at him. "That's one of the nicest offers you've ever made. But since neither of us has any prior pill-giving experience, I think four hands'd be better than two."

"You want to do it now?"

"I'd rather do it never. Let's have a debriefing first. You show me your findings, I'll show you mine."

"I got some background on Wiess and photos of him and Steve Frasier—that's the cop Corbin mentioned." His eyes narrowed. "How come you've got findings? You were supposed to be home this afternoon."

"I believe in taking advantage of opportunity when it drops into your lap." She told him about Lenny, Nikki, and Tiffany.

His jaw tightened. "If I'd used the fact that I was in the city as an excuse to go off on my own, you'd've reamed me out."

She chewed her lip. *Boy, are you ever busted. Doing the very thing you made him promise not to.* "Aren't you glad I got the information?"

He said, a growl in his voice, "I'm not at all happy that you talked to those people behind my back. I won't have you taking over my investigation."

She knew exactly how he felt. If it had been reversed, if he were encroaching on her territory, she would've been even more outraged than he was. "You're right. I had no business doing anything without telling you."

He gave her another angry look, then said, his voice curt, "I'm gonna get Starshine's pills." He went downstairs.

Still really pissed about my making him include me. Wonder how long before we have sex so he can get over it.

Zach reappeared and handed her the bottle. "I'll hold her mouth open. You stick it in."

He retrieved the two desk chairs from Bryce's room. Lifting Starshine onto his lap, he pried her jaws open. The cat's eyes went huge and black, her ears flattened and her body thrashed, but Zach was able to keep her mouth relatively immobile. Cassidy placed the pill at the base of the cat's throat and Zach clamped her jaws shut. A minute passed.

Cassidy said, "It must be down by now."

As soon as Zach loosened his hold, Starshine tore off his lap, shook her head, and streaked out of the room. "That was a quick recovery." Standing, he leaned against the doorjamb and crossed his arms. "I'm gonna visit the alderman tonight."

"My sessions'll be over at nine. Can I come?"

"I don't know." He was silent for a moment. "After what you did this afternoon, I've got half a mind to keep you out of it altogether." He gave her a long look. "On the other hand, you do get people to say remarkable things."

"Then I can come?" She glanced at the clock. Quarter to seven, time to change for her sessions. As she pulled off her jeans, she noticed a small white dot on the floor near the bed. Picking it up, she said, "The pill. Starshine cheeked it just like psychiatric patients do."

❦ ❦ ❦

As Zach headed north on Lake Shore Drive, Cassidy gazed out her side window at an endless expanse of gray, choppy water. The drive followed the curving Lake Michigan shoreline, a sandy beach to their right, a row of glittering high-rises to their left.

Cassidy said, "We're just going to ring this alderman's doorbell at nine forty-five and he'll invite us in and tell us about his relationship with Xandra?"

"If he's home and I can twist his arm."

"Why didn't you make an appointment like you did with Corbin?"

"I want an impromptu response. Now the guy's a politician, so he'll probably be able to keep a smile on his face the whole time. But I still want to see his reaction when I bring up the minister's daughter."

She wrapped her hand around her jaw. "Is Wiess one of your news buddies?"

"I don't usually cover politics but I've quoted him on occasion. He's an up and comer, a Lake Shore liberal with a lot of clout in the counsel and a ward that includes some of the most expensive real estate in the city."

"If Wiess and Corbin are both liberals, how'd they end up on opposite sides of that construction dispute?"

Disgust flickered in Zach's face, the expression he displayed whenever she articulated her vast ignorance of the world around her. "Chicago politics is not a team sport."

What is it then? Anarchy? Every man for himself? Survival of the fittest?

Wiess lived in the DePaul neighborhood, one of the liveliest and most congested areas of the city. After a long search for parking, Zach found a spot within walking distance of Wiess' residence. It was a three-story brick townhouse crowded into a row of similar buildings, all with six-foot deep front yards and wrought iron fencing along the sidewalk.

The door was answered by a trim, fortysomething woman who wore her hair in a ponytail and could've passed for a Land's End model.

Zach asked, "Is the alderman in?"

The woman crossed her arms. "If you need help with something, you'll have to see him at his ward office."

"Tell him Zach Moran from the *Post* wants to talk about a friend of his who was killed recently."

Skepticism registered on the woman's wholesome face. She hesitated, then replied, "I'll see what he says."

Minutes later a tall, athletic man with distinctive features, a chiseled jaw, and gleaming hair too golden to be natural appeared before them.

Nodding at Cassidy, Wiess said, "Isn't it a little late, Zach?"

"You gonna make me talk through the screen door, Gordy?"

"I'm not sure I'm going to talk to you at all."

Tennis-pro good looking. Cassidy thought of the preppy wife and wondered how Wiess handled the offers he undoubtedly received from other women. *Don't like gorgeous men. Always expect to be adored without lifting a finger to earn it.*

Zach said, "I understand Xandra Palomar was a friend of yours."

Wiess' mouth compressed into a thin line for one instant, then the amiable expression returned. His tone bemused, he said, "I understand she was a friend of *yours*." He opened the screen door. "All right, you can come in." They stepped into a flagstoned, vaulted-ceiling foyer. He took Cassidy's hand in a firm grip. "And you must be the unnamed woman from the article."

"Cassidy McCabe." *My claim to fame. I get to be Zach's mystery woman.*

"We'll talk in the den." He led them into a forest green room with a leather seating arrangement facing a heavy stone fireplace. Above the fireplace hung an oil painting, an abstract in black, white, and gray. Cassidy considered it rather boring.

Gesturing toward the painting, Wiess said, "What do you think? Joan and I were in Europe a couple of months ago looking at some of the new, young Italian painters. This is a Rizelli. Paid twenty-five grand for it and it's sure to double in the next ten years."

"I don't know, Gordy. Personally, I think the trend's away from abstract expressionism."

More male jockeying. Wiess shows off his painting, Zach knocks it. Wonder if Zach knows anything about art or if he just made that up?

Zach, sitting on the sofa with Cassidy beside him, pulled out his notepad. "Luther Corbin says he saw you, Xandra and Steve Frasier with your heads together at the Westin opening. A few minutes later Xandra approached him and specifically mentioned that she was a friend of yours."

Wiess, in an armchair to their right, tented his fingers beneath his chin. His Paul Newman blue eyes gleamed with amusement. "We all three went to high school together. Why are you here, Zach?"

"I'm working a story."

"No, you're not. You don't show up unannounced with your girlfriend for interviews. And the *Post* doesn't send you out to cover murders when you're a suspect. This is your private investigation you're running, isn't it? You interfering with the police here, Zach?"

Zach leveled his gaze at Wiess. "I'm working a story on how teenage girls get recruited for prostitution."

Wiess' placid demeanor changed not at all. He smiled slightly. "You still haven't said why you're here."

"Luther Corbin says Xandra was acting on your behalf when she persuaded his sixteen-year-old daughter to work for her."

"Corbin has a vivid imagination."

Picturing the strung-out girl, Cassidy felt anger rising in her chest. *This smug politician can sit and smile while Tiffany's dying.*

14. Cop Bar

Zach asked, "So why did Xandra go up to Corbin right after talking to you and make a point of saying she was a friend of yours?"

Wiess shifted in his chair. "I can fill in some of the details but only if it's on background."

Zach nodded.

"The three of us were discussing the discrepancy between the minister's straight-arrow public image and the way he finagles money behind the scenes. Now I do not want to go on record as making allegations against an icon like Corbin, but when it comes to finances, the guy's a shyster. If you don't believe me, check out who's making the payments on that Lincoln Town car he drives."

"So?"

"So Xandra got on this kick about Corbin being a sanctimonious hypocrite. Said guys like him stand behind their ten-thousand-dollar pulpits and point the finger at women like her, but at least she didn't pretend to be better than she was. Said she was going to go over and yank his chain a little. And then later on she told us she'd propositioned him, and the man nearly wet his pants over it. Her version is, he was dying to do it but since he knew she was a friend of mine, he didn't dare. Basically, she was waving a carrot in front of his nose, knowing he couldn't take it."

Zach said, "And I suppose his daughter starting to work for Xandra a few months later was pure coincidence?"

"How unusual is it for a girl with a serious drug habit to start turning tricks?"

He's got nothing to do with Tiffany's choice of profession but knows about the drugs.

"Corbin says you were getting even 'cause he walked all over you in that construction dispute."

Wiess cocked his handsome head thoughtfully. "I'd say this goes beyond imagination and verges on paranoia."

"Can I quote you on that?" Zach started writing.

Wiess chuckled. "Background, Zach. This is background."

"Since you're giving us background," Cassidy said, causing both men to give her a startled look, "I'd like to hear how the three of you got together in high school."

Wiess shrugged. "That's an interesting story, actually. It was because of Steve discovering her. Steve and I, we'd been friends for years. He was quarterback and I was class treasurer, so we were both firmly planted inside the inner circle. Xandra—her name was Sandra Schwartz back then—was a real nobody. Her mother was a notorious alcoholic and Xandra had to spend every spare minute baby-sitting just to get by. Her clothes were ridiculous. She cut her own hair. Basically, she was a mess." He shook his head slightly.

Cassidy said, "But Steve got interested in her?"

"That's about it. Somehow he saw the potential. He started taking her out, bought her some new clothes, got her hair done. And suddenly we all could see the drop-dead swan hiding beneath the ugly-duckling exterior. Steve and Xandra went together all through the last year of high school, and the confidence she gained from being Steve's girl was enough to get her launched."

So Steve played Pygmalion. Wonder what happens when the urchin-turned-beauty-queen gets tired of feeling grateful? "What about after high school?"

"Steve broke it off when he left for college. We both got our degrees and returned to Chicago. Then a couple of years later she called Steve out of the blue. At that point the three of us started seeing each other again from time to time, but just as friends. Steve was pretty outraged when he discovered she was working for an escort service. He tried to steer her in some other direction, but after she'd had a taste of the night life, there was no going back."

You mean, she wouldn't go from high-priced call girl to secretary? Maybe her typing skills weren't up to snuff.

Wiess gazed into space. "He couldn't get her to stop hooking, but he did get one message across that may have saved her life. When we first got together after college, she was flying high on coke. Now Steve's brother died from drugs, and he hates them. Somehow he was able to convince her to give up the cocaine, which kept her from ending up like so many of these girls do."

Cassidy rested her right elbow in her left hand. "So how did a politician, a cop, and a madam maintain a twenty-year friendship?"

"We didn't bring her along when we went out with our wives, if that's what you mean." Wiess laughed, showing teeth so symmetrical Cassidy thought they must be capped. *Wonder if that thin, straight nose came with the original model or was an add-on like the teeth.*

Wiess added, "Steve and I play golf. Before his divorce, our families used to barbecue together. Xandra was never part of our social life. Just the occasional lunch or charity event."

Zach asked, "How about the occasional favor?"

"We weren't keeping her out of jail, if that's what you mean," Wiess said humorously.

"I was thinking more along the lines of sending one of her girls up to a crony's hotel room. Bonus for a job well done."

Annoyance crossed Wiess' tanned face. "Don't insult me, Zach."

"You knew somebody put her in the hospital last January, didn't you?"

He shook his head. "We saw each other two, three times a year at most."

Keeping her voice casual, Cassidy asked, "You ever sleep with her?"

Wiess' sky blue eyes glinted with amusement again. "You don't really expect me to answer a question like that, do you?"

Zach said, "Why not? It's on background."

He gave Zach a long look. "Yeah, but this isn't for the paper."

Zach shoved the notepad into his pocket. "If it's on background, I can't use it."

"Sure, I slept with her a few times. How could I pass up an opportunity like that? Even though we didn't see each other all that often, we had a lot of history. I was fond of her." His face tightened as he looked at Zach. "When I saw that story in the *Post*, I wanted to go gunning for you."

Cassidy said, "Everybody both loved and hated her. Everybody had a motive."

"Loved and hated her," Wiess mused, his tone faraway. "Yeah, you could say that. At least back in the beginning when she was Steve's girl and she'd tease me, acting like maybe she would, maybe she wouldn't. That's how I felt then, but I got over it a long time ago. I sampled the wares, satisfied my curiosity, and put it behind me."

"Yeah, me too," Zach said. "Put it behind me, I mean."

A look of understanding passed between the two men.

Sampled the wares? Is that what it comes down to? A momentary distaste flared inside her, for Zach as well as Wiess, for all men who viewed women as a commodity to be sampled and put behind them, like little bites of food in the grocery store. She huffed to herself, then pushed the feeling away. "I was told by a knowledgeable source that Xandra deliberately set out to destroy Corbin's daughter."

Wiess shrugged. "I wouldn't know about that."

Zach said, "That's bullshit, of course."

Wiess stood. "I don't have any more time for you, Zach." As he walked them to the door, he commented, "You know, I'm glad you dropped by. I've always enjoyed irony, and after all these years of watching you uncover other people's fuck-ups, it gave me great pleasure to see your own rather impressive one appear in the *Post*. Best piece of irony I've run across in a long time."

🌿 🌿 🌿

In the car Cassidy asked, "Do all men act on opportunity like Wiess did?"

Kevin sure did. Any chance he got.

"Aren't you being a little indirect here? Isn't the real question—if some foxy lady invited me into her bed and I was certain you'd never find out, would I take her up on it? That's a question with only one right answer."

"So would you?"

"Why can't you just avoid touchy subjects like other people do? Cass, the truth is, I'm not sure. I'd like to think I'd never cheat under any circumstances, and the odds are I won't, because seductive women are not throwing themselves at my feet every day. And because I love you and don't want to screw up our relationship. But can I give you an iron-clad guarantee? I don't think anybody knows for certain what they'd do in the face of extreme temptation."

I want iron-clad. I want chiseled in stone, come rain or come shine, you can bet your life on it.

You keep hoping he'll say what you want but he insists on telling the truth.

Zach asked, "You up for one more stop?"

"Steve Frasier?"

"Gordy is probably on the phone to him as we speak."

"We gonna ring his doorbell too?"

"I thought we'd try this cop bar he hangs out at. It's just a couple miles north of here on Clark."

And who'd know better than Zach what bars everybody frequents? "What's he like?"

"Fairly easy to talk to. Doesn't make me play twenty questions like a lot of cops do. He's the violent crime commander at Area Three, which makes him Emily's boss. When she and I were an item, she used to talk about him quite a bit. Said he's great to work for as long as you toe the line, but don't cross him." He squeaked through an almost-red light. "The guy's as tough as they come. He took a bullet in the leg when he was a rookie. They said he'd never walk again, but he set out to prove them wrong and he did. Still limps a little but otherwise he's fine."

"Well, Emily's boss," Cassidy remarked, hating the sarcasm in her voice. "I suppose she's next on your list of people to call."

"You want me not to call her?"

"I'm sorry, you didn't deserve that." *Yes he does. They were an item, she tried to get him back, he refuses to hand out guarantees.*

He put his hand on her knee.

A moment later she asked, "What Wiess said about Corbin's financial dealings. You think that's true?"

"Sure."

I wanted him to be a good guy. "Is this something you knew already?"

"Not specifically. It's just that nobody gets into a position of power without being corrupt."

"The old power-corrupts dictum?"

"The old you-have-to-be-corrupt-to-get-power dictum."

Everybody we've talked to on this case is slime. "I don't know how you stand this world you work in."

"You think your world is any better? Everybody's corrupt to some degree."

"Oh? And how are you corrupt?"

"Same way you are. Either one of us sets our sights on something, we'll do anything to get it. Look at how we both bend the rules when we have to."

Not the same as corruption for personal gain.

You wanna believe you're better than power-brokers and pols. But are you really? Look at how you've been envying Xandra her power over men.

Not wanting to think about that, she asked, "Speaking of corruption, how much do aldermen make?"

"Just a minute." Pulling out his beeper, he read the number. "Shit, doesn't that woman ever sleep?" He stared straight ahead a moment, then glanced at Cassidy. "Aldermen get seventy-five K—same for all of 'em. Most of the fortunes are made by running some business on the side—a legal way to trade favors. You buy insurance from my agency, I'll support your zoning law. But Wiess is strictly a politico cum art collector. He makes a big deal about not owing anybody anything."

"His family have money?"

"He married it. His old man's a south side fireman. His father-in-law's a North Shore tycoon. For all I know, his wife gives him an allowance."

❦   ❦   ❦

Zach opened the door and they entered the dim, clattery interior of Dick's Den. The room was half filled, a mix of uniforms and suits, no other women in evidence. Peanut shells littered the hardwood floor and crunched beneath Cassidy's thin-soled flats at every step. Zach picked a table at the rear and they sat kitty-corner from each other facing the bar. Jerking his head to the right, he said, "Frasier's the big guy in the middle of that threesome at the far end."

Since the commander had his back to the room, all she could see were his thick mat of dark hair, longish for a cop, and his hefty, football-player shoulders beneath a wrinkled suit coat. *Kind of hours these guys work, nobody has a chance to get to the cleaners. Except Hathaway, of course. She could pull an all-nighter, come out looking like an anchorwoman on the ten o'clock news.* A waitress stopped at their table and Zach requested two Heinekens without consulting her.

Someday you're gonna have to train him to ask before he orders. Especially considering how much he's been ordering lately.

Frasier turned halfway around to nod at Zach, then returned to his conversation. Five minutes later he ambled over, his gait somewhat uneven, and sat across from Zach. He had a leathery face with thick, straight brows, sprightly brown eyes, and a nose that looked as if it had been broken more than once. Cassidy found him attractive in a thuggish sort of way. *The fastidious alderman and the hurly-burly cop. What an odd couple.*

Frasier chugged from the beer bottle in his right paw and said, "Why am I not surprised to hear that you and Ms. McCabe are ringing doorbells at all hours of the night?"

"Good to see you too, Steve."

The waitress set bottles, no glasses, on the formica table, its swirly gray pattern barely discernible beneath the network of scratches and cigarette burns. She took a sip. *If Mom could see me now. Swigging beer from a long-neck in an all-male cop bar. She'd be horrified. But Gran'd love it and beg to come along next time.*

"Nobody ever said you didn't have balls," Frasier commented, his robust voice making it a compliment. "Here you got Area Four dicks crawling up your ass and you come strutting into enemy territory to question me. I don't think my colleagues over at Harrison Street'd be too happy to hear I'd been aiding and abetting their prime suspect, especially considering that you're running your own investigation, which, as you know, is highly frowned upon."

"Since when did you ever care what anybody thinks?"

"Matter of professional courtesy." He plunked his elbows on the table, his good natured-expression giving Cassidy the sense that he was enjoying the exchange.

Zach said, his tone equally good-humored, "You afraid I'll embarrass the department by busting the bad guy first? It's no skin off your posterior if the Area Four guys come out not looking so hot."

Frasier chuckled. "You always could put an interesting twist on things. So, the reason I should talk to you is to obstruct another area and down the competition. You know that's not how it works, Zach. Cops always stick together."

Cassidy gazed at a wall plastered with signed photos, a mix of unknown cops and renowned Chicagoans. She picked out faces belonging to the deceased columnist, Mike Royko, and to the first Mayor Daley.

Leaning forward to fold his arms on the table, Zach said, "Xandra was a friend of yours. Area Four is spinning its wheels trying to build a case against the wrong guy. I have the advantage of knowing I didn't do it, so I can focus on other possibilities."

"So you're gonna whup the Area Four dicks. Emily'd like that." He glanced at Cassidy. "Or she would have a couple of years ago." He tilted his bottle, wiped his mouth with the back of his hand. "Okay, let's hear your questions and I'll consider whether or not I'll answer 'em."

Zach took out his pad. "Xandra knew she was in danger. Who might've been threatening her?"

Frasier tapped the bottom edge of his bottle on the table as he pondered the question. "She was a very savvy lady. There were times when something took her by surprise and she'd get temporarily shook, but once the crisis was over she'd be right back in control again. There wasn't much she was afraid of, although there were a couple of things she *should've* been afraid of. One was the possibility that some wigged-out john might come after her. The other was her habit of picking up boy-toys, having a fling, then dumping them. Some guys don't take too kindly to that." He locked eyes with Zach. "The first I heard from her after high school was when she called from that hospital you put her in. When the prosecutor let you off with a misdemeanor, I had half a mind to waste you myself. She talked me out of it, though."

Zach said in a laconic tone, "Just as well. It wouldn't have looked good on your record."

Frasier's face suddenly turned menacing, his weathered skin going a shade darker. "You think if I wanted to off you, I couldn't set it up so the case'd never be cleared?"

"What about the boy-toys? You know any guys she might've dumped lately?"

Cassidy noticed that her feet were sticking to the blackened floorboards. A picture came to mind of what she imagined the underside of the table to look like, all knobby with wads of used gum.

The cop shook his head. "Hadn't seen her since January. That was the second time she called me from a hospital bed. Something about getting beat up made her reach for the phone. And no, she didn't tell me who did it."

"You hear from her at all since then?"

"Oh, we talked a few times. She called the night of the burglary and—"

Zach sat straighter. "What burglary?"

15. Batterers and Burglary

Frasier sent Zach a superior smile. "You're gonna beat out Area Four and you don't even know about the burglary?"

"I'll know as soon as you tell me."

"She was planning to be out for the evening but she got a headache and came home early. Saw a light in her bedroom and called it in. Police caught the doofus red-handed."

Cassidy leaned forward to get their attention. "When did it happen?"

"Oh, about a month after she got home from the hospital. I got her call right after the uniforms cuffed him. She wanted me to come hold her hand but I couldn't get away. Evidently the guy'd turned off her security system, so somebody she knew pretty good must've set it up. I phoned the next day to see how she was doing, but she said it was all taken care of, didn't wanna discuss it. My guess is her musician boyfriend was behind it and she was embarrassed to tell me."

Cassidy asked, "Why Domingo?"

"He'd know her code. And they were always squabbling over money. She told me he had this fantasy of owning his own club, and in a moment of insanity she'd offered to bankroll it. About a day later she changed her mind, but he was always bugging her to keep her promise. So maybe he thought he had it coming, and if she wasn't going to follow through he'd send his buddy in to steal her jewelry. I could be all wrong about it, but that's what occurred to me at the time."

Zach asked, "You think Domingo might've whacked her?"

"I don't even know the man. I'm just passing along what she said."

Tilting her head curiously, Cassidy said, "When did you first find out she was hooking?"

"Let's see . . ." Rubbing his jaw, he gazed upward. "I think it came out when I was visiting at the hospital. You know, that first time when your boyfriend here punched her out." He shook his head. "Never could understand men pounding on women. But you know, Zach, after I calmed down about it, I decided you beating her up wasn't all bad. Gave her a taste of what she was in for if she wanted to be a working girl. It was the other thing you did that got me really pissed."

"What else did I do?"

"Supplied her with coke. After you were out of the picture, I had a hell of a time getting her off it."

Zach cocked his head in surprise. "She tell you that? I was working for a piddly ass suburban paper. Where would I get money for coke?"

"Your family."

"Well, to clear the record, it was the other way around. She was providing the drugs."

"Yeah, whatever."

"So," Cassidy turned her beer bottle in a slow circle, "when you first saw Xandra after high school, how'd you feel about her? Were you still in love with her?"

He waved one hand backward, brushing off what she'd said. "Didn't have anything to do with love. I was nice to her. She was excellent in bed. That's all there was to it."

Cassidy's eyes narrowed. *What's this? The only male in the universe she didn't have wrapped? That because she hadn't learned the art of holding out yet?* "What was the relationship like after you got together again?"

"I was this young, idealistic cop, and here was my old girlfriend turning tricks, so you can imagine what I thought about that." He took a swallow of beer. "I did everything short of busting her to get her to stop, but she refused, so I got out of her way. Things were kind of tense between us for a while, then we settled into a friendship of sorts." He thunked the empty bottle on the table. "Well, I've said more than I planned on. I sincerely hope none of it proves useful." Standing, he remarked, "I don't know, Zach. This pretty lady of yours may close the case before either you or Area Four figures it out."

❧   ❧   ❧

The Nissan turned south on Lake Shore Drive. At close to midnight on a Wednesday, the eight-lane highway that marked the boundary between city and beach was wide open and aglow with light from the myriad street lamps that marched along its perimeters.

Flexing her shoulders, Cassidy said, "Seemed like their stories matched except for one little inconsistency."

"You mean Wiess saying Xandra called out of the blue and Steve saying she called from the hospital?"

"Right." Cassidy nibbled her lower lip. "Since Steve's the one who received the call, he'd know for sure when it came. But wouldn't you think he'd tell his good buddy Wiess that their old friend Xandra was in the hospital? You know, time to rush those flowers and cards? I suppose Wiess might've forgotten the hospital bit, although you'd think all that history getting dredged up in the news story would've refreshed his memory."

"You think Wiess is being evasive?"

"Or, here's another scenario. Steve didn't tell Wiess about the hospital because he's the one who put her in it. Xandra said you were supplying drugs, he beat her up to get her to quit, then made her charge you so you'd go away." She gazed past Zach's head into a dark blur where sky and lake merged.

"Steve's got a real by-the-book reputation. It's hard to imagine him committing battery, but it does seem to fit." He paused. "The other questions are, did the same person put her in the hospital both times, and if he did, is he our killer?"

How many bad guys? One, two or three? She stared out the windshield as Zach exited the outer drive at Navy Pier, then went underground onto lower Wacker, a shortcut across the downtown area. With no other cars in sight, the Nissan rocketed along the brightly lit street, huge concrete posts flashing by on both sides. Minutes later he emerged onto the Eisenhower, also bathed in a dusky half light from the street lamps. He cut to the far left and drove west.

Cassidy said, her voice low and hesitant, "I went to the library and read up on batterers."

He glanced over at her, his forehead creasing. "Something about the way you said that makes me wonder if you're including me in that category."

"Not exactly."

You know he isn't a real batterer. At least most of you does. There's some little part that feels squeamish about it, thinks it's sordid. That has ideas like—if he did it once, he could do it again. Any male who ever hit a woman is bad. Which is really going overboard, considering all he did is push her around. Somebody else broke her arm and smashed her face.

"What does 'not exactly' mean?"

"Rationally, I know the fact it happened once doesn't mean anything."

"It didn't 'happen.' I did it. And it does mean something. It means—having discovered I can lose control like that, I need to make sure I walk away any time I start to get pissed."

"I don't think you're a batterer. It's just that, these revelations you've dumped on me are still a little raw. Inside my head, I'm tiptoeing through all this new information, trying to assimilate it into my previous image of you. I have to make internal adjustments, and the new pieces have sharp edges that create an occasional twinge." A silvery el train, its tracks running down the middle of the divided expressway, moved along nose to nose with the Nissan, then gradually fell behind.

Zach asked, his voice tentative, "Any idea what you'll end up with when you're done?"

She touched his leg. "Something good. Someone I can love." *For a nanosecond there, he actually sounded unsure of himself.* "You go around acting so detached, it's nice to know you actually care what I think."

"Yeah, I'm usually able to disregard other people's opinions. Times like this, it comes in fairly handy." He sent her a warm smile, letting her know he wasn't detached about her. "Go ahead, tell me about batterers."

"There are three types. The first are like you—not real batterers, just ordinary guys reacting on a one-time basis to an extraordinary situation. The second are men with serious problems, a lot of rage. These guys batter sporadically. The third are serial batterers—severely disturbed men who never stop."

His expression turned reflective. "Given the way Xandra jerked guys around, it's not surprising somebody'd take a punch at her on occasion. But from everything we've heard, it seems unlikely anybody'd get a second chance. Domingo was certain, if he laid a hand on her, that'd be the end of him. The only way she could've had a type two or type three batterer in her life is if she were the kind to keep taking him back, and everybody says she wasn't."

Cassidy nodded. "So the two beatings were either the acts of two different men or one man who wasn't a chronic batterer but got angry enough to lose it on two separate occasions. If it was the same guy, that means she had at least one relationship she kept going over a long period of time." An eastbound train shot past them, its windows revealing only a handful of passengers.

"We know she had a more than twenty-year friendship with both Wiess and Frasier, so it's possible one of those two punched her out twice, although Wiess didn't sound involved enough to get all hot and bothered. If you nailed it with your theory about Steve Frasier trying to get her off drugs, he could be a two-time batterer and the killer."

She pictured Frasier's dark, thuggish face, the humorous eyes. *Doesn't seem like he takes anything seriously enough to fly into a rage about it. What would piss him off enough to kill her?*

As if reading her mind, Zach went on, "I have to say, even though it's a nice, neat theory, it doesn't fit my image of Steve. The type one batterer you describe is somebody who acts out of passion, the heat of the moment, whereas Steve comes off as a guy with extreme self-control."

Exiting from the Eisenhower onto Austin Boulevard, Zach headed north toward their house. "So if we exclude Steve and Wiess, I'd say her musical-chairs-approach to boyfriends makes it likely the hospitalizations were caused by two different guys. Let's figure we have two separate batterers, with the first beating unrelated to the killing. The second beating, however, looks like a clear prelude to the murder. Especially if we assume the reason she started calling me afterward was her sense that she might be needing a safe house for Bryce."

They drove another mile in silence, passing well-tended homes and apartment buildings to the left, the Oak Park side, down-at-the-heels residences to the right, the Chicago side.

As they trekked from the garage to the gate, Starshine dashed across the street from the cat lady's house to roll at their feet on the sidewalk. A cool breeze had whipped up, making the treetops sound like ocean waves hitting the shore.

Cassidy sat on her heels and scratched the cat's neck. "What're you doing outside? You shouldn't be socializing when you're sick. Besides, those ruffians are the reason you have to take pills. You should stay away from them."

Zach stood beside her. "She's trained all your clients to open the door for her, and by now she's probably got Bryce jumping through hoops as well."

Starshine sprang to her feet and dashed for the door.

Standing, Cassidy allowed her eyes to sweep the softly lit street ahead of her, a view she always found soothing. Each dwelling had its own style, but all were set on trim lawns burgeoning with trees and shrubbery. The more time she spent in Chicago, the more she appreciated Oak Park.

Zach would insist that the village had its own brand of corruption, not so flamboyant as Chicago's fabled venality, but a subtler variety composed of arrogance and elitism. Cassidy, however, clung to her image of Oak Park as a place where integrity still thrived.

"C'mon." Zach tugged at her hand. "We have to make another stab at sticking a pill down the throat of a certain recalcitrant cat."

By the time they came around the oak room divider, Starshine was sitting next to her bowl on the kitchen counter.

"I'll get her meds," Zach said, heading upstairs. Cassidy started to dish up food. Moments later he returned, the pills rattling slightly as he came through the doorway. Starshine's ears flattened and she dove for the floor.

Cassidy spun around. "Damn, she's onto us."

The cat zipped past Zach, sped into the dining room, and halted beneath the teak table. Zach went to stand at one end, Cassidy at the other. Pulling out a chair, he reached beneath the table to grab her.

Starshine zoomed under the buffet standing against the north wall. Zach reached again and she scooted back beneath the table. "Shit," he said, getting down on all fours to crawl after her as Cassidy tried to block two sides at once. The cat raced toward the buffet again, saw Cassidy grabbing for her, made a sudden turn and fled between Cassidy's legs. Starshine was sprinting up the staircase before Cassidy could get herself turned around.

No live animal moves that fast. This is some kind of new rocket technology disguised as a cat.

Upstairs, the doors to the bathroom and all three bedrooms stood open. Cassidy and Zach searched for twenty minutes with no luck.

"I'm beat," Cassidy said. "At this point I don't even *care* if she doesn't get well."

Zach joined her in the bedroom. "Look at the time." The clock on the bureau registered one a.m. "Well, so much for curfew."

"Did you expect Bryce to just snap to and obey?"

"I guess that's unrealistic, considering I never did what anybody said."

Even people who've lived with children from the time they were born can't handle 'em. A hostile kid, you and Zach inexperienced. There's no way you're gonna get this right.

"I don't know what to do." She shook her head. "Bryce's life is even more of a mess than ours. His mother's dead, his girlfriend's a junkie, he's living with strangers, and he's trying his damndest to hate you. I don't know if we should be adamant about the rules or not. And if we should, I sure as hell don't know how."

"I know what I'm gonna do," Zach said, heading toward the doorway. "I'm gonna fix us each a drink so we can unwind and get to sleep."

Minutes later they sat in bed, Cassidy tucked under Zach's arm. He slugged down a portion of his bourbon and said, "You know what really surprises me? It's how pissed I am. Given the shit I got away with when I was his age, I would've expected to shrug off a few misdemeanors like curfew and pot. But I'm so furious that this kid's not obeying me—something I never did myself—I can't see straight. I'm definitely not father material."

❦   ❦   ❦

Mrorrr!

Cassidy opened her eyes. The clock said 3 A.M.

Of course it's 3 A.M. It's always 3 A.M. when you hear that sound.

She stumbled out of bed and opened the door. Starshine leapt delicately onto the waterbed, circled a few times, then curled into a ball between their feet.

❦   ❦   ❦

The next sound she heard was the front doorbell. When she opened her eyes this time, the clock said six-thirty. Zach got up, put on his robe, and went downstairs. Cassidy grabbed Zach's pillow and jammed it over her head. *I'm not getting up. Hathaway can throw him in a dungeon, hang him from wrist irons, stretch him on a rack for all I care. I'm getting some sleep.*

She opened her eyes again and saw that it was nine. In the kitchen a note from Zach was propped against the empty coffeemaker.

Cass,

Hathaway caught up with me, but I made her waste enough time chasing her tail that it was worth it. Don't know how long this'll take. See you when I'm done.

Love,

Zach

Noting the *love* at the bottom, she felt a sense of warmth rise in her chest. Getting that word out had been hard for both of them, but they were definitely doing better.

16. Cloud Puffs and Hot Fudge

The phone rang and Cassidy lifted it off the kitchen wall to answer.

"You two run down that killer yet?" Gran's perky voice asked.

"No, but we're working on it." Cassidy cradled the phone between her shoulder and neck as she started the coffeemaker.

"You'll get him. Anything you set your mind to, it always gets done."

Everybody oughtta have a cheerleader like Gran.

"And that man you share your garage with, he's okay too. Now I know Zach made his share of mistakes when he was younger, and considering what his mother's like, there's no surprise there. But most of us start off with our own set of problems, and it seems to me the main point of life is to see whether you're gonna beat them or they're gonna beat you. And it looks to me like our Zach's coming out a winner."

Gran knows about people. If she thinks he's a good guy, I must not be delusional, as Hathaway seems to assume. Cassidy poured coffee, adding cream and sugar. "Why don't I just send you over to Area Four and have you straighten out those two detectives who're doing their damndest to build a case against him?"

Gran let go with a boisterous cackle. "I can't even straighten out your mother. Now if you wanted me to give somebody the third degree, I sure could do that."

"Mom . . ." Cassidy said with a sigh. "How've you managed to keep her off my back all week?"

A groan came from the other end. "I been letting her wear out my ears talking. Every day we go 'round and 'round in the same argument. She wants to call you up and tell you how to live your life, which comes down to, you should dump Zach. Then she wallows around in this godawful drivel 'bout how men are no damn good, and in the end I have to yell at her and say—'Helen, if you don't leave her alone, neither one of us'll ever speak to you again.' "

"You said you wanted to help. Well, enforcing gag rule with Mom is downright heroic."

"I just wish you'd think of somebody I could pump for information."

I should let her pump Bryce. He could go live at her house. She'd win him over for sure, get him to spill everything.

But that'd be letting Bryce and Zach off the hook, not allowing them to beat their own problems, like she said.

"Anyway," Gran went on, "I got myself overbooked for this weekend, same as those airlines do. I've been trying to get Helen out more. The way she sits and broods in her apartment all day, it's got me real worried. So I told her I'd take her to the Farmer's Market for doughnuts this Saturday, but now I just realized I already promised Mabel I'd drive her to her cabin in Wisconsin. I hate to let Mabel down since we've been planning this trip for months. So I thought I'd call and warn you I'm gonna be gone a couple of days and I won't be able to stop Helen from bugging you."

The old bad-girl, guilty feeling settled in again. "I know she's depressed and I shouldn't be avoiding her. Don't worry, I'll take her to the Farmer's Market."

After the call she headed upstairs. A glance through the living room window told her that Bryce's car was in front collecting tickets again. In the hallway above she noticed his closed door. The boy's door seldom opened before noon.

You should make him get up and move his car.

I should also keep Starshine inside, stop eating peanut butter cups, and spend more time with Mom.

The cat, not seen since three a.m., had either escaped the house or gone into deep hiding. *Not about to try any single-handed pill-giving, anyway.*

Sitting at her desk, she stared at her client calendar, which displayed a week at a time. It was now Thursday morning, and in the two days since the *Post* had published the article about Xandra's murder, eight clients had canceled, although no one except Judy had mentioned seeing it. Ten other appointments remained standing. Cassidy had, in the past, experienced an occasional rash of unexplained cancellations, so she couldn't be positive that Zach's current notoriety had any bearing on her client defections.

Am I being paranoid if I assume clients are avoiding me because of the story? Am I being stupid if I don't?

She felt restless, wanted to get in the car and go rustle up suspects. Tapping her finger against the wine bottle she used for collecting loose change, she suddenly remembered Zach telling her he had brought home photos of Wiess and Frasier. *Could show the pictures to Nikki. Find out if they saw more of Xandra than they're willing to admit. It'd be better than sitting around waiting while Zach donates DNA.* She envisioned him tied to a table in front of a machine with octopus arms, the ends of which were little clamps that bit into his flesh.

She paged him, then paced back and forth in the small square of empty space between her desk and the bed. As time went on, excuses for visiting Nikki without his approval started popping into her mind.

Nikki isn't a new source, so talking to her wouldn't be an additional offense, just an extension of the old one.

Can't wait all day. Not my fault Zach isn't answering his page.

Besides, I'm not the one who's too close to it. He is.

Realizing she was on the verge of committing a second violation, she made herself stop listening to the seductive rationalizations bubbling up in her head. *You don't abide by the terms you set, Zach sure as hell won't either.*

When he finally called, she asked if he would mind her paying Nikki a second visit.

After a brief pause, he said, "Since you made the initial contact, I guess you might as well. The photos are in my briefcase." He did not sound pleased, but as long as he'd agreed to it up front he couldn't hold it against her.

ॐ   ॐ   ॐ

Nikki held up the Wiess headshot, a dozen silver bracelets rattling on her arm. "You could've saved yourself the drive down. All you needed to do was tell me his name and I could've dished up the dirt."

Her almond eyes crinkled at the corners.

Dirt on the politician who accused Corbin of hypocrisy? What could be better?

"But," Nikki's gaze met hers, "if it ever comes out that I told you, I could be in big trouble."

"No one will know where we got it," Cassidy said from her taupe chair opposite the matching sofa.

The younger woman studied her a moment, arched brows drawn together. "Okay, I'm going to trust you on this. Last night I kept thinking how bad it'd be for Bryce if his father got convicted of his mother's murder, so I'll do what I can." She wore her glossy black hair the same as before, pinned up in back with one loose piece along her cheek.

"So what's the scoop on the alderman?"

"He calls himself 'Bill Jones' but the alias is a joke since his picture's in the paper all the time."

Grinning, Cassidy visualized a headline: ALDERMAN CAUGHT IN VICE STING. *If only.* "I take it he's a john. Did he do business with Xandra or you? How does this work, anyway? Do johns pick one madam and stick with her the way women do hairdressers, or do they shop around?"

"Depends. The occasional customer is more likely to go back to the same madam all the time. The high-volume johns are always looking for new faces—I should say new bodies—so they call everybody. But as far as I know, Wiess used Xandra exclusively until three weeks ago when he called me."

"Well," Cassidy shook her head. "A gorgeous guy like Wiess. Probably has women falling all over him but he still goes to call girls." *Hope that didn't sound like "Yuck, call girls, why would he do that?"*

Nikki, not appearing offended, said, "Well, obviously, professionals do it better."

"I never thought about it before, but I guess the rest of us really are amateurs."

The younger woman's voice turned ironic. "Some people really believe—the more you pay for it, the better it is." Giving Cassidy an impish grin, she made it clear she considered people like Wiess absurd.

Cassidy had a sudden inspiration. "I'll bet he's one of those small penis guys."

"Hey, girlfriend, you're good." Nikki laughed. "Sometimes it seems, the smaller the dick, the bigger the ego." She wrinkled her nose.

"Well, anyway, the alderman was one of Xandra's biggest spenders. A regular call-girl junkie. Sometimes he'd do two, three hookers a day. The problem was, he couldn't afford it."

"How did he manage? She give him a price break?"

"Not in this lifetime. The way he managed was, he ran a scam on his wife, which worked just fine up until six months ago." Nikki rested one slender ankle on the other knee. "They own a large art collection, you see, and a lot of it's in storage. So Wiess'd run up this big bill, then sell a piece of art behind his wife's back to pay it off. Only the last time he tried it, she caught him."

"And they're still together?" *Lot of us never know when to quit.*

Nikki raised both arms to repin her hair. "I don't think she found out about his little hobby, just that he'd sold the painting and spent the money without consulting her." Nikki's eyes crinkled again. "So now she's keeping an eagle eye on the collection, and the alderman can't get his hands on any cash."

"Did Xandra cut him off?"

"Not immediately. Guess she figured anybody in Chicago politics could find a way to fill the coffers. But evidently Wiess lacks certain skills common to his fellow aldermen because he wasn't able to pay his debt off. So about a month ago, Xandra demanded the entire sum in full."

"And his wife refused to take care of it for him?" Cassidy let out a small giggle. "How uncharitable."

Nikki grinned broadly. "You got it. Now the way I heard all this is, Wiess called me three weeks ago and asked if I'd be willing to see him now and then at a reduced rate, cash up front. Well, I could use the money, so I agreed. We only got together once. Anyway, he'd been drinking and he went off on this rant about Xandra."

"What did he say?"

"Get this. He called her an ingrate. Evidently Xandra told him she couldn't wait any longer. Said she was in some kind of financial crunch and needed the money right away. And—this is the good part—if he didn't pay up by the end of the month, she'd send the bill to his wife."

Both women chuckled jubilantly.

Cassidy said, "Don't you love it when people get what they deserve? Hardly ever happens, but when it does, isn't it great?" Propping her elbows on the chair arms, she laced her fingers together. "So Wiess was really ticked off?"

"Guess he figured that since they had this long-term friendship, Xandra'd never put the screws on. Which just goes to show how little he knew her. He kept insisting he and his pal gave her her start, so she owed him."

"He shouldn't have to pay because his buddy dated her in high school?" Cassidy shook her head. "Amazing the rationalizations people can dream up."

She removed a photo of Steve Frasier from a brown envelope and handed it to Nikki. "This is the other guy I'm doing research on."

Nikki examined the picture for several seconds. "The face is familiar but I can't come up with a name. He wasn't a john and he didn't come over very often, but I remember a few times he'd drop by for dinner or drinks." She glanced up. "Which was unusual in itself, considering she rarely let any guy into the house except Lenny and her boyfriend du jour."

"Anything else?"

"Um," Nikki's dark eyes narrowed "Xandra seemed different when she was with him. Not so . . . I don't know . . . manipulative. I think he may've been the only guy she didn't look down on."

The only male she didn't have wrapped.

🍎 🍎 🍎

On the drive home, Cassidy's mind veered away from the case. Puffy white clouds floated overhead in a bright blue sky, the clouds reminding her of whipped cream, like the great globs that topped the hot fudge sundaes at Petersen's. Ever since she got her first bike, one of her favorite summertime treats was to peddle across Oak Park to the ice cream parlor that was already old when she was a kid, and was still in place, still the same today. Petersen's had to remain unchanged because it represented Oak Park's Norman Rockwell past, just as the glass and brick village hall represented its standing-tall present.

Thinking of hot fudge sundaes reminded her that there was life outside the case, and that it was close to one and she'd had nothing but coffee all day.

🍎 🍎 🍎

Spotting the mail on the porch, Cassidy felt a tightness in her chest as she wondered if today would be the day her sentence from the social work ethics committee arrived. She flipped through the pile, noting that the NASW envelope was not there but two greeting cards were, both addressed to Bryce. One had a return address; the other didn't.

Zach wants to hold onto them, find out who the senders are.

Don't like it. Not fair to Bryce. Certainly not trust inducing.

She opted for the direct approach. After taking down the return address, she would give Bryce the cards, ask who they were from, and hope for a loquacious mood.

She found Bryce in his room watching TV and eating from a blue bowl.

Crossing her arms, she leaned one shoulder against the doorjamb. "Would you turn that thing off for a minute?"

He cut the power.

His face appeared neither high nor sullen—appeared, in fact, fairly neutral, a distinct improvement over the other moods he'd displayed. She said, "That's not ice cream, is it?"

"It's all I could find to eat."

"What about the sugar frosted flakes and all the other stuff Gran brought over?"

"What am I supposed to eat the cereal with? Water? There's no bread for the peanut butter, and the rest of it's gone."

Taking the last bite of ice cream, he put the bowl on the floor and called "kitty, kitty." A wary Starshine slipped out of the closet to lick the bowl's interior, leaving it shiny and clean looking.

"You have some mail." Cassidy handed him the cards. He opened the return-address envelope and scrunched his face in annoyance.

"What's the matter?"

"Oh, it's just this dorky girl from school who has the hots for me." Tossing the first card into the trash on his floor, he opened the second.

"Who's that from?"

"This woman who used to take care of me." His voice softened. "You know, a nanny."

"You fond of her?"

"She's pretty cool. She used to play games and read to me when Mom was busy." His face darkened. "Things were just fine back then. I had a school I liked. Ellie was always there when I got home. Xandra didn't have any reason to send me off to that fucking boarding school."

Sitting on her heels, Cassidy extended her fingers for Starshine to sniff but the cat zipped back into the closet. "I ought to sue you for alienation of affection."

"What'd you do to make her so scared?"

"She got bitten by another cat and the vet said we had to give her pills. Turns out she's not fond of the pill-giving process."

"She doesn't need pills. Just look at her—she's perfectly fine. Doctors are always making you do things you hate." He spoke with the certainty of youth. "Anybody poked stuff like that down my throat, that'd be the end of them. They'd be history."

Oh, the blessings of clarity. Teenagers never have to struggle with shades of gray. No self-doubt, no shortage of self-righteousness. They've got the luxury of being moralistic, judgmental and ruthless. Zach screwed up so that's it, the end—he's outta the kid's life forever.

"What happened to Ellie after you went off to school?"

"She had MS and her symptoms were getting kind of bad so she retired. But she always sent me birthday cards. Even when Xandra forgot, Ellie never did."

"You ever see her after that?"

"Sure." He tossed the remote in the air and caught it. "Ellie was this neighbor that took care of Mom when she was a kid, and Mom, she was always nice to her. I think she gave her money, and every Christmas we loaded the car up with presents and took 'em to her house."

A compassionate side to Xandra? I'd never have guessed.

Just 'cause you're jealous, envious and judgmental yourself doesn't mean she was all bad.

🐾 🐾 🐾

Zach came home two hours later and went directly to the computer in his office. Cassidy, surprised that he hadn't poked his head in the bedroom to say hi, went to join him at the formica dinette table.

"I'm dying for a Petersen's hot fudge sundae. We have to ride there on our bikes right now before I faint from hunger."

Zach frowned. "I'm in the middle of typing up notes. You go."

Placing her hand on his arm, she said, "I need to relive my most cherished childhood memory and I want you to share it with me. I need hot fudge for comfort. I need it to help me forget my troubles, to give me the strength to endure my clients dropping away and the police snatching you out of our bed. Besides, I saw it written in the clouds: the real meaning of life lies in the small daily pleasures we so often neglect."

Irritation crossed his face.

"What, you don't like eloquence?"

"Okay, we'll eat hot fudge. But let's take the car. It's quicker."

"We have to ride bikes. I really need a little regression right now."

❦   ❦   ❦

Pedaling west on Chicago Avenue, she felt sweat burning her eyes and leaking out of her armpits. Her old wreck of a bike pinged at every rotation as she struggled to keep up with Zach, who raced ahead on his new Raleigh. *You should get outside more. Sure, as if my life were afternoon picnics and meandering down bike trails.*

A block east of Petersen's, she began noticing clumps of people, cones in hand. On a hot July afternoon, the renowned emporium drew ice cream lovers like the beach drew smooth-skinned bodies. The old stone-faced building sported two blue canopies, a blue RESTAURANT AND BAKERY sign, and blue gingerbread between the first and second floors. Teenagers, mothers with children, and elderly couples swarmed around the al fresco umbrella tables. On Sunday afternoons the ice cream cone line had been known to extend out the door and down the block.

Inside a smiling, apple-cheeked waitress in a fuchsia shirt seated them at a small, marble-topped table next to the window, then bustled off.

Cassidy put aside the menu. "I always order hot fudge."

"I always order the turtle."

Cassidy smoothed her hand across the orange-veined marble. The top half of the window was covered with a plastic shade that grayed out the light. She grinned. "This place always makes me feel like a kid again."

"I know this is sacrilege, but I lost interest in Petersen's after college. It's too old Oak-Parkish for my taste. My mother probably came here on dates."

She pictured Zach's mother, Mildred Lawrence, sitting at a table in a poodle skirt, anklets, and penny loafers, her aristocratic, old-lady face bobbing above the fifties' style clothes. Mildred was a thorn in everybody's side: Zach, because she had disliked him from the day he was born; Helen, because the teenaged prom-queen had looked down on South Oak Park kids; Cassidy, because the woman had belittled her at every opportunity. Even though Mildred lived only a mile from their house, Cassidy and Zach had nothing to do with her.

The waitress returned. "How about a sandwich or entree before your ice cream?"

They ordered sundaes.

Cassidy said, "Let me tell you what I found out from Nikki, then you can educate me about sample giving." She started in on her story, noting that Zach's face had darkened at the mention of Nikki's name. *Agreed, but he's still mad.* Finishing, she said, "Okay, your turn. What torture devices did Hathaway use?"

"Nothing to it. Slam, bam, I was in and out of the hospital in no time. All they did was take blood and saliva, then comb out my pubic hair. If I had more than five chest hairs, they'd've combed them too."

Their sundaes arrived, each in a large tulip glass with mounds of whipped cream, a maraschino cherry, and a pitcher of thick, rich sauce on the side. Cassidy carefully dribbled fudge on her ice cream, filled her spoon, closed her eyes, and blissed out as the first bite melted in her mouth.

Zach put his hands on the table but did not pick up his spoon. "When the police let me go, I decided that as long as you were tied up with Nikki, I might as well see what else Izzie'd dug up."

Tit for tat. Izzie for Nikki. "You do that to get even?"

"Probably. You know, I gotta tell you, I'm getting increasingly pissed. Mostly at myself for having caved."

17. Compliments Rolling In

She said in a small voice, "You wouldn't have caved if you didn't basically agree with me."

"Okay, I can see there's some sense in my not going completely off on my own. But having to take you everywhere is ridiculous. It looks like you're checking up on me, which you are. I've spent my whole life not letting anybody make me accountable or lay down rules, and that's what you're doing here. I can't live with it."

She hunched inward, hurt that he considered her so domineering. "I thought I was just tagging along."

"But I shouldn't have to tell you about every move I make or constantly take you with me." He dipped into his sundae.

Turning her head sharply to the left, she stared through glass and plastic at a family sitting around an outdoor table. "You're right. It isn't worth it. The last thing I want is to be a burden."

"You mean that? You're actually giving in?"

"I never realized this'd make you feel so … tied down."

He tapped his fingers on the marble for several seconds. "All right. Let's continue as is. You have been zeroing in on things I wouldn't've thought of. I guess I just needed to hear that you're not calling all the shots."

She said slowly, "I know I have an urge to get controlling, but I want you to stop me any time I do." *Yeah, right. Like telling him to stop the summer from getting too hot.*

He appraised her a moment more, then said, "Okay, I take you with me, you don't go anywhere by yourself. We'll stick with that for now."

Nodding, she poured more hot fudge on her ice cream, then tried to catch it as it dribbled over the edge of the dish.

Crunching a pecan, Zach said, "Here's what I got from Izzie. As it turns out, Xandra did not just sit on her hands when Nikki broke away. It seems our Madam X had a vice cop who did favors in return for free sacktime with the girls. So Xandra had her badge-toting friend hassle Nikki. She got arrested three times by the same officer. Even made her stay overnight in the joint once."

"Nikki gave me the lowdown on everybody else, but not herself. She told me everybody had a motive, and that's what makes this whole deal so confusing. We have all these people with a reason to want Xandra dead."

Holding his spoon aloft, Zach enumerated. "Wiess, because she was threatening to tell his wife where the money from the paintings went. Nikki, because she was trying to drive her out of business. Corbin, because she recruited his daughter. Domingo, because she wouldn't give him the money she promised." He stuck the spoon in his mouth.

Cassidy scooped up ribbons of ice cream running down the tulip glass. "There are two more names that need to go on the list. Steve Frasier and Bryce."

"Bryce." Zach's gaze drifted to the window. "I know we talked about it before but I've been trying to ignore that possibility." His eyes met hers briefly, then returned to the window. "Looks like I do need you after all. To keep me honest."

"I don't like it any more than you do." She smoothed out the napkin in her lap. "But if Xandra was threatening to split Bryce and Tiffany up, or maybe to harm Tiff . . . It's a possibility."

"And Frasier." Zach cocked his head. "I'm not aware of any specific motive, but that doesn't mean there isn't one."

"Here's another way to look at it." Cassidy scraped the bottom of her dish to get the last of the fudge. "Everybody says Xandra wasn't easily frightened, yet she tells you in the letter she's in danger. So which of the suspects'd be most likely to scare her?"

"I can't see her being intimidated by Bryce, Domingo, or Nikki."

"Wiess possibly, but he's such a pretty boy it's hard to imagine she'd take him seriously. Corbin might be scary. And Frasier definitely." She pictured the cop's face suddenly turning dark and threatening. "Frasier tops the list for dangerous."

Zach pushed his dish back. "Then there's the john she said beat her up in January. Tiffany talking about blackmail and a key. And that last little piece Nikki mentioned about Xandra needing money right away."

"This is pretty overwhelming." She licked her fingers, then dipped them in her water glass and scrubbed them with her napkin. "I'm glad you're in charge 'cause I wouldn't know where to turn next." *Oh come off it. Not only does modesty not become you, it sounds phony as hell.*

He nailed her with a skeptical look, then said, "We hit Bluestown tonight to see what Domingo can tell us about the burglary. After that—" He narrowed his eyes. "If blackmail was involved, the alderman, the cop, and the minister are the only ones respectable enough to qualify. With that in mind, I'd like to take another shot at Wiess and Frasier. We'll leave Corbin alone for now since your almost getting Tiffany into the hospital may've made him into an ally of sorts and I'd just as soon not piss him off if I don't have to."

🍎 🍎 🍎

As Zach dragged her through the impossibly narrow spaces between tables, an anonymous hand squeezed her left buttock. She jammed herself into a chair while Zach went to the bar to collect two foaming mugs of beer. The amped-up music surged thunderously in the small room, breaking against her skull like waves against a rock.

The room was dark and murky, smoke stinging her eyes and burning her nostrils. In the time it took her to drink half a beer, Zach inhaled his first two, then, she noticed with relief, slowed down on the third. Bobbing his head to the music, a tranced-out expression on his face, he looked as though he'd stay till closing if she didn't drag him away. *Right at home. In his element. Whatever made me think we had anything in common?*

Onstage Domingo, in an open-necked red satin shirt, hopped, bopped, cavorted, played and sang, all with supercharged, high-voltage intensity. The loose, floppy body had metamorphosed into a tightly coiled spring.

She yelled into Zach's ear. "This the same guy we saw two days ago?"

"Coked up. A lotta rockers can't perform unless they're wired."

During the break Domingo strutted up to their table, grabbed a chair, and straddled it, the pungent smell of sweat hitting her as he came into range. "Hey, man, you come back to hear me play." He swung his hand in a wide arc to slap palms with Zach.

Cassidy put her fingertips to her temples. *All this male revelry gives me a headache.*

Sitting straight, Zach leveled his gaze at Domingo. "We came back so you could tell us about the burglary."

Domingo pulled out a handkerchief to mop his sweaty face. "It's really hot under those lights, man."

"The burglary, Adonis."

"Oh yeah." Domingo bent over the table and began smacking it with his hands to the beat of the recorded intermission music. "You mean, when Jojo got caught in Xandra's bedroom with a bagful of her jewelry?"

Cassidy leaned closer to the musician, barely able to hear him above the loud voices and throbbing music.

Zach laid his arm on the table. "Now when exactly did this happen?"

Domingo stopped drumming and gazed into space. "Sometime after Christmas. February, maybe."

Zach asked, "How did Jojo get in?"

"Lenny brought him by the townhouse when he stopped to pick up some stuff from his room in back, and Jojo watched him turn off the alarm. He boosted Lenny's key, had it duplicated, then waited till Lenny was gonna be gone taking Xandra out for the evening. He would've got away with it, too, if Xandra didn't have that headache and decide to go home early."

Cassidy shouted at Domingo's bouncing figure. "Who's Jojo?"

He stopped and looked at her in surprise. "Lenny's brother. He couldn'ta gotten into her house if he didn't see Lenny turn off the alarm. Len, he felt real bad about it, too. It's been rough on Lenny, having to take care of that screw-off kid all his life."

She tilted her head curiously. "Why did Lenny have to take care of his brother?"

"Well, mostly 'cause there wasn't nobody else to do it. Their mother was never around, and since Lenny's five years older, it was always his job to see after the kid. Jojo, he always gets in trouble and then Lenny has to bail him out."

Zach emptied his mug and thumped it down on the table. "Why'd Xandra keep Lenny on after that?"

Domingo stopped drumming, sat up straight, and wiped his face again. "Oh, Lenny's been with her forever. I think she felt sorry for him too, stuck with that punk kid brother of his."

More compassion? Doesn't fit the grasping, narcissistic image I prefer to maintain of her.

Zach said, "He might even've been driving for her when I knew her before."

Cassidy propped her elbows on the table. "What was the relationship between Xandra and Lenny like?"

Domingo motioned to a waitress to bring him a drink. "He was sorta like part of the family. One thing though, Xandra told me a coupla times to make sure I didn't say anything in front of him."

Cassidy asked, "Why not?"

"I figured it was just her not wanting nobody to know nothin.'"

Power. You're the one with all the information, you control things.

Zach pulled out his pad. "I need Lenny's address."

"Shit, man," Domingo's broad grin tightened into a frown. "He was her driver. We didn't go to his house for fuckin' dinner."

"Give me both their legal names."

"Lenny, uh . . ." His face screwed up in concentration. "Silurski. That's it, Silurski. And Jojo, he was just Jojo."

The waitress placed a drink at Domingo's elbow and he drained half of it.

Zach said, "Where can I find a phone book?"

Domingo jerked his head at a hallway leading toward the rear of the building. "That office back there." He resumed drumming. Zach headed toward the hall. Five beats later, Domingo halted abruptly to stare at Cassidy. "You got nice tits but your clothes are all wrong."

Cassidy looked down at her swirly plum dress, an outfit she'd always felt good in. *What's wrong with my clothes? I should be wearing spandex? Sequins? What?*

🍂 🍂 🍂

As she climbed into the Nissan, a thought clicked into place. "I got it," she said. "I remember what it was."

"Huh?" Zach glanced at her briefly.

"When we talked to Domingo before, there was something that bothered me but I couldn't put my finger on it. It just now came to me."

"You wanna share this illumination of yours?"

"Remember the way Domingo kept saying he couldn't understand how a man could beat up a pregnant woman and abandon his child? He came on all accusatory about that incident from the past, but not one word about the present. All his anger was directed toward that first beating."

"Well, that is illuminating." He paused. "You think he knows I didn't do it?"

"Why else would he not consider you the likeliest candidate for killer? Everybody else seems to."

"So maybe it was Domingo after all." He scratched his jaw. "When Bryce said he was too much of a pussy, I was inclined to agree. But if the guy had enough coke in him, he'd probably be up for it."

"Does that mean we get to go home?"

"One more stop."

"Lenny's?"

"He wasn't listed so we'll have to get his address from Nikki or Bryce. But I thought we could swing by the cop bar instead. It's only a few blocks from here."

Slugged down three beers at Bluestown. He drinks three more, we're in for another fight about driving. Just tell him you wanna go home.

He'd drop you off and go to the bar by himself.

🥭 🥭 🥭

The man behind the bar handed four long-necks to a baby-faced uniform, then turned to Zach. His wire-rimmed glasses, ascetic features and bony frame suggested a downsized college professor, but the voice was pure south side Chicago. "What'llyahave?"

Zach leaned against the bar with the familiarity of a man who had considerable bar-leaning in his history. "I'm looking for Steve Frasier. He been in tonight?"

"He left maybe twenty minutes ago."

"On his way home?"

"He didn't confide in me where he was goin'."

Thought the reason guys liked bars is that bartenders, unlike wives, are supposed to be jovial and friendly. Or maybe sneering is the male version of affability, like punching is the way they show they care.

"He's probably at his house." Zach clasped her upper arm and moved her toward the door.

In the car she asked. "You know where he lives?"

"Sort of."

Suddenly went evasive on me. "So . . . " Her eyes narrowed. "What is it you're trying not to tell me this time?"

After a moment's silence, he said, "Couple of years ago, Steve had a barbecue for the department and I went with Emily. I couldn't give you the address but I think I can find it."

"And the reason you didn't want to tell me?"

"When it comes to women from my past, I never know what's gonna set you off."

For a guy who's generally pretty bright, he sure can be obtuse on certain subjects. "What sets me off is *not* the fact that you lost your virginity long before we met. I don't much care who you slept with in the past. I do, however, get miffed when former girlfriends circle back into your life." *Xandra's phone calls. Emily trying to push the restart button.* "I get particularly miffed when they circle back and you don't tell me about it."

"I always figure, if I tell you it'll stir things up. You'll ask a lot of questions and make me talk, and I'd rather just put it behind me."

He drove through a residential area containing modest but well-kept houses, the kind of working class neighborhood that was commonplace around the northern fringe of the city. They parked in front of a compact frame bungalow with lights shining from several windows on the first floor and one on the second beneath the pitched roof. Three birdhouses stood on tall poles in the treeless front yard.

Zach said, "Maybe we should get a couple of those for Starshine. Put 'em close to the ground and call it her entertainment center."

Frasier, in a plaid bathrobe, answered the door. "This is ridiculous, Zach. It's eleven-thirty. Your girlfriend needs her beauty sleep."

She gritted her teeth at the cop's patronizing tone.

"Where're your manners, Steve? Didn't your mother teach you that when old friends ring your doorbell, you should invite them in and offer them a beer?"

"You're not an old friend, Zach. You're an obnoxious reporter who currently has his ass in a sling and is thrashing around trying to avoid being charged with murder. But since Ms. McCabe here does not deserve to have the door slammed in her pretty face, I'll give you five minutes."

Nice tits, pretty face. Boy, the compliments are really rolling in. Maybe we should make a couple more stops.

As they went inside, Zach said, "This is only the first part. The second is, you offer us a beer." The front door opened into the living room, with the kitchen directly to the right, a short hall at the rear, a bathroom visible at the end of the hall.

Hands in his pockets, Frasier shook his head. "If you weren't good for a laugh or two down at Dick's, I wouldn't put up with you."

The cop led them into an old-fashioned kitchen, a formica table in front, a working area behind the table, a back door at the far end. Cassidy and Zach plunked into chrome and vinyl chairs while Frasier pulled three Buds from a nearly empty refrigerator. As far as Cassidy could tell from the beer bottles, styrofoam cups, ashtrays and newspapers that littered every inch of horizontal space, the kitchen was used solely for drinking, smoking and reading.

Taking a seat across from Zach, Frasier handed out the bottles. "What's so critical you have to come crashing into my house in the middle of the night?"

Zach chugged some beer, then asked, "Who was she blackmailing? Corbin, Wiess, or you?"

"Nah, you got it all wrong. If she was blackmailing anybody, it would've been one of her johns."

"She couldn't blackmail a john. It'd be unethical."

Steve snorted. "You haven't got a chance of busting this case. Outside of you, her johns're the best suspect pool going, and you don't even have their names. So what's gonna happen is, you'll keep running in circles while the Area Four guys quietly build their case, and then one day they'll show up at your door and read you your rights."

"Hypothetically speaking, Steve, if she were to blackmail one of the three of you, which would it be?"

"Well, it wouldn't be me, that's for sure. I'm the one she always called when she got herself jammed up. I can't see her alienating Wiess, either, given the clout he's got downtown." He tapped the edge of the bottle on the table, then shook his head. "Nah, he's too big for her to take on."

Not so big she wouldn't threaten to send his call-girl bill to his wife.
She didn't seem to think anybody was too big.

18. Porch Sitting

Frasier tipped his bottle back for a long swallow, then said, "Now Corbin, he's a possibility. After the way he hassled her, she might've wanted to get something on him to keep him in line."

Pushing a mass of snarly curls behind her right ear, Cassidy said, "I hear you insist your detectives play by the rules."

"Yeah, you could say that."

"So what did you think about Xandra's recruiting a sixteen-year-old?"

"The version I heard, the minister's daughter came to her. Either way, I didn't like it." That dark, dangerous look came over his face again. "I told her to leave the kids alone, but any influence I ever had was long gone. I considered locking Xandra up and sending the girl home, but from what I heard, Corbin's daughter would've headed right back to the streets—probably ended up worse off than she was with Xandra—so I let it be."

Zach set his empty bottle on the table. "So Corbin's your pick for blackmail victim."

Frasier's thick-lipped mouth widened in a broad grin. "I just thought of another scenario. Maybe Xandra'd reopened diplomatic relations with you, Zach. Maybe she started inviting you over for late night drinks. Then, all of a sudden, she presents you with this bill for back child support and threatens to blow the whistle to Ms. McCabe here if you don't pay up. So maybe you're the one who's getting blackmailed, and this whole pathetic investigation of yours is just a ruse to confuse the issue."

"Nope," Cassidy said, "won't work. Nobody could blackmail Zach. He doesn't care enough what anybody thinks of him to pay hush money."

❦   ❦   ❦

As they walked from the garage to the gate, Starshine, in a repeat performance from the night before, dashed across the street and rolled at their feet. After scratching the cat's chin and fussing over her, Cassidy stood and said, "Both Starshine and Bryce are completely out of control."

"You wanna take another shot at the pills? So far it's zero in three."

"When she jumps on the counter to get fed, I'll grab her. Once I've got a good grip, you can take out the pill. That way there won't be any warning sounds before I have my hands on her."

Starshine zipped inside the house ahead of them but did not follow her usual routine of stopping to check her food bowl. Instead, she raced across the kitchen and disappeared through the dining room doorway. Zach took off after her, and Cassidy came running behind.

When she reached the top of the stairs, Zach was standing inside Bryce's room, his gaze probing the corners. The sleeping bag and air mattress lay next to the wall on their left. The TV sat atop an old bureau, Cassidy and Zach's desk chairs lined up in front of it. The floor and bed were ankle deep in clothes, dishes, fast food containers and crushed Coors cans.

"I gotta get another TV," Zach said. "I'm going into withdrawal."

As he poked inside the closet, Cassidy surveyed the rumpled, bulgy, half-open sleeping bag. "It moves," she said, eyeing one of the bulges. Throwing back the top, she snatched Starshine by the loose skin on her neck. "Gotcha!" the calico dug claws into Cassidy's arm, flailed and squirmed, but Cassidy pulled up on the scruff until the cat's instinct to go limp, a residual response from kittenhood, kicked in.

Downstairs Zach seated himself on a dining room chair to hold Starshine and spread her jaws while Cassidy inserted the pill. Once it was in place, Zach clamped her mouth closed and Cassidy scrutinized her throat. After about a minute, she saw a muscle move, followed by a tongue curling over the pink nose. "I think that's it."

As Zach loosened his hold, the cat tore out of his arms and fled down the basement stairs.

"Well, we did it." Cassidy leaned her shoulder against the door-jamb.

"Only took two humans a total of three tries to get one pill down the throat of a pint-sized calico."

"She's small but mighty," Cassidy said with pride in her voice. "A cat to be reckoned with."

Zach smiled affectionately. "A lot like her mother. The both of you can be a huge pain in the ass when it comes to getting your own way."

Settling on his lap, Cassidy looped her arms around his neck and rubbed her cheek against the side of his face. "And you know how to make both of us purr." *Only he hasn't done it lately. Said he never holds a grudge past sex but there hasn't been any. Still pissed about the agreement, and until I can lure him into bed for something other than sleep, he's not gonna let go of it.* She pressed her body closer, hoping he would suggest they go upstairs, but instead he gently eased her back onto her feet.

"My night's not over. I'm gonna wait on the porch for Bryce and have a little discussion about curfew and parking."

She glanced at the clock above the window. "It's twelve-forty-five and you haven't had a full night's sleep all week. Do it in the morning."

He shook his head. "I wanna see what condition he's in, if he's doing any pot or coke. Besides, it's always more effective to catch somebody in the act." He took a fresh bottle of bourbon down from the cabinet.

Wants to bust Bryce on drugs but he's been drinking all night.

He dropped ice into his glass. "You go on upstairs."

No point. I'd just lie awake waiting for Zach. Besides, I want to see how the confrontation goes. "I need some time to decompress. Mix me one too and I'll wait with you." Her gaze fell on the food-encrusted cat dish on the counter. "Did you feed Starshine today?"

"This is the first I've seen her."

"As far as I know, she's hardly had anything to eat since she got bitten." Her chest went tight with worry. *Isn't eating, only had one pill. What if she doesn't get well?* She ran a can of cat food through the electric opener. Its whir had been known to bring Starshine racing from the far corners of the yard. Nothing. Carrying the open can to the top of the basement stairs, she called for a full minute. When Starshine still did not come out of hiding, Cassidy returned to the kitchen, washed out the bowl and refilled it. "Maybe she'll come up and eat while we're on the porch."

❦   ❦   ❦

They turned off the house lights so Bryce wouldn't know they were still up and settled on the wicker couch at the back of the enclosed porch. The street was clearly illuminated but the porch was like a cave, rendering them invisible. A breeze sloughed through the ancient, thickly leaved elms that arched across the street, creating a shushing sound and raising an occasional clatter from the wind chimes. Cool, summer-scented air riffled pleasantly over her skin. Given the parking restriction in effect between two and six a.m., only one car, halfway down the block, remained on the street.

Sirens wailed from Austin Boulevard. A bike carrying three medium-sized kids, two white and one black, labored down the middle of Hazel. Zach drank some bourbon, rattled his ice cubes, and said, "I oughtta call it in," but did not move to take his cell phone out of his pocket.

"Call what in?"

"More than one kid on a bike is illegal in Oak Park."

"Why?"

"Why do you think? They're obviously out to find preowned wheels for the two passengers."

Not liking his lecturing tone, she didn't respond.

Zach laid his arm behind her shoulders and said, his voice more conversational, "With all the crime around here, I don't know how you maintain your illusion that Oak Park's a safe place."

A dark sedan parked across the street in front of their house.

"Denial's a wondrous thing. It allows me to hang onto the sense of security I had as a kid before Chicago's west side went ghetto."

"Yeah, but it makes you careless."

"I have you to remind me." Putting her hand on his knee, she stared at the car across the street. The driver had made no move to get out. "Why do you suppose that guy's sitting in his car?"

"Too drunk to make it to the door?" Zach shrugged. "A guy in full view of a lighted street isn't likely to engage in any illegal activities, although criminals've been known to do some pretty dumb things."

From the alert set of the man's head and shoulders, Cassidy didn't think he was drunk. Ten minutes passed and he was still in his sedan.

An eastbound car approached on Briar. As it turned south on Hazel, she could see it was the yellow Miata. Bryce drove to the end of the block, circled the cul-de-sac, then returned to park at the end of the cement walk leading from the porch to the street.

"Okay," Zach said softly. "Here we go."

Just as Bryce emerged from the Miata, the sedan's driver jumped out of his vehicle. *What?* Cassidy's body jerked upright.

"Shit!" Zach mumbled, hurtling through the screen door and down the porch steps as Cassidy raced after him. Peering around the Miata, Cassidy saw the man, who was wearing something odd on his face, grab Bryce's arm. "Get your hands off him," she screamed. Zach, now at the sidewalk, spoke loudly into his cell phone, "Hazel and Briar. Kidnapping in progress."

The assailant made an attempt to drag Bryce toward his car, looked at Zach running toward him, then released his hold on the boy. Scrambling into the sedan, he gunned his motor, roared down the block to the cul-de-sac, drove over it, and disappeared on the other side.

Can't believe it. Right in front of the house. Lights flicked on at the south end of the block and a handful of people came out to stand in the street staring after the car. Cassidy gazed into Bryce's ashen face. His eyes were huge and dilated, his expression stunned.

She laid a hand on his arm. "You okay?"

"Huh?" He blinked, then continued to stare toward the cul-de-sac.

Zach paced in the middle of Hazel. *Full of adrenaline, no place to put it.*

An orange-and-white squad screeched to a stop in the intersection. Zach jogged up to the car as the uniform hopped out, leaving his door open. Cassidy, starting to shiver, hugged herself tightly and rocked on the balls of her feet.

Bryce looked down as if noticing her for the first time. He said in a shaky voice, "That guy tried to force me into his car."

She heard Zach say to the uniform, "I got his plate number." The cop sat down again and talked on the radio. Three more cars arrived, two marked, one unmarked. The police huddled with Zach, then two cops, one white, the other black, walked over to Cassidy and Bryce.

The black cop asked Bryce, "What happened, son?"

"I was just coming home when this guy jumps out of his car and grabs me."

"You recognize him?" The white cop placed a hand on his belt.

"He had on this sorta half mask that covered his eyes and nose."

"He have a weapon?"

"Said he had a gun. Said if I didn't get in his car he'd shoot me." Bryce shook his head. "I didn't recognize the voice. I don't think it was anyone I know."

🍎 🍎 🍎

When the police left, they went inside, Zach heading toward the kitchen. "Cass and I are gonna have another drink. You can have a beer. Then we have to talk."

Shouldn't be teaching Bryce to handle feelings with booze.

Yeah, but don't you need another small infusion of alcohol yourself right now?

The teenager stood in the kitchen doorway, face still white beneath the bronze skin. "Look, I'm really beat. Couldn't we—"

"No, we can't." Zach handed Bryce a Moosehead, Cassidy a freshened bourbon, then refilled his own glass.

For God's sake—the kid just escaped a kidnapping. Zach should leave him alone.

You know this is the opportune time. Right after a crisis. Defenses down. Our best chance of squeezing out some information.

They settled in the living room, Zach and Cassidy in the small armchairs, Bryce on the farthest end of the sofa.

Zach said, "Why would anyone want to kidnap you?"

Bryce took a long swallow, then slumped lower on his spine, dropping his chin onto his collarbone. He jerked his shoulders in a minimal shrug.

"The key." Cassidy sat erect, her gaze fixed on the boy. "Tiffany said somebody offered her money to get you to tell her where the key is."

"Yeah, but I don't know about any key." Pulling himself up straight, the boy emptied the can, crushed it and tossed it on the floor. "Can I go to bed now?"

"You completely ignored what I said about curfew and parking in the slot." Zach folded his hands on his chest.

"Yeah, well . . . "

"Well, what?"

Bryce glared at his father. "I got other things on my mind, all right?"

Cassidy asked, "Tiffany?"

Dropping his head, Bryce rubbed the back of his neck. "I couldn't leave till she went to sleep. I would've stayed except . . . "

"Except?" Cassidy repeated.

He muttered, "I hate how she is in the morning."

Tilting her head, Cassidy said in a low voice, "Trying to take care of Tiffany all alone has got to be overwhelming. It's too much for any one person."

He shot her a venomous look.

"You can't keep doing this," Zach said sternly. "It's not safe. Somebody's after you."

"Yeah, well, I don't just abandon people the way you do."

"Who did I abandon?"

"You left Xandra with a kid to raise." Zach started to speak but Bryce waved his hand to stop him. "I know, she had your butt arrested and maybe you thought that was a good enough reason to walk."

"I told you before, I didn't know she was pregnant."

"Yeah, well, maybe you can get *her*," Bryce jerked his head toward Cassidy, "to buy that story, but I know what really happened." He stood. "There's nothing you can do to stop me anyway. If you hassle me about taking care of Tiff, I'll just move in with her." He turned and stomped upstairs.

Zach sighed heavily. "I am definitely not father material." He met Cassidy's eyes. "Any suggestions?"

"I think all we can do is leave him alone and hope for the best." She sighed. "Any idea what he meant by 'what really happened?' "

Shaking his head, Zach got wearily to his feet. "I'm so tired I'm brain dead, but I still can't come down from being wired." He glanced at her. "I know you probably think I've had too much already, but I need half a drink more to get to sleep. What about you?"

"Nothing for me."

In the kitchen Cassidy noted uneasily that Starshine's food had not been touched. She leaned against the sink to talk while Zach poured. "After what happened tonight, I can't believe the cops'll keep wasting time on you. Now they'll have to come up with another suspect."

Bryce came into the room. Acting as if Zach wasn't there, he asked

Cassidy, "Where's Starshine?"

"Hiding in the basement."

He went to the head of the stairs, a place not visible from the sink, and called. Moments later he stepped back into view with Starshine in his arms. The cat flattened her ears and hissed at Cassidy and Zach.

"She eaten yet?"

"Be my guest." Cassidy and Zach moved away from the feeding station.

Bryce placed Starshine beside her bowl, then stood in front of her to block her view of the two abominable pill-givers. When she finished, he carried her upstairs.

Cassidy experienced a sinking feeling as she watched them leave. Glancing at Zach, she heard his voice in her head: *She never holds a grudge past mealtime, just like I never do past sex.*

🐾   🐾   🐾

Since Cassidy's Friday morning client had canceled and Zach had no real work to do, they slept in until ten. He brought up coffee, then went down to read the newspaper on the front porch. Sitting up in bed with her purple mug, she gazed through the north window at a splatter of sun-brightened green maple leaves. *Maybe it's good your clients are deserting you. Otherwise you'd never get any sleep, you wouldn't be available to run all over Chicago with Zach, and you'd constantly wonder how many of them were wondering about you. 'Course at some point not having an income'll become an inconvenience.*

The phone rang and she went to her desk to answer it. "This is Judy and ... well, I've finally made a decision." Her tone was apologetic.

She's leaving. I changed my mind—I don't wanna be deserted. Wish she'd just evaporate and I didn't have to hear the words. A squirrel skittered across the porch roof, standing on hind legs to look in the window. Cassidy wished that Starshine, who loved squirrel watching, was there to see it.

"So what would you like to do?"

"I'm sorry, but I've decided to find somebody else. Every time I think about coming back, those angry feelings get all stirred up again."

"You need to do what's best for you. Would you like one last session to terminate? Say good-bye and get some closure?" *Hope she says no. I don't wanna talk about it anymore.*

"I'd rather leave things the way they are. I just want you to know—until that article came out, I was really pleased with what we were doing. You helped a lot."

"Thanks. I enjoyed working with you, too. I think you'll get through this divorce and be fine. Do you need a referral?"

"No, I've already got a name."

Feeling a sense of defeat, Cassidy put down the phone.

Why do you care? This isn't really a reflection on you.

Oh yeah? Zach and your ex are both men who go outside the bounds. Rule breakers. Rebels. Guys who do the right thing bore you. You knew when you first met him, Zach's past was a little on the dark side—which was half the attraction. So don't play innocent here.

❦ ❦ ❦

Half an hour later Zach came in from the shower, his smooth dark hair plastered to his forehead, a towel around his waist. Cassidy sidled toward him with the idea of ripping it away, but his words made it clear his mind was elsewhere. "The first thing we have to do is get Lenny's phone number."

Disappointed, Cassidy dropped back down on the bed. "You mean, because of the burglary? You think there's a connection between Jojo trying to steal her jewels and the murder?"

"Probably not, but what else is there? Nobody's gonna raise their hand and say 'Here I am. I did it.' "

Watching him pull on his white jockey shorts, she was suddenly aware of how much she missed the physical contact between them. He dressed in jeans and a new black tee, its yellow letters proclaiming: BEER: PROOF THAT GOD LOVES US. The majority of his shirts had shrunk so tight he wore them like an outer skin. All were black; most shouted out his fondness for beer. His tight jeans were merely cheap and nondescript, not trendily ripped. His only interest in shopping was the discovery of new beer slogans. Cassidy had long since figured out that the purpose behind his style of dressing was to declare his disdain for appearance and to get mildly in the face of anyone who believed in a dress code, particularly the members of his own family.

So what's your excuse? Why are your clothes such a mess?

Other things are more important. I care a little about appearance but not a lot. The only time it bothers me is when I'm around someone like Hathaway.

Dragging her mind back to the case, she said, "You want me to see if I can pry Lenny's number out of Bryce?"

"Considering how heavy-handed I got last night, he's not likely to give it to me."

Alliances—always tricky. You form an alliance with Bryce, he may talk to you but he'll use you to go around Zach. You and Zach hold a united front, he can't get out of dealing with his father but he may not tell us anything.

Keep Zach out of jail first, worry about their relationship later. She said, "I'll give it a try."

After several loud knocks at Bryce's door, she finally extracted a sleepy, "Yeah?"

Peering inside, she saw the boy's head on his pillow, eyes closed, Starshine hunkered warily on his chest. The cat shot her a fierce look, growled, then wormed her way inside the sleeping bag. Cassidy said, "Can I come in?"

Opening his eyes, he raised his head. "Okay."

Cassidy eased into one of the desk chairs. Sitting up, Bryce leaned against the wall.

"Zach and I need some information."

He rubbed his eyes with his fists. "What?"

"We need to talk to Lenny. About the time his brother broke into your house."

"Lenny?" He scrunched his forehead. "He didn't have anything to do with it."

"We'd still like to talk to him. Have you got his phone number and address?"

"Yeah, I can give it to you." He yawned. "Just let me wake up first, okay?"

🐛 🐛 🐛

Zach sat at the table reading the newspaper. Cassidy leaned on her elbow, a frown on her face, brooding about Starshine and the pills. Bryce came downstairs holding the calico against one shoulder the way mothers carry their babies. He took her into the kitchen and gave her breakfast, chanting in a singsong voice as she ate, "What a pretty girl. What a good eater. You're such a nice kitty. I just wish you wouldn't bite my toes at three a.m."

Ah, toe biting. The price of catly love.

After she ate, Starshine slunk around the outer edge of the dining room and zoomed back upstairs. Joining them at the table, Bryce slid a piece of paper in front of Cassidy. "Here's that stuff you wanted."

"Lenny's number?" Zach asked.

Bryce didn't answer.

Cassidy turned it over. "What is all this?"

Averting his head, he looked at the floor. "That other stuff you wanted. The name of the john she said beat her up back in January, plus the date it happened."

Cassidy remarked in surprise. "He's an FBI agent?"

"That's who she said. I don't know anything else, just his name."

Studying his body language, she thought he looked embarrassed. "This is very nice, but I wonder why you decided to do it now?"

"No reason."

Zach said, "Thanks."

Bryce left the house.

19. Being Friends

"Well, an FBI agent." Cassidy tilted her head speculatively. "Maybe the FBI guy beat her up, she tried to blackmail him, and he threatened her. Even Xandra'd probably be scared of a fed."

"Yeah, but what evidence could she have against him?" He met her eyes, then gazed into space. "It's not likely anybody was peeking through the window to take pictures of him battering her. Somebody wants a key, which means Xandra must have physical evidence—a letter, a picture, a tangible item—locked up somewhere."

Fetching the bottle of pills from the kitchen, Cassidy said, "Before we start on the case, let's knock off the first unpleasant task of the day."

In Bryce's room, Cassidy yanked back the top of the sleeping bag to reveal a ferocious Starshine, ears flattened, muscles tensed, body poised for flight. Black eyes flashing, she hissed, then swerved around the hands that were coming at her, zipped past Zach in the doorway, and ran inside their bedroom.

Chasing after her, Zach said, "She went behind the waterbed."

Cassidy opened the hall cabinet and grabbed the water-filled spray bottle they used to dislodge the cat from her back-of-the-bed refuge. Zach moved his nightstand, lay on the floor, extended his arm as far as possible into the crevice, and squirted. Moments later, a damp, bedraggled, pissed-off cat dashed out of her hiding place and into Cassidy's arms.

Downstairs, after Starshine had swallowed the pill and disappeared into the basement, Cassidy leaned against the kitchen sink and said, "Let's try Lenny first. We've got both his home and cell numbers, plus his address."

"You start off. The fact that he's already met you oughtta lend some credibility. I'll get on the upstairs extension."

She reached for the handset on the kitchen wall next to the doorway. When Lenny answered, she said, "This is Cassidy McCabe. Bryce introduced us at the townhouse, remember?"

"Is there a problem with Bryce?" She heard concern in his voice.

Mention the kidnapping attempt? No, better not. "He's fine. Actually, the reason I'm calling is about the murder." She paused, hoping he'd say something that would give her a lead-in, but he didn't. "Bryce's father and I have been doing a little investigating, trying to find out what really happened." *You have any idea how ridiculous that sounds? A therapist and her boyfriend attempting to outwit the police?* She stumbled on. "So anyway, we'd like to talk to you. Just for background on Xandra's life." Gazing at the scuffed linoleum, she noted that even though the cat was missing, clumps of fur still drifted in her wake.

Zach's voice came on the line. "I'm Zach Moran, Bryce's father. Could we set an appointment to talk to you today?"

How simple. Why didn't I think of that?

"I don't have time." Lenny's affable voice went gruff.

What? He won't see us?

"Look, there're some details we really need to go over with you."

"I don't have to talk to you."

Cassidy said, "Lenny, please. Somebody tried to kidnap Bryce last night. Whoever killed Xandra is after him, too. I know you care about Bryce, so please help us out here."

"Sorry, ma'am." His tone apologetic. "I just can't stick my neck out. Besides, I don't know anything, anyway."

Cassidy felt as if he'd slapped her hand. Clutching Bryce's paper, she went upstairs to confer with Zach, who was seated at his desk. She plunked into her chair and swiveled to face him. "I'm amazed. Here I thought the minister, the cop, or the alderman'd be the ones most likely to refuse, since they have reputations to protect. But instead it's her driver."

"Public figures are used to talking to reporters, so it's wired in that if I ask questions, they have to answer. A schlub like Lenny who's never been in the public eye is more likely to be afraid of saying the wrong thing. Especially since he's got a brother tangled up in the judicial system right now."

"So we just have to drop Lenny?"

"For the moment." Zach took the paper out of her hands. "Let's move on to the FBI guy, whose name is," he glanced down, "Jesse Montez. After that, I want to run down the alderman again."

"I'll listen in downstairs."

She picked up the kitchen phone and heard Zach's voice. "This is Al Whitmore from the *Post.*

Whitmore—the reporter Zach suspected of feeding all that personal information to Izzie.

Zach continued, "Your name has come up regarding the murder of Xandra Palomar. I've got a few questions I need to ask, and these are not the kind of questions you want to answer at your office."

There was a brief silence, then Montez said, "If you're really from the *Post,* you should know you have to go through our media office to get an interview."

"An informed source has linked your name with the Palomar woman's. Now you and I can have an informal, off-the-record conversation, or I can take it to your media people. Your call."

"Your source is wrong. There's no point discussing this further."

Cassidy's eyes drifted to the window. The sky was as flat and blue as a painted backdrop, no whipped cream clouds anywhere.

"Then you'd prefer to have me print the allegation and quote you as a 'no-comment?' "

A pause. "That's entirely irresponsible—you know that."

"You want to keep your name out of print, let's discuss it on background."

"I could get in serious trouble for just sitting down at the same table with a reporter. Besides, the allegation is ridiculous. I've had almost no contact with the woman."

"Almost?"

Another pause. "Fifteen minutes, that's it. Meet me at the Einstein Bagels on Wacker, seven-thirty tomorrow morning." The receiver clicked down.

Cassidy hurried upstairs. "I just barely managed not to groan when he said seven-thirty."

"You don't have to go."

"You think you're getting out of here without me?"

"Now I'll have to explain you to a fed." He gave her a crooked smile. "This is my girlfriend. She's here 'cause I'm not allowed to leave the house without her."

"Ouch." Cassidy grimaced, then laid her hand on his shoulder. "I'm sorry to be so much trouble."

"I'll survive." He patted her hand. "Okay, I'm gonna call Wiess' secretary now. You go downstairs and pick up the extension again."

The call went into voice mail and he hung up. A moment later he appeared in the kitchen and said, "The secretary's probably on the phone so I thought I'd try again in a few minutes instead of leaving my cell number. I want you to listen in. I've thought up this great scam and if you don't hear it, there won't be anybody to appreciate how clever I am."

Zach returned to the bedroom and Cassidy decided to use the waiting time to make up a grocery list. Grabbing a handful of peanut butter cups from the cabinet, she opened the refrigerator and surveyed its contents: beer, wine, cheese, yogurt, fresh vegetables, and a carton of milk a week past its freshness date. Even with no drinkable milk, Bryce had found a way to consume Gran's sugar frosted flakes. *A complete failure at the care and feeding of a teenager. Nothing in the house for him to eat.* She bit a Reese's in two, sat at the table, and drew a forlorn cartoon face at the top of her notepad. After writing FROZEN PIZZA, TV DINNERS, and HOT DOGS she found herself at a complete loss as to what a seventeen-year-old might like. She tried to remember what Gran's bags had contained, but her mind was recalcitrant and refused to provide a single clue.

Zach came down to tell her he was ready to try Wiess' secretary again. This time an elderly female voice answered.

Bet his wife won't let him have any females under the age of sixty working for him.

"Well, hello there, Greta." Zach spoke in the thin, quavery tone of an old man. "This is Roscoe Fischer." He hacked out a dry cough.

Roscoe Fischer? Even Cassidy, who did not read newspapers, recognized the name of the famous *Post* columnist.

Zach went on. "Is that scalawag Gordy anywhere around?"

"I'm sorry, he won't be in all day Mr. Fischer."

"Just call me Roscoe. Everybody does. I thought we had plans for lunch but I didn't get it into my Day-Timer. One of those little slips that starts creeping up with age."

"Oh, I know exactly what you mean," she said eagerly.

"So would you mind checking Gordy's schedule to see if I'm on it?"

"I'd be happy to, Mr. ... uh, Roscoe." A pause. "Sorry, but I don't see your name anywhere."

Zach made a sound that approximated the chuckle of a septuagenarian. "Guess I must've dreamt it. Well, does he have anybody else down for lunch?"

Cassidy gazed across the kitchen at Starshine's bowl on the counter. *In the past—before she hated me—she always came begging for food whenever I stepped foot in the kitchen.*

The secretary said, "Looks like he's free today. When he doesn't have a meeting, he usually grabs a bite at Barney's between twelve and twelve-thirty. If you want to catch him, that's your best bet."

Zach made the chuckling sound again. "You've been very helpful, Greta. When I track him down, I'll have to put a bug in his ear about giving you a raise. That is, if I can hold onto the thought long enough."

❦   ❦   ❦

Cassidy and Zach drove into the Loop, paid twelve dollars for an hour's parking, then hiked to the corner of Dearborn and Washington across the street from Barney's Deli. There they took up their watch for the alderman. It was lunch hour in the business district and the sidewalks were jammed with expensively dressed, fast-moving professionals. Halfway down the block, a tall black man played a bluesy saxophone, the wailing, silvery sound rising above the traffic noises.

Zach pointed his head at a figure approaching the deli entrance. "That's him." They gave Wiess ten minutes to make sure he had food in front of him, an anchor to keep him from walking out, then Zach took her hand and they crossed Washington.

Cassidy said, "Don't forget—we can't use any of that juicy stuff I got from Nikki. It might give her away."

"Just one little piece."

Barney's was a brightly lit chrome and tile eatery decorated in a nouveau fifties diner style. Zach opened the door and they walked into a reverberating din of voices. Suited men and women stood in line to select food at the counter in front, carried trays to booths, and took not a minute longer than necessary to refuel their bodies for the afternoon round of corporate money making.

Whatever happened to STOP AND SMELL THE ROSES?

Wrong decade. This is the nineties. Besides, when was the last time you took a leisurely stroll or stuck your nose in any petals?

Wiess sat alone in a booth, a Caesar salad in front of him. Pushing his way through the crowd, Zach said, "Mind if we join you?" He slid in across from the alderman; Cassidy followed suit.

"You know, Zach, you epitomize the image of predatory reporter that's given the media such a bad name." He shoved romaine in his mouth.

"Wish I had time to debate the role of the press in watchdogging public officials, but that'll have to wait for another day."

Cassidy gazed at the alderman's thick, golden hair, chiseled features, and straight white teeth. *Even though you don't like handsome men—even though you know he's slime—it's hard not to drool.*

Zach said, "Who was Xandra blackmailing, Gordy?"

Wiess' high forehead creased slightly. "You really are getting tiresome. I told you already, we saw each other three or four times a year at most. I was not her best friend. If she decided to blackmail somebody, she would not've called me up to chat about it." He glanced at his watch. "I have somewhere I'd rather be."

"One more question," Zach said insistently. "Why was she particularly in need of money just before her death?"

Wiess gazed out the window for several beats, then turned back toward Zach. "She may've been considering a move out of the area. I called her about two weeks before she was killed, and she had a message on her machine saying she was away for a few days. When she got back to me, she mentioned that she'd been in Florida looking at property. I asked what was up, and she said she was sick of Chicago. She rattled off this long list of complaints, most of which I've forgotten." He paused, his forehead creasing again. "I think one was that Bryce'd refused to go back to his boarding school. She also said something about a girl who'd taken off with half her johns." He met Zach's eyes. "But you have to realize, she's been talking about moving to Florida for as long as I've known her. I just brushed it off."

❦   ❦   ❦

Zach parked in front of the house. "I'm going down to the office. Least there I can do some rewrites, make myself feel useful." He glanced at her. "You have any clients this afternoon?"

She pushed the car door open. "Just one."

"What time?"

Why does he care? "Three."

He kept his face forward, not looking at her.

"Why don't I call Bryce on his cell phone and ask if Xandra was planning to move. Catching him in person is always so iffy."

Zach handed her the notepad. "His number's in there."

In the house she sat at her desk and dialed.

"Yeah," Bryce answered.

"This is Cassidy. I just wanted to check out some information we heard today."

"What?" He sounded disinterested. She could hear Tiffany talking in the background.

"Did Xandra take any trips a couple of weeks before she died?" Cassidy took out a legal pad, swiveled toward the window, and propped her feet on the radiator.

"She went to Florida."

"What for?" Cassidy drew a sullen cartoon face on the pad.

"I don't know. She didn't say."

"She ever talk about moving?"

"Sure. All the time. But it didn't mean anything."

"Any chance she was planning a move in the near future?" She heard Starshine's dainty paws clumping like elephant hooves on the stairs, then the sound stopped. *Went into the kid's room.*

"Nah, she'd never move. When I was young I used to beg her to quit the business, and she always promised that some day she would. Some day we'd go off to Florida, she'd marry some nice guy, and we could be a regular family. But even then I knew she'd never do it."

"Why not?"

" 'Cause then she'd be just plain, ordinary Sandra Schwartz again. She loved being Xandra. She'd never give it up."

Cassidy replaced the receiver and stared at the mess on her desk, knowing she would never succeed in bending her mind away from the case and refocusing it on trivialities such as filling out managed care forms or balancing her checkbook.

The front doorbell rang, causing her shoulders to jerk wildly. *Classic conditioning. Front doorbell equals police equals panic.* Her hands and teeth clenched.

Can't be Hathaway again. She couldn't possibly come up with one more reason to hassle us.

Yes it can, and of course she could.

Standing, Cassidy looked down at the street for the detectives' sedan. Instead, she saw a Volvo. *Maggie's car.* She knew it well, having used it once to tail another vehicle. *Why's she here? We never drop in.*

Dashing downstairs, Cassidy opened the door, crossed the porch, opened the screen door. Maggie's pretty, no-makeup face registered surprise. "Well, I caught you at home." She stepped inside the porch, letting the screen door bang behind her. "I thought you'd probably be off chasing bad guys."

"I have to stay home sometimes. After all, I do have a few clients left who haven't canceled. People like me who avoid newspapers or haven't made the connection yet between the reporter in the article and the man in my house."

Maggie had a sheepish look on her face. "I realize I said I'd wait till you were ready to talk, but my curiosity got the better of me. Plus I wanted to make sure you were okay."

"Well, I'm not, but what else is new?"

"You have any clients this next hour? Or can I highjack you for lunch at Erik's?" Maggie, in beige pants and a cream top, waited quietly while Cassidy thought about it. Her friend never fidgeted. Simply being in Maggie's presence had a calming effect.

If you go, you'll have to tell her all the embarrassing stuff about Zach. You wanna do that? Her stomach reminded her that once again she'd forgotten to eat, the reason her weight remained low despite her chocoholic binges in times of stress.

Have lunch. Being friends means you have to talk.

"I'm way behind on overdue forms, unreturned calls, and unwashed dishes, mostly on Bryce's floor. No, wait, you don't even know who Bryce is yet, do you? But—as I started to say—I'm too distracted to get anything done anyway, so let's go to Erik's."

Since it was after one when they arrived at the deli, the lines were short. Cassidy and Maggie headed for the bountiful salad bar along the north wall. Behind them stretched a large room filled with blond wood, umbrella tables, and sprouting greenery. Located in the heart of the village's restaurant row, it was popular among all the various strata of Oak Park.

The restaurant manager, an enthusiastic guy working the cash register, hailed them with his usual "How's it going?"

The bakery display drew Cassidy like a tractor beam. Succumbing to her chocolate lust, she added a chunk of double fudge cake to her tray.

As they sat down at a window table, Maggie eyed the cake and said, "That bad, huh?"

"It's funny. When there's nothing wrong, I can go for months without the thought of chocolate entering my mind."

"When've you ever had even one month when nothing went wrong?"

"If I ever did, I'm sure I *could* go that long without thinking of chocolate."

Laughing, Maggie shook her softly curled head. "I said I wouldn't nag but I lied. I've been worrying about you ever since I read that awful news story. So I decided this time I'm taking care of me instead of you, which means making you talk."

Cassidy swallowed a mouthful of rich chocolate and sighed. "Zach hated having to tell me, and it's almost as hard for me to tell you, even though you're my best friend. But I don't want my stupid pride to make you give up on me, so here goes."

Maggie laid down her utensils, rested her chin on laced fingers, and gave Cassidy her full attention. Maggie's ability to listen with her whole self was one of the best things about her.

As Cassidy finished the story, relief washed over her. "I know talking's good for everybody else. Why do I always forget it's just as good for me?"

"I don't know. Why do you?"

Taking a deep breath, Cassidy said, "Tell me the truth, Maggie. Do you think I'm nuts to stay with Zach?"

20. Missing in Bar-Related Action

Maggie tilted her head slightly, poked at her salad, and said, "What makes you ask?"

Cassidy's brow furrowed. "Don't be a therapist. Be my friend."

Maggie laughed again, causing her delicate, silver earrings to glitter and dance. "I don't see anything much to hold against him, other than what he did when he was twenty-three and under the influence of hormones and cocaine. In the present, he seems to be handling himself pretty well."

Her voice barely audible, Cassidy said, "Except for the drinking."

"He's drinking too much?"

Staring at her plate, Cassidy mashed chocolate crumbs with her fork. "He always has a couple of drinks at night. Before this, he kept it pretty much under control. But now that we're spending half our life in these disgusting bars, it's escalating."

"Well, you've taken all the courses on alcoholism. What do you think?"

One of the questions you don't want to face. She turned her head to stare out the window at the brick bank building with its series of arched windows and entrances on the other side of Oak Park Avenue. "I can't tell yet. It could be just a stress reaction, like me with chocolate. Something that'll go away when this is over. Or it could be he's sliding into addiction."

Touching her hand, Maggie said, a note of concern in her voice, "What will you do if he continues drinking the way he is now?"

The other question you don't want to face. A sick feeling came over her. She knew what it would be like to live with an alcoholic. Several of her clients had told her. "I'd have to break up with him."

"Well, you're not required to think about it now," Maggie said, the same words Cassidy would have used with a client. "You can put it off until this mess is over and then decide. One thing at a time."

Sitting straighter, Cassidy gazed into Maggie's tranquil gray eyes. "You know, it's amazing. All these things we say really do help." Her stomach settled down and she finished her cake, then turned her gaze to the window again. Another day when sun poured out of a hyacinth sky like spun gold. A man with a shaggy white beard wearing spandex shorts and pads rollerbladed down the street. One of the clients who had canceled walked past on the opposite sidewalk.

Maggie said, "You're awfully quiet."

"There's one other thing I want to bounce off you. I told you I made Zach agree to include me in his investigation even though he was extremely pissed about it. And now there's this little therapist-voice in the back of my mind whispering, 'You should never force people to do things they don't want to do.' But that part's definitely not in control. The dominant voice is the one that's scared to death he'll get himself in trouble if I'm not watching over his shoulder." *Like a drunk-driving arrest, for instance.* "I know I shouldn't be thinking this way but I can't stop myself."

"So what gives you the idea he can't handle it by himself?"

"He's such a risk-taker."

Maggie sent her a pointed look.

Her cheeks growing hot, she said, "Okay, I'm probably worse than he is. But I've reformed. I'm not pulling any more crazy stunts without talking to Zach first."

"You'll talk to him, then do it anyway?"

"So you think I'm going to screw things up by getting so controlling?"

"Probably," Maggie responded cheerfully. "How do you make him do things, anyway?"

"Guilt." Cassidy grimaced, thinking how bad that sounded. "Oh God, I've become my mother."

Maggie said in her sensible way, "If you think you're jeopardizing the relationship, why not work on controlling your urge to control him?"

That's never gonna happen. "Because at the time I do it, I'm absolutely convinced that my way is right and that disaster will befall us if I don't."

❦ ❦ ❦

Her client, Pete, rang the back doorbell at three. When she met him in the waiting room he said, "I'm sorry—I let your cat out by mistake. By the time I saw your note, she was already gone."

The note, fastened to the inside of the back door, said PLEASE DO NOT LET THE CAT OUTSIDE.

❦ ❦ ❦

The phone rang during Pete's session. Afterward she went upstairs and pushed PLAY.

Zach's voice said, "Something came up and I'm gonna have to stay in the city later than I expected. Don't know how long this'll take, but I'll definitely be home before bedtime."

That's why he asked what time I had a client—so he could call when he knew I wouldn't answer. A jittery feeling started in her chest. Her back teeth clenched. *Sneaking around. Trying to get away with something.*

She dropped into her desk chair and swiveled to look out the window. A blue jay, landing on the porch roof, stared at her with one black button eye.

Maybe it isn't anything. Maybe he's just angry. Showing you he doesn't have to be accountable.

Then why not just say the deal's off?

She replayed the message and it brought back the memory of an earlier time when the same words had appeared on her machine. After three months of reliable courtship, he'd left a something-came-up message, broken their date, and proceeded to get erratic on her. It was the beginning of a no-Saturday-night-dates distancing routine that had signaled the near demise of the relationship.

How can he do this to me when we've gotten through so much?

She called his pager, then spent five minutes staring at the phone. Pacing back and forth in the middle of the room, she stopped to gaze through the west window at Hazel. A clump of small children played in the sprinkler across the street. An elderly couple walked hand in hand. A feral cat sniffed bushes two houses down.

She forced herself to breathe deeply. *Don't make this into more than it is. He's obviously following some lead he thinks you'd object to. Breaking into somebody's house. Stealing something. Calling Nikki and pretending to be a john.*

She took several more long, slow breaths but could not shake the anxiety twitches running up and down her spine. She'd been left too often. Every time it happened, the old feelings swamped her.

No idea when Zach'll get home. Bryce is indefinitely gone. Even Starshine's avoiding me.

She couldn't do anything about Zach or Bryce, but Starshine frequently went through doors when they were opened for her. Cassidy called from the stoop and Starshine came running up to the foot of the steps, eyed Cassidy warily, then pretended the human was invisible and slunk toward the door. Snatching her up, Cassidy carried the cat into the bedroom and held her squirming body captive in her lap.

"I know you hate being forced. I feel the same way. But relationships require compromise, and now it's your turn to do what I want."

As Cassidy petted and scratched, the calico gradually grew calmer, finally settling on her chest and starting to purr. "I'm sorry, but I can't stand total abandonment."

❦ ❦ ❦

The phone rang. Picking up, Cassidy heard a familiar female voice on the other end. "Zach and I are at The Hideaway. It's this little bar in uptown over on Broadway. Do you know the place I'm talking about?"

Emily? His old girlfriend who's also a cop? So she's the lead he didn't want me to know about.

"Uh, no. I've never been there."

"I took Zach's keys away from him. I think you better come get him." Emily's voice oozed sympathy. Pity for poor Cassidy who was still attached to this wastrel, this woman-battering male whom Emily herself had once been involved with but now was free of.

Humiliation burned hotly in Cassidy's stomach. *Would you, Emily, kindly get yourself transported to another planet? Turn to stone? Convert to Islam and jump on the first plane flying east? Anything so I don't have to look into your patronizing, sympathetic face, thank you humbly, collect Zach's key, and shovel his drunken self into the Nissan.*

She called a cab.

In the bar it took her a moment to spot Zach and Emily. They were seated in a booth in an unlighted corner, side by side, bodies touching. She gritted her teeth at the smell of smoke and overused grease. Crossing to stand next to the table, Cassidy forced herself to meet Emily's amber-flecked eyes. She refused to look directly at Zach, his frame jammed against the wall, because if he turned out to be as bleary and sodden as she expected, she would get even more embarrassed than she was already. She hoped Emily would give her the keys without another word. Failing that, she hoped the earth would open and swallow the honey-haired detective.

"You showed up sooner than I expected," Emily said, her voice chatty. She made no move to leave. Zach sat in the corner, arms on the dark wood table. An empty glass stood in front of each of them.

"Well, Emily," Zach said, his voice surprisingly unslurred and ironic, "you've made your point. What say we continue this conversation another time."

Emily turned toward Zach. "I'll let you know what I find out. We can get together then." Her tone was deliberately sultry. She handed Cassidy the keys and left. Sliding across smooth vinyl, Cassidy examined Zach closely. He smelled beery but looked all right. "You ready to go?"

"No, I'm going to order another drink."

Her fist drummed the scratched tabletop. She stared down at a squiggly cigarette burn reminiscent of a squashed, black worm. Choking back the haven't-you-had-enough speech, she said instead, "You think I have nothing better to do than wait around till you're ready to be driven home?"

"That's not bad. I expected a whole long sermon before I had a chance to get a word in edgewise." He wrapped his hand around the back of her neck. "Jesus, Cass, you're tight as a drum. Tell you what—you have a drink, I'll order Coke, then I'll drive home."

"Boy, you sure managed a fast sober-up." *What am I seeing here? The super high tolerance that goes with alcoholism?*

"You think I've had too much to drink?"

She studied him again. She had become very attuned to the nuances of his drunkenness and saw no sign of beer soaked brain cells. "Are you telling me you haven't? So why'd Emily call?"

"I asked her to meet me here because she's the only reasonable lead

I hadn't followed up on, and it seemed like finding out what's going on over at Area Four'd be a good idea. She doesn't have insider informa- tion at her fingertips, but she can get it." He turned his head slightly away, then looked at her again. "Remember, several months ago I told you she'd called to see if I was interested in getting back together?"

Cassidy propped her chin on her hand, a secret smile starting in the far reaches of her mind. "So are you saying she misconstrued your reason for wanting to see her?"

Zach twisted his empty glass on the dark, polished wood. "I guess I didn't make my agenda clear enough. It was also a mistake to suggest this place, which used to be our hangout. I just figured, given the story in the *Post*, she'd know I was after information. But apparently she made a different assumption."

"What happened?"

"She started off real friendly. She asked about you and how we were doing, and I made some crack about our only problem being that you think I drink too much, which is obviously where she got the idea. I told her we were working together, and then her voice got cold and she said she was surprised to hear it. Evidently she'd presumed that my inviting her to meet me meant my status had changed." He beckoned to a waitress.

Can see why she'd be pissed. If I thought my ex was gonna beg me to come back—even if I didn't want him—and he declared himself perfectly happy with my replacement, I might not take it so well either.

"Who's she getting even with, you or me? Probably me. Women have this unfortunate tendency to direct their vindictiveness at the rival instead of the man."

A cheerful-looking waitress with wild corkscrew hair came to take their order. Zach requested a bourbon for her, a coke for himself. "That's the beauty of it. She can stick it to both of us and come out looking like the sugar plum fairy." He laid his arm across Cassidy's shoulders. "I was on my first beer when she arrived. Then I ordered one for her, a second for me, and about that time she started insisting I was sounding incoherent and must've had several rounds before she got here. So then she whipped out her phone and called you."

"If all you had was two beers, why'd you hand over the keys?"

"Because I need her right now. I let her get away with her little game, so now she owes me and that'll make her more willing to give me what I want. This is a pretty major favor I'm asking. It puts her in the middle, and she wasn't too happy at the idea of trying to find some leak over at Area Four. But she said she'd do what she can."

The wild-haired waitress brought their drinks, setting them on cocktail napkins with cartoon drawings of voluptuous women dancing. "C'mon, Cass, drink up." He massaged the tense muscles at the back of her neck. "This week's been every bit as hard on you as it has on me."

She stared at a buxom blonde seated at the bar flirting with a man on the stool to the left. The woman, with bouncy, white-blond hair and a tight-fitting dress, looked like an overblown Marilyn Monroe.

Taking a large swallow, Cassidy felt her body loosen as the alcohol worked its way down. She twisted sideways on the bench, resting her back against Zach's shoulder. He wrapped his arm around her midsection and pulled her closer. Releasing a long sigh, she leaned into him.

He spoke next to her ear in a burry drawl. "I appreciate your taking this so well. I expected you to jump all over me before I had a chance to explain."

"Okay, I won't jump on you about drinking, but you deserve a major stomping about Emily." Her body stiffening, she pulled away from him. "How come the secret meeting? I thought we had a deal."

He slipped his hand under her loose tee, spread his fingers across her bare midriff, and drew her back. "I figured if I brought you along, Emily'd get jealous, and if I said I was gonna see her without you, you'd get jealous. Seemed like the easiest thing was not to mention it. I really don't need to deal with jealous women right now."

She removed his hand from her body and turned to face forward. Across from her a magic marker drawing of a heart with an arrow through it decorated the vinyl backrest. "I hate it when you go behind my back so I won't get jealous. I'm trying so damn hard to trust you and this doesn't make it any easier."

"I've told you over and over—I'm not gonna cheat."

"You've also said there are no guarantees."

He turned his head slightly away. "It's remotely possible that I might get attracted to somebody else. I've been moving from woman to woman my whole life and even though I want to marry you, it makes me nervous to cut off all my options. I think I can do this. If I can't, I'll tell you and we can call it quits. I won't play around on the side."

The fear she had almost managed to squelch rose up in her again. She drew in a long breath through clenched teeth, then let out a deep sigh.

Why does he have to be so scrupulous with me? Doesn't mind lying to everyone else. Why can't he just for once tell me what I want to hear instead of the truth?

Kevin told you exactly what you wanted to hear. Always. You want that again?

She watched the blowsy Monroe throw her head back and let out a raucous laugh. "Okay, what you said is fair. But it's not fair to say I'm jealous. After hearing that sneaky, evasive message, what was I supposed to think? If you're clearly doing something you don't want me to know about, of course I'm going to get nervous and insecure. So, no more secret meetings, okay?"

"I knew the message was lousy but I couldn't think what else to say."

"Why is it you can create all these clever stories for other people but you can't even come up with a decent misdirection for me?" She wadded the damp napkin into a tiny ball and jiggled it in her hand.

"I made up my mind not to lie to you. Even I know, if I started doing that it'd be all over."

"Oh." She felt more tension drain away. "So, tell me, why'd you break up with Emily anyway?"

Staring down at the table, he blew out air. "I'm not in the mood for this."

"Well, I am." She pulled herself up straight. "Having Emily tell me to come get you was not fun. So I think I have the right to know what led up to this little payback of hers. Besides, you owe me humiliation damages."

"I wish we didn't have to do this." Leaning into the corner, he turned to face her. "Okay, the way it was with Emily is pretty much how it was with all the others. It started off the same as our relationship. Once a week we'd go out to dinner, then she'd spend the night at Marina City. Or I'd meet her here after work. After a while she wanted more—that's how it always went—and I felt pressured. So I ended it."

Just enough to stave off loneliness, not enough to interfere with freedom. "So why didn't that happen with us?"

He was silent a long time. Then he said, "You made me talk. Like you're doing now. I always hate it while it's happening. But when I started my drifting off routine—"

"Yeah, I remember. You suddenly got busy on Saturday nights."

The outsized Monroe headed for the far end of the bar, a trip to the rest room no doubt. As soon as she was gone, the man she'd been flirting with, a good bit younger than she, bolted for the door.

Zach said, "It didn't feel right being without you. I wanted to come back."

Taking a deep swallow, she felt a glow spread over her that was some part alcohol, some part pleasure at what Zach had said.

Several moments passed. Then he slid closer, easing his arm around her again. She twisted so that her back was against him, making it easier for him to hold her. He pushed her hair aside, his lips moving warmly against the back of her neck. His hand wrapped around her breast, fingers stroking the nipple through her bra. A warm wet feeling started in her groin and spread outward, setting off small jolts of electricity.

Zach's voice flowed into her ear. "So you cast your spell over me and got more than you bargained for—Bryce in the extra bedroom and Hathaway ringing your doorbell."

❦   ❦   ❦

"Shared the secrets of my soul . . . " Kris Kristofferson's froggy voice rumbled from the speakers. Cassidy lay on her back, Zach on top of her, the water in the mattress surging with his movements. "I'd trade all my tomorrows for a single yesterday . . . " She trembled on the edge for a long stretch of time and then at last it came, an excruciating explosion at the core. Zach rolled over and she threw herself on top of him, clinging to his body through several minutes of delicious, shivery aftershocks. When she finally was spent, she turned on her side and he wrapped himself around her in a full body hug. ". . . blowin' sad while Bobby sang the blues . . ."

More time passed, then he rose and said, "I'm gonna fix a drink. You want one?"

"Mmmm. Okay."

She was sitting up in her long plum tee amid a pile of rumpled burgundy sheets when he reappeared and settled in beside her. He said, "Would you kick me out if I started smoking again?"

She pictured herself walking into a smoke-filled bedroom, then into a bedroom with clean air but no Zach. "It wouldn't be my first choice but I guess I could live with it."

"It's been over three years, but I've been dying for a cigarette ever since I walked into that townhouse and saw her body."

"At least you're holding out better than I do with peanut butter cups."

He gazed into space for several beats, then said, "In some ways it's worse now than it was before. When Xandra had me arrested, I was doing so much dope I went through that whole period in a kind of haze. It was only afterward I recognized how close I'd come to getting locked up. That's when I had my moment of enlightenment and realized I'd have to lay off drugs if I ever wanted to have a life."

She gazed at the arrangement of gold-framed photos on the dusty rose wall across from the bed. *Look at the way you scarf chocolate. How do people get through an ordeal like this without using something?*

Her chest tightening, she said, "You know, I've been worried that this case might push you over the edge in terms of alcohol."

"Yeah, I know. Every time I pour a drink you get this nervous look." He sighed. "And not without reason. There's a part of me that'd like to get drunk and stay drunk till it's over. Sleepwalk through the whole thing like a character out of a Southern gothic." He placed a reassuring hand on her thigh. "But there's some other part that won't let me, which probably surprises me even more than it does you."

She folded back a corner of the sheet, making it into a small triangle. "You mean you really aren't gonna turn alcoholic on me?"

"When this is over I intend to stay out of bars and get back to my two-drinks-before-bedtime routine."

That's what they all say.

Yeah, but Zach's been able to get himself straight before.

Letting out a long breath, she asked, "So what's this part that's keeping you from drinking yourself into zombiedom?" *The part that cares about me, doesn't want to let me down.*

"Actually, I've given that some thought. The obvious answer is that I need my wits about me. But I think there's something else I hate to admit even to myself."

"Which is?" She peered into his bronze-skinned face. He looked like his old self again, easygoing and unflappable.

"Growing up in the Lawrence household as the outsider—the kid who was always in trouble—I figured that since I had a different last name, I'd be immune to all that boring shit about standing tall and doing the right thing. But here I am, in one of the worst messes I've ever faced, and it's almost like I've been possessed by the spirit of some ancient Lawrence ancestor. It feels like it's simply not an option to fuck up the way I've been known to do in the past." He glanced at her furrowed brow. "I thought you'd be pleased to hear I'm not planning to get myself in trouble with booze."

She grimaced in embarrassment. "I was hoping you'd say it's because of me."

He stroked her hair. "Well, that too."

❦ ❦ ❦

They were nearly ready to turn off the light when Zach said, "Oh shit, we forgot Starshine's pill."

Cassidy groaned.

"Look, there's no need for you to get up. I can handle it on my own."

She briefly felt the old urge to fight against his doing things for her, then let it go and sank back down on the pillow. It felt good to have Zach take over sometimes, and he was usually more than willing to do it.

She heard Emily's pity-laden voice: *I think you better come get him.* But this time Cassidy felt no humiliation. Instead, her mouth curved in a small, gloating smile. She was the real winner, not Emily. *We'll get through this and we'll be fine.*

21. Farmer's Market

Cassidy was awakened the next morning by the phone, followed by Emily's voice from the answering machine. "I checked my log and the boss definitely was in the squadroom from sometime before six until around ten-thirty. I have it down in my notes—Sunday night we conferred on cases from nine-thirty until ten-thirty. I can't imagine Steve Frasier battering a woman, anyway. He's too much of a funda-mentalist when it comes to doing the right thing."

Yeah, but isn't it sometimes the most oppressively self-righteous parents who beat their kids in the interest of straightening them out?

Emily's voice continued, "Oh, and I was also able to pry one piece of information out of Area Four. The murder weapon was smudged, not wiped clean."

In the car on the way to the meeting with the FBI agent, Zach said, "I see the unwiped bottle as significant. No matter how drunk or angry Frasier might've been, I can't imagine him leaving without wiping the bottle. 'Course if he was in the station, that eliminates him anyway. It's possible Wiess or Corbin might've gotten that rattled, but I wouldn't bet on it. Now Domingo—he'd club her and run without a second thought."

Cassidy stared out the side window at a row of handmade crosses hanging on a fence along Augusta Boulevard in the heart of the Austin neighborhood, the crosses representing people who had died in street shootings. "I hate to say it, but I can see Bryce running as well." She shook her head. "No, wait. It can't be Bryce. He'd never've had sex with his mother." She pictured the photo of Xandra dancing with her son, then shook her head again. "No, I don't think there was any incest. He's certainly got problems, but not to the degree he'd have if she'd seduced him."

Zach's face turned grim. "Even though I'll come up negative on the DNA test, the police could still say she'd screwed somebody else before I arrived. Unfortunately, we could say the same about Bryce."

❦ ❦ ❦

Even on a Saturday, the Einstein Bagels on Wacker was swarming with business types. Cassidy, who'd thrown on clothes and left the house before she was quite awake, realized once again how ill equipped she was to mingle with the hordes of people who stormed corporate bastilles on a daily basis. In a washed out T-shirt and jeans, she looked more like she belonged on lower Wacker, the underground route that provided winter quarters for the homeless, than on the upper deck. She definitely did not match up to the image of a hotshot investigator ready to take on the FBI.

Yawning, she wondered how all these people who had real jobs, as opposed to vanishing clients, got themselves going every day at what seemed to her prime sleeping time. The morning was cool and gray, but she didn't know if the gunmetal feel and look to the air meant that the heat was receding, or if this was the early a.m. norm and the high temperatures simply hadn't started yet.

The clatter of voices, the gurgle of the expresso machine, the banging and scraping of chairs nearly drowned out the monotonous aerobic beat of piped-in music. Fresh bagel and coffee smells wafted around her, making her lust after a latté. Coffee was good at any hour but her stomach balked at solid food before the sun had risen substantially above the horizon.

Backing up against the wall to avoid the crush, she scanned for their fed. At least half a dozen guys were physically fit, crew-cutted, dark-suited, and ate alone.

"Him," Zach said, nodding toward a man in his early fifties who sat at a corner table and was scanning also.

Moving diagonally across the room, Zach said, "Montez?"

He gave a minimal nod, and they slid into black wooden chairs, Zach next to the fed, Cassidy at the opposite end of the two-by-three foot table. The empty paper plate, half finished coffee and scattered bagel bits indicated he'd been there awhile. He had dark brown eyes, light brown skin, and an expressionless face with tight lines around the mouth and eyes. Directing his gaze at Zach, he asked, "Who's she?"

"Cassidy McCabe. We're working this story together."

Glancing around, Cassidy noted that the bagel shop was a jumble of signage, placards hanging from the ceiling and cluttering the walls, a hodgepodge of different styles and colors that lent a junkyard look to the room.

Montez appeared skeptical. "ID?"

Zach laid his press pass on the green and gold formica table.

"You said your name was Whitmore."

"I lied. But this is on background so it doesn't matter. I'm investigating the Palomar murder and my source says you availed yourself of her services back when she was a call girl."

He stared stonily at Zach for three beats, then moved his eyes slightly to the right. "You're the guy who found the body, aren't you? So I'd have to guess you're a suspect yourself, which makes me wonder why you're questioning me."

"A little investigation of my own. Now tell me about your connection to Xandra so I don't have to go to the police with this information I have." A slim girl wearing a baseball cap moved through the crowd, a spray bottle and rag in hand, whisking off tables as soon as they emptied.

Montez looked straight at Zach a second time in what was almost, but not quite, a staredown.

Whoever blinks first loses, a manic voice chattered in Cassidy's head.

The agent said, "Yes, I availed myself of her services. Are we done now?"

"Did you beat her up on January ninth?"

"I didn't get physical in January or any other time. Why do you ask?"

"January was when she landed in the hospital. She told friends that a john who'd seen her in the past had moved back to town and was demanding personal service. When she refused, he punched her out. One of her friends put your name to the story."

"Wrong name. Wrong guy."

"So when did you avail yourself? You see her in January?"

Montez's eyes moved to the window. Following his gaze, Cassidy noticed umbrellas popping out. *Rain. First in two weeks.* The agent looked at Zach, then Cassidy. "You both guarantee total secrecy?"

They nodded.

Montez said, "Yeah, I saw her in January. And yeah, I left Chicago back in eighty-three. The first time I got transferred here was nearly twenty years ago. I was new in town, lonely, and I got ... very comfortable with Xandra. They transferred me again, I got married, forgot about her." He took out a pack of Marlboros, lit one, exhaled smoke from the corner of his mouth, aiming away from his tablemates. "Last fall the wife divorced me and I decided to return to Chicago. Try to recreate history."

Picking up a bagel crumb, Cassidy ground it to powder between her thumb and middle finger. "Xandra wouldn't see you?"

"What's the name of that Thomas Wolfe novel? *You Can't Go Home Again*? I never read the book but I always thought it was a great title."

Zach folded his arms on the table. "She said no and you knocked her around a little."

Montez's rigid lips relaxed slightly in a fractional smile. "I didn't knock her around. I didn't batter her. I didn't touch her. I don't need to beat women up to have sex."

His eyes locked on Zach's, then moved away. "I was frustrated and I told her so. Then I left and didn't go back. The date was January seventh, not the ninth." He looked at his watch. "Your fifteen minutes are up." He rose and walked away.

Cassidy watched his ramrod figure disappear. "You know, as much as I find his tight-assed, stiff-backed, unbending version of machismo offensive, I have to admit I believe him. He's just too arrogant to lie."

"Unfortunately, I agree."

"Unfortunately?" Her brow furrowed. "Wouldn't it be worse if we thought he was lying but we'd promised secrecy and couldn't use anything he told us? What, in fact, do you do if you go on background and the guy says he did it?"

"Circle around and get him from some other direction."

When they arrived at the house, Cassidy called her mother to say she would pick her up shortly for their Farmer's Market junket at Pilgrim Church.

Pilgrim was a heavy stone structure that hunkered solidly on the corner of Scoville and Lake. Unlike the heaven-reaching, gothic spires of First United, Pilgrim's Romanesque bulk was firmly planted on the ground. Cassidy thought that a church building like Pilgrim's would offer security, sanctuary, an earth-mother acceptance of the human condition with all its failings, as opposed to the gothic structure's more heavenly oriented disowning of what *is* in favor of constant striving for what can never be.

Aren't you being a little two-faced? Isn't it the constant striving that affords you an income?

Cassidy and Helen stood in line to buy fresh donuts and coffee. Helen muttered about the length of the line, which extended from the donut table on the east side of the church to the corner of the building and on into the alley in back.

Stop escaping into ivory towers. Your task here is to be nice to your mother. Get your therapist part in gear so you can listen calmly when she whines about Zach.

Someone opened a door into the church where the donuts were cooked and a sweet, cinnamony cloud blew over them. Coming around the building's corner, Cassidy looked down to see orange donut rings painted on the blacktop, the rings marking the path to the table where volunteers sold donuts to raise money for an Oak Park agency devoted to serving HIV sufferers. Farther on, a circle of musicians—guitarists, tin whistlers, banjo players—conducted a singalong.

They purchased their aromatic delicacies, then sat at a nearby card table. Talking around a mouthful of donut, Helen said, "I just don't want you making the same mistake I did."

"Okay, I'll make a different one." Cassidy tried to listen to the music but her mother's plaintive voice drowned it out.

"When Roland was giving me a such hard time, you helped me understand what was going on. After you explained things, it was a lot easier for me to give up on him."

"Glad it helped." *Way I remember it, you were truly pissed when I tried to warn you. Pissed, outraged, incensed, ticked off and generally out of sorts. Got up and left when I broached the possibility of a problem.* Squinting against the blaze of sunlight that had followed the early morning shower, Cassidy surveyed the crowd: young mothers, families, teens, elderly couples. No one in a hurry. Everybody friendly, happy to stop and chat.

Hardly any blacks. We try so hard to be integrated, but nonwhites seldom include themselves. Well, would you wanna be one of the few white faces in a dark-skinned group?

As they strolled toward the fruit and vegetable stands in the church parking lot, Helen said, "Remember when you were planning to marry Kevin and I didn't think he was all that trustworthy? But you insisted he was true blue, as honest as they come? Well, how can you be sure you're not doing the same thing now?"

Cassidy's lips tightened. *Like a heat-seeking missile, she never fails to zero in on my exact point of greatest vulnerability—my lousy track record with men. If I could be so totally and insanely wrong about Kev, how can I ever trust any male-related instinct again?*

Steering her mother toward a table loaded with greenery, she said, "Let's get some flowers to brighten up your apartment."

At the cheese stand, Cassidy inspected a white chunk flecked with green herbs. The sausage-shaped woman behind the table said, "Well, hello there, Helen. How you doing these days?"

As they turned to leave, Cassidy saw a tall, handsome woman in her sixties sailing toward them like a cruise ship. *Oh shit. Mildred.* She felt an urge to flee but Zach's mother had already spotted them, and dignity required that Cassidy neither run nor show her belly.

Taking her mother's arm, she moved directly into the other woman's path. "Good morning, Mildred." Feeling Helen stiffen, Cassidy realized that this encounter might prove less difficult for her than for her mother, who'd gone to high school with Mildred and felt forever intimidated by her.

"Well," Mildred said, chuckling softly, "if it isn't the little therapist person who's living with that scapegrace son of mine—the one I haven't heard from in the past two years. Although, given his present notoriety, I'd rather have him hanging around your front porch than mine."

"I'll tell him you send your love," Cassidy said sweetly.

A self-satisfied smirk appeared on Mildred's aristocratic face. She tucked a silver strand that had fallen loose from her French roll back in place. "I can't help but wonder when he's going to show up at my door with his hand out again. Criminal attorneys are so expensive, you know." She shook her head. "Too bad that little tart survived their initial encounter. If he'd done the job properly the first time, we'd all be spared the humiliation of an illegitimate child and a nasty murder case."

"Things just never go the way you want, do they?"

Mildred bent her head closer to Cassidy's. "I suppose you believed him when he said somebody else put her in the hospital."

"And I suppose you didn't."

"Do you honestly think he would've admitted it if he had?" Mildred raised her head, smiled malignantly, and swept on.

Cassidy gritted her teeth and swallowed the word that wanted to jump out. Glancing at Helen, she saw that her mother's body was hunched and shrunken, her face looking the way Cassidy imagined it might if she'd been run over by a six-wheeler and lived to tell about it. "Mom? You okay?"

"It's all right," Helen muttered. She gave herself a little shake and made an effort to stand straighter. "I always used to envy that woman. Her life seemed so perfect, and mine was always so plain." She lowered her forehead, her whole face wrinkling up. "But now I see she's even worse off than I am." She turned to stare at Cassidy, a sadness coming into her eyes. "Isn't anybody happy?"

"I think maybe Zach is. And I am a lot of the time." She smiled. "We like being together, you know."

"Oh." Helen turned her head to the side, then looked back at her daughter. "Well, I'm glad it seems to be working, but I still think you should be careful."

🍎 🍎 🍎

Cassidy went into the bedroom and sat at her desk, Zach rotating his chair to face her. He held an envelope in his hand.

"The report," she said, anxiety sputtering through her. "My professional sentence—handed down by the social work ethics committee."

He removed a letter from the envelope. "I read it so I could forewarn you. It's not that bad. All you have to do is consult an ethics specialist on a monthly basis. When you've done your time—eighteen months to be exact—he'll submit a report. If he pronounces you rehabilitated, it'll all be over."

She got a sinking feeling. "Well, I guess I can do that."

Zach's heavy brows drew together. "You're gonna hate it."

Lifting her heels to the edge of her chair, she pulled her knees up tight and wrapped her arms around them. "Whenever anybody tries to show me the error of my ways, it brings out this part that wants to argue and prove I'm right. I'll really have to work at showing the proper humility and remorse."

"You sorry you did it?"

"You mean, if I had it to do over, would I keep my ethical virginity? As far as that first incident goes—the time I accidentally blabbed after a grueling session—I'd definitely keep my mouth shut. That was a mistake, pure and simple. But the second violation, the time I decided that ignoring a murder was worse than giving up confidential information—I still can't get past the feeling that going after the Satanists was the right thing to do."

Zach reached over and patted her knee. "Since I'm the one who talked you into it, I certainly agree. Something there is about both of us that doesn't like other people's rules."

Shaking her head, she said, "I can never quite accept an absolutist approach to things. But if I buck the system, I've gotta be prepared to pay for it. Heretics have never been suffered kindly."

❦ ❦ ❦

At five o'clock Saturday evening Cassidy's desk phone rang. "This is Luther Corbin. I'm over at Illinois Masonic." His deep voice had gone hoarse. She sensed he was making an effort to keep himself under control.

Feeling shivery, she said, "Tiffany?"

"She's gone. OD'ed. We lost her a couple of hours ago."

Shit. Why didn't you follow her to the bathroom, stand outside the door, drag her back to the living room and sit on her. "I'm so sorry. This should never have happened."

"Goddamn right it shouldn't." Cassidy heard him take a long, indrawn breath. "She was still conscious when they brought her in. Told us she'd been getting these messages. Some cowardly fucker making anonymous calls. Calling and telling her she'd be better off dead, she was on her way to killing herself, she oughtta just do it and get it over with. I think he actually brainwashed her into wanting to die."

"Oh shit. The guy she told me about." She drew an evil-looking cartoon face on an unopened managed care envelope.

"You knew about this?"

Tell him about the key? What good would it do? "Only that somebody'd threatened her."

"This connected with that bitch madam's murder?"

"I don't know any more than you do." *God, you lie a lot. But why burden him with questions that don't have answers?*

"The goddamn phone calls had her going crazy. Pushed her over the edge. She just kept upping the coke to keep from being scared . . ." There was a long pause filled with the sound of his rough breathing. He sighed. "At least that's what I'd like to believe. I'd like to blame it all on some anonymous creep." His voice went lower. "But I can't stop thinking she never would've been out there all alone, drugging and hooking, if I'd been as concerned with my family as I was with promoting myself."

"You'll never know whether or not her life would've gone differently." *The downside of feeling so damn powerful. If you think you have control, if you think you can fix everything and then it doesn't get fixed, it has to be all your fault.*

"I try to tell myself she might've gotten in trouble anyway. But I just keep thinking—if only I'd cut her a little slack, if only I'd," he choked slightly, "if only I'd told her I loved her . . . These damn if-only's keep playing in my head."

Zach, coming into the bedroom, sat in his chair and listened.

Swallowing against the thickness in her throat, Cassidy asked, "How are you and your wife doing?"

"Brenda's been crying since we first got the call. I'm still mostly numb. We've known for a long time that this could happen." He paused, then said in a shaky voice, "There's almost a sense of relief."

She pictured the morning-after Tiffany. "Having something like this hanging over your head . . . It's almost worse than having it happen."

"Since you tried to get her into treatment, I thought you should know. She said she loved her mother and me but she just couldn't be the person we wanted her to be. God, I wish I could do it over. Anyway, she also wanted Bryce to know that she loved him and she's sorry for what she did."

Cassidy's stomach twisted at the thought of Bryce. "We'll tell him." She heard Tiffany's voice saying *They'll hurt me.* "There isn't any chance the anonymous caller helped her along with the overdose, is there?"

"Only by pushing her into it. He wasn't there when it happened. She was mixing all kinds of drugs. Her system just collapsed."

Cassidy closed her eyes briefly, then repeated. "I'm so sorry."

"There's one other thing." He cleared his throat. "After you made that effort with her, I decided to see what I could do in return. I know one of the guys over at Area Four. He told me the witness was the driver—Lenny something or other."

Lenny—of course. Drivers sit in their cars and wait. He's the only one who'd have a legitimate excuse to be watching her house.

22. Coming in Bunches

Cassidy replaced the phone, then turned to meet Zach's eyes. "The witness is Lenny—the only one who wouldn't talk to us."

"We finally got a break. Now all we have to do is find out who put him up to it." He tilted his head slightly. "Unless, of course, Lenny whacked her himself." He paused. "I'd like to take off this minute, go push him up against a wall and make him talk. But right now Bryce has to come first."

She couldn't think about the case, not with Tiffany just now dead. Her throat was clogged, her eyes moist. She stood and gazed out the window at two kids wresting on a bright green lawn across Hazel. Dropping back into her chair, she said, "Nothing makes sense. Corbin beat Wiess in a construction dispute and Tiffany's dead. And now we have to tell Bryce."

"Monday it was his mother. Today—not even a week later—it's his girlfriend. I don't know how he's gonna get through all this." Zach began flipping through his notepad.

"I better be the one to talk to him. We can't do it on the phone. We have to get him back here."

Zach placed the notepad on the desk in front of her, his finger marking the number, and she dialed.

Bryce said, "What's wrong?"

"This is something we have to talk about in person. Where are you?"

"The townhouse. Tell me now."

"Not till you get home."

Cassidy and Zach waited silently on the porch. She ate half a bag of peanut butter cups. He sat as still as stone. The light was just beginning to fade, and Cassidy thought it strange that it was still so early. *It oughtta be late. This day's been going on forever. We're all trapped in some kind of time distortion, doomed to stay right here in the present, living out the day Tiffany died till we get old and our own lives end as well.*

Bryce parked the Miata and joined them on the porch. "Well?" he said in an angry voice as he flopped into a molded plastic chair across from the couch.

Cassidy took a deep breath. "Were you with Tiffany today?"

Sitting straight, he asked tonelessly, "What happened to her?"

"She overdosed. They got her into the hospital, and she lived long enough to tell her father that she's sorry and she loves you, but . . ." *Mention the phone calls? Probably make him feel worse. Like he should've protected her.*

"Oh shit, oh damn, oh fuck." He bolted to his feet and hurled himself from one end of the porch to the other, half tripping over the clutter. He covered the porch's length twice, then dropped heavily into his chair and glared at Cassidy. "Why wouldn't she go in the hospital? If she'd done what you told her, she'd be okay and I wouldn't have to go through this."

"She couldn't. She just couldn't quit." Cassidy's eyes filled again.

Bryce covered his face, his shoulders heaving as he sobbed into his hands. Zach watched closely but didn't say anything.

The boy cried a long time, then dropped his hands, wiped his arm across his face, and said in an exhausted voice, "It was my fault." He looked at Zach. "I said I wouldn't abandon her, but I did. When I got to her place, she was pitching a fit. She kept riding me 'cause I refused to do coke with her. She just wouldn't shut up, so after an hour I left." A shudder ran through his body. Cassidy noted that his face was faded and bleary like a TV image that's gradually disappearing. "I knew she wasn't to blame. I knew it was the coke talking, not her. So if I knew she couldn't help it, I should've been able to stay with her."

He rose, turned his back, slammed a fist against the window frame. "Why didn't I stay?"

Coming up beside him, Cassidy laid an arm across his shoulders. "We're all to blame."

He sighed deeply and sat down again. "I don't know what to do."

Zach shifted on the couch. "Here's what we're gonna do for tonight. We'll pick up a pizza, make popcorn, get some videos. We'll move the

TV into our bedroom, then we'll all clump together and watch movies and eat greasy food on the waterbed. You can even rent something stupid like *Bimbo Babe's Beachparty* if you want."

❧   ❧   ❧

The phone rang. Cassidy's eyes opened halfway. She gazed into darkness, feeling disoriented and headachy. Zach, sitting on the side of the bed, picked up his line. "Moran here." The brightly lit 4:00 on the bureau clock stared down at her. Pulling a pillow over her head, she tried to weave Zach's voice into the dream that lingered just beneath her consciousness. She heard him say, "Hey, Emily. That's great. You really came through."

She removed the pillow, forced her eyes open and sat up. Pushing tangled curls off her forehead, she said, "What is it?"

"The cops identified the owner of the kidnapper's car. Ray Jojo Silursky, brother to Lenny." He looked away, then moved his gaze back to her face. "They just found Jojo's body. Executed."

"Somebody else died? How come everybody's dying?" She was not really awake; she was just pretending. *Deep down inside your real self is asleep. It's only this outer layer that's faking it.*

Standing, Zach picked up his jeans from a pile on the floor. "I better get to Lenny's right away. The cops'll be all over him."

"No!" Now she was awake. "You think you can get there before the police do? And if you did, that he'd invite you in for a four a.m. chat? You show up at his place now, the cops'll find out about Emily leaking information and you'll both be in trouble. Besides, why's it so important to break the case first?"

Rhetorical question. You wanna beat out that supercilious Hathaway every bit as much as he does.

Not enough to go ringing doorbells at four a.m.

"You've got a point." Dropping his jeans, Zach sat back down. "I suppose what oughtta be important is making sure they don't arrest me. Which is probably a nonissue anyway, now that they've got their hands on a dead kidnapper brother-to-the-driver." He paused. "However, I don't for a minute believe those bullshit words that just came out of my mouth and neither do you. If they find the killer first, I'm gonna be seriously pissed."

❧   ❧   ❧

At seven-thirty Sunday morning Cassidy struggled out of bed, put on shorts and a tee, and went down to the kitchen where Zach handed her the purple cat mug with just the right amount of cream and sugar. Gratefully wrapping her hands around it, she took her first swallow. *Coffee, the light of my life. Better even than chocolate. I didn't have coffee, I'd go around in a perpetual fog.*

Zach stuffed the last bite of cold pizza in his mouth. "Even though the cops probably have Lenny in custody, I'm gonna take a shot at running him down. But I was thinking it might be better if you stayed home with Bryce."

Lowering her chin, she glowered from under her brow. *How did I get put in charge of his kid. If Zach finds Lenny, I wanna hear what he has to say.* "Oh, I'm sure it'll be all right for us to leave Bryce alone a little while."

You just wanna go with Zach. You're not thinking about Bryce at all. A how-can-you-be-so-selfish feeling stabbed her. *Kid's been here less than a week—you're already experiencing mother-guilt.* She stared through her window into her neighbor's kitchen where a throng of kids jostled for breakfast and no one wondered why deaths were coming in bunches.

She said, "Why don't we wake Bryce up and ask him?"

❦ ❦ ❦

Pulling himself up from the sleeping bag, the boy looked even fuzzier than Cassidy had felt at four a.m. A sheet covered most of his jockey shorts and legs, the top half of the sleeping bag thrown off to the side. As Cassidy came into the room, Starshine ducked into the folds of the bag, her whole self hidden except for the ringed tail sticking out in back.

"Zach and I were thinking of driving down to talk to Lenny, but we didn't want to leave without checking on you first."

He yawned broadly. "Don't worry. I'm not gonna off myself or run away. I won't even clean out all the liquor in the house."

As he sat with his back against the wall, Cassidy marveled at how young and unfinished he looked, his naked torso not yet filled out. Her heart ached for him. Smiling weakly, she said, "What you're *not* gonna do is kill yourself or drink. So what will you be doing instead?"

He rubbed his eyes with the heels of his hands, then pulled his palms down his face, distorting his features. "Pet Starshine and feel like shit the rest of my life."

"I know right now you think it'll go on forever. It won't—it'll just seem like it." She sighed, thinking of the double whammy he'd sustained. "The kidnapper was Jojo. The cops found his body last night."

"Aw shit!" He appeared to be angry, but she'd learned by now that anger was the emotion he used to cover everything else. "Why would Jojo try to snatch me? I've never even met the guy." He shook his head. "This whole deal is so confusing. But you know Lenny's my friend, don't you? He'd never do anything to hurt me."

"The police'll be looking for Lenny. If he wanted to stay out of reach, where would he go?"

Bryce cocked his head and thought about it. "He might go to the townhouse. You know, he's got that room in back."

"Can I borrow your key?"

🍒   🍒   🍒

The grass in front of Xandra's townhouse was turning yellow but the weeds were doing fine. "Human beings have such an urge to make things difficult." Cassidy passed through the wrought-iron gate Zach had opened for her. "Here we plant grass, which is hard to keep alive and requires constant attention—cutting, watering, fertilizing—and we try to get rid of weeds, which is basically impossible. It should be just the opposite."

Zach unlocked the front door and they went inside. Cassidy caught a whiff of fried bacon. *Either is here or was here not long ago.* The fluffy white living room was pristine, the blood stains barely visible after the cleaning. *Xandra's whipped cream palace. Bryce here yesterday, but the place looks untouched. As opposed to his room in Oak Park, which nobody could miss as a teen habitation. Obviously trained by his mother to leave no sign of his existence in his own home.*

Anger at Xandra boiled up in her. *People who don't have time for kids, send them off to boarding school, make them come and go like fucking ghosts—people like that oughtta have their parent-licenses revoked.*

Moving quietly, they walked through the gleaming, marble-tiled kitchen, the remains of a meal strewn across a white, Corian counter, and into a short hall at the rear. Zach opened a door leading into a bedroom. With its smell of cigarettes and its shabby-comfortable furniture, the room emanated Lenny's presence as surely as if his name was written on the threadbare rug that lay on the polished cherrywood floor.

The small space contained a twin bed, a large television, an easy chair, a floor lamp, and a bureau. The lamp was on. Half a dozen garments were hanging in the closet. Zach started going though pockets. Cassidy discovered a wadded sheet of paper in a glass ashtray stuffed with coins, matchbooks and a crumpled cigarette pack. Scrawled across the paper was a telephone number.

"Look at this." She handed it to Zach, who headed straight for the phone that sat on one end of the kitchen counter.

He dialed, listened a moment, then hung up. "Luther Corbin's secretary."

"You know," she said, leaning one shoulder against the refrigerator, "the problem with this whole damn case is that we're overloaded with information and none of it fits together. Why would Lenny's brother try to kidnap Bryce? Does the kidnap attempt mean that Lenny's the killer? Why would Lenny call Corbin?"

"Lenny's obviously the key, and by now Hathaway's probably got him in the box." Zach's forehead creased in a deep frown. "Shit! The big mistake I made was letting him off yesterday. I should've tracked him down and pounded on him till I dragged out everything he knows."

"You don't pound on people. You walk away, remember?"

"Yeah, I know." He smiled. "But there's a certain satisfaction in thinking about it." He pulled the list of names and addresses Bryce had given them from his pocket. "Well, let's get on over to Lenny's apartment. There's not much chance he'll be there but we've gotta check it out."

🍎   🍎   🍎

Zach pulled into a small parking area in front of Lenny's expensive, Fullerton Parkway building. Cassidy, who'd pictured him in a dump, gazed in surprise at the sleek highrise. "How does a driver afford a lake-view apartment?"

"Obviously got a sideline. I'd guess he brings the girls their drugs."

"So he might've been the one feeding Tiffany her coke?" She pictured the driver putting his hand on Bryce's shoulder. "I know I'm being naive, but how could somebody like Lenny—a guy who actually seemed a decent sort—do that to her?"

"You're being naive." Zach's attention was focused on the building's entrance. "We're gonna get past the doorman by hitchhiking with a tenant. When I see somebody headed toward the entrance, we're gonna jump out of the car and intercept him about five yards in front of the door."

Ten minutes later Zach said, "That guy there," nodding at a paunchy, middle-aged man in running shorts.

Zach fell into place beside him and Cassidy followed a step behind. "Hi guy," Zach said. "How's it going?"

Pausing, Paunchy looked at Zach in confusion. "Uh . . . sorry, I can't remember where we met."

"Chatted in the elevator a couple weeks ago."

Most of the time you absolutely believe he doesn't lie to you. Then you hear him ad lib so smoothly and the doubts creep in again.

"Oh, right." The man still looked uncertain.

"Get in a good run today?" Zach asked as they passed through the glass entrance and turned toward a gate to their left.

"Not bad. My knee's acting up, though. The doc says it's okay to jog but I'm not totally convinced." The doorman buzzed the gate open and they went through it. Paunchy pressed the elevator button on the other side.

Putting his hands in his pockets, Zach commented, "Personally, I'm against exercise. Half the people I know've wrecked their bodies doing it." They boarded the elevator and Zach punched ten. "Me, I prefer to sit in front of the television with my pizza and beer."

The elevator stopped at five. Raising his hand in a parting gesture, Paunchy stepped off. At the tenth floor Cassidy and Zach exited into a short hallway. One door at the hall's south end stood ajar. Following the apartment numbers, Cassidy quickly realized that the unit with the open door was 1010, the address Bryce had given them.

Zach whispered, "Somebody's there ahead of us. Probably cops."

As they moved closer, Cassidy could hear Hathaway's voice emanating from the open door. *Of course Miss Perfect got here first. How could we possibly compete with an automaton who never needs to sleep?*

The senior detective said, "I knew we should've gotten here sooner."

Cassidy and Zach stopped to listen.

Torres responded, "What good would it've done? The driver was already gone when that dick who caught the brother's murder came by here at two."

A short silence. "I don't know why we're knocking ourselves out over a dead madam, anyway."

"To keep my clearance rate high." A pause. "Lenny's car is still in parking, there's no body in the trunk, and he's emptied out his closet. That means he's probably gone into hiding."

Torres said, "Too bad it's looking like the reporter didn't do it. I would've enjoyed throwing his ass in the slam."

"Because of all the dirty cop stories he's written?"

"On general principals. I don't like any media scum. They sit in their ivory towers and pick everybody else apart."

Hathaway said, "I can pick people apart with the best of 'em and you never seem to mind."

Torres chuckled, his voice loaded with sexual suggestiveness. "You see that fancy bedroom? Wouldn't you like to find out if it's better on satin sheets?"

Well, what do you know. You should've figured this one out sooner.

"Lay off, Torres," Hathaway said, her tone not matching the words. "We're on the job."

"So let's take a break."

The voices grew indistinct as the detectives moved deeper into the apartment.

Zach whispered in her ear, "You wanna stay and see if she's a screamer or give it up and go home?"

Cassidy flushed. *You would like to listen to her scream, wouldn't you? You suddenly turn voyeuristic? Or you just wanna get one-up on her for a change?*

She said, "Let's go."

23. Fairy Princess

In the car Cassidy remarked, "Hearing that conversation makes it easier to understand why Hathaway takes such a condescending attitude toward me."

"She does?"

Cassidy's forehead furrowed. "You didn't notice?"

"I was too preoccupied with warding off her attacks on me." He glanced at her. "So why does she have it in for you?"

"It's the pot calling the kettle black. Like the guy who's overweight and is the first to point the finger at anybody who's fatter than he is. By looking down on everybody who's in worse shape, he can convince himself he doesn't have a problem." A zippy little white sports car with a young male at the wheel zoomed past the Nissan, zigzagged from lane to lane, and disappeared into the distance. She hoped he had good insurance.

Zach frowned. "What's that got to do with Hathaway?"

"She's involved with a man who's got a bit of the street in him, who's basically a cocky little punk. Some part of her has to feel embarrassed about sleeping with this guy who's obviously beneath her. But she can tell herself that what I'm doing is so much worse, her little indiscretion hardly counts."

"Well, that makes sense," he said in his laconic voice. "If she's convinced that I'm a batterer or a murderer, and here you are still with me, you obviously can't have any self-respect."

As they sped south on Lake Shore Drive, Cassidy gazed out her side window at a broad strip of green parkway, highrises crowding up against its western edge. She turned back toward Zach. "Hathaway always looks at me as though I was a traitor to the sisterhood. Like one of those women who're lower than the lowlife males they cling to because they're siding with the enemy. Like a Nazi collaborator."

"Refusing to throw out an abusive jerk is not quite on a par with siding with Nazis."

She pictured the runty Torres and the ice queen Hathaway getting all hot and sweaty on red satin sheets. "Well, anyway, after eavesdropping on Hathaway and Torres at play, I can see why my staying with you pushed buttons for her."

"Why do you care?"

"Because I'm not so indifferent to the opinions of others as you are. Because I prefer approval to disapproval." Looking out toward the lake, she gazed at knife-edged sun rays reflecting off thousands of small wavelets, the dazzle as clear and cold as Hathaway's gray eyes. She suddenly felt lighter, not so burdened by the senior detective's contempt. "You know, when this is over I think I'll invite Hathaway to lunch." She envisioned herself sitting across from the sleekly appareled cop saying, "So, how is Torres in bed?"

They drove silently for a while, then she said, "What's next?"

"I think I'll go home and take a nap." His eyes looked flat and tired. "I'm all out of suspects, ideas and energy." He shook his head. "The police have the resources to hunt Lenny down. We don't. I hate to admit it, but it looks like the cops are gonna win."

Damn. I wanna make Hathaway look bad, stomp her into the ground. I want gloating rights.

Zach put his hand on her knee. "Let's go back to Oak Park and pill a cat."

🍎   🍎   🍎

They came in the back door and headed toward the stairs in front. On her way through the dining room, Cassidy spotted Bryce sprawled out asleep on the couch, his shoes, a pop bottle and a dish coated with soggy cereal on the floor beside him. *His mother, Tiffany, his home, his whole life. How'll he ever get through all this without being destroyed by it?*

They slipped noiselessly through the living room and up the stairs. From the hallway above she peered into Bryce's room and saw Starshine playing on the floor.

Continuing on into the bedroom, Cassidy said, "Let's skip the morning pill. I'm in withdrawal from cuddling. I want to see if I can coax Starshine into a petting session before we make her hate us again."

"Okay by me." Zach sat at his desk to tackle the week's accumulation of mail.

Sidling up to Bryce's doorjamb, Cassidy poked her head around it. The calico glanced up, then went on with her game. A bent corner of paper was sticking up from under the air mattress and Starshine was using it as the object of her hunt. She circled, pounced, withdrew to the corner, stalked and pretended to ignore it. As Cassidy crept into the room, Starshine stared with wild, dark eyes, then scuttled into the closet.

Punishing you. You force pills on her, she'll make you feel rejected and unloved. How does a cat know psychology so well?

Her gaze fell on the corner of paper. Pulling it out, she stared at a lined page containing a list of handwritten names and addresses. One edge was jagged, indicating the page had been torn out of a book. *Oh shit! Xandra's planner.* Anxiety snapped her nerves tight. *It was Bryce who planted it in our room for the cops to find.* Lifting the mattress, she uncovered a small pile of similar pages.

She went into the bedroom, plunked into her chair, and handed them to Zach. "Look what I found."

Zach leafed through the pages, his brow heavily ridged.

She pictured Bryce the way he'd looked the night of the police search, slouched in front of the television, a fourth beer in his hand. Taking a deep breath, she said, "This doesn't mean he did it. It could be he was just trying to get even with you."

Zach's eyes met hers. "You wouldn't've said that if you weren't thinking there's a good chance he did."

She spent a moment calming herself, then closed her eyes and thought hard. *Doted on his mother. Also must've had a ton of resentment. Strong mix of love and hate, lots of ambivalence.* She considered how gentle he was with Starshine, the same gentleness the cat brought out in Zach. She shook her head. "I don't think so. My intuition says he wouldn't do it."

"Your intuition's been pretty much on target before. Let's hope it stays that way."

They took the remains of the planner downstairs and settled in the armchairs. Bryce sat up and rubbed his eyes. They waited until he appeared somewhat alert, then Zach said, "We found these pages in your room."

Blinking, Bryce said in a belligerent voice, "Yeah, okay." He turned his head sharply away. "I did it. You nailed me." Standing, he started toward the stairs.

"Get over here and sit down," Zach demanded.

Bryce stood like a statue, shoulders defiantly squared.

"I said, sit down."

The boy returned to the sofa and sat low on his spine, glowering up from under his brow. "What're you gonna do? Turn me in to the cops?"

Zach folded his hands on his chest. "We'll make that decision after we find out why you did it."

Bryce shrugged.

Amazing. Tougher Zach gets, the more I want to let the kid off. Have to bite my tongue not to yell at Zach for being so hard on him. Here I am, practically an expert on triangles, getting sucked into this one. Crossing her legs, she locked her hands around one knee. "We need you to tell us why."

He twisted his head to look out the window behind the sofa. They waited. Turning to face them, he pulled himself straighter and gazed at the floor. "I don't know. I was in my room when the doorbell rang. After you went to answer it," he glanced at Cassidy, "I tiptoed part way down, stood just above the landing, and listened. I heard that loud cop say he was gonna search the house. The idea just came to me and I did it." His voice subsided into a mutter. "I was sorta buzzed so maybe that's why."

The living room was humid and airless. Sweat dampened the skin beneath her breasts. Cassidy remarked, "From what you said that night, it was obvious you wanted to see Zach charged with the murder."

Bryce shrugged.

"You still want that now?"

He slid back down on his spine, legs apart, knees jutting high in the air. His chest rose, then fell in a heavy sigh. "I don't know."

Cassidy tilted her head. "Why so eager to see Zach arrested?"

He stared at the ceiling for several beats, then sat up straight, bringing his eyes back to hers. "You wanna know? All right, I'll tell you." His face went dark and angry. One heel tapped out a staccato rhythm on the floor. "Because he almost killed my mother when she was pregnant, and his big bucks family bought off the law. He practically beat her to death, for Chrissake, and he never spent a night in jail. So I figure, even if he isn't guilty this time, he's got it coming. They bust him now, it evens the score."

Zach, his face remote, said nothing.

Cassidy felt hopelessness set in. *Xandra's got him so brainwashed, I don't know if we'll ever break through.* "You once told me I didn't know the whole story. What's the part I don't know?"

"The reason he did it." He banged his heel harder. "I bet he never told you he beat her up 'cause he wanted me dead."

She gritted her teeth. *Talk about hate-mongering. His mother, on a mission to instill disgust and loathing. And what a first-rate, A-plus, top-of-the-line job she did of it, too.*

"I'd like to hear all of it."

Bryce's dark eyes bored into hers. "Xandra told him she was pregnant. He ordered her to get rid of it but she refused. He said he'd never get another cent out of his family if they discovered he'd given them a hooker's baby as a grandchild. When he couldn't talk her into the abortion, he said he'd take care of it himself." He looked directly at Zach. "First you tried to kill me by beating on her, then you lied by saying you didn't know she was pregnant."

Starshine came downstairs and curled herself in Bryce's lap without so much as a glance in Cassidy's direction.

Zach shifted in his chair. "What makes you so certain your mother's version is true?"

"Why would she make up something like that?"

"Why do you think?"

"There isn't any reason." Bryce sounded a little less confident.

"Did your mother ever lie about other things?"

Bryce shrugged.

"She has lied to you, hasn't she?"

"Maybe."

"Have I ever told you anything that wasn't true?"

"You said you didn't know about me."

Zach leaned forward, forearms resting on his knees. "Bryce, what I did back then was really stupid and there've been plenty of times I wished I could undo it, but it was nothing like what your mother said. I was one of her playthings, and after three months she dumped me. She did not tell me she was pregnant. I went panting after her, trying to get her to tell me what was wrong, and after a couple of weeks she let me back into her place. We got high together and had sex, then she proceeded to dump me again. At that point I did something I've regretted ever since. I pushed her around. Maybe I even hit her. But when I left, her face was not bloody and her arm was not broken. Somebody else did that. The day I got rough with her was the last time I ever saw her alive, and I walked out of there not knowing about you."

Zach looked out the window, then back at Bryce. "I wish there was some way I could prove it, but obviously I can't. So that means you're stuck with having to choose between your mother's story and mine."

"Shit!" Bryce turned his face away again. "Why're you doing this to me? I don't need this."

Cassidy said, her voice gentle, "You're afraid to believe she lied about this, aren't you? You've always had her on a pedestal. All your life she's been your fairy princess. And now you're scared—if you accept that she lied about Zach—everything else you've always believed about her will come crashing down, too."

He covered his face with his hands.

"You've already lost her. Now you're afraid of losing your image of her as a princess."

"Will you just leave me alone?"

Zach stood. "We'll wait upstairs. You take whatever time you need, but you've got some more explaining to do before we're finished with this."

❦ ❦ ❦

An hour later Cassidy heard footsteps on the stairs. The light in the room was diffuse, the sun still too high for any rays to come slanting through the west window. She was sitting on the bed, a book in her hands, her mind unable to focus on anything other than Zach, Bryce, and the difficulties between them.

Above the hum of the air conditioner she heard a light tap at the closed door. Zach looked up from the bills on the desk in front of him and said, "Come in."

Bryce, face pale, eyes moist, shut the door behind him and leaned against it. "What else?"

Zach swiveled to face him. "How did you get the planner and why tear out the pages?"

"I was just going out the door to come here when Mom said, 'Wait. There's something else you have to take.' From the way she said it, it seemed like some new idea had just hit her. Well, then she just held it out . . ." He gazed into middle space.

Last time he saw her. "Bryce . . ."

He looked up.

"You don't have to go back there. Try to step away from the memory and just recap what happened."

"Oh." His shoulders jerked as he returned to the present. "Well, she just handed over the planner." He shook his head. "When she did that, I had this weird feeling that something bad was about to happen. She never let that book out of her sight. Never. It had all the names of her johns in it, plus everybody else she knew. She always said if the wrong person got hold of it, it could cause a lot of trouble."

Zach remarked, "Yeah, I'll bet it could."

Bryce scuffed his toe on the carpet. "I guess that's why she wanted me to have it. So the person she was afraid of wouldn't steal it. Anyway, she told me to guard it closely and not let anybody know I had it, and to especially make sure nobody got their hands on the section with names and addresses."

Zach's eyes narrowed. "So if you were supposed to guard it, why plant it for the police to find? And why tear out those pages?"

"She was dead. She didn't have any use for it. But since it always meant so much to her to keep the names of the johns secret, I had to take that part out." He looked at Zach, apparently thinking he was done.

"Go on."

"I put the book under your mattress, then I took those loose pages and slipped out of the house. I thought I'd just toss them in the river. But they were so important to Mom—they were almost like a part of her—I just couldn't do it."

Zach said, "So what do you think you oughtta do now?"

"Is there something I should do?"

"The police think I took the planner."

"Oh." A long pause. His eyes got scared. "What'll they do to me if I tell 'em?"

"Give you a lecture."

"Okay, I can do that."

Kid's not half bad. Much as I hate to admit it, Xandra must've done something right.

You don't have to admit that. Just call it good genes. From his Lawrence ancestry. Kind of genes that're keeping Zach in line. You don't have to give her any credit at all.

Bryce looked from one to the other. "You finished now?"

He went into his room and turned on the television.

Zach caught her eyes. "You have any idea whether he believes me or not?"

"I'd like to think so. But a big part of him probably feels that believing you means betraying her. Accepting that his fairy-princess mother deliberately poisoned his mind against his father might be too much for him." She shrugged helplessly. "I can't call this one. My psychic powers've crashed."

❦ ❦ ❦

Searching through all the pages, they found a number of well-known names such as Wiess', but nothing that advanced the investigation.

Zach dropped the pile on his desk. "Once this case breaks and I'm back to being a real reporter, I'm going after Wiess. Of all the slimy maneuvering I've ever come across, turning a teenaged girl into a hooker is the worst. If Nikki's willing to talk to me as a confidential source, I can do a story. How's this for a lead? SHOULD CHICAGO TAXPAYERS ENTRUST FIDUCIARY RESPONSIBILITY TO AN ALDERMAN WHO DEFAULTS ON HIS CALL GIRL BILL? A piece like that should shake up his marriage, if not the notoriously cynical Chicago electorate. He got such a kick out of reading about me, let's see how he likes it when the tables're turned."

Cassidy smiled inwardly. *Wouldn't it be great if what goes around really did come around? Some kind of natural justice so bad guys truly got theirs in the end? This has, of course, nothing to do with the real world. Just wishful, simpleton-type thinking.*

But wouldn't it be great?

24. Stupid Risks and Lost Causes

When the phone rang at seven that evening, Cassidy and Zach were both on the bed, the Sunday paper spread around them. She picked up at her desk.

"Is this the Moran residence?" A woman's voice, frail, a little shaky.

"Are you calling for Zach Moran?"

"No, actually, it's Bryce Palomar I'm trying to reach."

"Let me get him for you."

She brought Bryce in and handed him the phone. He said, his voice brightening, "Oh, hi, Ellie. How you doing?" They chatted for several minutes, then Bryce wrote down directions and hung up. "That's my old nanny. The one who sent the card. She wants me to come over."

Cassidy asked, "Tonight?"

"Yeah, I'm going right now."

Zach's forehead creased. "How'd she get the number? That line's listed under Cassidy's name."

"I don't know." He shrugged and left the room, his voice trailing off as he went downstairs. "I don't even know why she sent the card here."

Card's no mystery. Zach put our address in the obit. But she couldn't get my phone number from that.

Zach finished the news section, then removed all the papers from the bed. Pulling her closer, he ran his forefinger down the side of her cheek and across her lips. "Remember the excuse you gave for going off on your own—that you didn't want to miss an opportunity? Well, I don't like to miss opportunities either."

❦ ❦ ❦

They were enveloped in a long, warm, wet kiss when the phone rang again. They'd never allowed telephones to interrupt their lovemaking in the past, but this time Zach moved his mouth away from hers and said, "Could be Bryce. I better get it."

Can't imagine I ever wanted to be a parent.

Zach grabbed the receiver just before the machine cut in. After listening for several beats, he said, "Christ, he picked Bryce up right in front of your house?"

Cassidy started collecting her shorts, shirt and underwear off the floor.

"Yeah, I know who he is. I'm gonna go to his place right now and see if he's got Bryce there. Give me your number." He wrote it down and hung up.

Pulling on his jeans, he said, "Bryce was just leaving the nanny's when a big guy with a slight limp slammed him up against the Miata, cuffed him and forced him into a green sedan."

"Omigod—Frasier. How could a homicide commander just grab a defenseless kid off the street?" She shook her head. "Rhetorical question. Even I know about Chicago police corruption." Tying her tennis shoes, she asked, "You think he took Bryce to his house?" She pictured the small bungalow with its pitched roof and three birdhouses in the front yard.

"I'm hoping that's where they went. If they didn't . . . "

If they didn't, we won't be able to find him. If they didn't, Bryce'll be dead. "Even though Frasier is a police honcho, couldn't you call Emily or Hathaway and have them get over there right now? It's almost an hour's drive from here."

He gave her an are-you-nuts? look. "You think they'd ring a commander's doorbell and say, 'Listen, sir, I'm sorry to bother you, but did you just snatch a kid off the street?' All we've got is my story based on an old lady's description. Let me tell you, this is one time I don't wanna go charging in all by myself, but there's no other way."

Pulling herself up straight, she said, "You won't be all by yourself."

He stopped dressing and tried to stare her down. "Don't even think about it."

"I'm not staying home. You try to leave without me, I'll follow. If there's any chance at all of saving Bryce, it's gonna take two of us."

"It's too dangerous. If all three of us get killed, there won't be anybody to report what happened. Your job is to wait by the phone, and if you don't hear from me in about an hour and a half, call my editor," he jotted down the number, "and have him get in touch with the superintendent of police."

This is no time for single-handed heroics. Besides, Zach didn't mind having you turn up in time to save his ass last fall, even if you are only a "girl."

Her voice firm, she said, "I won't be left behind just because I'm a woman."

He made one more attempt to stare her down, then said, "All right."

"I suppose I'll pay for this later?" She spoke through teeth clenched in anger at the idea that she'd be punished for doing what she knew was best.

"You can count on it."

He may pack his bags yet.

As they buckled their seatbelts, Zach said, "Shit. I should've gotten a gun."

"I thought you had one."

"Since guns are illegal in Oak Park, the police took it away. But considering what would've happened to us if I hadn't had it, they decided not to press charges."

"Why didn't you get another one?" *Better yet, one for each of us.*

He turned east on Augusta Boulevard. "I was gonna. I almost did. I'm a procrastinator, remember? This may be the time procrastination really costs me." Zach squeaked through a light just as it turned red and sped around a bus, narrowly missing a van.

Clamping her mouth shut, she ordered herself not to issue a single warning about traffic tickets or accidents. *You've pushed far enough. Not one inch more. You can't change his driving, anyway.*

"So Steve Frasier killed Xandra." She shook her head. "Except Emily said he was in the station until ten-thirty."

"Must've hired it out." A pause. "And, I'd have to guess, Steve also administered those two beatings. You came up with a theory earlier that made a lot of sense. That he punched her out to make her quit drugs, then got her to press charges against me 'cause he thought I was the supplier." He hunched forward, both hands tight around the wheel.

"That last time I saw her—Steve must've come in after I left. He'd ordered her to stay away from drugs and from me, and she'd misbehaved on both counts. He could see she had a couple of bruises, so he decided to capitalize on what I'd started."

Cassidy nodded. "Not an out-of-control, crime-of-passion beating, but a parental-enforcer beating. He probably figured he was doing her a favor. And maybe he was, considering he got her to adopt his antidrug attitude." Her mouth tilted in an ironic smile. "The tough love approach."

Zach turned north on Humboldt Drive, the street that curved through the large green square that was Humboldt Park. He said, "But that first beating was irrelevant. It was the one in January that set off this whole chain of events."

"Steve tried to straighten her out again, only this time she didn't fall into line.

"She wasn't the same person nearly eighteen years later, any more than I am."

You wondered what would happen when the urchin-turned-beauty-queen got tired of feeling grateful. What happened is, she fought back. And then she got killed.

Cassidy gazed off to her left at an idyllic looking lagoon with brown-skinned children swimming in it. "So then Xandra reestablished contact with you so she'd have a safe place to send Bryce."

Zach stopped behind a double-parked Chevy, its yellow lights flashing. Waiting for a minuscule break in traffic, he pushed the nose of his car into the small space and zoomed into the left-hand lane. "She needed a person outside Steve's reach. Since she was dealing with a police commander, she had to find somebody he couldn't intimidate. So, even though she'd programmed the kid to stay away from me, I was basically the only person she could send him to. It was perfect on two counts. I was both his father, which gave me legal rights, and a reporter, which made me exempt from the kind of pressure Steve could put on a lot of other people."

She did have some motherly instincts after all.

Damn, and I wanted to make her into a cartoon villain, a seductress with no redeeming value.

❦   ❦   ❦

When they reached Frasier's block, Zach drove slowly past the small bungalow. The green sedan was parked in the driveway. Lights were blazing on both the first and second floors, with the large window in front shielded by miniblinds. *They've gotta be there.* Cassidy breathed a sigh of relief.

Zach parked in the alley behind the house. The sun was down but daylight had not yet started to fade. He removed a tire iron from the trunk, then led her through a rear gate. In front of them stood the backs of both Frasier's house and his detached side garage, as well as the backs of the houses on either side.

As they crossed the yard and entered the narrow passageway between house and garage, Cassidy visualized the interior layout. The rear half of the house contained two bedrooms with a bath in the middle. The front half was made up of the kitchen on the left, the living room on the right. They stopped at the bottom of a small stoop, the side entrance leading from the back of the kitchen to the garage.

She regarded the glowing windows warily. *Much rather break into a house that looks empty than one that looks like a party's going on.* Zach scrambled up the steps and peered in the window. "Nobody in the kitchen," he whispered.

"I'm gonna circle the house and look in as many windows as possible."

While he was gone she sat on the bottom step, scrunching herself into the smallest possible space in the hope of becoming invisible. *You've got it all wrong. You should make yourself conspicuous as hell. You get really lucky, a neighbor'll see you breaking in and call nine-one-one.*

Zach returned to stand on the side porch, Cassidy hovering beside him. "I got a look in all the windows except the living room, so that means he's either there or upstairs." He tried the doorknob, which didn't turn, then lifted the tire iron. "I'll take a stab at jimmying the door, but the odds of a Chicago cop not having a deadbolt are practically nil."

When prying failed, he tapped the tire iron sharply against the window. She froze at the clink of iron hitting glass, the clatter of falling pieces. Her heart hammered. *Definitely won't have the element of surprise, along with everything else we don't have . . . firepower, legal authority, any possible means of overpowering the cop. Talk about stupid risks and lost causes.*

Zach enlarged the hole by pulling away loose fragments, then reached inside and unlocked the door. The kitchen, as cluttered as before, was L-shaped. They picked their way through broken glass and crossed to the short leg of the L, which led into the living room. Zach paused. Cassidy listened intently but could hear nothing. The house, all lit up with no human noise, seemed eerie. *Like stepping into a nightmare.*

Zach slid quickly around the L with Cassidy behind him. The living room was empty. *Upstairs then.* In front of them a short hall connected the living room with the bedrooms and bath. In the hallway a door stuck straight out from the right wall. Following Zach into the hall, Cassidy noted that the doors of the other three rooms were open also. On the other side of the door that jutted into the hall, they faced a flight of stairs leading upward. The second story light, which had been on when they approached the house, was now off.

Grabbing Zach's arm, she whispered, "We can't go up there. Steve's gonna be waiting for us at the top."

Zach leaned in toward her ear. "Right. You high-tail it out of here and call my editor."

"Why not 911 from your cell phone?"

"Won't work. The responding officers'd never force their way in."

"Why don't *you* go call your editor. He's more likely to listen to you anyway."

Zach shook his head. "I have to get up there. There's no way of knowing how long he's gonna let Bryce stay alive."

There's no way of knowing if Bryce is alive now. Could be sacrificing our own lives for nothing.

"You go wait in the car, and if I don't come out, then you'll have a legitimate crime to report." Gripping her shoulders tightly, he turned her toward the door.

You can go up with Zach and maybe you both get killed. Or you can let him to do it alone, and he almost for sure gets killed.

You might die. But the two of you working together also might be able to take Frasier.

She removed his hands from her shoulders and turned to face him.

"I'm going with you."

"Shit." Despair came into his eyes. "Don't you get it? I love you. I can't stand the thought of taking you into a situation where you're probably gonna get killed."

"You think I could stand letting you get killed without me?" She rubbed her cheek against his arm. "Tell you what. I'll play dependent female and let you go first."

He sighed and started upward.

The old wooden steps were noisy. Cassidy groped her way upward in the murky light, her left hand against the wall, fingers brushing a sandpapery plaster surface. As her head emerged above the attic floorboards, she strained to see into the darkness. The top of the stairs faced the south wall, which rose two yards ahead of them. Zach turned around and started walking alongside the stairwell opening toward the opposite wall at the far end of the narrow room. Cassidy, coming behind him, still could not see Frasier or Bryce. The air was hot and stuffy, so smoke-filled her breathing turned raspy.

A light bulb at the other end of the room suddenly flashed on. Blinking, Cassidy stepped forward to stand beside Zach. They were facing Frasier, who had positioned himself near the north wall, about twenty-five feet in front of them.

The cop sat behind an old wooden dining room table, a gun in his hand. She was surprised to note that the face beneath the thick, dark hair seemed pleased, as if he were happy to see them.

Bryce was hunched in a chair pulled a couple of yards away from the table, his head twisted backward to observe their arrival. "Aw shit," he muttered by way of greeting.

Frasier, his voice jovial, said, "Hey Zach, come on over and join the party. But dump the tire iron first." He shook his head. "A tire iron, for God's sake. What a pathetic excuse for a weapon."

He pointed the gun at Zach, who laid the tire iron on one of the many boxes lining both sides of the room.

As Cassidy and Zach moved forward, the cop said, "This time I have to admit—I *am* surprised to see you show up here. How'd you find out, anyway?"

"You obviously underestimated me."

"You shouldn't have brought your lady friend. That was a mistake."

Lady friend, girlfriend, tagalong. An addendum. Of no consequence.

Frasier gestured toward two chairs drawn up to the table. Cassidy and Zach moved them backward, lining them up with Bryce's, then sat down, Cassidy in the middle. She noticed that the boy's wrists were cuffed in front of him.

Zach said, "I tried to get her to stay home but she wouldn't listen."

I heard. I just didn't obey.

"That's the trouble with women—they never listen. Here we are, two old friends in a situation where one of us is gonna die, and all because of a woman who wouldn't listen."

Zach folded his arms across his chest. "Why're we sitting on these hard chairs when there's comfortable furniture in the living room?"

"Just to be on the safe side. Nobody can get behind me when I'm up here." Frasier rested his bulky forearms on the table's scarred surface, the gun held loosely in his right hand.

Although Cassidy'd had some experience with firearms, all she could tell about this weapon was that it looked larger and more deadly than any gun she'd ever used. Newspapers, ashtrays and styrofoam cups were scattered across the worn rosewood table, mirroring what she'd seen in the kitchen. In front of Frasier sat a tape recorder and off to the side a coffeemaker, the carafe half full, its cord trailing off to an outlet in the wall.

Frasier said, "You got a piece?"

"No, of course not." Zach sounded offended. "Owning's illegal in Oak Park and carrying's illegal everywhere, so of course I wouldn't have a gun."

Looking at Zach's snug jeans and tee-shirt, Frasier said, "If I thought there was any place you could hide one, I'd have you strip. But it looks to me like you couldn't conceal a thimble in that wreck of an outfit you're wearing. Why you wanna go around looking like a bum, anyway?" His gaze shifted to Cassidy.

Thank God for my tucked-in shirt and shorts. And the reason he dresses down is, it used to make his mother mad and now it's just a habit.

"What're you going to do to us?" Cassidy wasn't sure she wanted to hear the answer, but she did want to interject herself into the dialogue between these two males who were focused so exclusively on each other.

"Well, now, I'm not sure." Frasier transferred the gun to his left hand, lit a cigarette with his right, and blew out a stream of smoke. "I'll have to think up a new plan."

"Won't it be hard to explain three bodies?" she persisted.

He chuckled. "I won't have to explain anything. Nobody's gonna associate your sad demise with me." Setting the cigarette in an ashtray, he rubbed his jaw. "How's this for a scenario? We make it a murder-suicide. Everybody already figures Zach clubbed Xandra in the heat of passion. When they find your bodies, they'll assume the stress of having killed his lover pushed him over the edge. Not bad, huh?"

Zach said, "Speaking of our Madam X, what'd she have on you, anyway?"

Frasier held up an audiotape in one large paw.

"You got it already?"

"It was tucked away in a post office box. After I grabbed the kid, I took the key off him, locked him in the trunk, and picked it up. Simple as pie. Problem solved."

Cassidy looked at Bryce. His eyelids drooped, his mouth turned down in what she saw as an attempt at defiance, but the fear beneath it leaked through. She said, "You claimed not to know about any key."

"I didn't until tonight. Ellie had it. She told me the whole deal when I got to her house." Bryce raised his cuffed wrists and wiped a forearm across his brow.

"That was smart," Zach said. "I have to give your mother credit. Who'd've guessed she'd give it to a woman with MS who's been out of the picture for years?"

Bryce said, "Actually, it makes perfect sense. Ellie was Xandra's neighbor when she was a kid. She took care of Mom all the time, kind of a second mother. Xandra trusted her more than anybody."

Zach said to Frasier, "What made you think Bryce could deliver the key? He obviously didn't know anything about it before now."

Frasier snorted. "Nah, he's just blowing smoke." He smirked at Zach. "Doesn't wanna admit he knew about it all along. That's the only reason Xandra'd make him go stay with you, Zach, after doing her damndest all this time to keep him away. She sent Bryce to you 'cause she had the dumb idea you could keep me off him, stop me from using him to get the key."

Shaking his head, Zach said, "She sent him to me 'cause she was afraid you'd try to control her by threatening Bryce. She figured he'd only be with me a couple of days and you wouldn't be able to find him."

"That's ridiculous." Frasier looked pained. "I'd never threaten a kid."

Talk about self deception. This guy's a rescuer-turned-persecutor who hasn't gotten around to adjusting his self-image yet. He wouldn't threaten a kid—just kill him. She said to Bryce, "Why'd Ellie have the key?"

"Okay, the way it went was, about the end of January Mom put two identical tapes in two different boxes. So there were these two keys. The first one she handed off to her attorney. He was supposed to take the tape to the feds if anything happened to her. The second went to Ellie as backup. That's how Ellie knew your number. Mom gave it to her along with the key."

"And the reason Xandra gave her *my* number is that Zach's number's unlisted." Cassidy sat with her hands in her lap, her left thumb rubbing her forefinger in small, circular movements.

Bryce continued as if she hadn't spoken. "Ellie's too sick to do anything now, but when Xandra first came up with her plan, she thought the attorney'd handle it and Ellie wouldn't have to get involved. Xandra figured if that jagoff cop," he glared at Frasier, "hurt her, the feds'd get the tape. That'd be the end of it."

Zach said, "What went wrong?"

Bryce drew his brows down even farther. "The jagoff cop got to her attorney and scared him off. Two days before Mom died, the attorney called and said he'd destroyed the tape without listening to it. So then Mom went straight to Ellie to warn her that the total responsibility for getting the tape to the right people was on her."

Cassidy commented, "Tough job for somebody who's sick and probably pretty frightened as well."

"Well, yeah, she was scared shitless. But she's the kind of person who'd never let you down. She'd've taken it right in to the FBI if she'd been able to get out. But she's been stuck in a wheelchair for over a year, and now on top of that she's started having these dizzy spells. She was hoping the dizziness'd clear up like it did before, but it just kept getting worse. So she finally decided to give me the key, even though she felt real bad about not following through." Bryce rested his arms on his legs, letting his hands dangle between them.

Frasier added, "And fortunately, I've had somebody on Bryce's tail since he first turned up at your house. Jojo was handling it till he got himself killed, then I took over. I figured sooner or later the kid'd connect up with somebody Xandra was close to, and then I'd know who had it. When I saw him go in the nanny's house, I knew I'd hit paydirt. So then, when he came out, I took the key off him. And if he hadn't had it, I'd've gotten it off the old lady."

"It was just dumb luck. Here you were operating on the wrong assumption that the kid knew where it was, and you still got the key."

His voice taking on a conspiratorial tone, Frasier continued. "Remember how it used to be, Zach, before you got so domesticated? You'd prowl the bars for hours till you found some wannabe model looking for a guy to take her home? Well, that's how I felt when I scored tonight."

"I never did that. You're thinking of somebody else." Zach shifted in his chair. "And Jojo, of course, was working for you. First you had him burglarize the townhouse looking for the key. Then you had him try to snatch the kid. He also must've been the one calling Tiffany. Why'd you have him do that, anyway?"

"Jojo was a moron. He should never've asked that cokehead to try to worm information out of the kid. I knew she'd end up blabbing and I didn't particularly want another murder that could be connected with Xandra's. So I just told him to keep at her till she took care of the problem herself. Anybody that messed up was bound to crack under a little applied pressure."

Cassidy glanced at Bryce, whose face was drawn into a dark scowl.

Frasier continued, "And as far as the kidnapping goes, that was Jojo's brilliant idea. I don't claim credit for that fool's screw-ups."

"Yeah," Zach leaned forward, hands outspread on his legs, "the kidnapping was a real farce. Jojo got himself identified so then you had to get rid of him."

Steve's thick brows drew together. "Too bad he was such a dumb fuck. I hate having to resort to violence. Goes against everything I stand for. But sometimes people don't give you any choice."

"Xandra didn't give you any choice?" Cassidy's back teeth clenched. "What'd she do that was so bad you had to kill her?"

Frasier replied in a low, deadly voice, "I didn't kill her. Zach did."

25. Women Never Listen

Zach? No, it couldn't be.

But why would Steve be lying now? She glanced at Zach, whose face remained as blank-screened as ever.

" 'Bout eleven-fifteen I came through the back door into the kitchen." Frasier looked directly at Zach. "The lights in that part of the house were off so you couldn't see me. I heard noises in her office and got up close enough to watch you going through her drawers. Your back was turned—you never knew I was there."

She looked at Bryce to see how he was reacting. He'd dropped his head and she couldn't make out his face.

"The blood wasn't fresh so I knew she'd been dead awhile. Since the two of you had evidently shared a bottle of champagne, I figure you'd fucked her, then gotten into a fight. What was it this time? She throw your ass out again?" His humorous eyes narrowed. "You know, I'm glad you showed up tonight. I'm gonna enjoy paying you back. What a dumb shit, thinking you could bash my girl's head in and I wouldn't get you for it." He chuckled softly. "So anyway, figuring the whole scenario had to have started four or five hours earlier, I decided to have you seen entering the premises at six-thirty." He ground his cigarette into the ashtray with more force than necessary.

That's what he'd like to do to Zach. Grind him into the ground.

Zach, his voice as low and dangerous as Frasier's, said, "You could've arrested me on the spot. But then you'd've had to explain what *you* were doing there. So you paid your gopher Lenny to take care of it."

"Good thing you got that scar." Frasier's weathered face broke into a jubilant smile. "All I had to do was make a sketch and he couldn't miss you."

Cassidy cocked her head. "If you thought Zach did it, why tell us about the burglary?"

Steve shrugged his huge shoulders. "Why not? You'd've found out anyway. Besides, I like to be helpful. I'm a friendly kind of guy—except, of course, when it comes to lowlife fuckers. I don't go around killing people because I *like* it." He looked at his watch.

"So, if you didn't kill her," Cassidy said, trying to make sense of it, "why so worried about the tape?"

Bryce turned his head in her direction. " 'Cause Mom had it set up so the tape'd go to the feds no matter who killed her. And this jagoff here knew about the back-up key. The only thing he didn't know was who had it."

Zach said, "Aren't you gonna play the tape for us?"

"Why should I?"

"We're old friends, remember? You said so yourself."

"As long as we've got a little time to kill." He inserted the tape into the machine.

The tape began with a woman's voice. "My name is Xandra Palomar. This tape was made January thirtieth. The two voices you'll hear are mine and Detective Commander Steve Frasier's. Frasier was unaware that the conversation was being recorded."

Xandra: "A couple weeks ago you told me you killed that guy in your department, remember?"

Frasier: "Yeah, Johnson. So what?"

Xandra: "I think you made the whole story up."

Frasier: (A chuckle) "That's a dumb thing to say."

Xandra: "To scare me. Keep me in my place."

Frasier: (Voice soft and deadly) "I got other ways to do that."

Xandra: "Back when I was pregnant, you put me in the hospital and I caved. Then, three weeks ago, I said I was moving to Florida and you did it again. But that's the last time it'll ever happen and I think you know it. Right now I've got a bodyguard sitting in the kitchen, and if I start yelling, he'll get between us even if you do have a badge. So, since you can't control me with your fists anymore, I think you lied about killing that cop. Because you know that from now on, the only way you can stop me from leaving is to kill me. And besides, you've always been such a law-and-order type, I can't see you pulling the trigger on one of your own."

Would he shoot me if I got up, walked over to the table? Police're trained not to gun down unarmed civilians.

Shot that cop. A wave of fear washed over her.

Cop was armed. Plus it was premeditated. I start moving toward him and he isn't expecting it, maybe his training'll kick in. He's the kind that'd have a harder time shooting a woman than a man.

Frasier: "Look, I told you, he didn't give me any choice. The moron was running his own burglary ring, for Chrissakes. I couldn't let him go on dishonoring the badge. And if I'd turned him in, there'd've been another big stink about police corruption. We don't need that, what with civilians already thinking we're a bunch of scum. This was the only way. Besides, he was asking for it."

Xandra: "You mean, like I was asking for that beating?"

Frasier: "You got it. How many times've I told you, you can't make it out there on your own. You need me now, just like you always have. Who do you think keeps the law off you? Who do you come crying to whenever there's a crisis? What we got going here is just fine. You give me what I want—no questions, no demands—I take care of you. You'd be nuts to give that up."

Xandra: "Oh, right, this situation we got here is just terrific. You keep your good ol' boy cops away from me and all I gotta do in return is pay your snitch's salary—this creep I can't get rid of no matter what he does—and make an occasional trip to the hospital."

Frasier: "C'mon, babe. You're blowing this way out of—"

Xandra: "Don't 'babe' me. I've been wanting out for years. Now that Bryce's refused to go back to boarding school, I can't put it off any longer. If I don't get that kid outta here, he's gonna start screwing the girls—if he isn't doing it already, that is. Once he heads down that path, it's only a matter of time till he turns up with AIDS. I can't put my own kid's life at risk just to keep you happy."

Cassidy's hands were cold, her mouth dry. *Too hard. Can't do it. Can't just get up, walk into a gun barrel.*

You don't do something, Zach'll jump him soon as he tries to take us outta here. And Frasier's primed to shoot Zach the first chance he gets. Dying to do it. Can't wait to put holes in him.

Her legs stiff, she stood and took a jerky step toward the table.

Punching off the recorder, Steve gave her a smile that made it obvious he considered her no threat at all. "Oh, and where do you think you're going?"

She took another step. "I need some coffee," she said, her voice raspy.

"Coffee? Who said you could have coffee?" He pointed the gun at her.

He's gonna shoot. He really is. He's gonna do it. She halted, her knees nearly buckling. Swallowing the lump in her throat, she said, "It's just that . . . I'm so scared. If I could please just have some coffee, it would . . . I could . . ."

"Cass," she heard Zach's voice, almost a whisper, behind her, "don't do it."

She picked up the carafe. Coughing, she swallowed again. "Could you please . . ." her tone terrified, begging, "Could you please tell me which of those cups," she coughed, "is the cleanest?"

His eyes dropped momentarily to the clutter in front of him. Pulling her arm back, she slammed the carafe into the left side of his face. A gasp came from Bryce. Frasier fired, the blast deafening. A stinging sensation sliced across the outside of her left arm near the shoulder. *Oh shit, oh shit.* Clutching the wound with her right hand, she felt a hot, oozing abrasion. The heavy table slammed into Frasier's chest, knocking him to the floor. Zach, lunging out of his chair, had pushed it into him.

Zach went racing around the left end of the table, Cassidy around the right, the two converging on Frasier from opposite directions as he rolled to his side and aimed at Zach. Just before he fired, Cassidy kicked him in the small of the back. The bullet missed. Zach dropped to his knees, got both hands around Frasier's gun hand, and forced the barrel away from his chest.

Immobilized, Cassidy squeezed her wounded arm and watched the struggle on the floor. Frasier, taller and heavier, was gradually moving the barrel back toward Zach's body. *No! Can't let him.* She grabbed two fistfuls of hair and yanked.

"Shit!" Frasier yelped as Zach pulled the gun out of his hand.

Got it! Thank God he's got it.

Zach stepped away and trained the gun on Frasier, the big cop lumbering quickly to his feet. He stood facing Zach at a distance of two yards, knees slightly bent, arms bowed at the sides, looking ready to leap straight into the line of fire.

"You gonna shoot me, Zach?"

"Yep." Zach fired, the bullet whizzing past Frasier's arm.

"Well, shit." Frasier moved backward, his limp causing him to stumble. "I never figured you to be so violent. I thought busting up chicks was more your style."

"Put the handcuff key on the table, then step away from it."

"What'll you do if I don't?"

"Blow a hole in you."

"Jesus, you don't give a guy any choice, do you?" His voice still carried an undertone of amusement, as if he knew this was just a diversion and everything would go his way in the end.

Should be scared. Feel better if he were scared.

Frasier put the key on the table and Cassidy took the cuffs off Bryce.

Zach said, "Lock his hands behind him."

Cassidy approached Frasier from the rear. The cop stood with his arms at his sides, refusing to move them into position. Zach fired into the ceiling directly above the cop, causing chunks of plaster to rain on their heads. Frasier thrust his hands behind him. Cassidy cuffed his wrists and stuck the key in her shorts pocket.

"Okay," Zach said. "We're outta here. Steve, you first."

They filed downstairs, Frasier, Zach, Bryce and Cassidy. As she stepped out of the stairwell, her gaze swept the short hall. At the end, a few feet to the rear of the stairs, the bathroom door was partly closed. *Thought all the rooms were open.* With Bryce about a yard ahead, she started toward the front of the house.

She heard a movement behind her. Twisting her head, she glimpsed a trim, gray-haired man just emerging from the bathroom. *Lenny?* His left arm shot around her waist, yanking her backward up against him. She felt a cold metal circle lightly touch her right temple.

The three males turned also. Zach's face got suddenly tense. Bryce gaped in surprise. Frasier started to move toward Cassidy, but Zach, standing behind him, jerked him back into place.

Frasier carped, "Well, it took you long enough."

"Leave her alone, Lenny," the boy demanded.

The driver said in an apologetic tone, "Sorry, kid, I gotta do what he says." He looked at Frasier. "I got here a few minutes ago, boss. Heard the shots, thought I better see what was going down before I made any moves."

Frasier gets his gun back, we're done for. She took the handcuff key out of her pocket and threw it as far as she could. Zach nodded his approval.

"Shit!" An angry flush rose in Frasier's cheeks. "Punch her out for me, will you, Len?"

Well, good. I've ceased to amuse him.

The driver said, "Bryce, you take that gun away from Moran and hand it to me, butt first."

Bryce hesitated but Zach handed over the firearm and said, "Do it."

Feeling Lenny's hands move behind her, she assumed he'd shoved the second gun into his waistband. She sensed him shift from one foot to the other and realized he was waiting for Frasier to tell him what to do next.

The cop turned to grin at Zach. "You go get that key or Lenny blows away your girlfriend."

Cop's the killer, not Lenny. "No, don't! They have to kill us anyway. Make 'em do it right here in the detective commander's hallway."

Zach put his hands on his hips. "I agree. If you're gonna do it, do it here."

Bryce stepped up close to the driver. "Jesus, Lenny, why're you doing this? You took me to my first ballgame. Are you really gonna pull that trigger and just shoot me down when your jerk boss tells you too?"

A long silence. Frasier, his broad face scowling and ruddy, seemed to puff himself up, growing larger and more menacing as she watched. He said to Lenny in his quiet, deadly way, "Don't you for one friggin' minute forget who's in charge."

"I don't know, boss. We're not really gonna shoot all three of 'em here in the house, are we?"

"If nobody unlocks these cuffs, we goddamn will."

Royal we. Meaning you shoot while I watch and then you probably get put away for it. If only Lenny's sharp enough to see it.

"I'm not so sure about this. I never killed anybody before. You expect me to just whack 'em the way you did Jojo? I don't know."

"All right," Frasier said gruffly. "You get the key, I'll take care of these bozos."

Pushing Cassidy in front of him, Lenny took an awkward step in the direction of the foyer where the key had landed.

"Wait." She braced her body, making his forward motion as difficult as possible. "You put a gun in his hand and he slaughters us, you think he's gonna let the only witness get out alive?"

Lenny halted.

Zach nodded subtly at Bryce, who seemed to be watching his father for cues. The boy said to Lenny, his voice calmer now, "I thought you loved your brother."

"I did."

"Then how come you're letting this jagoff give you orders?"

"He's a police boss. He could murder me the same as he did Jojo and just walk away from it. Or get me locked up for life."

"And don't you forget it."

"You're wrong." Zach jerked Frasier's cuffed wrists, forcing him to bend slightly at the waist. "He can't get outta these cuffs and he can't shoot anybody with 'em on. If we take him in now and all tell our stories, there's no way they're gonna let him off. I work for the *Post*, remember? If I stay alive, I can guarantee the paper'll be watching every move on this case. No matter how much the department—or even some judge— might want to cover it up, anybody who tries'll be throwing his own reputation down the toilet. Regardless of what he may have on you, Lenny, the odds are very high you'd get immunity."

"You know," Lenny said to Frasier, his voice growing stronger, "the guy's got a point. If there was any way I could see you go down for what you did to Jojo and not get dragged down with you, I'd jump on it." Cassidy felt the metal circle move away from her temple. She watched sideways as the tip of the barrel lined up with Frasier's body. Lenny's voice deepened. "You fucker. I never shoulda let you do it. I shoulda known what you were planning and come after you before you ever had a chance to get to him."

Frasier broke loose from Zach's hold, lowered his large head, and came at Lenny like a charging bull. Lenny fired. A rip appeared in the cop's khaki pants, but it didn't slow him down. The top of his head crashed into Cassidy's chest, setting off an explosion of pain and slamming her into Lenny. The driver banged against the wall, then went over backward, pulling Cassidy down with him. Frasier fell also, sprawling out on top of her.

She gasped, crushed beneath the weight of Frasier's bulky frame. The cop landed with his face inches above hers, his fiery brown eyes shooting sparks. The brown-stained teeth were clenched, lips drawn back in a death's-head leer, his expression one of pure determination. *Throw himself into a speeding train before he'd quit.* She felt a tiny spark of admiration.

Rolling the cop's body off hers, Zach straddled his barrel chest. Cassidy struggled to free herself from Lenny, who thrashed beneath her. Zach grabbed the gun out of the startled driver's hand. Pouncing from the other side, Bryce retrieved the second gun from his waistband. Cassidy scrambled to her feet and backed away from Lenny. The driver got himself upright, then sagged against the bathroom doorjamb. Bryce came to stand beside her in the living room, with Zach astride Frasier on the hall floor.

"Bryce, you hold that gun on your friend there while I make sure Steve doesn't attempt his battering ram routine again." Standing, Zach moved a yard back from Frasier. "Okay, you can get up now. You try anything else, I'll put five slugs in your good leg, and this time I guarantee you won't walk again."

Frasier heaved himself onto his stomach, raised onto his knees, and stood, Zach moving behind him to hold onto the cop's cuffed wrists.

"You pussy," Frasier said to the driver.

Lenny scowled at the cop. "This is the first time I ever *wasn't* a pussy. And you know what? It feels goddamn good."

Cassidy stared at the driver. "You said you never killed anyone before. So it was Steve after all? And that whole long story about Zach—that was just some kind of headgame?"

"No," Bryce said. His face had gone pale again. He took a deep breath. "It was my fault, really."

She felt a flutter of panic. *Bryce? Oh God, no.*

"Tiff's the one who actually hit her. But it never would've happened if I hadn't taken off."

"Tiffany?" Cassidy said, feeling an intense wave of relief.

Gazing at the floor, Bryce muttered, "I promised I wouldn't tell." He looked quickly at Zach, then back at the floor. "Shit. I guess there's no way out." He looked at Zach again. "All those years I was so pissed at you for not being around. But there're two people who fucking *died* because *I* wasn't around."

"We never get it all right. You try a lot harder than I did at your age. Hell, you probably try harder than I do now."

Bryce shook his head, dismissing Zach's comment. "Tiff and I had a big fight that morning over drugs. I'd just had enough of it so I took off driving. I didn't get back to the townhouse until four. That's when Xandra told me to pack a duffel and head out to your place." He sighed.

Hearing the self-recrimination in his voice, Cassidy closed her eyes briefly to shut out her sense of his pain, and sighed with him.

"What I did next was really dumb. I should've told Tiff where I was going, but I was still pissed, I wanted her to suffer. So I drove off to your place without checking in or anything. And then, to make it worse, after I left Oak Park I decided to stop at a movie just to drag things out a little longer." He dropped his head, rubbed the back of his neck. "That was so dumb."

"Will you get on with it?" Frasier started to take a step forward but Zach jerked him back.

"Let him tell it his way," Cassidy retorted sharply.

"Okay, okay. So anyway, when it got to be eight and Tiff still hadn't heard from me, she decided we had to have it out. She was high enough at that point to go storming into the townhouse. I'd given her a key, which Mom, of course, didn't know about. So she walked in and found Xandra and that jerk musician in bed, and the jerk got out of there, like right now."

So that's how Domingo knew Zach didn't do it. He was with Xandra at the time Zach was supposed to be coming through the door.

"Tiff started yelling about me running out on her, and then, of course, it all clicked in for Mom." He looked down, scuffed the toe of one sneaker on the floor.

Lenny whistled under his breath. "Boy, I bet the shit hit the fan about then."

"Xandra went off on Tiff like you wouldn't believe. She told her she'd be taking me to Florida in two days and Tiff'd never see me again. And then she said a bunch of other stuff." He shook his head. "Mom shouldn't've said those things. You can't blame Tiff for losing it after what Mom said."

Not too hard to fill in the blanks. And a lot of those blanks have four letters to 'em.

Taking a long breath, Bryce went on. "I guess Mom'd gotten rid of the bodyguard that night 'cause she wanted to be alone with Domingo for their little farewell party. So after she cut loose on Tiffany, she turned to walk away. And Tiff, she just lost it. She hit Mom with the bottle and then ran outta there. She thought Mom was unconscious. She didn't even know she was dead."

He paused to gaze into space, his features twisted in pain. "When Tiff got back to her place, I was waiting for her. She acted like everything was normal, didn't say a word about what'd happened until a few days later. I had no idea she was the one. I really thought it was you." He looked at Zach.

"The first I knew of it was the night Jojo tried to kidnap me. That's the reason I was out so late. Tiff finally told me what she'd done. That's why I gave you that information the next day. Guess I was trying to make up for being so sure it was you."

He's been through so much. And the worst of it is, thinking it's all his fault. "So you should've been Superman and realized that any time you weren't around, something bad'd happen to somebody you care about? Now how're you gonna manage to be everywhere at once so nobody else gets hurt?"

Bryce shot her an angry look, which she took to mean "shut up."

Know how he feels. Hate it myself when I wanna wallow in guilt, and somebody tries to talk me out of it. Kid's decided to blame himself, determined to hang onto it, won't let anybody take it away from him.

Frasier shook his head. "Well, shit. All this trouble 'cause of a fight between a coupla whores."

Zach said to Lenny, "Was Corbin involved somehow?"

"Huh?"

"We found his number in your room at the townhouse."

"Oh that. I was at Tiffany's when she crashed. She was looking real bad, so I called the ambulance, then I called her father."

Cassidy felt Zach's hand on the back of her shoulder. *Letting me know everything's gonna be all right.*

Looking at his watch, he said, "We better call Hathaway and see if she wants the collar enough to book an Area Four commander."

His voice bitter, Frasier said, "If only these bitches had listened, this never would've happened."

"No, Steve," Zach responded. "It happened because you were willing to break every law in the book to make people live according to your rules."

26. Power Struggle

Cassidy, in the body of a five-year-old, sat crying on a chenille bedspread as her father threw clothing into a battered suitcase. The male figure gradually metamorphosed into Zach. Removing a pile of black tee shirts from his drawer, he dumped them in the case, then looked straight at her. "I told you not to go to Frasier's but you wouldn't listen, so now you have to be punished. Women never listen and that's why all those people are dead—your father, Xandra, Tiffany, Bryce, Lenny. All dead because of you."

Guilt washing over her, she cried harder.

The waterbed surged. She opened her eyes to see Zach heading toward the doorway. "Coffee," she mumbled.

He turned to smile. "Soon."

His good-natured smile pulling her out of her bad-dream feelings, she snuggled down for a few more minutes of dozing. A throaty purr rumbled near her nose. Whiskers prickled her cheek.

Saturday. No clients till noon. Didn't all desert me after all. Only three permanently gone.

🐾 🐾 🐾

Half an hour later she sat up in bed with her coffee, fingering the scab on her arm and thinking about her dream. Zach was seated at his desk, the newspaper spread out in front of him. A week had passed since Frasier and Lenny were arrested, and Zach was back in the thick of things at the *Post*.

Picturing him with a suitcase, she asked, "So what's my punishment?"

He looked at her, his expression blank.

"You said you were going to make me pay for it when I insisted on going to Frasier's."

Swiveling to face her, he rested his forearms on his legs "You're right. That isn't finished." His eyes narrowed. "You and I have a real power struggle going on, and I can't help but wonder what it'll do to us in the long run."

Her chest tightened. "Create turmoil, cause fights." She took a deep breath. "You having second thoughts?"

"That's not what I said. But I do see it as a real problem. When you work with couples, how do you help people who run into impasses the way we do?"

Always there. With every breakup or breakdown, always a power struggle at the heart of it. "Teach them to compromise. Which we do most of the time. But when something comes up we both feel strongly about, neither one of us is going to just roll over—at least not without a fight. Which isn't all bad. Ultimately, I think the best relationships are those where people face their problems and work through them."

"Yeah, but it's really hard for me to take when you make demands like going to Frasier's or wanting to be joined at the hip during the investigation."

"It's just as hard for me when I feel I have to do something and you try to stop me." Finishing her coffee, she set the mug on her nightstand. "This isn't going to go away, you know."

"Two strong-willed people, each determined to have our own way." Lowering his brow, he regarded her intently, his dark expression in stark contrast to the sunlit window behind him. "Well, I've gotten this far, I'm not going to back out now. I guess all we can do is fight it out incident by incident and make up afterward."

She smiled, remembering her earlier concern that their relationship was too good to be true. *Well, you don't have to worry about that anymore.*

Later, when Cassidy and Zach came downstairs, they discovered Bryce's air mattress and sleeping bag neatly folded on the sofa, Starshine perched on top like a princess on her throne. Earlier in the week Bryce had announced his plan to move in with Ellie but hadn't named the day.

Cassidy said, "So this is it." *Now you can move the two dozen dishes off his bedroom floor and put them back in the cupboard where they belong. And you won't have to worry about him coming into the house when you're making love. So why don't you feel like cheering?*

They proceeded into the kitchen to make toast, Starshine jumping down and trotting ahead of them. After eating from her bowl on the counter, she gazed warmly at Cassidy and extended her nose for a nose-kiss. Now that the pills were over, diplomatic relations were back on track.

Cassidy carried her toast to the dining room table and sat kitty-corner from Zach. "I still think it's a mistake for him to go live with Ellie. He's always getting himself into these caretaker roles. I'm convinced he felt like he needed to keep his mother happy. Then he had Tiffany to rescue. Now it's this woman with MS. It's not good for kids. Turns them into little adults with way too much responsibility."

"What do you want to do? Tell him he can't go?"

"We should've tried to talk him out of it."

"You did. You wanna make him do what you think is best? You're turning into a menace like Steve."

She sighed. *I do have a part that tends to get preachy. Starts thinking I know what's right for everyone else. Bryce needs to make his own choices. All you can do is listen if he wants to talk, hope he lets you know if he needs help.*

She rested her chin on her hand. "What about you? How do you feel about his leaving."

"There you go again." Giving her a resigned smile, he said slowly, figuring it out as he went. "Relieved." A pause. "Happy to get out of being the enforcer. Glad to have our cat and house to ourselves."

There was something in his eyes that contradicted the words. "And sorry too?"

He shrugged. "Maybe a little."

Finishing her toast, she licked butter off her fingers. "What'll happen after this? Will you make sure to see him on a regular basis?"

"I'm not good at that." His shaggy brows pulled together. "People've never been very important to me. It's sort of out of sight, out of mind."

"Would you accept a little nagging?"

"I'd rather not."

"It's important, Zach. He needs you. You're all he's got."

"Yeah, okay."

☙ ☙ ☙

They were cleaning up the kitchen, Zach unloading the dishwasher, Cassidy rinsing yesterday's dishes, when Bryce came into the room. The boy reached down to pick up Starshine, who was rubbing her body fervently against his ankles.

Drying her hands, Cassidy turned to lean against the sink, Zach standing next to her. She said, "You sure you want to do this? You could always stay here, you know."

Bryce cradled Starshine as the cat sniffed his face and rubbed her cheek against his. "You've got your own lives. You never asked to have a kid dumped into the middle of things. I'd always feel like I was in the way."

Cassidy frowned slightly. "I'm sorry we didn't do better at making you feel welcome."

Bryce shrugged. "It's just how things are. Besides, I wanna stay at Ellie's. I always knew she loved me, and she's at a point now where she needs somebody there."

Cassidy asked, "How's she been managing alone for so long?"

"Xandra put a bunch of money in a trust for her. Plus she's got people who look in on her pretty often. Anyway, I checked out the public school and it's not too bad. I'm kinda looking forward to hanging around the neighborhood, not being so different from everybody else. And Ellie, she'll always be there, just like when I was little."

Zach said, "Well, I guess this is it."

Putting Starshine down, Bryce gazed at the floor. "There's one other thing." He looked at Zach. "I can understand why Xandra told me all that stuff about you. She was scared that when I got old enough to understand what she did for a living, I'd be ashamed of her. And it was true. I was always embarrassed, never wanted to admit she was a madam, even to myself. She was so scared I'd choose you over her, she had to make me hate you. She was always afraid of being left." Bryce's eyes held Zach's for an instant, then moved to the window.

Wonder how he feels about his father now. Probably can't risk feeling anything. Not till he finds out whether or not Zach can act like a parent. If Zach can do his part, maybe Bryce'll start feeling like he's got a real father after all. And here's Zach, with no great talent in that arena. She sighed. *Even with Bryce gone, this won't be easy.*

Cassidy said, "Will you come visit Starshine?"

"Sure."

"Maybe I'll try cooking Sunday dinner." The two males laughed. "You can bring Ellie. She sounds like somebody I'd like to get to know."

Cassidy, Zach and Starshine went with Bryce to the front porch. Cassidy stood on tiptoes to give the boy a good-bye hug, which he returned with a tenderness that surprised her. She said, "I'll miss you."

Stepping back, she watched as Zach and Bryce eyed each other warily.

"Well," Bryce started to turn. Zach thrust out a hand. Bryce put his in it, and they shook. The boy then sat on his heels and made mooshy noises at Starshine, who bestowed a quick love bite as he finished scratching her neck.

The calico jumped into her place in the open window as the two humans waved at the departing Miata.

"You should've hugged him."

Zach said, his voice growly, "Don't tell me what to do."

Cassidy watched the little yellow car disappear around the corner. The kids who'd been playing football in the middle of Hazel returned to their game. She said, "You know, at first I envied Xandra, but now I think I can almost understand the demons that drove her"—*not altogether different from your own*—"and even feel some sympathy."

"Xandra? How could you possibly be envious of someone as screwed up as that?"

She hesitated for several moments, then said in a sheepish tone, "Her power over men."

His eyes narrowed. "Back to wanting to control me, huh?"

She tilted her head in thought. "Actually, I don't. Sometimes I get controlling but it isn't what I really want. It's just that insecure part of me. I never want to be left either.

"Look, as much as I enjoy the sexy things you do in bed, I wouldn't be on the verge of a major commitment if you didn't have a lot of other qualities that are even more important. I like being with a woman who's sharp enough to keep me on my toes. And the fact that you have this warm, empathic, therapist side—something I could use more of—isn't lost on me. I'm in awe of the way you get people to open up about their personal lives, and I even like it that we can partner up on investigations—just so long as you don't get in my way. I never would've stayed with Xandra. I am planning to stay with you."

A giddy sense of pleasure bubbling up inside her, she wrapped her arms around his chest. *Eat your heart out, Spiderwoman. You were extremely clever at snaring people in your web. Better at making men desire you than I could ever be. But you'd never have kept either one of them—Bryce or Zach—forever. They need what we all need, something you couldn't afford to give. What we're all really looking for is someone we can love who will love us in return.*

She leaned backward to look up into his face. "Lately I've developed this unfortunate habit of gloating, which goes totally against my self image."

"What's wrong with gloating? Feels good sometimes." He pulled her closer, nested his cheek in her hair. "You still want to plan a wedding?"